Her Majesty's Will

Her Majesty's Will

A Tale of Will & Kit

David Blixt

For Patches, Fooles, & Rude Mechanicals
In short, the Shakespearean Actor

Contents

Act I
Art's False Borrowed Face

Scene One

Lancashire
15 July, 1586

In the long and amusing history of inauspicious beginnings, few can rival that belonging to young Will.

Let us for a moment ignore his humble origins, spotty schooling, and that early luckless brush with Law. If instead we focus upon his initial theatrical endeavor, we must agree that the likelihood of his ever attempting such a thing again was on a par with a Scotsman ascending the English throne. It happened, yes – but to this day no one quite believes it.

Which is all to say that Will's first play was a mitigated disaster.

To begin with, Lysistrata's balls were dropping, utterly ruining her song. What's more, Myrrhine insisted on missing her cues, and Calonike kept pulling off her wig. When Will chastised her for the third and a half time (the half having been an involuntary expulsion of air rather than proper words), she threw down her wig and ground it under foot. "But Master Falstaff, I doesn't wants to be a girl!"

"Fitting," replied Will tartly, "as I'm fairly certain she doesn't want to be you even more. But you're not a girl – you're a woman, a fine young woman that all the boys long for."

All the boys giggled, and Calonike flushed. "Why doesn't Booby-Tom play the girl?" demanded the boy in the dress, kicking the offending wig at Booby-Tom for further emphasis.

Booby-Tom wasn't paying attention, as he was occupied at the window with his hands down his braes. Will chose to not call attention to this activity, as experience informed him this would only disrupt his class further. All at once he felt cutting despair invade his liver, thinking of all the long nights spent translating Aristophanic Greek for these incurious offspring of rural imbeciles.

It was not that he longed for the adventure that was about to claim him. But had he been given the choice of facing death in the unknown or eternal life among this tribe of dwarfish tormentors, his preference was undoubted. Teaching was not in his veins.

But it was, at present, his profession. Disregarding Booby-Tom's self-abuse, Will decided to try reason. He stepped closer to Calonike, or Hemmings, as he was properly called. At once young Hemmings covered his bottom with his knuckles, thus hiding the two most often misused bits of him.

But Will did not use the cane. He tried words instead. "Master Hemmings, theatre is the gateway to understanding. It is not about story – stories can be told in a thousand ways: through song, through poetry, through prose, even through dance. But theatre is about *character*. It is the act of bringing people to life and keeping them alive. This play was written nearly two *thousand* years ago. Those who first peopled this story are long dead and buried. But each time it is performed, those people breathe again, as does the playwright. Can you imagine what a smith, a cobbler, a wainwright or carpenter would give to know that their craft would come alive again two thousand years from now? What has such permanence? Only God. As an actor you yourself become a god, performing an act of creation, breathing life into a statue and witnessing it quicken into being. You grant the people you portray, and moreover the playwright, a kind of immortality. The story may be silly, but the words are not. When they are spoken, given breath, these people become alive."

"Death ain't a person," cried another objector. "Nor is Love, nor Hope, nor Chastity…"

"I hope she's not real," leered Hemmings, which had the cruder boys laughing and the younger ones looking perplexed.

"You're quite correct," said Will, flouting the laughter by agreeing with it. "Those plays are not about people, they're about ideas. Which frankly is why they won't last. No one likes ideas – at least, not the kind that they are forced to listen to. But men will always respond to plays about mankind."

"This ain't about men, is it?" asked another. "S'about women."

Will could have argued further, drawing out the distinction between Man and Mankind. But he realized that he was growing guilty of the very thing he was objecting to – promoting ideas rather than people. He had to make this more personal. "Hemmings, think of it this way – theatre allows you to be something else, to pretend. Make free with your mind."

Hemmings scratched at a louse. "Sounds like lepers and thems what don't think well."

Will sighed with an ironical smile. "It's the 'well' that makes it art."

"Eh?" Hemmings had found the louse, plucking it free and eating it.

"Eh?" echoed Will snappishly. Mastering his temper, he attempted one more assault against a willful *won't*. "Isn't it better than just memorizing Virgil and parroting it back?"

"Nay!" retorted Hemmings. "It's just the same, only some of us gots to wear wigs and kits."

"And kiss!" cried another protestant, eliciting a huge response from the rest of the class. Though, Will noted, one or two boys didn't appear to object too strongly.

Stymied, Will unleashed his final weapon. "If you don't perform your parts this moment, we shall perform this play again tomorrow – and invite your fathers."

A tremor of fearfulness rippled through the room, bringing about a wonderful silence. Slowly Lysistrata began again to croak out her song. Myrrhine came in on cue, and Calonike recovered her wig.

Which left Will, lucky he, as the sole auditor to the travesty that was his first play.

Yes, *disaster* was the word. The only thing that kept it from being an unmitigated disaster, indeed the sole bright spot of the whole sorry affair, was that he did not have to endure the totality.

Mitigation came in the form of a timely interruption.

"Master Falstaff," said Booby-Tom, both hands now in sight. "There's a wench being swived outside. May we go watch?"

Cheeky. Under normal circumstance, Will would have insisted they press on. But in truth he was as eager to end this thespianic night-terror as they. Rising and striking Booby-Tom's pate as he passed, Will crossed to the door of the one room schoolhouse that was his abode. Home it could never be. His home was far away, and he was barred from it. Lord, did he hate being a schoolmaster. He often wished that some great plague would come and exterminate his bully pupils, or else a flood that would sweep him away from this place forever.

Little did he know, as he opened the door, that his wish – or at least a variation of it – was about to be granted.

Outside, it was indeed as Booby-Tom had described, at least at first glance. Not far from the door, just to the opposite side of the gravel path, it appeared as if two riders – one bald and squatty, the other bearing clear signs of the pox – had dismounted and were now groping and fumbling at a woman's clothing. To the childish eye, it certainly looked as if they were making a clumsy attempt at disrobement. But Will knew that if fornication was the aim, there were simpler ways to circumvent a woman's raiment. No, as he stood in the doorway watching it appeared, oddly enough, that the two men were searching for something hidden on the poor wench's body.

Until this moment the girl's face had been hidden from Will, turned away behind a curtain of curling midnight tresses. Suddenly her struggles and kicks turned her about to face him, and Will felt an ephemeral swordpoint enter his breast. Breath left him, his liver began to throb, his lungs turned to stone.

She should not have been beautiful. She was too dark, both in hair and eye. She was a raven, with the same mournful mockery in her eyes. Her skin was naturally fair, though recently burned by the sun.

This raven flicked a look to Will, who remained open-mouthed in the doorway, mere yards from where she stood protesting her molestation on the road. She did not cry aloud for aid, but a plea was present in her bottomless eyes.

The wise thing, Will knew, was to simply walk away. All that was required was a single backward step and let the door swing shut. In so doing, Will could banish this drama from his life and return to his promising career as a teacher.

"Hemmings, fetch my sword. Quick!"

The boys' excitement, already aroused at the prospect of watching the unwilling dalliance in the road, grew Cathedral high at the idea of their schoolmaster intervening. No doubt they would see him walloped, then watch the conclusion of the raven's rape. Better than the Christmas faire.

Waiting breathless for Hemming's return, Will listened to the grunts and cries from the road. The woman's words were curses, and those curses were far more creative and colourful than any Will had ever heard. The cries of "may the unholy angels bottle your filthy fiery farts and pour them down your throats" and "fut yourselves, you mewling doghearted flaccid-mouth wagtails" only made him respect this Dark Lady more. So too did her struggles, which were so far effective that only her bodice shoulder had torn and her over-skirt rent a little at the hip.

The accosters' utterances, in contrast to hers, lacked all originality. Only they repeated, "Where be it?" though they varied it by occasionally adding "whore" to the end. They clearly lacked her panache.

Hemmings returned pink and glowing from the loft that housed Will's truckle bed and basin. In his hands was Will's rapier, the hard scabbard bruised and nicked. Accepting it, Will didn't bother to fasten the sheath to his belt. Tripping lightly down the hill to the road, he removed the blade from its home. Unlike most scabbards, Will's had a metal ring in the mouth, that the two metals might scrape together. Though the resulting sound of ready steel was pleasing, it was, he knew, foolish – such a theatrical device might damage the blade.

Holding the scabbard of leather-covered wood in his left hand, his right forefinger and thumb found the grip within the sword's guard. It was a poor man's guard, simple, with only flat quillons to and fro and a single arcing knuckle-bow. But the thirty-three inches of steel were keen, shiny, and far from neglected – Will never knew if the Law would succeed in tracing him to Lancashire, so he kept his sword well-honed.

Stepping high upon the short stone wall, Will landed in the road. Keeping the weapon's tip down and the scabbard hidden behind his left leg, he said, "Release her, you varlets!"

It was said in his best voice, the one he had learned as a boy playing Aeneas in his own classroom plays – low but carrying, with the slightest edge of growl. He wished he were dressed for the part, instead of in his ugly master's robe. But his stance was perfect, and his tone remarkably commanding.

Grasping the Dark Lady by her shapely hips, the poxier of the two scoundrels covered her mouth and pulled her close. The squatty hairless one turned to face Will, his hand dropping with alacrity to the double-ringed hilt of his own rapier.

At close distance, it was obvious to Will's eye that these cads were something more than footpads. They wore fine if unmatched outfits of leather and rough silk, and their boots were tall. Not officers, but perhaps someone's personal guard? Confidence melting, Will quailed in his slippers. Somehow he managed not to tremble openly. *Alea jacta est.*

The front man was bearded and bluff, with a shattered hedge of teeth and a carbuncle nose. He told Will to sod off, though in language a shade courser and far more vehement. The second, a lean fellow with thinning hair and waxen cheeks, was less voluble, only grunting his assent.

With forced ease, Will brought his blade up into the basic invitation – feet shoulder width apart, right foot forward, the left angled a trifle out, knees at *demi-plie*. His scabbard played the part of a dagger on high, while the rapier aimed loosely for the talker's breast. "I say, release the lady and be gone." His voice did not betray a tremor.

Having abandoned their feminine attire, Will's young pupils drew closer to claim choice seats on the other side of the low wall. Some of them hefted stones and nocked them into the slings they were forbidden to carry. Will knew that he was just as likely a target for their missiles as his two opponents, but he chose not to share that intelligence.

The varlet that knew his tongue from his broken teeth said, "What does a schoolmaster know of fighting?"

"I may wear the schoolmaster's gown today," said Will, not in anger but again with that unconcerned combination of authority and growl, "but that is the fault of this blade – a blade that has skewered men for less insult that you have offered today. I swore never to raise it again in anger, but so help me God, if you do not release the lady in this breath, I will use the next to sing this blade through a measure of crimson music until my *forte* is cadent with your intermingled sanguinity."

As they remeasured him, Will feared he was a trifle over-playing the casual nature of his deadliness. Or perhaps they were merely negotiating his language. That he had certainly over-played. As per usual.

"Leave off, master," replied carbuncle-snout in a less strident tone. He was eyeing both Will's stance and the number of slings (a quantity which, in all honesty, astonished Will more than the varlet). "We're on orders to bring this thieving wench back to our mistress."

Will's arm was steady, his point unwavering. "Your mistress is no lady, to send such as you to retrieve such a woman in such a manner."

Carbuncle raised his voice. "You know fut all! She's a disloyal bitch, and has valuable property secreted on her person that does not belong to her."

"That is for the law to consider," said Will. "If you persist, it must perforce consider your deaths at my hand. I am content to have it so. Are you?"

The students began to crow in approval. Shouts of "That's tellin' 'em, Master Falstaff!" and "Give 'em what for, sir!" rang out through the sleepy pastoral landscape. Though they had often felt their master's cane, never had they guessed he owned such a murderously still temper! Rather than wishing him bested, they now began to hope he would exercise this new and unsuspected deadliness.

The two ruffians heard the boys' encouragement, gifting them further pause. If indeed the schoolmaster knew what he was about, slings and sword together would see them ended.

As the two men studied Will's stance, measuring his apparent skill against their own, the Dark Lady bit the hand that stopped her mouth, drawing blood. Her waxy restrainer cursed and released her. Carbuncle turned a mite and Will passed forward into the second invitation. Sensing the threat, both men leapt back and half-drew. This left the raven-haired mistress free to scamper behind the protection of Will's *en guarde.*

Carbuncle gave a final look of disgust as he backed away. "We'll be back for her," he growled, mounting his steed. "With a proper writ."

"You'd best have more than a writ, wit," replied Will with a squint he'd been told was properly stern. "A magistrate, one with proper manners."

"O aye," said carbuncle through his jagged maw as he sawed at his reins. "And she best be here when we do."

The waxen varlet articulated his emphasis with a grunt, and together they rode back in the direction of the town.

Watching them depart, Will released a little sigh of relief, lowered his guard, and turned to the lady. Who propelled herself into Will's embrace, her lips locked against his. When she paused for breath, she cried, "A hero, true!" before resuming.

Will's sword stood upright as he awkwardly accepted the kisses, even going so far as to put arm around the shapely hip. But as there was a bum-roll in the way, he was cheated of even a hint at the body beneath.

The children smacked their hands together in wild applause. Some twirled their slings, making a ripping sound in the air before loosing their missiles into the sky.

"Take a bow, lovely," said the Dark Lady in an unsuitably husky voice. "It's only polite. Everyone loves the triumphant end."

Flushing in embarrassed pleasure, Will did as instructed, breaking a leg. His students crowed with delight and he said to them, "That, lads, is Art."

After first ushering the Dark Lady up the stairs to his small loft to wash and collect herself, Will sent his pupils home – a triumph for them though it likely would cost him half the day's wages. He was expected to keep them until dark, and it was barely mid-day. But he happily resigned himself to his loss, hoping for a kinder recompense.

Belting his resheathed weapon, Will climbed the stair, already framing his advances. It was months since he had been alone in company with a woman, much less a woman who owed him her life. Or, if not life, at least her virtue. Will was not ashamed to hope that she might offer him the very thing he had preserved.

As he trod each creaking step he rehearsed each imagined approach in turn, discarding the coarser ones for quotes of Ovid or Terrence. A country wench was hardly likely to know they were not his own.

Mouth set in a deprecating half-grin, eyes full of salacious solicitousness, Will reached the top step and was taken aback.

The Dark Lady was nowhere to be seen.

In her stead Will found a slightly built man in a state of half-dress. Though wiry, his back rippled with a sea of taut muscles like a greyhound. His wispy hair was knotted at the back of his head, tawny brownish blonde in colour, not unlike a field mouse.

Taking no notice whatsoever of Will, the young man proceeded to tie up the points of his hose and codpiece. Flummoxed, Will said, "Pardon me, sirrah. But what on earth are you doing in my rooms, and what have you done with the maiden?"

"Why, I murdered her." The wiry fellow glanced over-shoulder with bland nonchalance. "And she was no maiden, I assure you."

Will's hand was cresting again towards the sword at his belt when all at once he saw a thing that made his blood not so much freeze as turn to sludge. The fell of magnificent raven hair lay on the bed, whole and alone.

For a wild moment Will imagined the youth had done as the New World savages and taken the Dark Lady's tresses, scalp and all. But then he saw further down the truckle-bed an unlaced and unoccupied dress. Over it lay the bum-roll and a device that Will at once recognized as a false-bosom.

Feeling faint and dizzified, Will turned again to the fellow dressing in the half-light of the single window. "Sir, pray tell me you are not she."

"I am not, though I was. But since she is no more, I cannot be anyone but myself." Shirted, the fellow now turned full-face and bestowed a bedazzling smile on Will. At once it was clear what had become of the Dark Lady. She had transfigured herself into a handsomely effeminate young man of Will's own age. The mournful eyes held more mockery than before, and the pouty lips seemed not wide enough for their thickness to belong to a man. It was an oval face, but with a jutting point of a chin and two magnificent cheekbones, sharp as a knife's edge.

Enjoying each fresh wave crashing over Will's countenance, the man grinned. "A thousand thanks, sir. If they had been allowed to continue in their hunt of my person they would certainly discovered more prey than they sought. May I know the name of my saviour?"

"Will," said Will, almost forgetting to lie. "Will Falstaff."

"A great delight," said the young man, breaking a leg in return. "I was Kitty, but now I think Kit will do. Tit for Tat, Kit for Kat. More low, far truer." The fellow flapped his arms in the loose-fitting shirt and gestured at the hose covering his legs. "I beg of you, Master Falstaff, assure me that these drab rags are not the best you own?"

In his confusion Will had not even noticed that the clothes on Kit's back were his own. "Indeed, I must do the opposite – they are my Sunday wear."

Sighing, Kit resumed slipping his arms through the sleeves of Will's best doublet. "Well, the indigent must not sneer at shillings, though they are not crowns. But truly we attired ourselves more handsomely at Corpus Christi, for all their sumptuary neversense. You don't happen to own any dags, do you?"

Still in a realm of utter befuddlement, Will replied that he hadn't any pistols.

"A fault!" groaned Kit. "But I imagine a man with such prodigious deadly skill at the fence must disdain the hackbut as a vile tool."

Will ventured a step, neither nearer nor further from his guest, merely a step for stepping's sake. "I am no swordsman, I must confess."

Fingers still at the laces, Kit batted his lashes in genuine astonishment. "No? But you handled yourself with such excellent poise, with balance and ease. I certainly believed you were deadly in your easy earnestness. Why, you performed the *imbrocata* so well I was tempted to applaud!"

"Pray, which is the *imbrocata*?" asked Will.

"The last invitation you issued, what George Silver calls the High Ward. Knuckles up, wrist high, point down."

"Ah, is that what it is called?" asked Will with shy pleasure. "I had no idea. I saw it done once, and practiced until I thought I had it right. But I've never actually potched and cut."

The man called Kit seemed never to be still. His hands flittered about his person, straightening, fussing, tying and untying, all in an attempt to present the best appearance. "But – surely, dear William, you are greatly skilled! You took up the invitation with the greatest of poise, and with greater calm, as if the thing were of no more moment than lacing one's points!"

Will was shamefaced, hangdog. "Alas, no. I know no more than you saw."

"And here I thought you were a deadly swordsman. Instead you are an actor! Bravo, sir! What a true delight, to find a kindred soul here in the blasted North. If that is where I am. In point of fact, would you be so kind as to tell me to what part of English soil do my boots currently cling?"

"Lancashire," replied Will. "You don't know where you are?"

"I am in Lancashire," replied Kit, casting a dissatisfied glance at the shortness of the sleeves of his stolen shirt. "Until I learn where exactly that is, I shall navigate by the stars." He re-lit his brilliant smile.

As this was not a particularly helpful answer, despite the smile, Will was forced to revert to an earlier subject. "A moment ago you referred to me as a kindred soul. What did you mean?"

Kit was casual in his response, but beneath the veneer was a delicious pleasure. "There are certain men – I am one – who seem to be that which they are not. Gifted? Perhaps. Dangerous? Often. Mercurial? Definitely. I spy in you, William my Conqueror, a kinship. With me, I am able to recreate much that I see with very little effort, and perhaps a dash more style. Do you find it so?"

Recovering a shred of the pride he had given up with his confession, Will bobbed his head. "It is as you say. I have seen swordsmen, studied them, and with a little effort can recreate whatever I see."

"Or hear," added Kit thoughtfully, though the meaning of this was lost upon Will. "What an actor you are! You fooled me, and I am no one's foole. Yet I was certain I had been rescued by some great but penurious duelist." For the very first time, he gave Will his complete attention. "Tell me, can you learn a thing just by watching?"

Will reddened. "No, I —"

"O, please sweet William. Bestow your total confidence to me. I will do the same for you."

"Very well then." Will cleared his throat. "I often practice things, willy-nilly things, at night when there's naught else to do."

"What kind of things?"

Will felt as if he were being pressed by a confessor. "Oh, juggling, tumbling, attitudes, voices – whatever has caught my fancy." It was a trifle thrilling for Will to be thus confiding in someone – especially a figure as outlandish as this Kit. Will's wife was a distant woman, and had never understood his addiction to these nocturnal distractions. Though that was hardly the cause of their frosty relations…

"Marvelous." Kit paused for a length of a single pulse, then gestured briskly at Will's ransacked wardrobe. "Hurry, man, and pack."

"Pack?"

"Are you an aural as well as a muscular mimic? Yes, of course you will pack, unless you prefer to leave your admittedly trifling raiment behind us. Truly, friend, it might be for the best. Make a clean break."

Will stared, his face a *tabula rasa.* "I am not going anywhere."

"*Au contraire, mon frère!* We must be gone this hour, you and I, lest the foe return to molest us both with greater numbers."

"Sirrah," said Will slowly, as if to an idiot, "I cannot leave with you. I am hired by the city to instruct the boys this whole year. Nor do I have cause to go."

Kit had begun to gather the remains of his disguise in a bundle, but he paused. "Master William," he cried in earnest dismay, "you have the greatest cause in the world – the preservation of life, limb, and liberty! If you were the swordsman you seemed, I might feel secure in leaving you to fend them off at your pleasure. But your chivalry, though misplaced, has nonetheless misplaced *me* in your debt. It would be poor repayment to allow you to be hanged from that fine oak by the road. For that, I assure you, would be your fate. They are in earnest. Their goal? No less than treason. Your mere murder pales in comparison. Therefore you must travel with me to safety, or else far too soon expire the term of your brief life."

These words rattled the cage of Will's skull, ricocheting like balls from the absent hackbuts. Hanged. Treason. Murder. Will opened his mouth to venture a question, but was swept up in the other man's frantic and repeated orders to pack. Without quite knowing what he was about, Will threw together his few belongings into a satchel while keeping one wary eye on his companion. Kit was finishing stowing the pieces of his female guise, more voluminous by far than Will's own meager clothings.

Fortunately Kit had overlooked Will's good boots, or else decided they were too large (though generally much Kit's size, Will owned fabulously huge feet). As he donned them, Will said, "Where are we going?"

"Away from here," replied Kit evasively. Realizing the churlishness of the answer, Kit bowed in apology. "Forgive me, darling man. But if you are taken, it is best that you know nothing of my destination. Surely you see that it is better for us both. However I am free to assure you that we are off to save a nation, this emerald isle, and that together we will be rewarded for our selfless duty. Past crimes will be forgotten, our futures assured, and all will be well once we have reached our destination."

Will felt a dizzying excitement. Already he was eager to abandon his snot-nosed, mewling pupils for this adventure. The added enticement of a pardon for past crimes, innocently offered by Kit, bore such appeal that Will was prepared to throw Kit's slight frame over his shoulder and carry him to the Antipodes, if that was their goal.

But this was all a touch too fantastic. Hating himself for doubting yet knowing his doubts were sound, Will forced himself to speak. "If the matter is as urgent as you imply, I will never falter. But I require proof."

"Wisely, wisely. 'And whoso list to hunt, I know where is an hart.' " The quote from the poet Wyatt, though heartening, was not reassuring. Next, like a traveling magician plying his trade, Kit waved his hands and produced a small wax seal with a flattened face. "Behold, the private seal of Lord Walsingham, close counselor to Her Majesty Elizabeth, long may she reign."

Will did not belong to such exalted circles as would recognize said seal. But Kit spoke with such casual conviction that, in Will's already willing state, he acquiesced at once. "I am your man. But, hear me, I must know more, in time."

Kit patted Will's cheek in tender comradeship. "And you will, Will, you will! But first we must be craven and kick up our heels for our skins. Let me ask a base, vulgar question – have you any coin?'

As it chanced, Will had recently received his modest monthly stipend and had not yet found opportunity to send it on to his dependants. But it seemed imprudent to inform Kit of his modest wealth. "I have a few crowns," he said, feigning embarrassment as he touched his purse.

Kit shrugged. "T'will have to serve. I have none myself, and there is no time to borrow or beg more. We must fly, or else we—" he paused, his best ear cocked to the air. "Do you hear, Will, do you hear?"

Will did hear. Horsemen in the road, several by the mingled shouts and clops. The threatened traitors had returned, and in greater numbers.

Throwing his satchel over a shoulder, Kit skipped down the stairs to the schoolroom and opened a window that did not face the road. Will joined him, heaving his own small fardels through the opening into the descending twilight. But before he could himself follow it, he felt a hand at his waist. He grasped at his rapier's hilt, but it was already in Kit's long dexterous fingers.

"Forgive me, friend," said Kit, "but it is of more use in my hands. In such numbers they will not be thwarted by display but by deed."

Will was more relieved than dismayed at this presumption of his weapon, as he had momentarily feared some cross. Kit's argument was quite sound, and Will was not to be left defenseless. He still had the hard scabbard in his belt, and in extremis the small paring knife he had secreted in his boot's leg.

"Now, swiftly, my lovely," said Kit with a grin so joyful as to belie their urgent straits. He swung his legs over the low sill. Will mimicked exactly Kit's easy roll, then reached up to pull the shutters close behind them. Kit was waiting, bouncing back and forth upon his toes, readying his joints for flight.

Just as Will lifted his satchel there was a crash from within the schoolhouse, followed by several smaller bangs as pews and desks were overturned. As he took to his heels alongside his unorthodox friend, Will hoped that Kit's pursuers, in their thwarted rage, would set the place alight.

Throwing a final glance at the worm-eaten, mouldering, chill tomb that had been both abode and prison to him lo these many weeks, Will further wished – on the off-chance that the Lord in His Heaven was granting sinners' wishes this day – that he would never set foot in a schoolroom from now until the end of the world.

With that, Will and Kit ran for their lives.

Scene Two

Sad to say, in those days it was perilous for two men to travel across the English countryside. Notwithstanding tales of wolves and bears, of demons and rangy hogs, every village and hamlet had their own ideas of how to handle unwanted strangers – which is to say, all strangers. Stocks and whips for some, hanging and flaying for others. Unless one could produce a letter from a lord or local magistrate, civilization in those days held more perils than the wild. But then, let us be frank – when hasn't it?

Most pressing to our hero, however, was fear of their pursuers. "Are you certain we are not exposing ourselves to capture?" asked Will furtively, not for the first time. "Could we not," he gulped, "be *gallowed?*"

Kit was blithely scoff-full. "Why should we be? They are in the hunt for a man and woman. What do they care for two poor blighted fellows who have been robbed of their horses and are forced to finish their travels afoot?"

It was just morning, with an unseasonable dew weighting down the lesser plants. The eye of God was just risen over the horizon, still red and bleary from a night spent watching heathens a world away.

Will's own eyes were in hardly better condition. They had slept in the embrace of an oak after a half night of being chased across fields by dogs, recalcitrant geese, and the occasional witch (Will imagined she had been a witch, the way she cursed them). After too few hours of sleep, Kit had roused Will with a series of cheerful kicks and pinches, and together they were on their way again.

Kit glanced around him, his face screwed as if he were chewing something distasteful. "A grey eye looks back towards Erin, as the Irish say. The North is a dismal kind of place, is it not?"

This observation came as they passed through a smallish hamlet. Indeed, the deprivations of the people were difficult to ignore. Good Queen Bess had never forgiven the North for the Catholic rising seventeen years previous. Two magnates, the Earls of Northumberland and Westmorland, had armed the people and marched to free Mary, Queen of Scotland, who was then as now an enduring "guest" of the realm. As a result Elizabeth had kept the Borderers down by any and all means possible. Roads were not kept, sheriffs had free licence to hang and plunder, and the taxes were so onerous that no one was surprised when they went unpaid. Extreme poverty was a defining characteristic of the lives of Border dwellers, so much so that they took pride in their deprivations and kept themselves aloof from law and civility. As lawless a place one could find outside of London, and far larger, with far more places to hide.

But calling Lancashire the North was rather like referring to Wales by the name of Ireland – a comparison not without merit, yet offensive to both. When Will tactfully pointed this out, Kit merely shrugged. "I have no idea where I am, truly. Two days ago I was playing the serving wench in Staffard—"

"Stratford?" asked Will in a sudden flush of panic.

"No no – Staffordshire. Dear lord, my friend, you are white as a sheep in snow!"

"I – it's nothing," replied Will lamely, studying the sky.

Kit made a silent study of his companion until Will pressed him to continue his tale. "As I mentioned, I was in Staffordshire, which is many miles from Stratford – that's in Warwickshire, no? – pretending to be the creature you first met me as." Kit frowned, his gaze wandering off. "In which guise—no, whom I was portraying—no. Feh. Guise, dis guise, de skies…"

"Whyever were you in such a guise?" pressed Will.

"Hmm? Oh! To gain intelligence against the insidious foe," replied Kit, who so far had supplied no surname. It gave him a moral superiority to Will, who had provided a false one. "The castle was rife with treason. When I had procured enough evidence to prove said treason, I hid upon a wagon and departed the castle grounds. I had thought the wagon headed for – well, elsewhere than here. Where did you say we are? Lancashire? Where is that, in relation to where I started?"

"Some seventy miles north, I think."

"Ay me!" cried Kit in real dismay. "That wagon must have been on the way to her son, not…" He paused, then smiled. "We must head south-east from here, to more populated lands."

Will surmised that their unsaid destination could only be London itself. A flutter of excitement filled Will's chest. London! How he had dreamed of London. Full of excitement, learning, spires touching the clouds and fathoms of precious, precious books.

But London was several days march distant, an unwelcome fact that had not escaped Kit's understanding, for he said, "Today's object is to discover first food and drink then, with any kind of luck but bad, a horse. Two, if we can manage such a tremendous coup."

Feeling an imaginary unweighting of his purse, Will said, "How do you propose we find mounts?"

"By asking for them, naturally. But first, we shall break our fast. Do you think your few coins could run to meat and eggs, or must we suffer through weak beef tea?"

Hard learned frugality coupled with the suspicion of several days of travel ahead led Will to buy them porridge and bread from the hamlet's single inn. At the last moment added two pints of wheaty ale to fill their stomachs. They ate for a time in relative cheerfulness on the bench in front of the inn, until the stern eye of a passing patrol of the sheriff's men made Will uneasy.

"Do not fret, my dear," said Kit. "Unless the disease is more rampant than we know, it is not the sheriff's men who will be hunting for us. No, our vultures are an altogether more dastardly band."

"Then why not apply to the sheriff for asylum, even transport?"

Kit smiled in a wily way. "Because the result would benefit only the sheriff, not ourselves. If we approach the local authorities, be they earls, knights, bishops, or sheriffs, their humanity will rise to the fore."

"I fail to understand you," said Will.

"A common failing, I'm afraid. My meaning is this: to gain the aid we require, I would needs must impart some of the intelligence I have gathered. Once a nobleman hears of this treason, a vision will perforce descend upon him, as in the days when angels visited the Hebrew prophets. He will see not us in the part of the hero, but will instead take that role unto himself, imagining the riches pouring into his purse rather than ours. A noble seeks only advancement. Now, it is true that we might find ourselves with a generous new patron, but experience tells me that such honest dealing is far from the norm. Besides, why be pensioners when we may be made noble ourselves? I'd rather live on my own land than subsist at the whim of another landowner. For us, *ad lucrandum vel perdendum.* Does it not follow?"

"Certainly," said Will, having absorbed this discourse in duplicity with fascination. "You make all as clear as a sky rubbed raw by rain. We shall either win all, or lose all." He longed to ask what intelligence Kit possessed, and against whom the charges of treason would be lain. It had not escaped Will's attention that he was risking a great deal – perhaps all – for a cause he knew a handful of nothings about, and that the scenario Kit presented applied to his present as well as some imaginary future. Kit held the knowledge. Will held only the bag.

Their breakfast finished, they returned their bowls to the suspicious landlord. As if by cue, Kit launched into an ingratiating discussion of the small hamlet and their surroundings. "We are traveling acrobats, you see, earning a weak living by moving from town to town, performing for pennies."

This parcel of news surprised Will more than the proprietor, who seemed bemused by this declaration. *Vagabonds*, was the thought clearly etched across the man's craggy brow. They were moments away from being stocked when Kit suggested they provide a demonstration – "free of charge, of course!" – at mid-day in front of the inn. "And as we do our tricks for the few inhabitants of this charming village, you can serve them drinks and meat pies and such trifles as I'm sure you are well renowned for."

"What's in it for you, then?" demanded the landlord squintily.

"A chance to perform is all a true actor desires," said Kit loftily, but then added in a confidential tone, "However, the charity of those who have been entertained never goes amiss. And perhaps we might earn a free supper before we are on our way." He followed this with a knowing look and a finger laid alongside his nose.

Scenting a chance to make money and secretly amused at the concept of any charity on the part of the locals, the landlord agreed to the arrangement. He shook Kit's hand and sent his boy up and down the single street, informing all the other boys of the hamlet of the impromptu performance. Boys being the best means of spreading information quickly, this ensured a decent audience, and the display was scheduled for mid-day.

Will was signaling desperately to Kit, who smilingly ignored him with equal urgency. Still speaking to the proprietor, Kit requested the use of the back yard beside the stables to practice their routines. The landlord agreed, and Will found himself arm in arm with the man he was fast suspecting was no friend but instead a kind of living goad.

"I have never been taught acrobatics!" hissed Will in a sibilant whisper as they entered the yard.

"A hindrance," admitted Kit, "but not insurmountable. And did you not mention tumbling and juggling among your nocturnal peregrinations? Certainly a sufficient base for a routine routine. There are four daytime hours between ourselves and our scheduled performance, and if the Admiral's Men can put on a full play after a day of rehearsal while half in their cups, surely we two creatures of far superior talent can produce something twice as spectacular in half the time."

Will protested that the Admiral's Men, of whom he had heard but never seen, were professional actors. "And so shall we be, by day's end!" retorted Kit, still tugging on his borrowed cuffs as if hoping they might have grown overnight. "If by 'professional' you mean 'paid for their labours,' I assure you we twain shall have a new profession."

"Gecks?" asked Will, meaning professional Fooles.

Kit cocked his head, then said with suddenness, "You, my dear heart, are no Lancastrian!" It was not a question, but rather a pronouncement made with delighted finality.

Startled, Will blenched. "Why do you say so?"

Kit ticked off the points on his fingers. "Firstly, geck is a regional noun, as gallow and potch are verbs. They do not speak so in these parts, nor in London. Secondly, in your more careless moments your accent slips, coming something decidedly more southern to my ear. Your Fs turn to Vs, your Cs into Zs, and you have the roundest Rs I've ever encountered." He grinned fleetingly, then pressed confidently on. "And thirdly, you blenched when you thought I had said Stratford. Is that your home?"

"My birthplace," admitted Will unwillingly. His obvious reluctance ended the inquest, though the thoughtful expression in Kit's eye was troubling. Then, with an air of decision, he removed the scabbard he wore and handed Will his own sword back. "Well, take this up. It is time for your first true lesson in swordsmanship."

"Now?"

"T'will delight the crowds and save your neck, both at once." Kit was rummaging about the yard, and finally he emerged with a sturdy stick that he used as a mock blade. "Ah-ha! The very thing." Returning, he took up a stance just to Will's right, with a long stick held loosely in his grip. He looked relaxed but taut, if a thing such as that were possible. At once Will lowered himself into the pose he had used so successfully the day before.

"Very good," said Kit, observing Will sidelong. "Your poise requires no comment, though perhaps a trifle more bend in the knees? Excellent. Now, when you think of fighting, what do you see before your mind's eye?"

"Blood, and – blood," said Will.

"Aye, blood will have blood," said Kit wryly, dark eyes twinkling. "If the thing's done right. But if you fear the sight of blood, then the blood you see will be your own. Now, close your eyes and picture instead a dance."

Will's eyes remained doggedly open, gazing with undisguised skepticism at his companion. "A dance?"

"*Absolutement.* Fighting is dancing. There is a sequence of accepted steps, and their order matters. But most importantly, there is always a leader. It is the role you must always assume if you can – you must lead the dance. That is why I will reverse the usual order of instruction, which is foolishly defensive, and teach you the good bits first. Let us cut and thrust!"

For an hour Kit led Will through the killing and wounding strokes, first the most basic, then as Will showed himself exceptionally adept, the more exotic blows.

"Around, around!" he cried at one point. "The *punto* is a circular step, not an advance. And the blade follows the same arc, around *com ça*, and *za!* The point is buried just below your opponent's shapely buttock, where a longish doublet meets the thigh."

During another sequence, Kit said, "Yes, my dear, but pray do not over-extend your knee, keep it above your ankle. It is the back foot that must do the work. That and the arm make the *passado* with a *demi-volte* so effective."

Panting, Will slumped to sit upon the ground, his knees curled up to his chest. "Where – did you learn this?"

It was not a passing question, though it was framed as such. Will was hungry to know more about the fellow to whom he had tied his star.

Kit showed himself affable to interrogation. "At college. I have mentioned Corpus Christi, no? I did not receive my degree, alas. But I did take my turns at the post and pillar with some of the finest gentlemen of the age, and the disgrace was not mine. Though I tended to drop my point at inopportune moments. Mar 'em low, that was my sad inclination. One that cost me dear, I assure you." Kit chuckled at some private jest or memory, then urged Will to drink from the nearby well before starting again.

For the second hour they focused on defensive moves, and again Kit was complimentary in his corrections. "Just so, my dear, except you must bring the circle of the blade in the opposite direction, else you will drag his point into your own breast. As you see," he added, nodding to where his stick was pressed against Will's chest.

Will imagined the stick in Kit's hands to be unbated steel and felt faint. "The circle of the blade? I do not understand."

Kit dropped the point of his stick into the earth and leaned upon it like a cane, in an entirely affected attitude. "Like certain aspects of dancing, mathematics are involved in the art of the fence. In this case, geometry. Attacks are linear, defences circular."

"The *punto* is a circular attack," noted Will, not in protest but in attempted comprehension.

"There be exceptions to every law," snapped Kit huffily, "both of man and nature. Do not focus on this as a rule but as a trend. There are circular attacks and linear defences, but they are uncommon, which in turn renders them valuable in the arsenal of your memory. But trust me, a circular defence will protect you far more than a linear one. The goal is always to clear the incoming point from your breast, high, or loins, low. Only the keenest swordsman can feel confident in a linear parry. I myself only use them in one out of ten duels."

"You've dueled?"

"Yes, but never for anything so pretty as a woman's honour," said Kit, bowing a little to Will. "Or, for that matter, even my own. Petty insults and broken wagers, mostly, resulting in petty blows and broken shins. I have never killed a man."

Will's unexpected and, for him, rare silence to this statement caused Kit to arch one eyebrow in interest, but Will again took up his defensive stance, effectively ending the conversation. Kit obliged him with an attack that Will parried perfectly.

After that second hour they rested for a time. Then, armed with only some bits of wood and a filthy pear, Kit tried Will's hand at juggling. In this Will required no instruction – at least until it came to performing jointly, for he had never before worked with a partner. But within minutes he was able to catch and release without much overt concentration.

Pleased, and declaring them well ahead schedule, Kit then led Will through a series of light tumbling. At this too Will also proved quite adept, so much so that it was his own suggestion that they combine the two, juggling and tumbling. To their mutual surprise, and Kit's cloudy consternation, it was not Will who had the first miss.

"It was a poor throw," said Will, correctly judging his companion's pinched mouth.

"It was a fine throw!" snapped Kit, liverish for the first time in their acquaintance. "Modesty is as false as exaggeration, and I beg you not to indulge in it while in my company!" Rising suddenly, he stamped into the inn and for a moment Will feared he had committed some cardinal sin. When the seconds lengthened to first a minute, then two, he had a wild idea that Kit had departed in a fit of pique. On the verge of rushing inside to check, he was relieved when at the end of two hundred seconds Kit returned – relieved, that is, until he noted the rusty sword in Kit's grip.

"The landlord has been kind enough to give us the loan of this raw blade for the duration of our performance. Come, let us work up a sequence – and a tale to go with it!"

There was a glint in Kit's eye that boded poorly for Will's chance of winning even a choreographed duel. But as soon as Will missed an early exchange, Kit let loose a bark of triumph and the evil spark disappeared. Apparently Kit was correct that Will was a born actor – he had missed deliberately.

After rehearsing their whole short routine three times, Kit insisted that they rest. Waiting for his turn by the well, Will said, "I appreciate the instruction, and understand the need for funds, but surely this is time lost on your urgent journey, is it not?"

Kit wiped his mouth with the cuff of his shirt, which had been Will's best. "We will travel further mounted in the afternoon than we would afoot all day."

"How does this gain us mounts?"

Quickly Kit threw an arm about Will's neck, drawing him close and pressing the forefinger from his free hand to Will's lips, close to his own. "Mum's the word. Allow me to surprise you." Kit's long lashes were brushing Will's brow, and though the small gesture was intensely communicative, its message did not penetrate Will's preoccupied brain.

Mid-day came too soon. Hearing the crowd assembling at the front of the inn, Will felt a frightening exhilaration. Would he remember the sequence Kit had led him through? Even if his mind served him, would his body follow? Would he carry it off? The rabid bat flapping in the gaping hole of his abdomen contrasted marvelously with the lively beating of his heart, the throbbing of his liver, the constriction of his throat.

"Come," cried Kit, clapping Will about the shoulders. "Time to rub your antlers on the fraying post, and leave the velvet behind!"

When the landlord finished dispensing drinks and roughly-made pasties, Kit stepped out from the lee of the inn to stand in the centre of the road. In a carrying voice, he introduced himself by the name of Virgileous Humanus and Will by an equally unlikely pseudonym, and expounded for a few witty impromptu stanzas on their stellar abilities and sordid past. They had traveled the world from infancy, it seemed, learning to imitate the monkeys of Africa and the lemurs of Asia. They had learned the fence from the greatest swordsman in Italy, the fabulous Fiore de Liberi, and performed before the great Cham himself.

Then came the moment Will dreaded and longed for in equal measure. Crooking a finger, Kit signaled his partner forward. Will obeyed, and instantly found an apple pitched at his head, not from the audience but from Kit in an improvised start. Will caught the missile and launched it back as another came speeding at him – Kit was performing at a greater speed than they had rehearsed. But, much to his own delight, Will found himself able to match it.

Soon they added tumbling, all the while keeping three apples, two pears, and an orange aloft. The only embarrassment came when Will, relaxing slightly now that his nerves were passing, let loose a windigall mid-roll. His face reddened at once and he almost let the orange drop to run for shelter. However it was such a delight to the crowd that Kit quickly did the same, though Will suspected him of cheating and supplementing the sound with his mouth. Soon the crowd was adding gaseous brawps of their own to punctuate each roll, and the landlord was able to sell another round of drinks for further production.

At the end of the tumbling and before the swordplay, Kit made an announcement. "Soon, my friends, I will perform the greatest feat I know, learned from the *jighitovka* in the land of the great Cham! But for this magnificent display, I will require the use of the best and swiftest horse in this fine land. Who owns such a beast?"

There was a good deal of argument among the men in the crowd, and it seemed to come down to two who obstinately stuck to their exclusive claim on a faster horse. Kit listened intently, then with the air of a man who enjoys a good quarrel, suggested that both horses be saddled for his trick. "I will try each. Who knows? Perhaps when the trick is done, you two shall race to have a conclusive decision made." Agreeing wholeheartedly, the men sent boys off to saddle the mounts.

Will's growing suspicion about the horses was supplanted by fear as they started their fencing display. This time Kit did not speed up but kept time and measure, whistling a low tune for Will's benefit. Will timed each stab and parry to the music, and as he knew the tune, he began to sing:

There was a friar of order grey, *Inducas*
Which lov'd a nun full many a day

In temptationibus

A look of delight spreading from brow to chin, Kit joined him:

This friar was lusty
Proper and young, *Inducas*
He offer'd the nun to learn her to sing
In temptationibus

O th' re mi fa the friar taught, *Inducas*
Sol la this nun he kiss'd full oft
In temptationibus...

They continued to sing of the singing nun, the groping friar, and of his rocking the nun's *quoniam*. Consequently their 'duel' took on a strange air, more musical than martial. It was a familiar song, the better for its rudeness. By the third verse the crowd had joined in with gusto.

When the song concluded and Will had 'lost,' Kit made a leg to the assembly. As their cheers died down, he asked if the horses were prepared. Seeing they were, he ordered them to opposite ends of the single street, each tethered to a post. Then he said, "Now, for your entertainment and at the risk of my very life, I shall leap atop a charging horse and unsaddle the armed rider with nothing more than a look. Moreover, I shall do so while burdened with weights upon my arms so that you may be sure I strike no blow!"

Will began to sweat as Kit gestured him close. In a hurried whisper he said, "Mount, and ride full tilt for me. I will move out of your path, and you will continue to ride. Nay, no qualms, please – remember, this is a matter of national vitality!" Turning back to the crowd, Kit told a boy to bring him his satchel, and Will's. Then he lifted them and, declaring them too light, asked for something heavy to weight them down. "Lest I be tempted to use my arms," he explained. So the two satchels were filled with a loose brick on one hand, and a block of wood on the other. When Kit declared one still too light, he demanded one of the stone bottles of wine that he had seen on the landlord's shelf.

"Now I shall march to one end of the pitch, and holding these twin weights by my sides, stare down the mighty beast that comes a-charging at me."

The crowd was packed cheek by jowl, craning forward in anticipation. If any among them smelled the rat they did not dare comment for fear of looking the foole.

At the west end of the road Will mounted the waiting mare. The saddle's girth was a trifle loose – apparently the boys had hurried their saddling in their fear of missing the show.

When Kit, far down the road, gave the signal, Will urged the horse forward. It responded eagerly, launching into a gallop and gathering a goodly amount of speed.

Some among the crowd might have, by now, begun to fret. And when Will passed Kit by there were a few shouts and jeers for the scrambling Kit. Those turned to a chorus of outrage when Kit used his borrowed sword to sever the second horse's tether and stepped into the stirrup. Standing sideways in the saddle, held in place by the weight of the two bags draped on the horse's far side, Kit somehow got his mount moving along behind Will's. In moments they were galloping full out on their stolen transports, the fastest the hamlet owned.

They quickly veered off the main road, crossing a brook and tearing through a batch of flowering trees. There were shouts from behind, but distant. Never did Kit pause to look back, leading them this way and that, laughing to himself the whole time.

Surely with all this to-ing and fro-ing, thought Will, *we shall be caught.* Yet somehow, despite being complete strangers to the region, they returned to the main road with not a pursuer in sight.

"Two horses, a sword, and a bottle of fine wine!" crowed Kit with glee. In response to Will's sour look, he laughed. "Oh, sulk! Tell me you have never stolen before, and I will tell you that you are a fibber, a teller of lies, a weaver of falsehoods!"

Ready to answer, Will had to close his mouth. It was true, he had committed a kind of theft. He had also tasted of Law. The combined experience made him undesirous to repeat the performance.

"No, my dear," continued Kit, uncorking the stone bottle and drinking deep, "save your pity and remorse for the next strangers who enter that Godforsaken hamlet, for they shall certainly be flogged and stocked on sight."

Riding off into the warm English afternoon, Will was quiet. Though he admired Kit's devil-like ingenuosity, now the sheriff's men would be after them as well as their unknown pursuers. And Will could no longer claim to be an innocent passenger on this darkening and mysterious voyage. He was no mere traveling companion. He was an accomplice.

He wondered if that hadn't been Kit's intent all along.

Scene Three

Having ridden through the entirety of that afternoon and night, and then again the whole of the following day, the oddly matched pair of fugitives made their way through huge swaths of Cheshire, Derby, and Leicester.

Unbeknownst to them, the redoubtable Bill Camden had recently immortalized their environs in his massive tome, simply entitled *Britannia*. In it, Camden described Cheshire thusly:

'*This country* (as William of Malmesbury saith) *is scarce of courne, but especially of wheat, yet plentifull in cattaile and fish.*' *Howbeit Ranulph the Monke of Chester affirmeth the contrary:* '*Whatsoever Malmesbury dreamed* (saith hee) *upon the relation of others, it aboundeth with all kind of victuals, plenteous in corne, flesh, fish, and salmons especially, of the very best. It maintaineth trade with many commodities, and maketh good returne. For why, in the confines thereof it hath salt pits, mines, and mettals.*'

Proving unequivocally that Master Camden had never traveled to Cheshire. Indeed, so unwilling was he to do so, he would instead simply repeat whatever dross was said about the place, no matter how contradictory, rather than make the trek. Yet on one topic he waxed knowledgeable:

'And this moreover will I adde: the grasse and fodder there is of that goodnesse and vertue that cheeses be made heere in great number of a most pleasing and delicat tast, such as all England againe affourdeth not the like, no, though the best dayriwomen otherwise and skilfullest in cheese making be had from hence.'

Will himself sampled very little of the cheeses, as they were doing their best to avoid human habitation. But the one wheele he did lay hands upon was, in fact, exceedingly fine.

If the aim was indeed London, theirs was an indirect route, to be sure. But Kit had expressed a desire to altogether avoid Staffordshire. Just as well, as far as William was concerned. From Stafford, they would necessarily pass through Warwickshire, and Will was content not to further risk dancing with a hempen wife. He had enough troubles.

He also had a companion now as interested in his past as Will was in their present. When they stopped beside a stream to wash themselves, Will tried to keep his back away from his companion, but Kit spied the marks at once. "My dear friend! You've been flogged!"

Will nodded. The memory of the whip cut deep, hurting more than the dozen spindly scars upon his spine. Kit pressed him on the cause, but Will demurred, saying only that it was an injustice.

"Aren't they all?" replied Kit as they remounted.

On their third evening since feloniously acquiring mounts, they came to rest in a Northampton glade within a single day's ride of London. Kit had at last given up any pretence of a different destination. Yet beyond their physical goal, Will knew nothing more solid than what he had been able to divine through guesswork. During the journey he had attempted to draw out further intelligence from his companion through half-jests and leading remarks, all of which Kit deflected with careless ease.

When they tired of their saddles and needed diversion, they prac- ticed their fence. Will was surprised at how many simultaneous ele- ments had to be at the forefront of his mind. He was lightly prodded and slapped with the blade, in moves that would have maimed or bled him dry in a true fight. But he twice managed to disarm Kit, which gave him a satisfying thrill.

Then came a new lesson. "Being able to use a sword is all well and good," explained Kit sententiously on this, their final day on the road. "But the real skill is knowing how to walk with one. An actor must imitate a gentleman – indeed, so must a spy! And to a gentleman, there is nothing so natural as wearing a sword. So put on this scabbard and let me see you walk!"

It was a fascinating half-hour. Lounging languidly by the fire, feet outstretched, Kit called out corrections to Will's gait as he perambu- lated back and forth. "Try turning. No, you'd've whacked anyone be- hind you. And never grip the hilt while you're walking. If you must rest your hand, do so loosely, not with the fingers. Rest your wrist on the pommel, that will let you guide the blade without being offen- sive. Step up on that stump. Ah, if you were climbing stairs, you'd've tripped yourself. Longer strides…" He seemed to be training Will for something, but what that might be – a test, perhaps, or some kind of performance – went unmentioned.

At the end of the lesson Will sat grimly by the meager fire. Arm weary, saddle-sore, hungry and faint from fatigue, he set his mind to either have the truth of the matter or insist upon parting ways. The promised reward, so alluring and enticing four days earlier, had grown less positive in Will's imaginings with each passing mile, in direct con- trast with Kit's assurances. Indeed, the more Kit spoke of their mutual well-being at the end of this trek, the less Will believed it.

Thus Will sat in quiet determination. Kit, ever the contrarian, was sprawled upon the earth, bootless toes enjoying their freedom as his fingers prodded the collection of twigs and leaves that did little more than smoke. Frustrated at his lack of skill in kindling, Kit happened to glance at Will's unshod feet. His eyes traveled upwards, an appreciative smile growing. "Damn me! You have the most excellent calves!"

"Should I not?" asked Will.

"I never trust a man in tall boots," answered Kit knowingly. "Most often he is disguising the disgusting turn of his misshapen legs. But you would not be ashamed to put forward your best foot – indeed, there is little to choose between them. I—I—Achoo!" A stray wasp of smoke had ventured up his nostrils.

Will laughed as Kit stamped and swore. Brushing an exasperated palm across his face, Kit paused to stroke his chin, his mood brightening visibly. "Ah! The delight in not shaving – I have missed that simple pleasure. Perhaps by Sunday next I will own a mustachio as trim and pretty as yours."

Seeing a possible line of attack, Will lunged. "How long were you forced to maintain your female guise?"

"A whole fortnight," admitted Kit with evident pride.

Will gazed in wonder across the feebly smoking fire. "And you were not ever discovered?"

"Never even suspected!" crowed Kit. "I tell you, what espionage has gained in me, the stage has lost." He wilted a little, a film misting his over-large eyes.

Will found himself moved by Kit's suddenly mournful expression. "How did you come to such a trade? By family, acquaintance, or accident?"

"All three at once," replied Kit, punctuating his sour words with a single bark of laughter. "My father provided the tools, my mother the wit. My college provided the background, as well as a lure. The accident was my own folly, in seeing too late… Well, my better nature never seems to dominate my actions." Here Kit paused to eye Will keenly. "But why such probing queries? Surely after a few days in my company your keen brain has plumbed the depths of my spirits and determined that I am as trustworthy as the hound's paw, as sharp as the falcon's pounces, and as noble as the lion's mane."

"All of that may indeed be so," said Will stoutly. "Nevertheless, I consider it past time I learned a trifle more about our cause."

"Indeed? Even when it is the absurd nature of the world that one may learn more and know less?"

"Profound as that may be, Kit – well, let us begin with that. Is Kit your Christian name, or a diminutive?"

"Tis, tis," said Kit. "Short for my Christian name, which has more Christ in it than most."

"Christopher, then?"

Kit sighed. "A name that I have never enjoyed. Perhaps because I have so often heard it spoken in tones conveying disapproval. In Kit I have discovered another New World, a wondrous land of freedom. Freedom from inflection. Kit. Kit. You see? It is quite past the hedge of the teeth before it can be laden with want. It is quite impossible to imbue Kit with overtones or undercurrents. You are equally fortunate in Will, Will. Also short, though perhaps not quite as good as Kit. My hard, decisive ending is better than your almost indefinite one." Kit paused to applaud himself. "Ha! That is as true of life as it is names! And it is especially true in theatre. You are fond of theatre, no?"

"No," said Will. "I mean, I am, but do not seek to put me off. I have risked my life in this venture. I feel I am entitled to know why I might soon encounter that decisive ending you refer to. Surely I have proven my constancy."

Kit considered for a time, eking out the moments by prodding the smoking embers of the fire he had so far failed to kindle to life. "You asked how I came to this sordid business. As a schoolmaster you will appreciate this irony. It stems from education."

"Education?"

"Indeed." Kit was smiling now, the corners of his mouth curling tightly. "My father taught me well, though the Lord knows he had little but self-tutelage to guide him. Because of his insistent schooling and a bit of chicanery that I need not enter into, I was admitted to Corpus Christi College in Cambridge on a scholarship. I am certain you will find this difficult to credit, but at college I became something of a rakehell."

"No!" gasped Will, throwing his hands to his cheeks.

"I assure you, it is true," said Kit proudly. "I was nothing like the sober, respectable fellow you have come to love these last few days. Well, to shorten a lengthy tale to its component parts, it befell thus: in my worser moments, I committed an indiscretion that needs must be expunged from my records before I may earn my degree. I was on the brink of expulsion when I was snatched back from the precipice by, not a savior, but a fiend, a very devil. Like Satan summoned from the depths of Hell, I was approached by a man in the service of the Queen. Quite unbeknownst to me, Corpus Christi is the breeding ground for government agents, and between admonishments, one of the professors – or perhaps it was a classmate, I was never certain who – passed along my name as a candidate."

"You were offered your degree in exchange for a service."

"Hardly." The fire in Kit's eyes burned hotter by far than the poor kindling before him. "I was told to go to France for a term of three years."

"France! Whatever for?"

"To spy. The assumption was that a man of my – talents? Predilections? Leanings? Skills? – that a man such as myself could infiltrate various societies that were closed to their usual agents. At the end of that time, provided I had performed up to their expectations, I would then, as you say, be granted my degree and be free to exist again as I pleased."

Greatly moved by this tale, Will shook his head angrily. Having himself been exiled from his home for a pseudo-crime, he felt for his newfound friend. "That is monstrous! To banish you from your own life for three long years!"

"Calm yourself, my dear," said Kit, reaching across to pat Will's forearm consolingly. "I went willingly. What's more, Paris proved far from unpleasant, and I made many friends and had a good deal of amusement. However, *caelum, non animum mutant, qui trans mare currunt.*

After nearly a year abroad, I saw in Stafford an opportunity to deliver to my governmental masters such a coup as would put them forever in my debt, rather than the reverse. It meant returning to England and taking on the guise I was wearing when first we met, and required much that a mere mortal actor could never endure. Fortunately, I am a god among actors."

"Is that your chosen profession?" asked Will in wonder.

"Rather, it is my nature," corrected Kit. "I have maintained one guise or another for, oh, all my life! I wonder at times if I have no genuine personality at all, only whatever airs suit the moment."

"What do you mean?"

"Well, for example, at my father's side I was the witty pupil with no aspirations beyond that of shoemaking. At school, to please my classfellows, I turned prankster, the witty slack-all who maddened the professors through my dedicated lack of dedication. In France I took on the part of the dissolute poet far from home. To me, it took no more effort to change my persona than it would for you to change your hose. I fear sometimes that under it all there is no real person, just another player waiting for his roll of parchment. The world is a stage, Will. Our parts depend greatly upon our setting, and the expectations of our audience. You enjoy theatre?"

Will answered with a slight shrug of his shoulders. "I enjoy plays, yes. But I have never been in a theatre."

Kit goggled. "You have clearly performed!"

"In school. And once, when a traveling troupe came through Stratford, they required a local boy to speak a few lines." Will flushed even as he raised his chin. "I believe I did not discredit myself."

"I am sure you did not." Kit's voice was smooth and soft as the skin of a peach. "As I imagine the scene, you are a supremely gifted and handsome boy. The player king comes forth and asks for a volunteer. You are too shy to raise your hand and put yourself forward, but you have a mischievous friend who pushes you from behind. All eyes go to you as the player king asks if you are interested. You say 'Aye, sir' and at once you're whisked up to trod the boards, a small roll in your hands. You con your piece well, and in no time it is your turn to speak. Your voice warbles a bit on your first line, but in moments you find your inner voice and you orate to the crowd in the guise of Cupid, or Mercury, or perhaps some manifestation of Love."

"Actually, I was a herald," said Will, shifting a little away from the fire.

"The herald of Love," purred Kit. "You must have cut a fine figure. *Amor ordinem nescit.*"

Love knows no reason, translated Will. He coughed, though he was nowhere close to the smoke from the fire. "So – acting. You have studied it?"

Kit grinned as though Will were being amusing. But his voice did exchange a trace of purr in return for something brisk. "Yes. Well, there is no formal instruction in acting at Corpus Christi, it is far too low. We read the Greeks and Romans, of course. Aloud, but without staging. However we did see the plays around Cambridge, and moreover we performed them, but amongst ourselves, for ourselves. Nothing more. Several of us have tried our hands at playwriting. And in immodest truth, it is without question that I excelled all my classmates in inking the most moving verses, as well as displaying a genius for low prose."

"But how did that aid you in playing a woman's part, and for such duration?"

Kit became crafty. "Contrary to what most theatre-dwellers will spout, Will, acting is not an art. Unless you take art to mean artifice, in which case that is precisely the truth."

"But surely plays are Art!" protested Will.

"The written words strung together may indeed constitute Art. And in performance, the end result can become what we define as Art – an edifying sensual experience that enlightens as it entertains. But acting is not an Art. It is a craft, just as smithing or cordwaining are crafts. The setting of words to paper is likewise not always Art. Sometimes words, alas, are merely words."

"I do not understand." Will's face conveyed his confusion. "Surely the taking on of a part is an Art."

"Not at all. Tell me, what is an actor's goal?"

"To become someone else," said Will at once.

"Absolutely not," said Kit emphatically. "Acting is a matter not of becoming the part, but of fooling an *audience* into believing you are someone you are not. Actors forget their audience at their peril. Two sides of a coin. Or – better! – they are as flintstones! Useless alone, but in meeting they blaze to life."

Considering this for a moment, Will could not bring himself to agree. "Surely the best way to create that belief in the audience is to become the thing itself!"

"On an abstract level, I might concur. But with new plays to perform every three to four days, your professional actor would go absolutely mad. The skillful actors, the craftsmen, they know how to create a belief in someone else by using their bodies, their voices. What does it matter if an actor believes, so long as the audience does? It is the audience that matters."

Though this explanation did not please Will, he was uncertain how to counter it. Kit's firm passion had the weight of both experience and consideration behind it. Whereas Will's protest was amorphous, the root of it entirely out of reach. It wasn't that Kit's thesis was demonstrably false. It just *felt* false.

Instead of pursuing the argument, Will returned to the more immediate tale. "So you returned from Paris before your time to foil some plot. What plot? And how? And did your masters know?"

"I have no master," said Kit coolly. "But if you mean, did my backbiting tormentors know – no. I prefer to present them with a *fait accompli*. So I used my disguise to infiltrate the insidious household."

"How?" demanded Will. "Sure and you fooled me, in the road, for minutes. But day after day..."

"As with any audience, I showed the household what they expected to see."

"By doing what?" pressed Will, all innocent curiosity.

Kit's head took on an odd cant, and the smile in his eyes became something more than amused. "You haven't inquired as to the nature of my educational indiscretion," he observed through batted lashes.

"In respect to your privacy," said Will, shyly looking back towards the kindling.

"I respect your very respectable respect," said Kit. "Well, I allowed the men of the castle to see what they expected to see: a classless wench of no family or standing, willing to perform any act – any at all – to gain advancement."

Will had a sudden difficulty in swallowing. "You can't mean—"

"Ah, Will!" said Kit with low laughter. "How very prosaic you are. You betray your country origins. But let us agree that sex is a woman's best weapon, and while disguised as a woman, I would have been quite a foole not to make best use of it."

"But how – surely they discovered that you… that you lacked, or rather did *not* lack…"

Kit threw back his head and laughed at Will's new level of imaginings. "Have you never taken the pleasure of a hurried pinch and push in a forgotten corner, with the fear of discovery adding spice to the act? Clothes are rarely removed, and when pushing and pulling there are ways of managing. Besides, there are other more tried and true… But I'm embarrassing you."

"Not at all," said Will, standing swiftly. "The fire is dying. I should go to find some more kindling."

There was a hitch in Kit's breathing as he said, "Stay, and we shall make a blaze to rival the stars." He took Will's hand and pulled gently. "Come, do not deny that you and I shared a spark upon our meeting. Shall I resume my wig and bosoms? Is that the way to tempt you?"

This was a clear hit. For each night in Kit's company, Will's sleep had been tortured with images of that Dark Lady he had seen on the road. Only in his dreams she was truly a lady, both in spirit and form.

"I did – I thought you a woman. What I saw in you, it was not…"

"A false pretence," said Kit, his fingers brushing lightly across Will's forearm.

"That is a t-t-tautology," protested Will feebly. To his great shame, he was hiding himself from the confrontation, taking refuge as he always did, in language. "Pretense is by nature false. The redundancy is unnecessary."

"Save for emphasis," said Kit, with an emphatic caress of his own. "Language is not always helped by clarity and concision. What is woman but woe of man? Remove the woman, remove the woe. Without Eve's daughters, the act cannot be sinful, for it was Eve who first made us blush. You need never blush for me, Will. It's not something I ever—"

It was possibly the most wrenching moment of young Will's life, desire mingling with horror and prudery all at once. The rebel in him, never far from the surface, shouted to be freed from Will's moral prison. Yet his own sense of decency and, yes, convention, strove to quell the desire. "Kit, I don't think I…"

But Kit was already reaching for him, placing a hand over Will's mouth and dragging him to the ground. Will struggled as Kit threw his wiry frame across Will's legs, pinning him to the earth.

A bristly chin scratched Will's ear. "They've found us!"

An entirely different kind of panic flooded Will, and he had no time to even regret the shameful thoughts he had conceived of Kit's violence. Laying flat to the ground, he raised his head just enough to gaze at the far end of the clearing where hooded figures were emerging from the thicket. The night sky illumed the earth just enough to reflect light upon their drawn swords.

Scene Four

The feeble fire provided no heat and even less light, but of the four men facing them, Will thought he recognized two. When the leader threw back his cowl, he was proved correct. No amount of darkness could diminish the ruby glow of the carbuncle at the end of that nose.

Will scrambled to his feet, his hand dropping to his side, only to realize his sword lay on the ground nearby.

"Well well," said carbuncle-snout, grinning in recognition. "If it isn't our fierce schoolmaster! We're ready to learn you a lesson or two."

Too long a pedagogue, Will could not resist the impulse to correct his antagonist's grammar. "You teach. I learn."

"That's what I said," said carbuncle with sneer.

Will chose not to further argue verbiage. The rapier's tip was pointed at his liver, and carbuncle's pronated hand showed not a quiver.

The other men took up aggressive stances, and Will noted each in turn, a study in contrasting threats. Carbuncle's waxen-faced companion wore his sword still upon his hip, as his fingers were engaged in gripping the bulky handle of a wide-mouthed hackbut. His two near allies were armed with similar instruments of fire-filled destruction. All four were dressed in the same fine but unremarkable fashion. Not sheriff's men, certainly. One of them even wore the brand of *M* upon his cheek, meaning he had murdered, but called upon the clergy for salvation.

Will was no longer the empty-shirt who had fooled these men in their last encounter. His skill at the fence had grown by exponential factors this last week, and had there been only one man facing them, or even two, he might have tried to take up arms and put himself to the test. But three firearms, mostly aimed at him, were enough to make him keep his hand well clear of his sword's pommel. No, rather than action and swords, it would have to be guile and words.

Carbuncle looked about the clearing. "Where is the woman? Tell me true now and I might leave you to live."

Will looked unwillingly to Kit, who was making a determined study of the night sky. So much for steadfast aid.

"I said where is she!" For emphasis, Carbuncle tapped his rapier's point against Will's sternum.

At this, a flash of something very like gunpowder ignited within Will's eyes. But no gun had fired. Indeed, the only sound was of his heart throbbing in his ears. Will felt an increase in breath and stature as his blood raced through his veins, filling his vision with a purple rage. He knew these signs too well, the telltale approach of the beast that had already made ruin of his life once before – his temper. Once again, Authority was impressing itself upon him and, no matter how justified the imposition may be, he rebelled.

Without thought and with a speed that caught every man unawares, Will's right hand rose to knock the offending blade away with a back-handed slap. Before the surprised soldier could raise it up again, Will had closed the distance between them, pressing his chin almost against the uniformed lout's ruby nose. "Do not presume, sirrah, to poke at me. I do not know who you believe me to be, but I assure you, I am not a fellow to trifle with."

"Oh, I ken who you are right enough!" The stinking breath that emerged from between those broken teeth was nearly enough to make Will retreat and beg for mercy. Eyes watering, he forced himself to hold his ground as Carbuncle continued. "We spoke with the Lancashire magistrate, we did, who gave you that cozy job with the mites. When we told him what you'd done, and that you'd legged it, he said you was already on the run from trouble in your hometown, and as a favour to an old mate he let you run the school."

This did not assist Will's deception, as facts oft foul falsehoods. But Will's leaking eyes had caught hold of something, an object hanging from a cord about Carbuncle's neck. Clearly it was meant to go unseen, but the device had worked its way free from the tunic to lay sideways in the folds of the uniform collar.

Though the path to escape was still shrouded, upon catching sight of that tiny symbol Will saw his next step. "Dolt!" he cried. "Clod! Zed, that most useless of letters! Did he tell you what I was running from?"

"Don't you take on airs with me..!" began Carbuncle.

"How could I not, when you befoul the air with your every utterance!" Will's voice was again the bass authoritative tone he had used upon their first encounter. "But I will make known to you what I am, and all will become clear." By now their noses were almost dueling.

"We know that you are not who you say you are, Master False-Staff!" sneered Carbuncle. His friends cackled at this limp rejoinder, angering Will still more.

"Huzzah! He has ears and therefore can hear. You know who I am not, but not what I am." Before the man could answer, Will stepped back. Raising his right hand, he moved his fingers and wrist in an elaborate series of three gestures.

His reward was a gasp from every man save Kit, who for once appeared gratifyingly confused. Warily lowering their weapons, each man in turn repeated the sign. Kit managed to imitate the gestures well enough, and he reluctantly followed Will's example of kissing each of their foes in turn upon the mouth – a horrendous exercise, hardly worth the chance of freedom.

"For the Father, the Son, and the Holy Ghost," gasped Will in Latin, with a meaning-filled side glance at Kit. At Will's words, understanding flooded Kit's eyes, though his face remained commendably unchanged. These soldiers were Catholics, damned in this realm by the practices of their faith as any English Protestant would be in Spain or France. The device about Carbuncle's neck was an elaborately carved cross, a tiny figure of Jesus upon it. Recognizing its import, Will had made the only action in the world that would convert these men from foe to friend.

Of course, this raised the issue of how Will knew the secret Catholic sign. Feeling Kit's questing thoughts probing that matter, Will reminded his companion there was much to do before they were free by saying to their dangerous gulls, "Come, stand by this weak fire and threaten us no more."

"Forgive us, Master," said the Carbuncle, obediently sheathing his weapon. He gestured to one of his fellows and that man began building their kindling into a proper blaze. "We had no way of knowing…"

Having gained this unlooked-for ascendancy over their foes, who looked to be more than twice his age, Will decided to display magnanimity in victory. "Of course you did not. You could not. My posting was God's doing. But I believe introductions are in order."

Carbuncle introduced himself as Matthew Derby. His waxen friend was another Matthew, surnamed Rookwood. The man with the branded *M* on his cheek was Francis Higgins. The last was called Robert Brockhurst, who had pinkish skin and a wicked-looking crossbow slung over his shoulder.

As the names meant nothing to Will, he listened with only half an ear as his thoughts leapt from point to point as a frog does upon a pond, so swift that he reached the end with hardly a ripple to show.

Point – When accosting Kit days before, they had demanded an object of some kind, indicating Kit possessed a tangible thing that these men desired enough to travel many miles to recover.

Point – A thing so precious would only be kept concealed on Kit's own person.

Point – These men still believed they were hunting a woman.

Their foes having completed their introductions, Will found himself weighted with their expectant stares. Mentally tucking away these points, he swiftly thought of a man he owed an ill-turn. Picking up his sword, he sheathed it and took up the pose of a gentleman, learned only an hour before. With the same poise he bowed, extending his left leg and stepping back on his right, hands before him. Unlike the Eastern form of bowing, where one presented the back of the neck in offer to chop off the head, European bows were designed to show deference, but also allow quick access to one's sword, the feet perfectly poised to lunge.

Will was grateful for it now, as he conjured about for a suitable false name. Finding one, he smiled inwardly. "I am Sir Thomas Lucy. My companion…" He gestured to Kit, who so far had been quite useless in this deception.

No longer. With a flourishing bow that bespoke absent ruffles and feathers, Kit intoned, "Don Crithtoforo Rodrigo de Luna y Thalamanca, Marquis of Theville and Grand Counthilor to His Majethty Philip of Thpain." His accent was without flaw, right down to the Castilian lisp.

Again the four men gasped and hastily bowed, much lower than they had bowed to Will. Their firearms, already pointed at the ground, edged behind them almost out of sight.

While their heads were low, Kit launched a winning smile at Will. There was a malicious twinkle in Kit's eye that bespoke his delight in assuming a disguise so monstrous.

Attempting not to burst with mirth, Will said, "Now, you seek the woman I prevented you from molesting in the road two days past. Yes?" There was assent. "Very well." Pointing to Kit's satchel, he said, "Everything she had on her person is in there."

"I – she – what?" demanded carbuncled Derby. "In there?"

"Yes. You may search it if you like," added Will offhandedly. Kit's lack of protest informed him that his assumption was correct – Kit had the thing, whatever it was, on his person.

Derby sent Rookwood to riffle the satchel, then asked Will, "Sir, if you please, where is the little b— the, ah, female at now?"

"She no longer exists," said Will seriously.

"Dead?" demanded Derby squintily. "How?"

Before Will could craft a suitable lie, Kit drawled, "'Twath I mythelf who am ending her mitherable exithenthe. After taking my pleathure and leithure, of courthe. The was extraordinarily, how you thay, fetching. Would not you agree, Thir Tomath?"

Will's pursed lips served as both the real answer and the veiled one. Meanwhile Derby's face was all over confusion. Turning back to Will he said, "But then – why did you rescue her at all?"

"To prevent a scene," said Will as if speaking to an idiot.

"And to lull her into a fraudulent thense of *thecuridad*," added Kit. If his moustaches had been long enough, he might well have twirled them. "Before the died the condemned herthelf most magnificently." He said the word *con-dim-ned*.

"But," protested Derby, whose confusion was entirely understandable, "begging your pardons, but how did you even know she was..? Everyone else thought she was going direct to London!"

"You are not the only, how you thay, toolth in thith enterprithe!" proclaimed Kit loudly. "My perthonage was informed of the woman'th fly, and I horsed north to undo the damage the do."

"But it was Sir Thomas here who stopped us from taking her," protested Derby, whose wits were having difficulty parsing both the tale and Kit's adopted speech.

Kit frowned at Derby, implying the fellow's foolishness. "For reathoning obviouth even unto a perthonage thuch as yourthelf, I could not take pothethion of her." *Dear lord*, thought Will, listening to the lisp. Kit was surely over-playing the role. "The would hardly trutht thuch a one as mythelf. *Qué láthtima!* Even were I able to hide my magnifithenthe in these drab garbth," he plucked distastefully at his clothes, "alath, my thtyle of the thpeak would betray me. Thuthly I was forthed to visit upon my friend Thir Thomath, who ith, as you have learned, living in thecret because of his great devotion to our cauthe, to enlitht him and make of him a prime party to ending that vile woman'th vileneth!" Kit's smile of pleasure was the perfect illusion of a man pleased with how he had spoken.

Derby was staring suspiciously at Kit. "My lord, if you don't mind my asking, who..?"

"No nameth, *por favor*," said Kit, pressing a finger to his lips and eyeing Derby's companions with a jaundiced eye.

Rookwood made a startled cry. He came away from the satchel with Kit's wig in his outstretched fingers. "Fut all! What's this, then?"

At first it was difficult to distinguish the words coming from Rookwood's mouth, and Will perceived why the fellow hadn't spoken up to this moment: he had the mightiest lateral lisp it had ever been Will's fortune to hear, far more disabling than Kit's affected one.

"O, *thi!*" cried Kit, recoiling in similar horror. "Imagine my dithtathte in dithrobing her and finding her to bear no hair upon her body! None at all!"

"None at all?" repeated Higgins with overt interest.

"Not a thingle hair, anywhere. *Ay ay dioth. Y cuando…*"

"There's naught here," said Rookwood, dropping the false fell and wiping his fingers on his doublet. "Fut that."

"Pardon, masters," said Derby, "but she had a papers on her…"

"*Papier*," said Kit.

"Aye, papers," said Derby shortly.

"Non, the paper, *uno*. A thingle theet, with much writing. Thith ith what you are meaning, no?"

"Yes!" cried Derby. "You have it?"

"Had," said Kit. "We have thet it to the fire."

Derby looked at once at the poor blaze beside them as if the document might appear there. Will, meanwhile, was growing more and more delighted. Through this interrogation, all his questions were being answered.

"What is this paper she had stolen?" asked Will.

Derby looked startled, then suspicious. "You don't know?"

Will blenched, fearful of having ruined what so far had been a marvelous display of *extempore* guile. Fortunately Kit was prepared. "I did not tell him. In point of fact, until thith moment he knows nothing of thith paper. We men of the world extend our living by murdering our tongueth." He issued a significant stare, and Derby looked ashamed.

Will was busily piecing together disparate parts of the tale. Kit had disguised himself as a serving wench to serve a woman, someone important, and Catholic. Kit had run off with a paper taken from that important personage. From what Derby implied, the paper was fatal to whoever carried it, and to its owner as well. And Kit had referred to treason.

What woman lived in Stafford under guard that might be engaged in treason?

All at once the heart within Will's breast stopped. Air ceased to reach his lungs, his blood stopped in his veins, he grew dizzy and faint.

For once the question was posed, the answer that leapt to mind was obvious to any man with half a brain. A lackwit would have made this simple deduction days before, but Will's supposed cleverness in tempting an answer from Kit prevented him from seeing the matter clearly.

One woman in all the realm stood to gain more than any other by treason, and the restoration of the old faith to England. Mary Stewart, who had both English and French royal blood in her veins.

Mary, mother of James VI of Scotland.

Mary, Queen of Scots.

"Fut all," murmured Will.

Scene Five

The relationship between Good Queen Bess and Mary, Queen of Scots was firmly established at an unlikely meeting near Haddington in 1547, at the right tender ages of 14 and 5, respectively. While the English stomped around growling and the Scots traded hard cheese for French troops, the two future Queens met quite by chance in Countess Ada's nunnery. Five year-old Mary, being of French extraction and already a queen, pointed to her Protestant princess cousin's freckles and said, "You have a dirty face, did you know?" The young Elizabeth, who disliked the French not half so much as she did girls named Mary, responded by locking her little cousin in a cupboard for eighteen hours, then buying up all the make-up in the realm. Sadly, this entirely set the tenor of their relationship to the end of their days.

In due course little Princess Betsy became Queen of England. She emerged from the clutches of her half-sister Mary only to find Mary of the Cupboard angling for the throne of England as well as Scotland. The Catholics, in a severely disappointed protestation that Bess meant to continue her father's Protestant ways, decided the throne should pass from Sister Mary to Cupboard Mary. Luckily for good old England this did not transpire, but it did lead to rather hard feelings between the cousins.

Perhaps to compensate for Elizabeth's lifelong lack of a spouse, Mary took marital vows three times (*bella gerant alii; tu, felix Scotia, nube!*). Alas, each marriage only proved Bess' wisdom in remaining foot-loose and fancy-free. Mary's first husband, King Francis II of France, died of an ear infection that burrowed into his brain. Her second, a handsome strapping fellow too magnificent to be let live, expired of strangulation, explosion, or both. Her third husband died the most ironic of deaths, being chained to a pillar in a Scandinavian dungeon for ten years by the relations of his first wife, whom he'd divorced twelve days before taking Mary in marriage.

Heartbroken and seeking sympathy from her cousin for all her personal woes (and also having been chased by her subjects across the border in a leaky rowboat), Cupboard Mary appealed to Bess for comfort in the form of both sweetcakes and an army to regain her throne. Taking prodigious pity upon the renegade queen, her cousin gave her both sweets and soldiers, though not in the manner hoped. Elizabeth placed Cupboard Mary in 'protective custody' – though whom the custody protected was a matter of furious debate. For eighteen years the Scottish Queen had been shuttled from one noble lodging to another, furnished with the finest cupboards that could be imagined. Placed with Elizabeth's most trusted lords, Cupboard Mary was kept studiously away from harm and worldly cares.

It was the height of ingratitude, then, that Mary should be planning escape, murder, usurpation, and revenge. But she was, we must always remember, half-French.

The rest of Will's night was a harrowing humour, at once frightening and festive. Keeping to his outrageous role, Kit played the perfect Spanish host, inviting their pursuers to dine. Wine flowed, and while Will sank deeper and deeper into thought, Kit kept their foes-turned-faux-friends entertained with stories and Spanish songs of an obviously ribald nature:

> *...Làvanthe leth galanath*
> *con agua de limoneth*

*lávame yo, cuitada
con anthiath y passioneth!*

Drunk, they slept close to the fire, all six of them. In one way, Will was grateful of their presence – Kit could hardly make further advances now. Although, knowing Kit, he might enjoy the challenge.

Throughout the night Will flogged his most excellent memory for details regarding Mary Stewart, once Mary I of Scotland. Born in the same year that good King Henry of England had executed his fifth wife for the treasonous act of adultery, the infant Mary had thrived for an entire week before ascending to the Scottish throne. Years later, at the ripe age of sixteen, Mary made claim to the English throne as her own as well. Too many Catholics agreed, leading to the failed uprising in the North that still smarted. For that reason Mary was now both a pampered prisoner and the focus of Catholic hopes in England.

Turning all this over on a mental spit, Will roasted his thoughts. Had the wily Kit uncovered a Catholic plot? Was that the content of the message that would earn them praise, profit, and position?

Will marveled that he, of all people, should be thrust into such a circumstance. And what on earth had prompted him to appropriate the name Lucy for his misuse? There were few greater scourges of Catholics than Sir Thomas Lucy, as Will had excellent cause to know. He at last nodded off with visions of angry bishops dancing along the inner lining of his skull.

In the morning the odd company had lost none of their bonhomie and parted on the best of terms, with the four Catholics riding west, Will and Kit east, paying the tolls out of the money they had taken off their hounders.

"Why do you need our money?" demanded Rookwood of Kit in the one uncomfortable moment of their parting. Behind him, Brockhurst's fingers were questing again for his hackbut.

But Kit was carelessly assured. "Alath! Our amigo Luthy here did not athitht me out of pure, how you thay, charity. *Qué láthtima!* Among hith thinth ith the gamble, and he lotheth *mucho dinero* at the horthe

– he cannot rethitht a wager! What money I had, I gave him. Only – *idioto!* – he lotheth it the next night over the cardth!" He swiped the air as if asking God to smack Will. "To bring the proper newth to London, we mutht have the funding. When you tell your mathterth the *papier* is dethtroyed, I am thertain they would not only approve, but altho repay – even if you were to, how you thay, exaggerate how much you give to uth? Neh?"

Brightening at this thought, the four men pooled their funds into Kit's purse. Will's new failing, fresh-minted in the fires of Kit's mind, did nothing to help Will's financial state. Due to his having lost the imagined funds, he didn't receive a brass farthing.

But he did not mind. He still could not bring himself to believe their luck in having men so foolish as to credit their deception. He only relaxed when the four men disappeared over the horizon.

"All due to you, William!" cried Kit as they rode merrily on towards London. "If you had not produced that miraculous heathen sign, they would never have believed us their fellows. How lucky I fell in with a traitorous Papist heretic, versed in the apish toys of the Antichrist!"

"I'm not," Will protested.

"O, please say you are! It makes you that much more appealing!"

"I regret diminishing my appeal," offered Will wryly. "My mother is – was, related to some."

Kit looked pained. "I sincerely hope it is the relations, and not the mother, that is deceased."

"Yes," assured Will. "And I've met a few priests."

"I see your habit of living upon the knife's point is nothing new. Being a Catholic priest is death by law, and harbouring one is treason."

"I am well aware." Will lowered his voice so that not even the horses could hear him. "I once tutored in a household that harboured Campion."

"Damn your eyes!" Kit's sudden exclamation sprang from a bucketful of pure jealousy, a scandalous wish that he could claim acquaintance with the notorious Jesuit priest who had decimated the Protestant theology, despite the ruin of his earthly frame by torture and neglect. Not even the cold embrace of death had silenced Campion's ideas. Five years after wriggling free of the mortal coils, his book *Decem Rationes* remained the touchstone for Catholics in England.

"Well," shrugged Kit, "it's simply marvelous you knew the signs. That's twice now I owe my life to you. Never fear, dear heart, I am keeping a tally!"

"I am astonished we survived," admitted Will.

"We cannot hope their masters will be so credulous," warned Kit. "By nightfall at the latest they will be after us again. But by the time they catch us up, we shall be residing in the London public houses with more coin in our purses than we could spend in a year."

"Truly?"

"A knighthood may be a trifle ambitious," admitted Kit, his eyes atwinkle. "But we may safely assume Her Majesty's gratitude will not be stingy in terms of earthly rewards. Surely, love, you have sussed out the treasure I possess."

Will nodded. "The *papier* you have incriminates Queen Mary of Scotland."

Kit grinned. "I certainly hope so, after the trouble I went to in obtaining it. Would you like to see it?"

Will almost fell from his saddle. "Yes!"

Chuckling, Kit produced the small twist of paper from his sleeve and handed it across. Will read:

CFPXCFXSPBCTPW†CJGWCFWCNJYWCNKYESN
EYLYNNPSWNNQLNNCRBEPCFQI‡XJELTBCEQPFN
NPRWWECHPCRCORBFQROAJPCFOPCROOPWCQB‡

"It is, of course, in code," observed Kit, plucking it back.

"But what does it say?"

"Therein lies the sport – I have no earthly notion! The Queen's code-breakers will tell us – or rather, they won't, but they'll tell someone – and our reward will be a monetary and personal freedom for which we both long. Doubtless you wish to return to your home of lovely Stratford. It sits upon the Avon, does it not?"

Ashen and chilled, Will was not to be diverted. "Wait a little! You're saying you have *no notion* what this message reads?"

Kit joyfully abandoned his arms into the air. "None! The heretic Scottish Queen has a method of sneaking messages out of her confinement in the bung of her beer barrels. I managed to distract her clark," here Kit winked, "and copy down the note he was about to seal. But he realized what I was about, for no sooner had I escaped the castle but the holy hounds were at my heels."

"You don't know what it says," repeated Will woodenly.

"'Tis as meaningless to me as a Bible to a Saracen," replied Kit with glee.

Enough proved too much. This admittance served as flint to spark the explosion of Will's temper. "Tell me, sirrah, that you are not serious! Tell me this is yet another of your elaborate pranks! Tell me that I have not risked wrack and ruin for this inconsequential string of letters! That I have not run away for the second time in my life, consorting with Catholics and murderers and – and *you!* – all for what might very well be Mary Stewart's request for fresh linens!"

"Oh, it can hardly be that."

"Kit, this might be a trifle!"

"I think not."

"And what do you base that upon?"

"Upon the degree to which they desire it regained. They would not expend so much effort if the message were inconsequential."

Considering, Will was forced to bow to this irrefutable logic. "I suppose that is so," he relented.

Kit clapped his hands together. "Of course it is! I am a man of parts, Will, and every part sound as a bell. By this time tomorrow we shall be entering London, our fortunes forever changed! See if they are not!"

♦ ◊ ♦

London
21 July, 1586

"London. Gem of all joy, jasper of jocundity!"

While Kit recites his Dunbar, history and reverence demand we pause a moment to savour Will's first view of the great city of his dreams. For London had indeed been his dream for so many years, a glistening, gleaming conglomeration of ideas and intrigues, of nobility and native-pride, of the impossible possibles and the known unknowns. To him, London was as attractive and seductive as that first glimpse of a Dark Lady in the road, all promise and mystery – a heat felt not merely in the heart, but in the loins.

But just as the Dark Lady had shed her guise, revealing both more and less beneath, so too was up-close London something altogether different from his fanciful fantasies.

Much like the outer-skirts of a lady's gown, the London's outskirts were bemoiled with the dirt and grime that rubbed up against them. Will's first impression was not of grandeur, but rather of teeming squalor and undulating vice that had a grandiosity all its own. Cottages held together by filth, workshops that smoked beside huge heaps of refuse. With a population nearly a hundred times that of his native Stratford, the sheer press of humanity inspired fear and awe in equal measure.

Nothing in his life experience to date had prepared him for the smell. Mingled in the streets were nightsoil and offal, blood and viscera he could only hope came from livestock. Barring rain, the only cleansers were pools of horse urine, cow urine, dog urine, and doubtless human urine as well. Never had he dreamed that with so many creatures packed together, there would be so many varieties of dung. Had he been able to breathe, he would have been impressed.

But still, he told his doubting self, it was London! Like the Dark Lady's transformation, it was both less and much, much more. And what did it matter how he came, or that he was just one more cork bobbing on a sea of human hopes within its walls? He had come, at last! A childhood dream fulfilled. In spite of his senses, he felt a surge of hopefulness, that he might at last reach down within himself and fulfill the potential that until now had gone untapped. In London he would make his mark. In London he would find his muse. In London he would finally find his home.

How many of us, in our lives, have come to such a moment? Arriving at a cherished place, be it a building, city, or country, and placed in it all our future hopes and dreams. Do not, then, think less of Will's need to externalize his creativity and nascent genius. It is a human failing, seeking without that which is within. And despite what we are told, Will did not invent humanity. He embodied it, in every sense.

Worried that the Catholic guests of the other evening might have followed or even preceded them, the wary duo circled around south, crossing the Thames further inland. Thus they now approached the great city by its busiest path, up Southwark High Street and across London Bridge. Not that Will could tell it was a bridge, so crammed with shops and stalls that even on horseback one could not see the Thames. Kit sat astride his mount cloaked in deliberate world-weariness, whereas Will had to fight the urge to gawp at every turn. Men and women wriggled and wrestled their way through the heaving throng, and progress was slow, allowing Will to marvel at the goods sold along the eight hundred foot length of this architectural wonder. A silken doublet! A velvet hose! A scarlet cloak! A copatain hat! Every trick, knack, bauble, or drapery imaginable (and some decidedly un–) was there for the asking. He noted that the sartorially obsessed Kit was fingering his purse and casting a wistful eye over, of all things, a woman's gown. Will flushed and looked away, trying to banish all thought of his Dark Lady in such a garment. This procession into his dream city was above base humanity and low, unnamable desires! This was a moment for transcendence. This moment had to be momentous – a metaphorical shaking of the earth. Let the word go forth: Will had come to London!

It would be a simple and pleasant story-telling task to comically undercut poor Will's attempt to imbue the moment with importance. But truth is ever stranger and more appalling than fiction. For, as he made his way across the bridge, he was shaken from his grand thoughts by something far more Tragic than Comical, and entirely mortal.

Looking to his sinister side, Will spied a thing that made his bowels clench and almost felled him from his horse. Mounted at the far end of the bridge was a collection of severed heads, a potent warning to evil-makers.

Among them was a face Will recognized. "Edward…!"

"Eh?" said Kit, distractedly.

"Nothing," said Will at once, blood draining from his face, his tone belying his word.

Taking note of his companion's horrified stares, Kit said, "Ah yes! Traitors and scoundrels. Fear not, my friend. The fate that awaits us is quite the contrary of those poor souls, may the holy Jesus spit in their eyeless pockets."

"I hope so." Against his desire, Will perused the other faces, feeling the heavy hand of inevitability. Yes, sure as certain, there was Edward's son-in-law, his expression mournfully maskish.

It is often in the nature of the universe to answer prayers backhandedly. For weeks Will had longed for the sight of some friendly faces. Hideously, his wish had been fulfilled. And there was more than a trace of grim irony. But for Edward Arden and his foolish son-in-law, Will would be in Stratford still.

Old Edward's face was nearer, and it was old Edward's face that spoke to him. How often had old Edward bounced Will upon his knee as a lad? How often run through the streets with Will upon his back? How often had they sung together, laughed together, jested together?

And look at him now. The executions were more than two years past, yet Edward's visage, though forlorn, was mostly intact. Yes, the eyes were gone, taken for jelly by carrion birds. But the face was mostly whole. His own flesh nightcrawling, Will realized the skin had been tanned, a process with which Will had been acquainted since childhood, though he'd never seen his father apply it to human flesh.

Thus we will note that Will's first impression of London was that of a *momento mori*. Like the Triumphing generals of Roman times, he heard a whispering in his ear, *"Respice te, William, hominem te momento."*

Look behind you, William, the city was saying. *Remember you are only a man.*

As Will gazed on at these grinning grislies, Kit waved a cheery hand at the bustling metropolis before them. "Welcome to the faire that never ever ends!"

Act II
Bearded Like The Pard

Scene One

Filled with an unnamable dread, Will followed his companion's unwavering path into the heart of the great city. Kit never hesitated, guiding his mare with unnerving certitude. To Will's foreboding ears, each crack of their horses' hooves sounded like cannons. Or perhaps that was a deceit of his racing heart.

At last he could bear to keep silent no longer. *Sotto voce* he asked, "Kit, where are we heading?"

"Why, we are off down Seething Lane!"

An answer without an answer. But the name alone added a knot to the growing rattail in Will's stomach. Why could their destination not be Tranquility Lane or Unthreatening Street?

The knot tightened as Kit turned east up a street marked in chiseled stone 'Great Tower.' Will looked up over the low houses ahead and beheld that unmistakable monument synonymous throughout the realm with death – the Tower of London.

The Tower was actually three. A fortress begun centuries before by Julius Caesar and finished by William the Conqueror, it had expanded over the last five centuries into a massive walled keep, but rather than sheltering those within from harm, in recent years the occupants had more to fear from their hosts than anyone outside those formidable walls. Few invited to stay in the Tower ever left its walls – except perhaps in the bellies of worms.

Navigating the wending streets, Will noted at once an abundance of riches. The homes here were well-made and tall, with liveried servants scurrying about. The crush had abated, as the poor had little business in this area. Riding tall, Kit reeked of respectability and Will attempted to do the same. But almost at once they were stopped by three city guards. "Oi! Whereabouts be ye heading?"

Will felt faint. Fugitives and horse-thieves, they were also potential traitors, carrying treasonous coded messages. Hanging would be the least of their punishments. The boot, perhaps? Or the rack? He ran a finger over his thumbs, wondering if they would be whole by nightfall.

But Kit wagged a finger. "Not now, my fine fellow," he replied in a crisp London accent. "I'm off to see the Master of Seething Lane."

The guards backed away, and under their helmets Will saw a veritable rainbow of reactions: fear, respect, disgust, guilt, dismay. But they were allowed to pass, and as they arrived at their destination moments later, Will understood at least the fear and respect. Seething Lane sat literally in the shadow of the Tower's wall.

Turning past a remarkably small medieval church, Kit dismounted and hitched his (stolen!) steed to a ring on the stone wall across the street. Then bold as brass he climbed the few stairs to an impressive abode and knocked. When the door opened, Kit said, "Please inform Sir Francis that Mr. Marlowe is here."

Left alone in the entry chamber, Will muttered, "Mr. Marlowe?"

"Is my father, and he's none too happy when I throw his name about. But it had to come out, William, it had to come out!"

"And Sir Francis?" asked Will with real trepidation.

"Ah-ha," grinned Kit, "I hear by your voice that you've deduced our host!"

Will wished he had not. Fingers of fear creeping up his spine, he realized they were standing in the home of Sir Francis Walsingham, Principal Secretary to Her Majesty Queen Elizabeth I, her master of spies. Suddenly Will felt the watchmen's mixture of terror, respect, disgust, guilt, and dismay swarm upon him like an angry hive, pricking him inside and out. It was difficult to imagine the man without horns or cloven feet, such was the reputation he had cultivated. To be in his home was akin to brazenly stepping into a spider's web and waiting to be spun up and dried of blood.

Through the entranceway there appeared a man, too short, stocky, and swarthy to fit Will's mental portrait of Walsingham. And it indeed proved not to be him, as Kit reached out a hand and said, "Walter! My dear William, allow me to present Mr. Walter Williams, Walsingham's Welsh right hand. William, Williams. Williams, William."

Williams did not even nod Will's way. His frown was fixed on Kit's whole person, his jaw jutting like a mastiff's. "Mr. Marlowe. You are meant to be in Paris, are you not?"

"Alas, Master Williams, Paris proved too dull! I pined for the cut and thrust of my native land, and so stole out of my French hose and into ones with more frills and thrills."

"Why have you come here?" articulated Williams through gritted teeth.

"I – we, that is, mustn't forget my valued and most handsome compatriot – *we* come bearing a message for Sir Francis. The rest I refuse to say in the foyer, as pitchers have ears, even in this most impenetrable of domiciles."

"Mr. Marlowe, I do not have time—"

"O, I assure you, you have time for nothing else! For this is a message comes straight from the ink-stained quill of—" Kit leaned down to whisper into Williams' ear. The Welshman showed no reaction whatsoever to the name Kit supplied, but by his very stillness Will perceived that the name Mary, Queen of Scots, had proven Kit's point. Lower lip over his upper, Williams beckoned them both into a side door that led to a plainly-furnished office. "You have this message?"

"I do, but I will place it only in Sir Francis' hand. I do not mean to impugn your intentions, my dear sir, only to say that in a matter of this import I should not wish my message to go awry in translation."

For the first time Williams took in Will. "Who is this?"

"My rescuer and savior, William Falstaff! He heroically unfaced the hounds set upon me as I escaped the Scottish Queen's lair."

Williams returned his gaze to Kit. "And you stole a message."

It was not a question, but Kit treated it as one all the same. "Aye, I did."

"Do you know the contents?"

"Alas, I am no cryptographer, as you well know. I imagine my messages from Paris were nigh on undecypherable." Williams' stony face confirmed this statement. "But once I place it into Sir Francis' hands, he will pass it to the right honourable code-breaker, and hey presto! I am certain you will have all the proof you need of treason, treason most hideous and impolite. Now, may I please see Sir Francis?"

Williams glowered. "He is out at present."

"Then we shall wait," answered the unperturbed Kit, sitting on a low bench and crossing his legs.

"That you shall not," answered the Welshman. "Go find some lodgings – the Elephant. Stay there, within doors. Do not come until we send for you."

"The Elephant," repeated Kit, his tongue practically withered on the sour name. "I prefer the Peacock, or else the Belfry."

"The Elephant, if you please. You will draw less attention there."

Kit shrugged. "I'm afraid I had not anticipated this delay, and we are a trifle out of purse to take rooms…"

Williams brusquely took a purse from his belt and tossed it onto a side table in the hall. The small leather bag clinked as it landed. Kit snatched it up and headed towards the door, calling out loudly over his shoulder, "Many thanks, friend Walter! Give my love to Sir Francis, and tell him this paper will be the settling of all accounts. Come, Master Falstaff! Until Sir Francis calls, we shall revel it as bravely as the best!" Pausing in the doorway to send a sweeping bow to Williams, Kit removed himself from the foyer. Will did a half-hearted bow to the frowning Welshman and quickly followed his friend outside.

Kit was already unhitching his horse when Will caught him up. "He doesn't seem pleased."

Kit shrugged. "He never does. Still, compared to his master, he is as gregarious and chatty as my old nurse, who was I think a hen in a prior lifetime." Kit tossed the small bag of coins into the air. "But this is well! Come, Will, we shall drink and dine in as fine a state as the poor Elephant will allow."

Reversing their previous route, Kit led the way back across the Thames into some southern suburbs called Newington. Arrived at a crossroads, they dismounted and entered a public house next to a locksmith's shop. Above the locksmith's door was a massive sign displaying a carved and painted elephant bearing a castle upon its back. The public house had its own sign over it displaying a faded pig and a dragon. But no one ever said, *I'm staying at the Pig.* No one named it the Dragon either, perhaps out of pitying respect for the pig. Instead, Elephant and Castle had become the default name of shop, house, and intersection all.

Kit took a room for them both, and ordered a midday dinner. The meal consisted of a loaf of bread, two pints of thin beer, as many pints of thinner porridge, and two slabs of meat (provenance unknown), accompanied by some kind of vegetable soup – what kind Will could not discover as the vegetables in question had been boiled past all recognition. Still, it was the first proper meal they had eaten in several days. Sitting against each other at table, both tucked in with gusto.

"Tell me now, sweet William, and tell me truly too, is not London a magnificent feast for the senses?"

Will was eyeing a slab of cheese upon the landlord's table. "It is more in all things, certainly, than I ever imagined. Humanity at its rawest."

Pleased, Kit nodded agreement as he ladled his porridge. "Just so. London is like woman in all her forms – loving mother, devoted sister, nagging wife, sultry mistress, and the toothless old hag who begs for coins. Only she is all these at once. Most people do not recognize her living nature, but she has a robustly sticky ticky heart, and if you listen you will hear it beat…"

"KIT MARLOWE!!"

"O God," groaned Kit, his gaze skipping over Will's shoulder. "Speaking of sultry hags, here comes Huffing Kate."

A large-boned, broad-chested wench plopped down at their table without asking. She smelt of weeks-old lavender. Dressed in a russet gown over her kirtle, the laces in front, the horn of her busk was alluringly visible. She proceeded to give Kit a dark stare. "You owe me—"

"A drink!" exclaimed Kit, forestalling whatever else she might have demanded. "Landlord, some wine for Kate, and another pint of beer for my own self, if you please. And may we trouble you for a slab of that fine cheese?"

"You took my best gown, Christopher," said Huffing Kate. Will understood how she earned such a name – with every breath she expulsed air in loud, angry gusts, while at the same time heaving her impressive cleavage. She may have been twenty-five or twice that, so expertly was her paint applied. But the flinty glint in her eye proclaimed her to be, in experience, as old as time itself.

"It was, and remains," said Kit, "a fine gown. The fineness was what made me have need of it."

"Gave it to some wench, did you?" roared Huffing Kate. "My best gown, as a gift to some other girl?"

"I assure you, no other woman has worn it. I kept it only as a token to your memory."

Huffing Kate huffed. "A likely story!"

"And absolutely true," added Will, who received a glower for his trouble.

The wine arrived, and Kit offered it to her. "Drink, and be friends, then we shall make amends."

Huffing Kate raised her chin imperiously. "'Tisn't burnt. I like my wine burnt, you know."

Kit smiled. "It shall be burnt. I know how to burn it, without fire."

Huffing Kate eyed him suspiciously. "How?"

"Marry, thus. Take this cup and place it, with the greatest care, between your knees." She obeyed, and Kit picked up the pitcher of wine and poured some into the cup she held. "There! In so fiery a place as that, the wine must be near scorched black!"

As Kit roared with merriment at his own jest and Will hid a grin behind his hand, Kate leapt to her feet. Enraged, she threw the drink all in Kit's face – or tried. Kit was already halfway under the table, and the liquid merely grazed the shoulder of the doublet he wore – Will's best. Dropping the cup as though it did burn, she pointed a finger at Kit. "You just wait here, Kit Marlowe. I'll return, and bring with me the spirit of Revenge!"

By now the whole room was uproarious with laughter, and Huffing Kate's attempt at a dignified exit only added to the mirth. Kit resumed an upright position, muttering, "Damnable cockatrice. Dame Coy. A very cursed shrew, by the blessed Trinity, and a very devil. She is an angry piece of flesh, and soon displeased, quickly moved, but not lightly appeased." Finished with his theatrical quotation, he said in earnest, "Avoid women, William! Avoid them altogether. If you must make a child, make it from clay, or from your own ribs. You will have less trouble."

Amusement fading, Will thought of home and his own children, whom he had not seen in almost a year. He stood. "I need to walk. The seams of my belly threaten to burst."

Kit leapt up. "Excellent notion! We shall amble about before the bellows of Kate's breasts cause the coals of her temper to roar anew. In fact, ah-ha-*ha*-ha-ha, I have it! Follow me. We'll just have time."

Will had intended to walk about alone. "Shouldn't you wait for—" he glanced around furtively, "—the summons?"

Kit flapped a hand in the air. "Pish. If they mean to keep us waiting, I shall do the same to them. Come, I'll show you Newington Butts!"

Leaving their few possessions in their room as proof they meant to return, Kit and Will took the air, heading further south. At once they entered a thriving district with signs proclaiming goose-pulls, cockfights, and baitings of bears and bulls.

"I've seen bears at bait," commented Will, "but never a bull."

"O, aye!" said Kit, rolling his eyes and adopting a withering visage. "'Tis a riotous affair, pleasing to all the senses. They get the poor animals drunk and then tease them to death with a thousand cuts. With luck, they may gore a man or two before they expire. The crowd drinks it up like a dog does vomit."

"I take it you do not care for such sport," remarked Will dryly.

"Sport, is it? Perhaps so, like the bull-jumpers of ancient times. But it is hardly what I might term *entertainment*. Ah, there is our destination – the Newington Butts!"

They had turned a corner and were now in view of an octagonal building of nearly three stories, with an angled thatched roof and a crowd around it.

Expecting to see an archery yard, Will exclaimed in joyful surprise, "Why, 'tis a theatre!"

Back before the invention of the hackbut and the gunpowder cannon, England's greatest defence had been her Archers. Consequently, large swaths of land were set aside for their continued practice and skillful mastery. As the targets they shot at were called Butts, these large pieces of property were colloquially referred to by the same name, and in the process giving birth to many fine puns – the butt of many jokes, as it were.

Yet archery had given way to musketry, and these practice yards had fallen into disuse. In the case of the Newington Butts, it proved an ideal site for an amphitheatre – wide, disused, far from Authority, and surrounded by brothels, cock-fights, and bear-baits. The dyer-turned-landlord Philip Henslowe was said to have invested heavily in the enterprise.

But it was not Henslowe's name and crest that adorned the flags. It was a device unknown to Will. He asked, and Kit squinnied at it before replying. "These are the Earl of Oxford's men. Surely you have heard of him! He's a rogue called de Vere, always in some trouble or other with the Queen. Quite the opposite to us."

Will had to confess that the name de Vere meant nothing to him.

It was two o'clock or thereabouts, explaining the crush of men at the theatre door. "Excellent!" effused Kit. "Such a gathering means a new play!" And indeed when they reached the door they saw a sign that read as follows:

The Spanish Tragedie:
or Hieronymo is Mad Againe
Containing the lamentable end of Don Horatio, and
Bel-imperia; with the pitifull death of olde Hieronymo

"May we?" asked Will, eyes wide as a child's.

"Whyever not? Let us hear a play!" Paying a penny into the box, they passed within doors and Will experienced a true Theatre for the very first time.

The open-air amphitheatre, called the Pit, contained a raised stage at one end, and was ringed all around with galleries and balconies. The stage itself thrust nearly halfway into the Pit, placing the actors in the middle of their audience. Back of the thrust, the stage floor was made of wood and bestrewn with straw rushes. A mere twenty feet wide and barely fifteen deep, the shallowness forced the actors to come within olfactory range of the stinking masses in the audience.

Jostled on all sides, Will asked plaintively, "How many people fit in here?"

"Over a thousand, they say. I've never counted."

"Cannot count so high?"

"Mm. Quite."

The rear wall of the stage looked, oddly, like a house supported by two Herculean pillars made of massive tree trunks. High overhead was a roof like a temple, the underside of which was painted like the night sky, with astrological signs and sigils. "Those are the Heavens," said Kit. "There's a door in the centre, and sometimes it opens and a man flies down upon a rope. *Deus ex machina*, my dear, is the very definition of trust. Can you imagine being the man hanging from a slender thread so high?"

"No," admitted Will.

Behind the pillars, the wall contained two doorways to right and left of a curtained arch. Above the door area was the *Frons Scenae*, an elaborately painted screen. Today the setting was clearly Spanish, based on the architecture and banners that flapped frozen in the paint.

A sudden flourish of trumpets and two men emerged from the center curtain. One was dressed in a rich Spanish doublet, the other in a scarlet robe, his hood hanging over his face like the Grim Reaper. The Spaniard spoke:

When this eternal substance of my soul
Did live imprisoned in my wanton flesh,
Each in their function serving other's need,
I was a Courtier in the Spanish Court.
My name was Don Andrea...

"He's a ghost!" exclaimed one of Will's neighbours.

"Who's the other?" demanded his companion.

Soon they learned that the Scarlet fellow was not Death, but Revenge. Kit rubbed his hands together. "Ooh, I know who wrote this! 'Tis the lost little lamb!"

Will heard not a word of Kit's derisiveness. He was transfixed, gazing in rapt attention as living, breathing actors gave life to lines upon a proper stage. He had seen players in times past, as the travelling companies came to Stratford for an odd week-end. But this, Will thought, *this* was what it must have been like in the ancient times, when Julius Caesar and Pompey the Great went to take in a play.

The central wheel of the story turned on a father's grief over the murder of his son, and his revenge upon the murderers. Clearly the author had been influenced by the classics – specifically, Seneca. If the presence of a living personification of Revenge upon the stage were not signal enough, soon men were dying right there upon the stage, crimson cloths flowing like blood. The show was hideously, hypnotically violent, and the crowd lapped it up.

Watching the son's murder and the Machiavellian scheming of the two villains to remove their own henchmen, Will could appreciate the artistry of the killing. But his attention wandered to the theatre itself. Pointing up to the balcony directly above the stage, presently empty, he nudged Kit and whispered, "Who sits there?"

Kit scoffed. "Those are the Lord's Rooms. Noble nobs and their friends, who prefer being seen to seeing. I've always wanted to see someone use the balcony in a show, just to tweak their noses. Ooh! Madness!"

Back on the stage, the parents of the dead man had gone insane. Attempting to relieve their grief, the father turned to murder, the mother to suicide.

In the Fourth Act the grieving Hieronymo, lamenting the death of his son, spoke these lines:

> When I was young, I gave my mind
> And plied myself to fruitless Poetry;
> Which though it profit the professor naught,
> Yet is it passing pleasing to the world.

Will was mightily affected. It were as though the playwright had stepped inside Will's skin and unearthed a golden kernel of truth – true for Will alone while also true for the world at large.

The story neared its end, leading to an ingenious device Will had never heard of before. To gather all the guilty parties together into a single room, the better to act out Hieronymo's revenge, a trap was set for the villain: the characters in the play staged a play of their own called *Soliman & Perseda*. Both villains were convinced to be actors in this play, not knowing the knives that would stab them were real. A play, within a play. Inspired!

As Hieronymo stood before the king at the end of the 'play,' explaining all that had gone before, Will listened with both awe and hunger. Then he shuddered in shock as not only trumpets but real cannons full of shot sounded a dead march. The King of Spaine mourned his brother and the King of Portugal carried away the body of his son. The ghost and the spirit of Revenge had a final exchange, then all the players came to the edge of the stage and bowed, breaking their back legs as the nobility did. As swiftly as it had begun, it was now over. Barely two midday hours had passed.

The crowd roared its approval, and Will cheered himself hoarse. Kit clapped lazily, affecting a yawn.

Exiting this humble marvel of timber, nails, flint, plaster and thatch, containing all the wonders of the world, Will eagerly followed Kit around to the rear where resided another modest structure. "The Tiring House," explained Kit. "Above it is the Hut, where they store their properties. Holla! Thomasina!"

A reddish-blonde man with a pointed beard turned and immediately emitted a heartfelt groan. "O fut. Marlowe."

"Excellent well, thank you!" answered Kit genially. "Seldom better. The only trouble I have was this piece of derivative tripe they just threw on the stage like some day-old fish! They should have you writing, Thomas, not whoever scrubs out their chamber-pots."

"Thank you," answered the playwright with a nastily satisfied grin. "If you had truly hated it, you would have complimented me. Your praise always lies in your most insulting nature. Jealous, are we?"

Kit turned to Will. "Jealous? Are we?"

Will held out a hand. "William Sh– I – Falstaff. William Falstaff. And I certainly am, if not jealous, then at the least envious. A marvelous effort, and not at all derivative." Will was consciously distancing himself from Kit's disdain. "The *stichomythia* was used to great effect, the references to *The Aeneid* were a marvelous homage, and rather than remain confined within Seneca's frame, you expanded his borders. The play-within-a-play was a triumph all its own."

The pointed-beard jutted upwards with the man's stunned smile. "Damn me, learned praise, and honest!" He seized Will's hand and wrung it. "What are you doing in the company of a dullard like Marlowe here? One of his Corpus Christi friends slumming, no doubt. I am Kyd, Thomas Kyd."

"Ah," said Will, perceiving Kit's mention of a 'lost little lamb.' "A pleasure."

"*Assai sa, chi nulla sa, se tacer' sa,*" said Kit sourly.

73

"I would love to hear your thoughts," expressed Kyd to Will, "but I must away. There is another play that I am to prepare for the morrow – I am to be prompter, not author."

"Ah!" cried Kit. "The price! All is now clear. Did they not pay you for your fine play, but rather force you to drudge and toil it in their stews? Are you paying them for putting it up?"

Flushing red as a beet, Kyd ignored Kit and addressed Will instead. "If you are still in London the day after next, Master Falstaff, then I beseech you to come and crush a cup with me." He eyed Kit ruefully. "Bring Marlowe if you must. I shall bring a halter and bit to check him. A pleasure," he added, wringing Will's hand again before ambling back into the Tiring House.

As Will and Kit retraced their steps towards the Elephant, Kit summed up his impression of Kyd. "A good fellow, but a little jaded. Six years my senior, he's tied to an Earl who demands he do actual work – hunting Catholics, I believe," he added with a malevolent twinkle. "No, actually he's a scrivener, using letters for base profit, not Art. But the best Art comes out of trying times, as history tells us. Based on what we just witnessed, Kyd's times are extraordinarily trying."

"You mean you thought the play was good?"

"It was excellent," replied Kit savagely. "Too good for Kyd. I wonder if someone wrote it for him."

Will did not like the notion of taking credit for another man's work. "Perhaps you don't fathom the full depth of his capabilities. As you say, hard times bring out the best in men."

Kit shrugged, then rubbed his hands together. "There is a pork pie at the Elephant that has me salivating just conceiving of it. There is some ingredient that I cannot yet determine, and I always think one more serving will solve the puzzle. Tonight I shall try again. How discerning is your palate?"

"I know a horse from a hen," said Will. "And an eel from an elk."

"Mmmm. Perhaps I shall invade the kitchen and watch the food being prepared. I'll claim I fear poison!" He laughed at the notion.

Arriving just as the reddish sun was dipping below the buildings, Will remained without doors. "I must make water. I'll be in presently."

Kit waved his assent and stepped inside, his thoughts fixedly upon his stomach. After his companion had disappeared within doors, Will stepped to the left into the shade of a hedge and opened the points of his codpiece.

While he was relieving his trunk on the Elephant's brick hide, several footsteps caused him to look away from his work. Four men had gathered on the front step. Their hoods were up, and they seemed sharp set and tense. As they opened the door, a blazing light illumed their visages.

Jutting forth from out of one of the hoods was a nose bearing a massive carbuncle.

Scene Two

Will was grotesquely thankful he had just relieved himself – the sight of Matthew Derby's red-splotched nose might have caused him to perform the act involuntarily.

Several questions leapt fully-formed from his mind: *What in God's name is he doing here? How did he find us? What does he have in mind?*

Seeing swords on their hips, the answer to the last was excruciatingly obvious.

To Will's great credit, he did not even consider leaving Kit alone to meet to his fate. Hurriedly retying his points, Will raced around to the rear of the inn – and checked. Two more men lounged menacingly by the kitchen door. One was Higgins. Both were armed. Receding into the lee of the wall, Will looked for a window large enough for him. Alas, too many attempts by patrons to escape their debts had caused the proprietors to shutter their windows tight.

Will thought briefly of running to the house on Seething Lane and returning with aid, but by then Kit would surely be dead or gone.

There was nothing for it. Bracing himself, Will walked up to the front door of the Elephant and Castle and entered.

The room was thick with heat, as the whole neighbourhood had gathered for an evening of companionable carousing. There was smoke from the weak lamps, more from the kitchens, and half the room was indulging in the new fad of drinking upon pipes of tobacco, puffing the smoke and releasing it into the air. It was the nature of

Will's mind that, even in danger, he thought there must be a better word for the act – smoke was not liquid, to be drunk like ale or wine. *But time enough for that later,* he reminded himself. *If there be a later.*

He spied the assassins at once, sitting in twos at opposite ends of the room. But he made certain he did not meet their eyes as he searched for Kit.

Kit was not in the great room. *Terrific,* thought Will. *He likely saw our friends and, believing me safe without, escaped. Which means I just walked needlessly to my doom.*

But then he heard the casual bray of Kit's good cheer from the kitchens and remembered the pork pie. Forcing a smile across his lips, Will sauntered with what he hoped was a casual gait across the rush-strewn floor and through to the portal through which some truly re-markable odours emanated.

Kit was perched on a stool, hands about his knees, watching fasci-nated as the Elephant's fat cook explained his concoction. "One full onion, but sliced thin. Two crushed garlic cloves. A handful of flour. And the pork, naturally. Now, here's the secret – nutmeg."

"Nutmeg!" cried Kit, clutching himself with glee.

"Pepper, and red wine. And now, you'll never guess – a dollop of honey. Add some dates and potatoes, and whatever fresh plants we have to hand, and *voah lah!* Your pork is ready for pying!"

Kit shook his head in wonder. "Delicious to think of! And you're right, I'd never have guessed the honey. It makes me buzz" Kit spied Will standing in the door. "Will, come and see real perfection in the making!"

Will thought it better to remain in the door, where their foes could see him – if he disappeared, they might follow, driving them out the rear door to their death.

Yet he had to warn Kit somehow. "Nay, nay, I think real art was in that play this afternoon! Ah, how the actors played their parts. 'Hi-eronymo, beware: go by, go by.'"

He spoke not as one delivering a warning, but as one appreciating poetry. Nonetheless the line from Kyd's play made Kit start off his stool. He had Will's measure, and the odd nonsense quotation raised his hackles, even as his voice remained casual. "My dear, this is the landlord's best dish, as I described it to you."

"I see. A pity 'tis a Thursday and not a Friday, for then should we have had fish by the score." Will could see that the Catholic reference did not escape quick-witted Kit, and he continued, "Surrounded, as it were – fish to the front of us, and behind us as well."

"I could wish all fish far behind us," said Kit, lounging in the doorway, his eyes unfocused. Half-in, half-out of the main hall, he had certainly picked out at least two of their antagonists. Unlike everyone else, these hooded Catholics were making no effort to enjoy their evenings. Their very attempt at inconspicuity defeated their aim.

Knowing that the eyes of their enemies were upon them, Kit decided to put on a show. "When it's done, make another for my friend here!" he called overloud to the landlord. "We'll be sitting with these fine fellows!" He elbowed into the most crowded table and sat. Will took a place beside him.

By the smell of them, the occupants of this bench were tanners – a profession Will knew well. Before they could object to the intrusion, Will seized upon their conversation. "Gentlemen, who buys your glue?"

"Eh?" said several at once.

"Your glue," repeated Will with a smile. "My friend and I are interested in starting a business. My father was a tanner, and I know the trade well. But I'm not interested in starting such a business in London if it means competing against the likes of you!" He made a show of admiring their bulk. "Rather I thought we might become purveyors of glue."

To hide his utter bafflement, Kit was particularly earnest in his affirmation. "Ay, glue."

"We make no glue," answered one man, waving Will away.

"No? Do you have no scraps of leather or hide strewn across the floor? You must be the most efficient tanners in the history of the world if you have not!"

"Ay, we are," retorted one man, drinking the heavy beer that made up most of his meal.

"Well done," said Will. "'Tis boon for you, if ill for us. There's a pretty penny to be made in glue. Perhaps even a tanner for the tanner!"

There was a good deal of laughter at that jest, tanner being slang for six-pence. Their new friends began thawing to their presence. One said, "Go on, then. Tell us about the glue."

"O, it's ever so simple," cried Will. "You take whatever scraps you have about and boil them. Then let them soak in a vat for two or three months, boil them again, and you have glue!"

"We knows how to make it, y'daft git," protested a burly tanner. "How's we make money on it?"

"Books," answered Kit at once. "Book-binders need glue, don't they? That's where my friend and I come into it. We know book-binders, and can sell them on a new source of their precious glue."

Several tanners looked thoughtful. "Figures it's books ye like," said the burly drunk. "The pair of yeh look more like worms than men."

"Perhaps when we've all dined," said Will, seizing on a possible avenue of egress, "you can show us your workshop, and we can discuss the business—"

"*Christopher Marlowe!* What scheme is your fluttering mind hatching at now?"

Kit winced as Huffing Kate appeared at the top of the stairs, her voice loud enough to make all heads turn. She flounced down the steps and took up station across the table from him, fists on the bum-roll at her hips. "Whatever'e tells you, lads, trust him no further than you'd trust a Spaniard with your gold or a Frenchman with your wife! He's got no honest heart in him, and he can't but open his mouth but a lie escapes the hedge of his teeth!"

The tanners looked angrily at Kit and Will. Rather than protest, the duo stood and crossed to another table. Kit grimaced at Will. "Women. Woe, man."

As their pies arrived, Kate sat opposite them with a wide smile plastered on her plastered face. "That serves you, Kit Marlowe!"

"Ay, so it does," answered Kit. "More than you can realize. I don't suppose you'd feel like doing me a favour?"

"What can she do?" demanded the angry Will, who had been quite proud of the escape he had almost engineered. "She can't seduce four men at once."

"Can't I, though?" asked Huffing Kate huffily.

"Kate, my love, you are quite correct," replied Kit distractedly. "A whole cohort of men might parade your nethers without so much as a mention."

"O, that's done ye, Kit Marlowe! I'll go fetch Blacke Davie for thee!" Huffing Kate flounced to the exit.

Kit smiled slightly. "I adore that woman-like creature."

"She cried your name for all to hear," warned Will.

"Our friends would have it easily enough off anyone else here," answered Kit lowly. "By the by, that was an excellent bit of wit, says Kit – the business with the glue. If not for the bonny Kate we might well have made it out. Now, how to remove ourselves from our plight. Are there only the four?"

"No, there are two men without the rear gate."

"Our friends brought friends. Confederates in conspiracy."

"Perfidious perpetrators."

"Diabolical... no, it's escaped me. Damn."

"I hope we can escape them as easily. I assume they'll wait us out."

"Aye. If we bolt, they'll run us down. If we stay, they'll outlast us. What we need is – singing!"

"I beg your pardon?" said Will.

"And you shall have it!" cried Kit glowingly. "Do my shell-like ears deceive me, or do you hear singing?"

Will listened, and indeed he heard a pair of voices raised in song. "Aye, I hear singing."

Kit looked positively gleeful. "A chorus of angels could not sound sweeter. Salvation lies in the foole, Will, always in the foole."

"Christopher, for the love of God, what are you—"

The door banged open so sharply that every man jumped, and the two pairs of Catholic killers in the corners reached for their weapons. But the men entering were not soldiers or officers of the crown. One was a man short and broad, with a cheerfully ruddy face and curling hair on his head and face. The other was slightly taller and far leaner, his neat beard jutting out while his eyes were sunk deeply into his head. The lean man carried a lute, while the stocky man bore a drum on one hip and a sword upon the other. Both were playing and singing vociferously:

Come thou Monarch of the Vine,
Plumpie Bacchus, with pink eyne:
In thy vats our Cares be drown'd,
With thy Grapes our hairs be Crown'd.
Cup us till the world go round,
Cup us till the world go round!!

"Heaven be praised." Exhaling in excited satisfaction, Kit rose and waved. "Tarlton! Armin! Join us, won't you?"

The stocky older man broke off singing and cried, "Tarlton is no carpenter, to join mismatched pairs."

Kit showed his teeth in a belligerent smile. "Will my purse purchase your fellowship?"

"Depends how deep your purse reaches."

"For you, to the depths of Tartarus – which is where you belong!"

"Do you make the squinty-eyed knave of me?" demanded Tarlton genially as he sat on the bench opposite Kit, just beside Will. His loud voice carried as if he were upon a stage.

"I was merely referring to your infernal destination, not any yellow hue to your blood. But if you will Orient yourself to your left, you may meet my dear friend William Falstaff, late of Lancaster and harbinger of all things troublesome."

"Me?" demanded Will.

"Dick Tarlton," said the stocky man. "Forgive me if I don't make a leg, but I just sat down and don't think I can rise again. I was supping at Court and was mightily over-served. May I introduce Bob Armin, my claque." Armin broke his leg, and Will rose to offer the same compliment in return.

"At Court?" asked Will.

Armin answered. "Maestro Tarlton here is the Queen's favourite foole."

"Or so she says," interjected Tarlton. "There are many fooles she favours far more – the porky Bacon, the devious de Vere, the stalwart Stanley, to say nothing of the dubious Dudley. But 'tis me they call foole, and perhaps I am, as they profit by their foolishness, while I sew patches in my hose. Sit down, Bob, else I shall swoon looking up at you."

All four seated, Kit called for ale. As soon as the landlord had brought it, Kit leaned in close. "Dear Spotted Dick, there is a price for wetting your lips."

"When is there not? Too often now I wake to pay it with blindness and ill-humour. Ah, the vicissitudes of age!"

"That will seem small price, Dick, compared to this. Will and I are in pendulous peril, and require aid. There are four men in this room who wish us ill."

Tarlton quaffed his cup in one draw. "Far more than four, Marlowe, I assure you."

"Yes, but few of them will actually see me spitted upon a dagger's point. I'm on Queen's business," he added in confidential tones.

Will saw Tarlton's beard quiver, and the ruddy-faced foole blinked his understanding. Was he too in the service of Walsingham? What kind of man was advising the Crown, who employed so many men of low arts?

"Say no more," said Tarlton, laying a finger along his nose and sharing a significant look with Armin. "Do you wish their arrest, or your escape?"

"The latter would suffice. We know not who to trust at present."

Tarlton smiled expansively and looked to Will. "Who now is the foole, that he places his trust in a foole?"

"At the moment, sir, the foole is we. We must turn the tables, and make the foole he." Will nodded towards the corner where sat Derby the Carbuncle-Nose. As he did, they made eye-contact. Rather than look away, Derby removed his hood in a menacing fashion. Obviously it was pointless for anyone to pretend any longer.

Tarlton examined the man himself. "I see why you fear him – he bears a portal to the Underworld on his snout. What d'ye know of him?"

"His name is Matthew Derby," said Kit. "A Catholic in the service of Mary of Scotland, and through her the great lemand lamp of lechery."

"By which you mean the Papacy?" asked Will.

"Right."

"Perhaps it's only an ecclesiastical cold in the head. He might sneeze and find himself reformed."

Tarlton's expression seemed to blaze to life, some inward fire stoked. "I think it best we have all the players on the board."

Kit groaned theatrically. "O fut, he's inspired again."

"Beware, friends," said Armin. "When the age is in, the wit is out."

"Stuff yourself, you cod." Fixing a smile across his visage, Tarlton rose and waved. "Matthew Derby! By God, what a surprise to find you here! Kit, do you see? It's Derby! Derby, come and join us! You, and your friend!"

Will's horror was amplified when Kit jumped up and shouted to the other end of the room. "Rookwood? Are you here, too? Come and crush a cup! Come along, we're all old friends! Don't be afraid – come and join us!"

When it became clear that they would not stop shouting out their would-be killers' proper names for all to hear, the purple-cheeked Derby rose from his seat and came over, joined by his three companions.

Of the four men who had waylaid them on the road to London, one was missing – Higgins. In his place was a man unknown to either Will or Kit. Broad and mustachioed, he bore the menacing air of a professional soldier. His gimlet gaze bored into Will's skull as if it were itself a weapon.

"Please, sit," waved Tarlton. Poxy Rookwood and diminutive Brockhurst shared the bench with Kit and Armin. The new man joined Derby in bookending Will and Tarlton.

"You're dead men," whispered Derby in Will's ear.

"Kit," said Will, attempting unfelt bravado, "Derby says we're dead men."

"Well, my mortality has been weighing heavily of late," answered Kit. He nodded at the mustachioed man. "Who's your dire friend?"

Derby waved a hand. "This is…"

"No names," growled the big man. "You're foole enough for letting them know your own."

"I told you, they said…" protested Derby.

"I know what they said. You're more of a foole for believing their lies. That whore was right – you know you can't trust them just by looking."

"Insults!" cried Tarlton. He turned to Will. "Are you going to accept that?"

"I'd offer to challenge him," said Will, "but I rather think that's what he's after."

"You rather think," sneered the stubbly soldier. "Listen to yourself. Real men don't talk that way."

Will bristled, the danger rising within him. "Pericles, Caesar, Charlemagne – well, perhaps not Charlemagne – but men of action who enjoyed their language. Great minds use great words as well as great swords."

"Well said!" cried Armin. He faced Brockhurst. "Sirrah, would you kindly shift your sword's hilt? It is impacting my ribs."

Rookwood leaned across the table towards Will, sharing the perversely sweet smell of his licentious disease. "So what's *your* true name, then. T'isn't Lucy for certes."

"It's Lousey," answered Kit. "Reflecting his conversation."

"Thank you," said Will caustically.

Derby rounded on Tarlton. "What do you stare at?"

Tarlton's eyes were fixed upon the other man's nose. "Your bubukles. They're wonderful. Can I buy them off you, to keep me warm this winter?"

Derby scowled as Brockhurst said accusingly to Kit, "You're not Spanish!"

"Alas, the span of my Spanishness is spent," admitted Kit. "Now I am only Spanish in my troublesome spirit."

"That's for certain!" cried a joyful Tarlton.

Kit appealed to the heavens. *"Ay ay dios. Y cuando…"*

"Fellows," said the soldier to Tarlton and Armin, "I know you not at all. I'd dearly love to break your heads for insolence. But our quarrel is with these two men, not you. Clear off, and leave this pair to us."

An expression of indignation crossed Tarlton's face. "You mean that I am not the center of your world? I refuse to believe it! I am Dick Tarlton! I am the Queen's own Foole!" With that, Tarlton stood and, despite his age, flipped over backwards, somersaulting across the bench and landing again on his feet. All eyes were upon him. He grinned. "You really have no use for me?"

The unimpressed soldier misliked the number of eyes upon him. "None."

Tarlton leaned over the bench and, left hand dangling near his sword, brought his right hand up in a slow and deliberate gesture. "The *fico* for thee, then."

It was a huge insult, especially with all the room watching. The soldier blanched and seemed to swell. But Derby reached across Will to clasp the man's arm. "Savage – nay!"

The tall and muscular man was aptly named, for he turned a savage look upon poor Derby. Rather than speak, he stood and crossed back to his former table, throwing himself down and staring at Will and Kit.

Tarlton made a sad mewing sound. "Neighbours, we are tedious. Or so Monsignor Savage finds us. As Mark Antony said to Augustus, *Aut bibat, aut abeat.* What, Papists sans Latin? Tis a pity. I mean, drink, or get out."

At that, Derby, Rookwood, and Brockhurst all stood and retired together to Savage's table. Tarlton laughed and resumed his seat. "Damn, I was certain he'd draw."

Will was astonished. "At the cost of your life!"

Tarlton merely arched his eyebrows. Armin explained, "Dick here is one of the best swordsmen in England."

"Truly?" demanded Will.

"A silken tongue, a heart of cruelty," confirmed Tarlton.

"All players are great swordsmen, Will," said Kit, rolling his eyes for their companions' benefit. "They have to be. How better to ape the nobility than to outface them at their own skills?"

Blood still high, Will didn't care for being treated like a lackwit. "Well, what now?"

"I don't rightly know," said Tarlton, chewing his lip. "I'd hoped to fight him, and purchase you a distraction. Now we need something—"

He was interrupted by the door to the Elephant slamming open and a huge man with bristling black beard and wild eyes took two steps into the room. He filled the doorway, but just behind him Will could see the red hair and buxomate heave of Huffing Kate.

The massive man bellowed, "Where be he? Where be Kit Marlowe!?!"

Will leaned over to Kit. "Blacke Davie, I presume?"

Tarlton smiled broadly. "Perfect."

Scene Three

"Marlowe! Where be ye?" cried Blacke Davie, a man so wide he had to sidle through the open door. "Marlowe, you have an appointment with Blacke Davie's fist!"

"You tell 'im, Davie!" cried Huffing Kate, leaning upon the wooden doorframe as if it were a lover.

"I'll avenge ye, Kate!"

Davie's bellow had the landlord already scurrying around collecting his best dishes and cups, while sending a boy for a city guard.

Davie spied Kit. "Marlowe!" Kate squealed with delight.

Kit started to rise, but before he could open his mouth, Tarlton stood and turned. "'Twas I, Blackie, who put the lad up to it!"

Blacke Davie checked, confused. He obviously knew Tarlton, and was a little afraid of him. This flagging fire required oil, so Tarlton blew a kiss to Huffing Kate and said, "What demon have ye brought with ye, with teeth longer than her beard?"

Kate gasped and leapt forward, shoving past the stunned Davie to pummel at Tarlton. But Tarlton somehow stepped aside and Kate went flying over the wooden trencher and headfirst into Kit's lap. Foregoing witticisms, Kit grasped her waist and hauled her heels-over-head over his shoulder, to the approving roars of the watching patrons – her bumroll was clearly visible, but that accounted for all her smallclothes.

Blacke Davie's roar was far from approving – the rude fellow clearly thought himself a knight defending a lady's honour. He drew and tried to stab Kit, but Tarlton's blade was already hissing the air. He chopped down on Davie's rapier and in an instant they were at it.

Kate howled in dismay as Kit finished flipping her, dropping her onto her feet as he stood to draw. Will had already drawn, certain this commotion would be a ready invitation to the Catholic pawns. He was correct. Derby came a-stabbing, and Will made good use of Kit's tutelage, whipping his blade around to halt it.

Armin had drawn and was outfacing Brockhurst and Rookwood both. Lifting a flat tin dish, Kit hurled it as a discus then leapt atop the table to fence with the soldierly Savage, kicking dishes and cups at him as he parried and slashed.

"A pretty plan!" piped Will.

"Needs only refining!" countered Tarlton, busily fending and proving with Davie. He was indeed a master swordsman, parrying Davie's cuts with the ease of a grown man warding off a child. He continued to taunt, saying, "Davie! These men have all tried Kate's virtue, and found it wanting!"

"Raaahh!" replied Davie. His manner of swordplay was more like punching while holding a sword, but he was so big, his swings so wild, it was rather effective. Tarlton positioned himself next to the man called Savage, then ducked as Blacke Davie swung. The soldier had to break off his attack on Kit to defend his flank, and Kit jumped for the door as Tarlton cried, "Sweet William, go!"

Will was a bit entangled with Derby at the moment, so he abandoned gentleness. Sliding in for a *corps-a-corps*, he locked his guard tight to his opponent's and with his free hand tweaked the carbuncled nose. "Suckle my cod, you Papist twat!"

The ecphonesis uttered by the injured Derby was worthy of the finest actor. Disengaging his blade, Will ducked Blacke Davie's next wild swing and ran to join Kit at the door. "After you," said Kit, glowing with glee.

Will and Kit bolted into the open evening air just as Higgins and his friend came in the rear of the tavern. By now the whole place was alive with fighting, the landlord weeping in a corner, watching his establishment suffer wrack and ruin for the third time this fortnight.

Sheathing their blades, Will and Kit started to run. Hearing crashes and cries behind them, Will became concerned. "What about Tarlton?"

"He'll handle Davie. By the hour the others return, he and Armin will be well gone."

"Others return?" asked Will.

Kit's lips turned down in unmerciful derision. "William. They are chasing us. *Cache-cache.*"

Will glanced back, then redoubled his pace. With Savage leading the pack, all six assassins were in hot pursuit of their prey.

"Turn left!" called Kit. In his panic, Will almost confused his right and left, and barely made the correct turn. Kit was ahead of him by several feet, but Will proved to be faster, and soon they were running side-by-side down the muddy busy thoroughfare, pursued by crazed Catholics.

Will glanced back. "They're closing."

"It's the press!" snarled Kit, complaining of the crowded street. "Left again! And right! *A sangre! A fuego! A sacco!*"

They sped along the unpaved street, leaping over horse-pies when they spied them. "Where are we going?" demanded Will.

"Away from them!" answered Kit snappishly.

"Yes, but eventually we'll run out of city."

"We're in London! It's one magnificent warren of hiding places, an escapade of escape. *Cache-cache!*" He pointed. "See! Opportunity presents!"

His index finger was directed at a cluster of twenty men standing without a wooden theatre – not a proper theatre such as the Butts, but one that was far stronger-looking, and more used.

Puffing for breath, Will gasped, "I thought we were avoiding—!"

Kit was already off. "Less thought, more haste! Chop chop!"

Wondering what value Kit had seen in this knot of men, he squinted. They were dressed in white linen shirts and hose, and plain wool doublets and capes. The black of their outer-things had faded, looking to be a pasty brownish-grey. In one man, it might be neglect. In a group, it was a statement – they were refusing to spend money on frivolities such as re-dying their plain, functional garments.

Instantly a quotation sprang to Will's mind:

"No doubt but this poyson hath shed foorth his influence, and powred foorth his stinking dregges ouer all the face of the earth; but yet I am sure there is not any people vnder the Zodiacke of heauen, how clownish, rurall, or brutish soeuer, that is so poisoned with the Arsnecke of Pride or hath drunke so deepe of the dregges of this Cup as Anglia hath; with griefe of conscience I speake it, with sorow I see it, and with teares I lament it."

Those words had been written by Phillip Stubbes, in a wide-ranging diatribe entitled Anatomy of Abuses, decrying among other things the fanciful nature of fashion.

These men were Puritans. And they were protesting whatever was going on inside the theatre.

Swiping his hat from his head and putting upon himself even greater heights of breathlessness, Kit threw himself at them. "The Catholics! The Catholics are rising..!" Then he collapsed in one man's arms as if in a faint.

As Will knelt beside his friend, gasping for his own breath, a nearby the Puritan leader gazed wide-eyed in an almost erotic excitement. "Catholics? What Catholics?"

Will pointed at their pursuers. "There! Them! Those!" He found he was quite skilled at screaming in panic.

"Catholics?" demanded the Puritan again, as if in his mind Pandora's jar had just opened.

"Denizens of Hell!" exclaimed Kit, eyes still shut.

"How can they be Catholic?"

"They're rising – all over the city!" gasped Will, his terror genuine as the Savage crew drew ever closer.

"But how do we know they're Catholic?" demanded the Puritan, who evidently expected fire, brimstone, and forked tails.

Exasperated, Will exclaimed, "They're wearing Spanish hose!!"

Nonsensically, this was the linstock to the Puritanical cannon. With an outraged howl, the mass of them surged forward drawing up clubs and cudgels from the detritus of the roadway. Savage and the rest found themselves faced with fanatics, willing to die to protect Kit and Will, Queen and Crown, and this blessed Isle from the Papists.

Recovering from his feigned faint, Kit guffawed. "Spanish hose. Well done."

There was a scream as one Puritan fell, skewered on the tip of Savage's blade. The man was a terror, and far more martial than the Puritans had perhaps expected. In seconds their reserve would leave them, and the hunt would resume.

"Shall we join them?" asked Will, uneasy at duping men into fighting for him.

"Certainly not!" cried Kit. Taking hold of Will's shoulder, he shoved him forward into the theatre.

"Oi!" protested the Box-Keeper. "Oi! It's a penny to enter—"

They leapt past him and towards the entrance to the groundlings, meaning to get lost among the thick crowd. The Keeper shouted urgently behind them, and Will briefly wondered why, unlike the Butts, there was no curtained entry into the ground-level, but only into a raised gallery above. They had to push together on a heavy door, swinging it wide. As they did, they heard the excited shouts of a crowd cheering on a performer: "Or-si-no! Or-si-no! Or-si-no!"

The view that spread before them was both astonishing and terrifying. The smell was worse, and Will suddenly understood what it was the Puritans outside had been protesting.

There was no stage, but rather a pit below the stands where three giant bandogs were conversing in snarls and barks with a huge figure in a shaggy brown coat. The roaring of the crowd above was quite deafening, but all at once the shouting and growling stopped as all eyes turned to gaze at the two intruders in the pit. All eyes, including those belonging to the massive beast tethered to the center of the ring. Orsino.

Will and Kit had stumbled into a bear-baiting.

Scene Four

Animal sports had declined greatly since the days of the Roman Colosseum. Gone were the days when hundreds of beasts were imported in chains from the far corners of the world for fantastical battles – lion v. ostrich, elephant v. bull. In the 1500 years since the Emperor Titus inaugurated his glorious monument to blood sports, the games had become sordid and squalid – *visera sans valore*, guts without glory.

There were three men in the bear-pit already, holding their great mastiffs by the ears. The bandogs strained forward, eager to leap up and take their share in the blood-letting.

The redundantly christened Orsino was angry, excited, and frightened all at once. Diseased, flea-ridden, and far from proud, he was fastened by a rope about his waist to a stake with an iron ring in it. The rope was fifteen feet long, confining the beast to a diameter of thirty. The pit itself was perhaps fifty feet from end to end.

Just as the intruders entered, taking stock of the affair, one of the keepers, be it from shock or pique at the rude interruption, let loose his animal. The creature was momentarily uncertain, choosing between the lesser and greater targets. But he stayed true to his training, leaping off his powerful hinds to wrench at the bear's bare rump.

The bear's aggrieved roar did not muffle the clatter behind Will and Kit as the Savage band knocked down the Box-Keeper and chased through the short corridor to where the two fugitives stood framed like portraits of fear.

"In a choice between them," opined Kit lightly, "I'll take the Deep Blue Sea over the Devil." And with a laugh meant to be fearless but that emerged almost hysterical, he ran into the ring. Will paused a moment, then with a deep breath plunged in as well.

The bear was engaged with his first conversant, the two of them debating the finer points of tooth against paw. A solid smack seemed to win the argument for Orsino, as the dog did not rise to contest the point. While the shaggy brown wall faced the other way, Kit and Will scrambled by his left side, heads low.

Will found himself spewing a quote. "Bears have the weakest heads, as lions have strongest."

"Feeling baited?" laughed Kit.

"I wish his claws were bated," replied Will, looking at the air-slashing sharps.

"So as to abate your fate," said Kit, backstepping wildly.

"Now you're baiting me," said Will.

"I'm a master of it!"

"You've been saving that jest, haven't you?" laughed Will, never taking his eyes off the bear.

"Get out of it!" roared one of the mastiff masters, barely holding his animal in check. The crowd above jeered and shouted, complaining of the spoiling of their wagers. But Will only had eyes for the latest Savage entrant to the fray.

Unlike Kit and Will, the pursuers entered with swords drawn and ready. Sensing what was in the offing, the crowd scrambled to make new wagers. Savage said nothing, but began circling the outer circumference of the pit, just out of Orsino's reach.

"William, dear?"

"Yes, friend Christopher?"

"Release the hounds."

Will had already had the same notion. Drawing his blade, he jabbed at the nearest dog owner, who instinctively released his grip on the beast's ear. Kit did the same, and at once, eager to continue their fellow's argument, the two dogs leapt at yellow-eyed Orsino. One plucked him by the throat. Orsino answered by traversing the ban-dog's scalp with an open claw. The other nipped his heel and the great bear cried out, as if confessing a fair point made, while the second mas-tiff leapt to clamp his hideous teeth on the bear's most potent debater, his arm.

Will and Kit kept well back, circling the pit to remain out of both an-imal and human clutches. Their goal was to edge back to the door and sprint to freedom, leaving Savage trapped on the far side of the bear. But Savage had dealt with that, leaving Derby to guard the escape.

They had to dodge as one of the hounds was knocked their way, yelping in offended protest. With all the fending and proving, plucking and tugging, scratching and biting, plain tooth and nail on both sides, such expense of blood and skin was spent between them as a months licking would not recover.

Savage found his path blocked by one of the dog owners, and with no thought whatsoever ran the man through the shoulder with his blade. The crowd was now torn between watching the trio of animals or the septet of humans. Rookwood and Brockhurst had begun to circle the other way, pinning their true prey, Will and Kit.

Orsino proved himself an old hand at argument, strangling one dog while lashing out at the other in a spine-breaking blow. The debate in the pit's center was almost concluded, and the one at the outskirts was about to begin. Savage was drawing close on the left, and Rookwood on the right. Encouraged by the bloody mess of the dogs, the crowd was calling blood of a more human, if not humane, nature.

Under his breath, Will was muttering. Kit cast him a glance. "What?"

"Nothing," grunted Will, shaking his head.

"You sounded like you were—"

"Singing, yes. Nervous habit. Like I said, nothing."

"Not nothing, a thing of brilliance. Sing out!" And Kit launched into song:

Ah, Robin, jolly Robin
Tell me how thy leman doth
And thou shalt know of mine.

Will swiftly joined him:

My lady is unkind, perdie,
Alack, why is she so? (cried the others)
She lov'th another better than me
And yet she will say no.

Orsino cast aside the spent form of the choked mastiff and shook his ears thrice, spraying high and low with his blood and slather. Then his muzzle dropped as his ears pricked. Amid the shouts and clamours, the singing had momentarily soothed him. Or simply confused him.

Shoulder to shoulder with Will, Kit paused in his singing. He had a feverous look in his eye, and a dangerous smile. "Do you recall our horse-thieving days?" he asked.

That act seemed already months behind them. But Will understood at once, and acted without hesitation. Without sheathing his sword he cupped his hands.

Ah, Robin, jolly Robin
Tell me how thy leman doth
And thou shalt know of mine.

Kit stepped up and Will heaved him, leaping, towards the center of the ring. The back of the victorious Orsino was to them, and Kit lighted upon it for a split-second. Using the bear's shoulder as a step, he launched up and over the bear and towards the egress. Startled, Derby tried to raise his sword, but Kit's blade knocked it aside midair, followed by Kit's whole frame knocking the Catholic bodily to the dirt.

The bear felt the step and, startled from his reverie, imagined a new tongue was joining the violent debate. Enraged, he swung his great paws up and behind him to swat at his back. As he did, Will dove forward, rolling and cutting at once. His target was not Orsino, but the rope lashing the bear to the floor.

A scream of terror arose from the stands. Those at the front attempted to climb over their neighbours in a hurried retreat. Used to watching such debates from on high, they had no desire to test Orsino's Socratic skills themselves.

Will finished his roll and ran for the door. He leapt over the supine Derby, whose nose was now crimson from blood as well as treasure. Kit was waiting, and together they ran. Casting a final look over his shoulder, Will saw Savage and the others show real fear, trying to reason with Orsino with the pointed arguments of their blades. But the bear showed no sign of being impressed by their points, and the men were scattering, attempting to climb the walls or run for cover. So too the three dog-owners who raced after Will and Kit down the corridor to the exit. They turned and barred the door, trapping the Savage band within.

Through the outer-most door, Kit called out Satan's lament from the pious play *The Harrowing of Hell:* "Out, alas! Now goeth away my prisoners and all my prey! Ha!"

Will and Kit reached the street a second before the fleeing crowd. Sheathing their swords, they blended into the panicked mass. It wasn't until they were several streets away that Kit plucked Will's elbow and lead the way into an alley so they might recover their wind.

"I retract all I ever said against bear-baiting!" gasped Kit in exhilaration.

Temporarily unable to conjure words, Will just nodded. He was relishing the horrible glory of his survival, and pitying the bear Orsino, who was not suited for such a life. Clearly the noble animal had a more musical soul.

Perhaps the same notion was in Kit's mind, for he quoted John Skelton:

Wolde to God it wolde please you some day
A balade boke before me to laye

And lerne me for to synge re, mi, fa, sol
And when I fayle, bobbe me on the noll.

Scrubbing the spatters of bear and hound blood from their faces and hands, they set out to find a new lodging. "For I fear the Elephant has closed itself to our trunks," said Kit. *"Cache-cache!"*

That statement started the wheels of Will's mind turning again. "But how on earth did they know where we were?"

Kit sighed theatrically. "O, 'tis an indigest world, William. I am afeared, and I hope I am much mistaken, that we have been most foully and brutally betrayed."

Scene Five

"Betrayed?" echoed Will hollowly. He had not even considered the possibility. "By whom?"

"There is but one choice," explained Kit with resentful patience. "Lord Walsingham's own Wit, the Welsh Walter Williams. He alone could have told our pursuers where we'd lighted. Which means," added Kit, his keen eyes living their own life, "we have an added value to present his Lordship Sir Francis."

"You mean we deliver both the message and that he has a traitor on his staff?"

"Just so. Come!" Kit whirled and started off in a new direction.

"Back to Seething Lane?"

"Not directly. The house will now be watched by Derby and his savage companion, assuming they survived the embrace of our orsine friend. So we cannot just walk up and knock. Walter the Welshman might simply lock us out, placing us between Scylla and Charybdis."

"Then where, pray, are we going?"

"Why, to hunt the most elusive and rare beastie in creation – a gambling Scotsman!"

Will threw up his hands. There was never a direct answer from this walking goad, this fiendish fellow who had so upheaved Will's life. So why was it he was enjoying himself so much?

Hours on, our heroes – or at least our unheroic leads – were to be found standing in the lee of a quite fashionable building. Not only was Will tired and hungry, but the reaction to their earlier adventures had given him the shakes. With his arms folded tightly to hide this, he blinked hard to keep off the weighty blanket of sleep.

All Kit had conveyed so far was that there was a man who liked the odd game of chance – cards, mostly. Being in the employ of the Queen's spymaster, he could not indulge himself openly. "Sensing the danger if this temptation went long unacknowledged, our lovely Sir Francis arranged for this house to be the gambling den of men who should not be compromised. They play an elegant game of Primero, for stakes as high as Heaven."

Primero was a card game Will had played back in the days when he was on the road towards becoming a gentleman. The 8s, 9s, and 10s were removed from a deck, then four cards were dealt. Aces, 6s, and 7s were the highest scoring single cards, and the hands were known by names such as Primero, Maximus, Fluxus, and Chorus. It was not a game he had enjoyed, but he had been good at it. Then the prospect of being a gentleman vanished, and with it his need to understand the game.

"There's our Judas goat," said Kit.

Roused from his sour thoughts with a nudge, Will spied the mannish goat as he stepped into the moonlight. It had to be nigh on eleven o'clock, but he seemed fresh. Medium height and sturdily built, their goat had a thick moustache and no beard. He breathed deep, coughed, then stepped over a pool of horse urine and set off.

Kit held up a hand. He ticked his fingers down, three, two, one, then he and Will set off in pursuit.

"Who is he?" whispered Will.

"In France I knew him as Peter Halins, but for certes that's not his name."

"It's so late, he must be heading home."

"I doubt it. And no whispering – if he hears men concealing themselves, he'll vanish. He is, after all, a spy. So, tell me what you thought of the play – and do try not to piss yourself."

Will understood – it was again time to play a part. Unfortunately, Will knew precisely how a drunkard behaved. Slurring his words, he loudly quoted several lines from *The Spanish Tragedy:*

> *O eyes, no eyes, but fountains fraught with tears;*
> *O life, no life, but lively form of death;*
> *O world, no world, but mass of public wrongs,*
> *Confused and filled with murder and misdeeds.*

Kit chimed in, adding superlatives of praise. Their quarry paused to piss against a wall, probably to let them pass. Kit kept his face obscured and let Will do all the talking. The moment they turned the corner, they hid, but continued the conversation in lowered voices, as though they were drawing further off.

"What now?" asked Will lowly.

Pressing his lip so close to Will's ear that the new beard tickled him, Kit said, "There is a secret entrance, I'm sure, to Walsingham's lair. We must follow this Halins and force into the light that which is obscured. Ah. Here he comes."

After that it was harder, as they had to trail the man in silence. But the distance was not great. By the signage they had arrived Crutched Friars Street when the man vanished into an alley. Kit grinned as his feet gave a little skip. "I was right! He's off to work – Seething Lane is just around the corner. This must be a back way in. Come on – quick!"

The goat man not called Halins did not enter a house facing Seething Lane. Instead he approached a side-gate to a house on Crutched Friars a full block away. Just as the gate was swinging to, Kit pounced, placing a knife at the spy's neck. "Not a sound, dearie. Simply show us the way in."

"Dunno—" the man protested in a perfectly Scottish lilt, but was cut off by Kit's free hand tugging his ear.

"Ah ah! No sound, Peter-not-Peter. What name are you using nowadays?"

The goat gasped. "Marlowe?"

"Nay, that name is mine, you may not take it. Passing that by, I guarantee that I have news that'll make grim Sir Francis dance like a satyr. What rewards and riches will ye reap, if ye but take a gamble upon us."

"What do you—?"

"My companion and I cannot use the front door, as I'm quite sure it's being watched for our arrival. But we have vital and urgent news regarding a plot against Her Majesty. You will be doing God's own work if you show us the way. And not the Catholic God of Rome."

The man had steel, that much was clear. He weighed Kit's words, the knife at his throat frightening him not a jot. At last he nodded. "Put away yon dagger, man, and follow me."

Resheathing, Kit nodded for Will to close the gate behind them. Then they followed the goat spy not called Peter towards a side door to the grand house before them. He jangled some keys and opened the heavy portal. Inside he nodded to a woman sitting with a load of laundry she was folding. Will thought it was late for that, until she drew from the many folds a massive hackbut and aimed it at him.

"Who are these?" she demanded.

"They're in Sir Francis' employ," said not-Peter.

"They must leave their swords."

At once Kit obeyed the gatekeeper, and Will followed suit, unbuckling his scabbard from his belt and laying it on the rush-covered flagstone floor. Seconds later these rushes were rushed aside to reveal a trapdoor. Not-Peter hauled on the large iron ring, and soon Kit and Will were descending a wooden staircase to an airless stone passage.

Ten minutes later they emerged from the far side, into light. There was a gatekeeper at this end as well, a man this time, who gazed hard at three where he'd expected one. "Thomas, what the blazes..?"

"They are here with me, with news for Sir Francis. Is he..?"

"In his study," answered the guard reluctantly.

"Hullo Skeggs," said Kit brightly.

"Marlowe." The man made it sound like a curse.

The spy called Thomas (was that his first name or his last, wondered Will) led them around a corner and up a flight of ornately-carved stairs. Arriving at a large door made of oak, he paused to turn a gimlet eye on Kit and Will. "If you have lied to me," warned the Scotsman, "I'll have you flayed alive."

"And I'll deserve it," agreed Kit with perfect amiability. "And more, *un fate plus mal que mort.*"

Already regretting his decision, Thomas-not-Peter goat-man pursed his lips. Bracing himself, he knocked on the dark door.

"Come."

Invited, Will stepped into the private study of the Queen's spymaster. It was dark, but he imagined over the door the words of Dante: *All hope abandon ye who enter here.*

The man behind the desk was dressed all in black, and not the faded black of the Puritans but the rich and expensive black of the most binding dyes. His hair, too, was dark, though not as pure a black, more a deep brown. But the widow's peak was sinister, and the neat beard and thick, jutting moustache were menacing.

Blackest of all were his eyes. Set in the deepest, saddest pockets of human flesh Will had ever seen, the eyes were offset by the sallow skin, making them appear bottomless, unearthly. The candlelight striking them seemed to be swallowed, not reflected.

Those eyes now gazed at the trio as they entered, carrying no hint of surprise – or any expression at all.

"Sir Francis, forgive me," said Thomas-not-Peter. "Christopher Marlowe waylaid me on my entrance. He claims to have news fit only for your ears."

There was a long silence as the spymaster digested this information. Then to Kit he said, "You went unobserved, I trust."

"Yes, my lord," said Kit, in what seemed like genuine obedience.

"Very well. Thomas, step down the hall and tell Faunt that I am expecting our Swedish friend, but may be delayed to the meeting. If

I am, he may conduct matters in my stead. Then return and stay by the door in case I need you."

Thomas-not-Peter obeyed, and Will watched him go with unease. Being alone with Kit and Walsingham was unnerving to say the least. He felt like a kitten standing between a lynx and a leopard.

Walsingham remained seated. At his back there was a great window, but shuttered, allowing in no light at all. "So, Marlowe, you're back to playing the rogue. You've abandoned your post in France. I suppose you know what this means."

"Why, nothing short of utter disgrace," answered Kit in an over-cheery cadence. "Unless, perhaps, I have something of far greater value than seducing young Parisian secretaries for you."

"Your companion looks startled," observed Walsingham, referring to Will's expression. "Is he not one of those conquests?"

"Not yet, at any rate." Kit threw the ghost of a wink in Will's direction. He seemed supremely confident, so much so that he took a chair unbidden and stretched out his legs before him. "No, William here had the misfortune to save my life, and has assisted me ever since in my quest to reach you with what is, I assure you, the thing you have craved most in all the world."

"An end to the Spanish?" asked Walsingham, proving he owned something resembling humour.

"The next best thing, then. An end to Mary of Scotland."

Walsingham was silent for a long moment. Then he held out his hand.

Kit made a show of retrieving the twist of paper from inside his shirt. He placed it in the waiting palm and sat back. "Copied from her clark's desk. I made watch, and very cleverly deduced the means by which she is communicating with the larger universe outside her circumcised sphere. How does she do it, you ask? Sometimes she receives small slips by hand. But for letters of import, she sneaks them out through the bung of the ale-casks she's allowed, and receives them the same way. You'll want to arrest the beer-man, I daresay. This was a message brought in for her to read, and I had it before it had been decyphered, which means it is still, alas, in code. But I'm confident, after all I have achieved so far, you can deal with such trifles."

Walsingham rose as he unfurled the deadly missive – deadly to Mary, if Kit was correct. He frowned down at the unbroken string of letters, arching an eyebrow. "And you come pell-mell in the dead of night because…"

"We tried to deliver it earlier in the day," added Kit airily. "We left a message with Welshman Willie, and told him where to find us. Oddly enough, we'd hardly sat down to our supper when we were attacked by Mary's men – the same men who pursued us all across the country-side." In a whisper of dramatic mockery, Kit added, "I'm quite afeared, my lord, that you have a spy here."

"Several, in fact." Walsingham crossed from behind the desk to its right side, closer to the thick-wicked candle that provided light for the desk. He leaned towards the illumination. His hooded eyes burned brighter than the candlelight. "Copies?"

"None!" exclaimed Kit, sounding offended. "I know my business, my lord."

"I see. Forgive me, I had to check." And standing upright, Walsingham held the twist of paper over the flames and set it alight.

Will felt his heart skip a beat, then double its paradiddle. Kit fell sideways in his seat, barely catching himself from hitting the floor altogether. "My lord! What–"

"Christopher Marlowe, you are the king of fooles! Do you think that you, in your wig and false bosoms, could discover a truth hidden from the entire British government? From this office? From me?"

Kit's smile was no longer real, he had simply forgotten to remove it. "You – you knew?"

"Of course we knew." Walsingham towered over Kit, still, calm, cold. His words were crisp and clipped. "And do you presume to think that Williams can do anything without my knowing? It was not he who set the Papists upon you. 'Twas I."

Kit's bravado vanished altogether. "You?"

"Yes. I hoped they might kill you both before you reached this office. That they did not is disappointing, but as you assure me no one saw you enter, we are safe. They will not know that you delivered the message, and when your bodies are found, they will believe you were accidentally killed on the way to my door."

Eyes wide, Kit's jaw seemed unhinged from his skull, yet he still managed something like speech. "My Lord, I don't—"

"Worse than disgrace this time, I'm afraid, Mister Marlowe. Your actions—"

"I don't underst—"

"*We own the brewer!*" snapped Walsingham. "We receive the whole of every message Mary sends out, not this mere snippet. It was quite a trial, actually, engineering a method for her to send treasonous communications without her suspecting us."

Shaking, Will wondered if it was not too late to slip out unnoticed. *Probably.* Beside him, horror had settled over Kit's features.

"You see it now, I think," said Walsingham in a tone so icy one could skate upon it. "Rather than do us a service, your idiotic lark has risked an operation that took months to put in place. This is why we professionals behave professionally – *and obey orders*. To keep from ruining the well-laid plans of our betters." His voice grew low, almost a hiss. "So, on behalf of Her Majesty's government, I must convey my thanks, Mr. Marlowe. By tripping in and playing the hero, you've damaged the nation, and quite possibly imperiled the throne."

Kit reached out a pleading hand. "That message…"

"Whatever was in it, I promise you, we've already seen and done with it. And now, alas, we must be done with you as well." For all the force of his words, only now did he raise his voice. "Phelippes! Skeggs! Come at once!"

The door opened, and without it stood the two men, hands on their swords.

"Take these two and have them killed. It must seem accidental. And put a paper on Marlowe that is smudged beyond recognition, preferably by his own blood. That is essential."

The man called Skeggs grasped Will by the elbow, without any re-sistance. Thomas-not-Peter whose surname appeared to be Phelippes put a hand on the stunned Kit's right shoulder, meaning to haul him out of the chair. Only then did Marlowe shake himself and speak a protest. "I have another piece of information."

Walsingham waited with a bored expression on his face. Will was eager to hear Kit's latest stroke of genius to remove them from harm – in all their short acquaintance, Kit hadn't yet failed him.

Still, Will was surprised when Kit twisted and pointed at him. "This man calls himself William False-staff, doubtless an alias to shield him. He's from a Papist family in Stratfordshire, has a grudge against a man named Thomas Lucy, once studied with Campion, and likely commit-ted some crime in Stratford itself for which he was flogged. Interrogate him and he will surely yield up other names."

Though Kit's finger was directed at Will, his eyes were upon Wals-ingham, searching for salvation. Will dragged his own eyes away from that Judas finger and did the same, wondering if he were about to be put to the torture before he was put to death.

"I very much doubt the names of a rural recusant or two is worth the risk of compromising Her Majesty's safety. Take them away."

Will felt a surge of anger – not at Marlowe, but at Walsingham himself, who had to this moment not even deigned to address him. Here was Authority personified, and Will was being arbitrarily and summarily sentenced to die without even a word being addressed to him. No!

His passivity to date helped him. Skeggs thought he was re-signed, and was focused instead upon Kit. Wrenching his arm free, Will reached down and drew Skeggs' sword from its scabbard. He slashed confidently, making Skeggs weave and skip backwards, then he whirled just in time to strike Phelippes' half-drawn sword. "Kit, you bastard, stir yourself!"

Kit was still sitting boneless in the chair with an expression that seemed hammer-struck. Forced to engage two men at once, Will shouted, "Christopher! You got me into this!"

As Will turned to shove Skeggs away while keeping his point on Phelippes, the devastated rogue Marlowe shook himself like one of the Orsino-struck bandogs. Rolling out of his seat, he grabbed it by the arms and heaved it madly across the desk.

The near-imperturbable Walsingham shouted as he ducked. But Kit hadn't been aiming for the spymaster, but for the window behind him. The shutters splintered, the glass shattered, and the balmy night air entered the room, snuffing the candles.

In the darkness, Kit wrested Phelippes' sword free and leapt onto the table. "Will! An exit, I think, is called for!"

Will jumped up beside him. Together they hopped onto the window's sill, then with a held breath, threw themselves into the night.

Act III
A Skirmish of Wits

Scene One

"Tumbling, tumbling!" cried Kit in mid-air.

Will obeyed, performing the old acrobat's trick of rolling as they reached the earth. Even so, it was a miraculous landing, coming down without breaking bones. Will felt a sharp pain in his knee as he rose, but was able to ignore it as he took to his heels.

They were at the front of the house, with the high gate before them. There were no guards at the gate, but Will recalled that some of Savage's allies were likely without, watching. And from inside the house orders were being shouted for their instantaneous demise. Will had no idea how they would extricate themselves from this. All they could do was run.

Kit lifted the latch and heaved the gate wide, then turned right. Will was tempted to dart left in the hope that their pursuers would deem Kit more valuable. But his star was now firmly tethered to the comet that was Kit.

As they ran, he called out, "You betrayed me!"

Far from looking abashed, Kit shrugged. "It was not my tongue that was loose. You knew I was involved with the craft of spyhood, and should have guarded your secrets properly."

Not an answer to mollify. "If we survive, I'm going to strike you on the nose."

"If you devise a way for us to survive," laughed Kit sourly, "you may do so and welcome!"

Turning left onto Crutched Friar's Street, they saw men emerging from shadows on both sides. Together they dodged into the center of the street, feet pounding the cobblestones. The pain in Will's knee, until now merely annoying, became more insistent. He would have to stop soon. It was not a matter, then, of out-running their various enemies. It had to be guile, or daring.

Ahead there was a carriage coming towards them, drawn by a trotting pair of dappled mares. Will wondered who was inside, and decided it could hardly matter – there was no shelter to be had within its walls. And it was heading back the way they had come, exposing them to two very dissimilar packs of hunters…

A wild idea, glorious in its stupidity, coming to him, Will hissed to Kit, "Take down the driver!"

Stunningly, Kit did not question, argue, or even comment. He ran for the carriage, sword in hand.

Will stopped running, a blessing to his throbbing knee, and turned to face the mass of men – perhaps a dozen – that were in the street behind. "Spies for Elizabeth, meet spies for Mary!" he called out loudly. "Mary's spies, meet those of Her Majesty the Queen!"

This revelation was a sharp shock to those men who worked in Walsingham's home – they had been under the cruel misapprehension that the Catholics were men from their own side. Suddenly both sides ceased running, busily hiding their faces while peering suspiciously through their fingers at the men nearest them. To know the face of an enemy spy was more valuable than gold.

There was a scuffle to the West, and Will ducked as a hackbut was fired. Though it came from the carriage, it served as a reminder to everyone in the street of the gravity of matters to hand. The Catholics turned to flee and Walsingham's men tried to catch the enemy nearest them, while Will turned to see the carriage clattering at him at an alaruming pace. Knee protesting wrathfully, he started to run with it, then leapt aboard.

Kit was sitting atop the box, laughing and swearing. "Almost lost an ear! How daring would that make me look?"

"I can oblige you," retorted Will. "But later!" Clambering up on the side of the stage, Will swung his sword in great downward sweeps as they hurtled through the men still in the street, sending them diving for cover in the muck-filled gutters. They passed Seething Lane once more as they continued down Crutched Friar's, then Kit turned them north.

"Where's the driver?" Will asked – or started to. He was cut across by a second hackbut blast from the street behind them. Clearly the driver was striving to catch them up. Ducking, Will climbed around to the driver's perch.

"Any notion who's inside?" asked Will as he settled in beside Kit.

"I saw a feminine face peeking through the curtain below."

"Who?"

"Oh yes, I stopped and chatted her up," snarled Kit, holding the reins uneasily – skill upon a horse obviously did not translate to driving a pair from atop a rattling box.

"She must be afraid," protested Will.

"Your chivalrous bent is admirable, under the circumstances. But she has nothing to fear. I am quite frightened enough for us all."

As Kit drove them around another corner, Will looked at the carriage roof. There was a small door for the driver to speak to the occupant. Will lifted it, intending to assure the occupant that no harm was intended her. But as he leaned forward a flash of steel nearly took out his eyes.

Will closed the hatch again. "She's armed."

"Naturally," snorted Kit. "The way this night is progressing, I would not be at all surprised to find that we've abducted the Queen herself."

Will had a horrible moment. The face he had seen briefly had indeed been in the middle of life, about forty years, with pale skin and bright red hair. The very image of the Queen, at least by her portraits on coins and placards. "No – it can't be…"

"I was joking—" began Kit, turning their carriage again. He glanced Will's way and saw the horror. "No. No no no… William, please tell me –"

"I don't – look out!" Will pointed at the obstacle in their path, a pair of kites feasting on some dead or foul thing in the roadway. Kit shouted and they flew past his face, shrieking their rage that their midnight meal was interrupted.

"Where are we going?" demanded Will.

"Out of the city, then out of the country, I imagine. Do you speak French?" With the shouts of pursuit now faded away, he slowed the carriage to a modest trot, just fast enough to keep their passenger from throwing herself out. It was a highly unlikely course of action, for a noblewoman's many layers of heavy skirts would get dragged under the wheels. But red-headed women were unpredictable – as one look at Huffing Kate would confirm.

"Fut!" swore Kit.

"What?"

"I can't think of a way out of the city that doesn't mean passing through a gate. And at this time of night…" While the name London encompassed all the various municipalities, boroughs, and villages in this area, the city itself was just a square mile, entirely enclosed by walls. The only way out was through the walls, over the walls, or down the Thames, also guarded.

Kit muttered something, and Will understood that he was talking the problem through. "Can't do the—or the other—if we perhaps—it's not as though…" Trailing away, he shook his head vigourously then began chewing on his lower lip, sucking the hairs that grew just below it.

"Kit, if we don't hide soon…" The alarum would be spreading now to all the gates. It was merely a matter of minutes before they were apprehended. "This carriage is too noteworthy to—"

Suddenly smiling, Kit cut across him. "William, can you drive?"

"No," said Will, unwilling to even try. He now suspected Kit of intending to throw him to the dogs, while escaping unharmed.

"Pity," said Kit. "I'd hoped to spare you this. But if I am needed up here, you must step below and convince our guest to aid us."

"Aid us," repeated Will with a dull groan. He perceived what Kit had in mind.

"Just so. Open the hatch and see if you can speak sense to her."

Will did as bidden, and was again repelled by the flash of steel. He slammed the hatch shut. "She does not seem particularly communicative."

"Nonsense, you're just not speaking her language. Look, I'll open the hatch and distract her. Then you may step inside."

"So said so done is well," replied Will, looking at the cobblestones racing below. But he obediently clambered up and over the hatch and poised himself above the carriage door. He nodded to Kit, who took one hand off the reins to lift the hatch.

The knife came again, and Will was already hanging heels-to-heaven, opening the door with one hand and poking his sword in with the other. He was afeared that she was not alone, that someone else held the warding dagger. But within the dark interior there was only the one occupant, poised upon her knees under the hatch, slashing wildly upwards. She turned and saw Will's inverted face hanging just inside the open door. Recoiling to the farthest corner of the carriage, she turned upon him a fierce glare. "You dare draw your sword upon a lady?"

Will felt a moment of blissful relief. The Queen was pure English, whereas this woman had the hint of an accent, possibly Scandinavian. He felt foolish for even imagining that they had actually kidnapped the Monarch.

"I apologize," said Will, wondering how he would swing himself down into the carriage.

"Are you highwaymen? Are London robbers grown so bold?"

"We are not robbers and have no intent to molest you in any way. I am a gentlemen," added Will. That was stretching a point. Though they had been well upon the way, his father had never been actually granted gentle status, lacking only the funds to purchase it. But in the moment it could not hurt.

"Prove it, then," she told him. "Release me."

"I cannot."

"Then you are no gentleman."

Will thought for a moment, then threw his sword upon the carriage floor. "There. I am no longer a gentleman. No arms. Now, may I please enter and speak with you?"

She paused, evidently surprised by both his actions and his accent – not London, but not unpolished either. Placing one foot atop his sword to keep him from taking it up, she said, "I am keeping my knife."

"As long as you do not seek it a new sheath." He rolled himself lithely down and into the vehicle. He swung the door shut behind him, plunging them into near-darkness. The only light that remained came from the hatch by Kit's seat.

"Whom may I have the honour of addressing?" he asked.

She paused, then said, "My name is Helena." Noble and rich, she was clearly unwilling to provide her captors with additional information that might lead to her ransom.

"Time, William, time!" called Kit from above.

"Lady Helena," said Will quickly, "my friend and I are in terrible danger. Through patriotic actions, with no malice in the world, we find ourselves chased by both our nation's enemies and its defenders. Either will, catching us, end our lives at once. We seek only to escape the city and go to earth until we can prove our innocence." He spoke earnestly, and only the last word stuck in his throat. Whatever they were, it was not innocent. However accidentally, they had become traitors to the Crown.

But he must have been at least somewhat convincing, for Lady Helena said, "What, then, do you wish of me?"

"Only the use of your carriage to leave the city bounds. If you can pass us through the gates, I swear to you that we will leave your presence as quickly as we came."

While the wheels clattered without, there was silence within. Will had stated his case as fairly as a desperate man might, and he sensed that further pleading would only harm his cause.

When at last she spoke, her voice was raised. "You there! Driver! What is the nearest portal?"

"We're close to Cripplegate, my lady," said Kit hopefully.

"Very well. Take us through."

Will sagged in relief. "Your ladyship, I cannot thank you enough."

"No," she agreed from the shadows of the carriage corner. "You cannot."

Will was again struck by her accent. Something about it made his palms itch. It hovered in his memory like a half-remembered song. He was certain he had never heard it before. There was something...

But they were already drawing up to the gate. Will heard the shout of the guards and Kit pulled the carriage to a halt.

"Stand!" called a guard.

"Stand?" answered Kit in a bored tone. "If I stand, I'll fall, and the horses will be masterless."

"Ye wot well what we want, saucy fellow," answered a second guard. "Who have ye within?"

Not knowing, Kit made the best answer he could. "A lady."

"We'll be seein' abou'tha," said the first guard, whose voice sounded closer. He was approaching the door Will had entered.

This was the moment of truth – would she preserve them, or betray them? He wondered what words her accent would shape—

Then he remembered. Walsingham had said he was expecting a Swedish visitor. Had he been referring to this woman? Was she, too, one of his army of agents? Had they all unknowing delivered themselves into the maw of another trap?

There was a bustle of movement, and Will heard the scrape of his sword being taken up. *We're through*, he thought. Already he was raising his hands in surrender.

"Here!" hissed the lady, thrusting the sword into his hands. "Hide it!"

Astonished, his heart beating anew, Will quickly sat upon it. And just in time. A moment later the door was wrenched open and a bearded face poked in, accompanied by a lantern.

He took in Will, who looked rather the worse for wear, but then his eyes came to the lady and his jaw dropped open. Seeing her in proper light for the first time, Will felt much the same. Here was beauty if one talked of beauty. Red hair and deep brown eyes, a fine forehead and modest chin. Like most women of her colouring, her eyebrows were so fair that she did not have to pluck them. Her ears were slightly pointed, giving her a look more Irish than Swedish. Her lips might have been full, had they not been pressed together so very tight, and the flush to her cheek might just as easily have been excitement, or anger.

More, she was dressed for court. Between puffed shoulders and below a gold-fringed ruff about her neck, a large emerald hung at her throat. There were several jewels about her fingers as well. This was not only a lady, but a lady of substance.

"Who are you?" she demanded of the guard. "Why do you open a door without knocking? Cannot you see the seal on the door?"

Stepping back under this verbal attack, the guard lowered his lamp to gaze in horror at the seal painted on the door's exterior. "Pardon us, your Ladyship. But at this hour—"

"Does the hour excuse rudeness? Vulgarity? Insolence?"

A second guard appeared, roughly dragging the first back. He was at once deferential, removing his helmet and bowing low. "Pardon me, my lady, but we had no anticipation of anyone leaving the city tonight. And though it may be rude, it is our commission to ask the names of the people who pass in and out after daylight hours. I'm certain you understand."

The lady who Will knew only as Helena lifted her chin imperiously. "I do. And had you but asked, I would have answered. I am Helena of Snakenborg, Marchioness of Northampton, wife of Sir Thomas Gorges, and Lady-in-Waiting to her Majesty the Queen." She waved a hand at Will, then above. "These are my servants."

The man knuckled his forehead swiftly, bowing so low he almost disappeared from view. "Begging your pardon, my lady. We'll open the gates at once."

This remarkable lady turned her face away from the light, as though offended by the sight of the fellow. Will had a quick glimpse of her in profile before the door was shut, taking with it the light. In moments they were moving, and Will was breathing again. "I cannot thank you enough."

"Don't let it prevent you from trying," she said wryly.

"Thank you," he said at once.

From the darkness, Will would have oathed he heard a smile cross her lips. "So, I presume your trouble stems from the Moor?"

"The Moor?" repeated Will dully, and Helena laughed.

"Forgive me," she said. "It is the name Her Majesty gives him. Sir Francis affects a somber wardrobe. I swear, if it were permitted, his ruff would be black as well."

Clearly she was referring to Walsingham. "Aye," said Will, answering her earlier question. "We are running from Walsingham. There was a – misunderstanding."

"That happens quite often around Sir Francis. I trust I will not regret aiding you this night."

"I hope not. But have we imperiled you?" asked Will with genuine concern. "Your driver will have told them whose carriage—"

"You are sweet, for kidnappers. I'll say I was held at sword-point by two desperate men. It is true, if briefly. Now, why are we stopping?"

Kit opened the hatch once more. "We're well outside the walls, so we will trouble you no more, my lady."

In the moonlight Will saw her eyes grow wider. Had Lady Helena owned eyebrows, they would have been arched. "Will you leave me driverless? Stranded here, alone on my own? Why not just cut my throat and have done?"

Staring at her, Kit's voice held strained amusement. "Where would you like us to deposit…"

"My home, of course. Then you may lay before me the nature of your indiscretion, and we may see how it may be mended. Head west, to Whitefriars. My husband's town home is there – we happen to be in the city for his knighting," she added with wry pride.

Kit obeyed, the carriage rattling down the rough road. Will sat in silence, trying to peer at the lady in the dim light coming from above. "We won't be able to stay," he said suddenly. "They'll trace us to your home, and put you in danger."

"And you don't know how far to trust me," she added smoothly.

"I trust you as much as I trust anyone in the world, at present," said Will.

"Either you are simple, which I doubt, or bitter, which I abhor. Life is too grand to harbour bitterness, young man. It makes the living acrid. Try to live without it."

"As you say," replied Will dubiously. Then he added, "In the interest of fostering trust, perhaps you can tell me why you were calling on Sir Francis so late?"

The lady laughed. "It's no mystery, nor even a scandal! He is merely having trouble decyphering – I should say, parsing – a phrase in a diplomatic communiqué from my native land. The nature of the hour is dictated by the bawling of my youngest child. Bridget is teething at present and refuses to be soothed by her nurse – who in turn is grateful, having the marks of new-minted teeth about her bosoms already."

Having experienced the squalling of infants, Will joined her in laughter. But even as he slipped into comfort and relief, he recognized how dangerous it was, the most insidious of traps. Nor did he quite believe her – if it were not urgent, then why the midnight ride? But he was keeping his secrets, and she had at least made up a pleasant lie to cover hers.

After ten miles of the most pleasant conversation of his life, they arrived at Whitefriars. She called directions up to Kit, and soon they were at the gate of her husband's town home.

As a groom was roused to take charge of the horses and the maids called to wait on the lady, Kit bounded down from the box and plucked Will out of the carriage. "Time to go, I think."

Will nodded. Gratitude and caution both demanded they not stay.

Kit heard the rustle of the lady's skirts as she began to emerge from the carriage. With his usual drolling tone, he thanked her in his own fashion. *"Be not forgetful to entertain strangers: for thereby some have entertained angels unawares."* He was smiling at his own cleverness when he caught first sight of her. Involuntarily he whistled softly between his teeth, and Will felt his internal fire of joy heaped with coals – twice tonight he had seen Kit flummoxed, a wonder indeed.

They both broke a leg to the lady, and amazingly she offered Will her hand. "I would like to know how your misadventure ends – so long as it ends well. I do not like tragic tales. There's too much real tragedy in the world."

"If it ends well, my lady," answered Will, lowering his face over her hand but stopping short of kissing it, "I shall return. If it does not, I won't be able to."

"I look forward to your return, then." With that, the Lady Helena turned and strode toward the house door, where lamps were being lit. Despite the many pounds and layers of fabric, she walked with purpose and poise.

"I'm damned," said Kit appreciatively. "Why, there's a wench."

Will nodded, then punched Kit full in the mouth.

In the far distance there was a clatter of hooves. As Kit touched his bloody lip, he raised his eyebrows as if to say, *Satisfied?* Will grimaced, then nodded. In mutual consent, they left the carriage to the confused-looking groom and walked swiftly off into the embracing darkness.

They circled around to return to London proper by a different route, coming down by the road to Bishopsgate. Moving furtively in the predawn light, they maintained a tense silence. Now the immediate crisis had passed, Will was fuming like a coal-furnace. Finally he could no longer contain himself. "What now, O soul of cleverness?"

His tone was acid, and Kit responded in kind. "You tell me, then. It's time you contribute something to this debacle."

"*I?* Aye, I agree. 'Tis a debacle, and that's entirely due to your leadership. I still haven't decided to forgive you."

"What's to forgive?" demanded Kit, looking remarkably like a man with a severe toothache. "As Abel said to Cain, 'Brother, why art thou so to me in ire?' Did I break my word? Is it my fault that things took an unfortunate turn?" As Will thought it was indeed very much Kit's fault, he opened his mouth. But Kit barreled on. "I was improvising in a moment of distress. Tell me you've never done the same."

Will's words were as sharp as a blade. "Not at the cost of anyone neck but mine own."

Kit made a gesture Will couldn't quite see, but interpreted it correctly. Feeling bilious, he was on the verge of leaving Kit to his fate. *But I am in the tongs, suspended between hammer and anvil. What choice do I have?* Swallowing his betrayed outrage, he gave it one last go. "Do you have any–?"

"Nothing!" cried Kit, now gesticulating wildly. He caught his tone and lowered it, but his hands continued to trace invisible sigils in the air. "My intent was to expunge a bad deed in my past with a far greater service. Now I've committed a far worser deed, and would require a far greater service! O, if only we had copied the note! I see it curling into ashes before my eyes. Damned if I can't taste them in my mouth. The smoke of that fire lingers in my nose like Huffing Kate's breath! With that note we might have stood a chance! Decypher it and save good Queen Bess ourselves. That would force Sir Fucking Walsingham to give us knighthoods instead of nooses!" He slapped his pate with his open palms. "If you want to hear me name myself foole, I do it gladly! Foole! Foole! FOOLE!"

Will waited until Kit's self-venom was spent. "When you've quite finished."

Kit seemed to snarl. "Aye?"

"If that is our sole obstacle, you may consider it solved."

Kit gasped. "You copied it? But when – was it while I slept, you naughty boy..?"

"No. I memorized it."

Kit's delight turned to derision. "You memorized it."

Will closed his eyes, and as if he were looking at the lines of letters afresh, in daylight, he began to recite: "CFPXCFXSPBCTPW, symbol rather like a cross, CJGWCFWCNJYW… Need I continue?"

Kit was agog. "What – how –? You saw it for all of ten seconds!"

"I have an exceptional memory, I think I told you," said Will smugly, sensing a turn in their relationship. "A gift from above, or my grandmother, who had a similar talent in music. Besides, in Stratford there was little to do but memorize. And like the muscles of the sword-arm, the more a thing is used, the more it strengthens."

"Ha-*ha!* Take that, Sir Fuckall Francis!" Kit capered in the street, his clicking heels caught in the first dim glow of a distant sunrise. He then grabbed Will by the shoulders and stepped into a passionate kiss that surprised its recipient.

But Will did not struggle to be free. In point of fact, the kiss became angry and impassioned, hands clutching and grasping at shoulders and hair. Breath became secondary, and the gnashing fury of the kiss left them both gasping for air.

Stepping back, Kit's eyes blazed. "My dearest, darling William, you are *full* of surprises!"

Scene Two

Kit and Will took their time approaching the city wall, lingering in shadows – they had to wait until they could merge with the morning bustle of men entering the great city. The time was not wasted. The seal of indecency having been broken, the two young men continued to explore the thrill of the forbidden. Will's shyness was less of an impediment than Kit's bloodied lip.

They broke apart when they heard a whistling tune approach. Their blood raced for a variety of causes, not least being the stimulating threat of death that hung over them both.

The whistler was as cocksure as a man carrying a barrel on a pair of spindles could be. He led with that belly as if it were a weapon, a cannonball that dragged him behind it on his thin knobbly wobbly legs. He was clearly a military man, but gone to seed – or to trough. Certainly not to stud.

The whistler came not alone, but with a dogged companion bearing a lantern. The companion was like one of the yapping dogs favoured by court ladies, furtive and bouncy all at once, eager for approval and wary of careless kicking.

The smaller one spied Will and Kit almost after they had passed them by, and he tugged on the whistler's cape. "Eh? What drags me so? Gheroff!"

"Tis I, Sir Oliver," said the little puppy man, eyeing Kit suspiciously.

"No, tis *I*, Sir Oliver!" retorted the knight with military precision.

"I mean, Sir Oliver, tis I, your faithful Virgil."

"Ah! Then from henceward keep your own name for yourself, and make certes it follows mine, for tis improper for once such as yourself to proceed a knight of the realm." He began to resume his whistling and walking, but dogged little Virgil waylaid him.

"But Sir Oliver, there are two men over there."

"Eh?" Sir Oliver whirled about, his hand reaching for his sword, but unable to reach it across so vast a belly. He tried again, and failing, struck out at Virgil with the back of his hand. "Damn your eyes, Virgil, why do you never buckle the thing right?" Smiling in embarrassment, Sir Oliver approached Kit and Will as he might two companions. "A fine old man, but something past it, if you take my meaning, masters." He laid his finger alongside his nose and tapped it. "When the age is in, the wit is out, they say."

"They do say so, friend," agreed Kit. "Don't they, Bill?"

Will nodded. "That is what they say."

The knight arrived and bowed to them. "Sir Oliver Sutton, at your service." He began to wobble halfway down and both Will and Kit leapt forward to grasp his arms to keep him from landing ignominiously on the filthy pavement. Virgil raced up and pushed from behind, and in moments they had the portly knight righted.

"Ah, thank you! These uneven streets." He slapped at Virgil, who was attempting to straighten his cape. Sir Oliver's style of speech was that gruff military manner peculiar to the English, so low and cunning that it was nearly impenetrable. "Masters, I am constable for this whole borough, and we are on the hunt for two notorious benefactors of the crown, who have this very night made a bald and daring rescape from the Tower."

"Not the Tower," whispered Virgil. "Near the tower."

"Near is as good as," scowled Sir Oliver. "If a man be in the cowpie or near the cowpie, he smells it all the same, I daresay! Don't you daresay? Who dares not to say?"

"I daresay you daresay," said Will.

"I daresay I do!" agreed Sir Oliver, beaming. He slapped Virgil again. "Do you dare say I daren't daresay?"

Virgil was covering his head, bobbing in either agreement or avoidance. "Sir Oliver, I know not what to say!"

"Then you are a wise man," said Sir Oliver sententiously. "For the wise man knows when he has nothing to say, and therefore says his fill of nothing."

Kit found this irresistible. "But Sir Oliver, surely there are many fooles who say a great deal of nothing."

"There be such, yes," agreed Sir Oliver at once with his grumbly mumbly military briskness. "But such as they don't know they have naught to say, so say what they say in ignorance of all they know."

"Master constable," said Kit joyfully, "your mind is a wonder to behold."

At which the knight threw up a hand to his pate. "Oh! Thank heavens. For a moment I thought I had lost my hat."

Kit had to turn aside to keep from laughing outright. Will was less amused – he had little taste for drunkards. Yet there was no reek of sack from the man. Perhaps he had been too long at war. Such things happened.

Despite Sir Oliver's obvious and easily-bestowed camaraderie, Virgil was eyeing them suspiciously. Will decided to take charge by asking, "So we must be vigilant for two men escaped from the Tower. What was their crime?"

That had both Sir Oliver and Virgil frowning. They exchanged an almost panicked glance. "They—"

"They—"

"They have escaped!

"Aye, escaped!"

"From the Tower!"

"Near the Tower."

"From near the Tower! That shows them to be the most vile of criminals. For why should a man be in the Tower if he be not a criminal?

And why should an honest man escape the Tower, if he were in it? No, an honest man would stay and be hanged for the criminal he was."

"Then," said Kit seriously, "these men are accused of the crime of being criminals."

"That, sir, is the very defect of the matter," replied Sir Oliver.

"Then we shall be watchful for just such men as look like criminals. If we see them, we shall come and fetch you at once."

"Me? Nay, fetch not me, masters. For while you were fetching me, they might know my vast repudiation and prove what they are by stealing away. Arrest them yourselves, and bring them back to the Tower in my name. That's the eftest way."

"Sir Oliver," cried Kit, "you are as wise are you are intelligent."

The knight glowed. "Kind of you to say so, master! Kind indeed! But it bears nothing to hide one's covered lantern under a barrel."

"Nay, you must expose it," said Kit.

"Just so! Exposure, exposure is the key. Why, I exposed myself to the Queen once, and she very kindly made me a knight afterwards. Twas no less than I deserted." He started to bow again, and they had to repeat the affair with catching him up and steadying him. "These streets. Fare you well, masters! And thank you!"

"Thank you, Sir Oliver!" waved Kit, beginning to walk in the other direction. In a low tone he said, "Perhaps we should choose a less guarded place to wait for the dawn. That constable is far too shrewd for such low criminals as we."

Chuckling, Will concurred.

They ambled about, feigning inebriation whenever they passed a night watchman or random beggar. As it grew so late as to warrant their arrest for sheer loitering, they took refuge beside an alley wall and tried to sleep.

Suddenly from above came a most wailing cry that made them start and look about for pursuit. But it was not a guard or man-at-arms. The noise had more pity than fury in it, and when Will tried to parse the words, he found them of no sense: "Fathom and a half! Fathom and a half! Come, snulbug, and feed ye!"

"Who's there?" demanded Will over Kit's insistent shushing.

A chorus of voices called out in response, "Who's there! Whose their! Whoos stair!" But his answer from the original caller was in the form of a song, in a mad passion sung:

> *From the hag and hungry goblin*
> *That into rags would rend ye,*
> *And the spirit that stands by the naked man*
> *In the book of the moons, defend ye;*
> *That of your five sound sense*
> *You never be forsaken,*
> *Nor wander from yourselves with Tom,*
> *Abroad to beg your bacon.*
> *While I do sing: any food, any food,*
> *Any feeding drink, or clothing?*
> *Come, dame or maid, be not afraid,*
> *Poor Tom will injure nothing!*

As the eerie singing swelled, Kit plucked urgently at Will's sleeve, pulling him away from the great building at their backs. The other voices had risen with the first singer, joining in the chorus. Not trained performers nor drunkards, these men and women sang with vicious and desperate glee:

> *I know more than Apollo,*
> *For oft when he lies sleeping*
> *I see the stars at bloody wars*
> *In the wounded welkin weeing,*
> *The moon embrace her shepherd,*
> *And the queen of love her warrior,*
> *While the first doth horn the star of the morn,*
> *And the next the heavenly farrier!*
> *While I do sing: any food, any food,*

Any feeding drink, or clothing?
Come, dame or maid, be not afraid,
Poor Tom will injure nothing!

Across the street, Will whispered, "What the Devil..?"

"Invoking the fallen lightbringer is apt," replied Kit, "for all light has left that place. I did not recognize it in the dark. That be Bedlam, and therein madness dwells."

"Bedlam." Will glanced back at the wall surrounding three stone buildings and a church. Even as far away as Stratford had he heard of the dustbin of the mad men, the lunies of London. Properly titled Bethlem Royal Hospital, this place had existed for nigh-on three hundred years as a repository for those men whose personal reality was too far outside the common to be allowed to roam free.

Kit was drawing him further off still. "Ay, Bedlam. Sometimes they allow the lesser mads to wander in daylight, begging in the streets, and they spout such gibbers as you've just heard. Poor Toms, all."

Will shivered. The harrowing voice was still singing, barely audible now over the howls of the other two dozen inhabitants. And now rose the shouts of attendants using sticks and whips to beat the zanies into silence.

But that one lone voice had been beautiful and earnest, so clear. "Poor Tom," he sang again. "Poor Tom will injure nothing…" It now sounded like a plea. The saddest sound Will had ever heard. Then it was cut off.

Scene Three

Hours later Will and Kit joined the throng pressing into the city. Though they were nervous, no guard passed them a second glance.

"I told you," crowed Kit. "No one would think us so foolish as to attempt to enter the city. They're still watching to see if we try to leave!"

Once within, they fleetly lost themselves in the bustle of the busy streets of Greater London. As these were two men incapable of walking in silence, conversation kept burbling up like amphibian farts from just below a pond's surface. Most of the time it was Kit, pressing his companion to further expound his declared powers. "Anything you see?"

"Read, more like. I have a terrible faculty for faces," admitted Will.

"But if you've read it, you can – what, see it?"

"Almost as if I had it before me," confirmed Will.

Shoving past a beggar, Kit shook his head. "I am consumed with envy. Had I such a skill, I would – I don't know, but I'd do something more than teach school children in the wilds of Staffordshire! Will you tell me now what sent you to the hinterlands to tie yourself to such a grindstone?"

"Later," said Will, mistrusting. Kit had violated their burgeoning friendship, creating a rent that might not be mended. But Will also felt that alone he would be even more lost, while together they might at least try to escape the pit Kit had dropped them in. "Our first mission is to uncypher this code. We must also devise a way to uncover what Walsingham knows of Mary's messages. With that in mind, the time has come for you to be glass-clear. No more prevarication. Tell me how you came to possess the message."

Kit recoiled, not from the demand, but from the stench – the sun was warming the nightsoil in the road, releasing foul humours into the air. "Let us find a finer abode where we can abide the reek, and I'll spill all my heart to you."

They wisely chose an establishment Kit had never entered before. Ordering beer and cheese, they sat in the center table – hiding in corners, Kit suggested, would only draw suspicion. "Doubtless the order for our arrest has gone out far and wide."

Seated and swilling their awful small beers, Will said, "Now. Tell."

"My past being our prologue? Very well." With aplomb, Kit launched into his tale. "As I may have mentioned, I was stationed in France as penalty for my collegial misdeeds. This was nine months past. As you may surmise, my behavior at college led Walsingham to believe that I might be able to gain the confidence of men of certain – predilections. One such man was called Gilbert Gifford, an apostasy of alliteration, but he has a decent wit and a handsome dimple in his chin. His is a Catholic family, and he has been a-study of Church matters in both Rome and Rhiems. He was expelled from the Roman college for transgressions I surmise were close to my own – for all their commonality, they are inexplicably frowned upon in the priesthood. The French, being more liberal, took him in and made him deacon and a reader in Philosophy.

"This man Gifford was one of my targets, and with modest claim I must say I made short work of him – with my charm, my beauty, and my silver tongue I soon had his confidence. While he was taking holy orders, my most unholy ones were to gain entrance to his circle of friends and so compromise them. But before I could overcome his barrier of shame and have him introduce me to his confederates, he was sent across the Channel on some errand of import for the imprisoned Catholic Queen. Naturally I passed this information on, but to my astonishment nothing seemed to come of it. I continued to receive letters – such letters! – from him, and his movements seemed open and unhindered. With each one, I confess my frustration grew large, whittling away at my own monumental patience. He mentioned visiting the Scots Queen at least three time, in an attempt to impress me. After six months I'd had enough. If Sir Francis would not grab hold of the golden opportunity, I would!

"I took ship in secret and returned to this glorious nation, came to London and prevailed upon my dearest Kate for the loan of her best dress. Then, with all the arts of the stage to assist me, I called upon my dear Gifford. How amazed he was, to find me transformed into the woman of his dreams! I convinced him I was madly in love, and hoped to aid him in his cause.

"Between giggles and fits of passion, and more wine than my purse could ever afford, we concocted a plan to place me in the Queen's household. He was reluctant, naturally, to deceive her Majesty, but the prank was too good to resist. I told him I could protect dear fat Mary from harm, pass her messages from him, and be his eyes and ears within Chartley Hall.

"By this time, Gifford had the Queen's complete confidence, and so she accepted me as a scullery maid. I must say, playing the part of a woman is no great feat, but hiding the beams of my natural brilliance under a bushel was perhaps the performance of my life. I spent two weeks in the castle, shaving in secret and thanking the Almighty for the invention of the bumroll. The hardest part, I found, was the wind."

"The wind?"

"Windigalls, which is to say foul humours, which is to say the fart. The woman, in her ongoing act of deception that is her Edenic heritage, constricts her waist with the aid of corsets and laces. As you know, I did the same. But wearing such a device for hours on end does terrible things to your gizzard, your liver, and the balance of your humours. Imagine your stomach being compressed against your kidneys, and everything shifted up against your lungs. It cuts down the appetite, for certes. It also gives one the anal flutters something fierce.

Fortunately the skirts are heavy, and trap the air down below. Have you never been to a fancy ball? Ah, well, had you been, you'd have seen women over to the sides, well away from company, rocking back and forth to let loose the foulness their vanity had created, so it didn't well up on the dancing floor." He laughed. "Gives new meaning to the question 'Sits the wind in that corner?', I'll tell you!"

Fascinating as this undoubtedly was, Will was not to be diverted. "Kit, to the point."

"Ah. Yes, well, after some little time there, at last I sussed out the trick with the beer-kegs. The Queen has two secretaries allowed to her, one French and one English. She would dictate her message to the one, who would translate it into English, then the English one would put it in code. After that it was sealed up tight and stuck in the bung of the empty beer barrel."

It was plainly spoken, which was pleasing. Perhaps Kit was attempting to regain a share of Will's confidence by a forthright confession. More likely, given Kit's nature, he was behaving like a peacock, demanding praise for the cleverness God gave him.

But William had many questions, so he boldly interrupted the tale. "I don't suppose you were ever allowed near enough to hear the dictation."

"Never," said Kit, with a measure of rue. "If I'd even tried they'd've known right off I was spying. I had to be as unobtrusive as possible."

"Pity, but you're likely right." Will couldn't imagine that Kit was entirely reticent, but he allowed that to pass unremarked. "Now, you've come to the same conclusion that I have, no?"

"That I was entirely, utterly mistaken?" answered Kit. "That Sir Francis did indeed stop my dear Gifford the moment his boots trod upon good English soil and forced him to turn traitor against the Scottish Queen? That the silence I took for inaction was actually the silence of protecting a valued pawn on the chessboard of international intrigue? That by intruding myself into the matters I did in fact, as Sir Francis was too kind to say, make an utter cock of it? Is that what you are alluding to?"

"Yes," said Will.

"I agree," nodded Kit. "How else would Sir Francis know of the trick with the brewer and the beer barrels?"

"Quite." Will noted that the innkeep was drawing near, suspicious of two men in such deep conversation. "Have you finished? Shall we take the air?"

Exiting, they walked a ways in uncommon silence before Will said, "What I fail to see is Sir Francis' aim. If he had isolated Mary, why then provide her a means of communication at all?"

"Entrapment," answered Kit. "Ensnarement. Entangle-ment. While our good sovereign may be too tender-hearted to end her cousin's life, in Sir Francis' mind there is no greater threat within our borders than the grown child of the Stewart and the de Guise."

"Another tautology," said Will. "*De* means *the.*"

"Tell thou the tale," snapped Kit. He made an aggressively inviting gesture. Will tried to apologize, and Kit said, "Nonono, please! Mm?"

"I beg your mercy. Pray continue."

Kit pressed his lips tight, then sighed as if he were granting a life-time's worth of favours. "The threat of the Stewart *et* the de Guise bloodline." He gave Will a gimlet eye, daring him to object. Will shook his head, and Kit nodded. "Well, there is none greater within the realm. She is Catholic, of royal blood, Scottish, English, and French, already a queen twice over – a natural nexus of revolt. Of course conspiracies revolve around her, so why not take control of them? Invite her to commit the treason she longs for and ensure both Elizabeth's survival and Mary's demise?" Thinking as he was speaking, Kit suddenly whistled. "Walsingham must want my guts for lute-strings."

Will was concentrating. "So you copied a note that came from the barrel, as it sat on the desk of Mary's English Secretary, before it was decyphered."

"Actually, no. This one bypassed the brewer, I think. It came direct from Gifford, since he had come for a visit. But the process is the same."

Will walked on for a moment, a frown across every one of his features. "But is not Gifford acting as Walsingham's agent?"

Kit affected a disappointed expression. "Don't be thick, my dear. Of course he—"

"No, wait!" Will held up his palm. "This message you stole, it wasn't part of the normal route you described."

Now it was Kit's turn to frown. "What?"

"Mary to the French secretary, French Secretary to the English Secretary, English secretary to the barrel – is that correct?"

"Aye, that's just what I said."

"Then why did Gifford bring it?"

"I thought—" Kit's eyes lost focus. "I thought – I thought they were just by-passing the system out of convenience. But it does seem a risk, doesn't it?" His pace quickened unconsciously. "And why, why did he go along with me posing as a wench in the house? I thought he was besotted with me, and liked to gamble. But with his balls slung up in Seething Lane, he knew what a dangerous game he was playing at. Why would he take part in something so patently absurd?"

"Did he think he was doing Walsingham's work?" asked Will charitably. "That you were part of the plan?"

Kit shook his head. "No. Absolutely, no. It was our little secret, he had no notion – to him I had fut-all to do with Sir Francis."

"Then I ask again, why did he have a message at all? Why did he risk detection by bringing it in?"

"But it wasn't a risk, was it? He knew he'd not be searched well, because he's Walsingham's creature."

"Though the fact that he brought it in might raise Mary's suspicions instead," objected Will. "This makes no sense."

"It does," said Kit slowly, "if you shave it with Occam's Razor. Never forget the Oxfordians! The simplest answer is usually correct. In this case, the simplest answer is that friend Gifford is playing his own game."

"Does that mean Mary knows about the duplicity with the brewer?" mused Will, more to the air than to Kit.

But Christopher Marlowe was never a man to let a question go unanswered, regardless of whether he knew the answer. "Possibly, but

I doubt it. Instead it strikes me that he's playing both – betraying Mary to serve Sir Francis, while carrying secret messages for Mary that may help her escape. That way, whoever wins, the victor is in his debt." The corners of Kit's mouth turned down. "I confess I am impressed. I had no concept he was such an accomplished back-biter – and I've tasted of him!"

Will blushed, but refused to let his mind be untracked. "He might have brought you in as a warning to Mary – there are spies in your midst. He expected you to be caught, exposed, and for her to take measures to protect herself. It was a warning without a warning."

"O, I continue to be proved a foole," said Kit without rancor. In fact, he seemed almost amused.

"Our only hope is that Walsingham is wrong, that the message you stole isn't one he's seen, that it's a separate set of instructions. That Gifford is giving Walsingham the double cross."

"Making him a triple-crosser. Talk about cross-gartered," laughed Kit grimly. "Well, Gilbert Gifford, you shall receive six inches of steel and have done. Come, William!" With the air of a man minded to murder, Kit started purposefully in the direction of Gifford's London abode.

Will clasped Kit by the arm in prevention. "No! What will that help?"

"It will make me feel better," offered Kit. "Besides, if he has a message on him, we can prove to Walsingham that he's been deceived."

"And if he doesn't have a message?" demanded Will. "Think, Christopher! Our best hope is decyphering the message we do have, while at the same time watching Gifford to see with whom he converses. Walsingham must be watching him as well – and Walsingham knows of your acquaintance with Gifford. They'll be waiting for you."

Kit pulled free, but did not continue his trek. "I notice the singular. What, then, do you propose?"

"That you find some manner to break this code, while I watch Gifford – he doesn't know my visage, and Walsingham's men will hardly know me. If necessary, I'll shave and trim my hair. What say you?"

Kit considered for some little time. "It is a plan both reasonable and wise."

"And therefore you loathe it."

"Exactly. But I see little choice in the matter."

"All that remains is finding ink and paper for me to put down this code, and to find the means of breaking it. Do you have any thought of where…"

The smile that spread across Kit's face filled Will with foreboding.

"I do," answered Kit with dark delight. "I do, I do, I do. While you and I are, we shall imagine, the smartest and handsomeset men in London, we require the aid of minds as devious as our own. We must seek out those notorious fiends, those men of no standing, those devils incarnate. We want wily Watson, lithe Lyly, lodgy Lodge, poor Peele, and the great Greene – in short, the Wits!"

Scene Four

In the London of good Queen Bess' day, it was no small thing to become a man of literature. One had to turn one's back on family, friends, prosperous employment, decency, cleanliness, sobriety, and even health. But to the self-proclaimed Wits, what was endless suffering against the contribution to the world of a perfect line of blank verse?

"Watch out for Watson," advised Kit earnestly. "And Greene. Well, all of them, really. Hide your purse, never offer to buy, and for the sake of the Almighty don't let them know you're a school-teacher."

"If they're your friends," said Will, "won't Walsingham be watching them?"

"Worse! Several of them have worked for him in the past, and he has no doubt told them to report me the moment I appear. So we beard the lion's cubs, if not her den. But have no fear! They'll not betray a University man!"

They first tried a tavern in Bankside, to no avail. As they wended the London streets along the Thames south bank, Will began to take the sense of the city, orienting himself to landmarks he could spy. Always there was the monumental, crenellated Tower of London, foreboding in its menacing stone.

To his left was the truncated spire of St. Paul's cathedral, charred and jagged. Years earlier it had been struck by divine wrath in the form of lightning, giving both sides in the religious divide a sign from above that they were in the right. Like the nation, the spire had yet to be mended. Further off was the façade and arched colonnades of the Royal Exchange, holding the promise for generations of buyers and sellers of wares.

"You mentioned one Lyly. Would that be John Lyly?"

"It would. You know him?"

"Of him. I read *Euphues: Anatomy of Wyt*."

"But not its descendant, *Euphues and his England?*"

"Alas, no."

"No alas about it," clucked Kit. "Brace yourself should you meet him to engage in an euphuistic debate."

Will was absurdly excited at the idea. Not to be confused with euphemism, Euphuism was a style of speech popular in court these last ten years, bursting as if from a cloud to drench the speech of anyone daring enough to try it. The torrent had sent ripples as far as Stratford. The style was tricky, with short staccato bursts of wit back and forth, dense with verbiage, alliterations, oppositions, and all the rhetorical tricks one usually found in the French language – hence the inevitable condemnation of it by the French, who called it *la Préciosité*. It was said that any beauty at court was not counted worth a groat if she could not bandy the badinage of Euphues. Much of Kit and Will's natural exchanges had been done in a euphuistic vein, and the thought of trying his brain against the inventor of the style was as tempting as it was daunting.

Will and Kit arrived at a particular street in Southwark, Borough High Street, that positively teemed with inns. Most were well-kept and ostentatious, with fresh painted signs and scrubbed steps. Will saw a sign and gasped – the Tabard was known to him at least by reputation, having been the inn owned by one Harry Bailey, the fictional host for the travelers in Chaucer's *Canterbury Tales*.

"*Bifel that in that season on a day, In Southwerk at the Tabard as I lay...*" quoted Will.

Kit made a sputtering sound and rolled his eyes. "Hot pokers! Ridiculous stuff. He should just have written about Edward II outright…"

Further along was The George, formerly the George and Dragon. The dragon had either retired or expired, and only George remained. Outside both the Tabard and the George, passengers waited for coaches to take them as far afield as Canterbury or Dover.

Ignoring both of these coaching inns, Kit entered the walled yard of the building beside the George. The cobblestones here were much used and beaten down by horses, with a stable off to one side. But upon the right-hand there was a raised platform as one might see used in public executions.

"They oftimes stage plays here," said Kit. Passing the stage, he knocked on the boards for luck, then crossed the yard and tapped his fingers on the building's stone exterior, as if communing with an old lover. " 'Glorious Odysseus, what you are after is sweet homecoming, but the god will make it hard for you. I think you will not escape Shaker of the Earth, who holds a grudge against you in his heart.' Coming, William?"

Staring up at the faded hanging sign, Will saw the remnants of a painted stag and read the inscription, *The White Hart Inn.*

No one remembers today that the White Hart was the noble symbol for His Royal Highness Richard II, which he took from his mother, along with his gentle nature. We may today see his adoption of such a symbol as perhaps a sign of opposition to his Plantagenet father, familiarly known as the Black Prince. But I think we must agree that so gentle a soul opposed no one so well as himself.

This inn, however, had a less benign history, having housed the rebellious Jack Cade when he led his forces against the good (if befuddled) Henry VI. Since that time it had been forced to suffer all sorts of malefactors – brigands, rogues, rakehells, scoundrels, varlets, whores and their pimps, cony-catchers and their marks, and most recently the worst of the lot – writers.

These last were counted worst because, though they paid for less than they ate and almost none of what they drank, they insisted upon putting on airs, demanded better quality service, and insulted the proprietors in such dense and unfathomable language that one could hardly take offence because one had no idea what they were saying.

The air was thick with tobacco mixed with the reek of stale beer and burnt meat, making Will sweat the moment he stepped within. His feet scuffed the straw rushes strewn to soak up ale and piss alike. Whereas Kit entered like a husband entering his mistress' house. "Where the devil is a drink for me!"

At this hour the room was mostly deserted, and of the few men present in body, most were insensible. Two of the sensible heads came around, and with them came groans of dismay, followed by airy darts of ridicule.

"It's Morley," sneered one, a lean and noble fellow with yellow hair and reddish beard. "Quick, hide your wit, lest he steal it."

His companion, grossly fat and bearing great splotches on his complexion, took a moment to puff his pipe and frame his insult. "The great walking spur, that makes a jangling noise but never pricks!"

"O, that I could see the brains that coined such a jest," cried Kit nastily, "that I could hug them, you fat-kidney'd rascal."

"Am I wise, or no?" countered the fat man, rising to his feet. He had a thick moustache and a jutting, bristled beard.

"Otherwise," answered Kit. For a moment they stood with hands hovering over their sword-hilts. Then, laughing, they stepped into a hearty embrace.

"You rogue!" cried the fatty man, pounding Kit's back with hands that looked like hams. He did not look like a man who came by his size naturally, but rather by great effort.

"If I had a glass, Roberto, you would quit me and condemn yourself." Kit glanced around. "Wat's son not about?"

"He was in a foul mood, and decided to lighten it by stepping out to hear his fellow members of the bar engage in low matters."

"You mean matters of law," said Kit.

"I know what I mean," said the fat man, "and say what I know."

"But rarely know what you say," replied Kit.

"Or pay what you owe," added redbeard.

"Shall we retire to a private room and crush a cup?" The fat man glanced Will's way. "Is this yours?"

"Indeed! A fine fellow, and witty, with gifts I can only dream of. His name is William. Dear Will, this," he indicated the thinner man, "is John Lyly. Lyly, Will's read as much of your work as a man might stomach. And speaking of stomachs," he smacked the fat man's protuberant belly, "this is the great (and I mean *great*) Robert Greene, who like me is a man of discernment and culture – meaning he hails from Cambridge, while John here rose from the stews of Oxford."

"I studied at both," said Greene, bowing to Will. "So I am twice the man they are."

"Twice?" demanded Lyly, also bowing. "Thrice at least."

"In wit, I am twenty times your better," grunted Greene, struggling to rise from his bow – the drink already in him had him unbalanced. "'Tis only fitting that I try in girth to match my genius."

"*A whoremonger,*" expounded Kit, quoting once more, "*a haunter of stews, a hypocrite, a wretch and a maker of strife,* as Heywood makes the Husband. *Chargé d'ans et pleurant son antique provesse.*"

Will returned their bows in his best manner. Both men were older than he. Lyly looked the younger, but was in fact the elder, having a full decade of life more than Will. Greene was only five years Will's senior, but he looked three times that, the fee-paid for gross excesses. As Kit had said in his Frenchified way, "weighed down by years and weeping his former glory."

It is an unfortunate moment in life, but all too common, when one judges a man harshly because he resembles someone else, someone known in days past, someone held in low esteem. In this case, Greene's appearance – his broken cheek veins and marks of pox, his gross belly and reddened nose – all these gathered together to remind Will of the true villain of his life, a man once admired and now loathed. It was a pity. Had he not taken an instant coolness to the man, the following exchange might not have taken place, and they might just have ended as friends.

"Shall we adjourn to a side room and tap a keg?" asked Greene innocuously.

"Why not converse here in the open?" asked Will lightly.

"Because some men have things to hide," answered Greene with a broken-toothed smile.

There were indeed several low characters in the room, and though none looked his way he felt that they had measured him, found both his purse and his liver, and were waiting for opportunity to remove both. Even the inebriates reeked of danger as much as beer.

In a low voice Kit said, "You've heard, then, that we are hounded."

"Foxed, more like," said Lyly. "'Tis they who are the hounds."

Still staring at Greene, Will let some of his mistrust show. "Do you mean to tree us? Hold us at bay until the hunters arrive?"

"What an uncharitable thought!" cried Greene.

"I thought you might prefer the charity of the informer's fee," countered Will. "With so many chins to support, you must welcome income from any source."

Greene looked taken aback. "Why, I would sacrifice one of my chins to preserve a fellow University man! What school did you say you hailed from? Not Cambridge, surely!"

"Nor Oxford," offered Lyly.

"From the University of the universe," said Will, "with providence as my professors and my opinions, unparrotted, entirely mine own." He could smell the ale on the fat man's breath, and the reek of it took him winging back to Stratford, which only strengthened his disgust.

Lyly was smiling. "Well said."

Greene sniffed, the phlegm rising within him. Quaffing the last of his flagon, he wiped his lips with the back of a fat paw, sending drops of it through the air at Will. "I knew you at once. Had you been a university man, you would never have asked such a question. We do not peach on each other – 'tisn't done. Little bull's pizzle," he added with a belch, turning away.

It was as much the dismissive belch as the insult that did it. Once more Will's temper ignited his wit. "Massive tallow-catch."

The words had slipped out before he knew it. Kit exclaimed in mild shock, while Lyly laughed aloud, which caused Greene to turn his full flabby face towards Will. "Will you turn your knavery upon a gentleman? Will you clout the air with your petty insults?"

"Would they were less petty, that my knave's clouts could fan the air of the gentleman's ungentle breath."

"You miserable little sheath of eel-skin!"

"You grotesque great bombard of sack-lees!"

Lyly howled with mirth as Greene shouted, "You little upstart crow!"

"You upended elephant!" shouted Will.

Greene's swelling face had turned a most royal shade of purple. "You mizzling, pizzling, untutored, unlettered, decency-breaking, puny insult to the very idea of manhood!"

Trembling with outrage, Will was entirely unwilling to have any but the last word. "You grizzling, fizzling, unmannered, unsobered, horse-collapsing, tubby insult to the very idea of humanity!"

Three of the inn's low characters had lifted their heads to follow the exchange, and two had stood, hands inside their doublets on hidden hilts, ready to come to Greene's defence.

For a moment it looked as though Greene were a cannon, with his head as the ball, so ready it was to explode from its body. Then all at once he burst, not to pieces, but to laughter. Lyly broke into applause, and Kit had given over to mewing with delight.

"*O* it is a world to see," cried Lyly, quoting only himself.

"Well done, boy." Greene reached over and pinched Will's cheek. It looked friendly, but the force behind it left a bruise that lasted all day. The piggy eyes were no longer blurred, but hard and clear, daring Will to ever attempt such an exchange again.

"Down, lads, down down to Hell." Waving his would-be defenders aside, Greene turned to the innkeeper. "A keg of ale, landlord – on this young cockerel's tab." Low he added, "And not a word to the constables about young Marlowe here, or I'll refuse to pay my bill, and you'll lose a year's wages! Ha! Come," he said, draping a weighty arm about Kit's shoulders. Together they made for the stairs, but were forced to part, as the narrow steps could barely contain Greene alone.

Kit allowed Lyly to pass him, which afforded him the chance to hiss in Will's ear. "Well, Odysseus, you've certainly found your Earth Shaker. Though the homecoming was mine, you made it into a crucible. What, pray tell, was that?"

"He rubs me wrong," said Will shortly.

"He rubs against everything," admitted Kit, noting the man's girth. "But we require him – he's the best among us."

"I highly doubt–!"

"I mean only that he's the only one of the Wits that can support himself solely through his verses. A remarkable achievement!"

"Indeed," agreed Will, in a tone of awe that anything could support such a monstrous mountain.

Kit shrugged. "Well, don't try it with Watson. He'll have your gizzard out of you."

Will nodded absently, his face flushed. In truth, he was feeling the churl – his had been the first insult, an unworthy suggestion that Greene would sell them for a pint of ale. Taking a deep breath, he followed Kit up the stairs resolved to attempt civility. This man Greene was, after all, a professional writer, something Will had only ever dreamed of. And they needed his help.

Greene led them to a private room, and said, "There. It faces the front, so you'll have ample notice of any invasion, while this side window provides rooftop access for a swift egress." He spoke only to Kit, avoiding Will with his eyes. Will sulkily took a seat beside the open window that looked down over the roofed horse-stable of the inn next door.

Greene sprawled himself upon a bench beside the front window. "A pity you were not present yesterday, Christopher. We were taking to pieces that new, dare I call it, play that the jump-up ewe has fashioned at the Butts."

"We saw it," admitted Kit.

"And liked it," said Will, incapable of refraining.

Greene answered Will without looking at him. "Predictably, such a blood-soaked mess would appeal to the masses. But hardly to a man of substance. How dare he, a scribbler and scrivener, try to emulate men of learning and education. How dare he!"

Lyly joined in, with less invective but more snobbery, comparing *The Spanish Tragedy* to his own works, *Campaspe* and *Sapho & Phao*. To Will's dismay, Kit added his voice, poking fun at the rude confluence of history and Senecean blood. For ten minutes the three University men heaped coals upon the head of the absent Kyd and his play. Through it all, it was hard to say which offended them more, the fact that Kyd had attempted the feat, or that he had pulled it off. Unable to fault the end result, they took turns abhorring and lamenting his audacity for daring to write a play in the first place.

If ever there was an unlikely moment upon which history hinged, it was this. Will had never before dreamed of being a playwright. Actor? Yes, that profession had fascinated him since his first taste of the stage in his tender years. But never had he thought to set quill to paper and become a joiner of words. Somehow it seemed presumptuous to even apply to join the ranks of Aristophanes, Aeschylus, Sophocles, Euripides, Plautus, Terrence, and Ovid. How could a tanner's son rise to such elevated heights?

Yet, hearing the litany of abuses hurled at a humble man of no formal education just because he had attempted to write a play, the forge of Will's temper fashioned a new weapon. This time his anger was not hot, but coolly calm as he found himself with an unlooked-for yet all-consuming desire.

When this was all finished, when their lives were safe and the threat passed, he would spite these pompous, self-indulgent, self-congratulating men of high birth and low morals by bending his mind to do the very thing they were ridiculing.

Will would write plays.

Scene Five

When the theatrical abuse was finished, and all unaware that they had spurred the silent Will into a new profession that would change the shape of history, literature, culture, and the very language they spoke, the Wits turned to the problem at hand. Greene paused in rubbing his poxed inner thigh to clap his hammy palms together in gleeful anticipation. "Now, Christopher, do entertain us with the tale of your transgressions, that we might take catharsis for our lives by seeing you brought low."

Laughing as if it were a matter of no consequence, Kit launched into a tale that was, for the most part, the truth. There were some omissions. Gifford for one. Will's history for another, for which Will was gratified. At the conclusion, Kit asked for paper and ink, which was sent for.

As they waited, Lyly made a summary. "So you have a coded message that must be turned to plain text to save you. Do you wish us to do this decyphering?"

"I have no doubt," said Kit bravely, "that given time I should bend this combination of letters to my will. But time is a luxurious and harsh mistress. So I will appreciate any aid the Wits can give."

"My wits are sodden, as has been mentioned," said Greene, with a nasty look that only reached halfway to Will. "I doubt I have the sense to make sense of anything."

"Where is the good Doctor Lodge, then?" demanded Kit cheerfully. "Amateur that he is, certainly he can bleed the wine out of you, and so restore you to your senses."

Lyly answered. "Lodge is off to the Canary Islands."

"Why, for God's sake?" demanded Kit.

Lyly frowned, resisting the admission. It was Greene who said, by way of explanation, "Chased by usurers."

This sad statement was perfectly true and utterly ironic. Just the year before, Thomas Lodge had published a tract called *An Alarum Against Ususers*, which spoke from great experience of the dangers of young men borrowing money. That he had escaped debtor's prison was due to the felicities of his parentage, as both his father and step-father had been Lord Mayors of London. Being disinherited for penning *Defence of Poetry, Music & Stage Plays* apparently did not mean his parents meant to suffer the dishonour of seeing him gaoled.

"Alas," cried Kit as the paper arrived. "He might have been a help. Who else is about?"

"Watson, only. Shall we send for him?"

"No," said Kit. "He's not one to take kindly to a summons. He'll turn up in his own time. Ah, the paper! Thanks, lad." Relieving the serving boy of the tray of paper, the rude pen, and the bottle of ink, Kit carried it to where Will sat.

Greene frowned. "What, wasting paper on that mewling child?"

"This mewling child is about to vomit forth the message in question," said Kit, responding swiftly so as to cut across any tart reply from Will. But Will was already settling in to copy, from memory, the vital, fatal message. He repeatedly closed his eyes, the better to re-call the sequence. Twice he paused, checking his own memory before setting it in ink. Finally he was through and he handed it over to Kit.

Kit at once set to copying it over again on a separate sheet of paper, while Will wrote another copy out fresh. When he was finished he compared it with his last, and was gratified to see they matched exactly:

CFPXCFXSPBCTPW†CJGWCFWCNJYWCNKYESN
EYLYNNPSWNNQLNNCRBEPCFQI‡XJELTBCEQPFN
NPRWWECHPCRCORBFQROAJPCFOPCROOPWCQB‡

Watching this display, Greene was impressed despite himself. Still, his compliment offered less of the palm and more of the back-hand. "The *idiot savant.*"

Will swallowed the insult with no more response than a cheerful fig in Greene's direction.

Four copies made, Kit passed them around and they each set to studying the letters.

"There were no breaks between words?" asked Lyly.

That question Kit could answer. "None."

"Pity. But I suppose that's part of the cypher, to make it more difficult to determine the beginning and end of words."

"Well first," rumbled Greene as he scratched his groin again, "I think we should examine the frequency. E is, I think, the most common letter in the English language."

"How do we know it's English?" demanded Lyly. "The Scots Queen is a French-woman at heart, and she intrigues with both French and Spanish. And being Papish, would they not use Latin?"

Will had not even considered this hurdle, and it seemed insurmountable. How could they translate the message, when they did not even know what tongue they were translating it into?

"It would help if we knew to whom the lady was corresponding," observed Greene, raising both his furry eyebrows in Kit's direction.

But Kit was evidently unwilling to give over the name of Gifford. Will suspected he was holding back that essential piece to shield Walsingham's network of spies – they were in enough trouble to be getting on with. "He's an Englishman who speaks the *lingua Franca* fluently. Besides, he may only be a courier."

"How do we know this is not a message *from* the Scottish queen, rather than *to* her?" asked Greene.

Kit oped his mouth, then halted as if a statue had been caught in mid-yawn. He threw a glance to Will, who did not catch it but let it sail by. Kit shrugged. "We don't."

"Does that help us?" asked Lyly.

"Not in the slightest," answered Greene. "But 'tis better to know than not to know." He gave a significant look, if not to Will, at least towards the corner where Will was residing. "He who knows nothing, knows enough to keep quiet."

But Will was studying the page intently. "How many examples of double letters are there in English? I see four examples of NN, and one of WW."

"Could be double letters," mused Lyly, "or else two words butted up against each other. Damn! I do wish the English could agree on formalized spelling – it makes this so much harder!"

"If we standardized the formation of words," intoned Greene gravely, "it would stifle man's creative freedom. We write as freely as we speak. To take that away from a man is to bind him, confine him to a circumscribed world of lesser men." Satisfied that the others were aware of his awesomeness, Greene returned to the paper. "If this can be trusted – I say *if!* – I count 16 Cs, 11 Ns, 8 Ps, 7 Ws–"

"9 Ps," corrected Will.

Greene spent a moment counting and grunted. "9 Ps, 7 Ws, then. And one pricked Ell," he added. An ell was a measurement, translating to 45 inches. That Will was the prick was self-obvious. Thus, Will was a massive prick.

"Better than a furious inch-wick swallowed in grease."

"Does frequency matter?" demanded Kit, forfending the coming renewal of hostilities.

In Lyly he had an ally. "Only insomuch as there are common letters. It is high likelihood that either C or N represent the vowel E. We are fortunate that the message is so long."

"Oh?" asked Will. It seemed to him the longer the message, the harder to translate.

"O, *absolutement*," replied Lyly. "The more message, the more clues, the easier solved. I propose, fellows, that we first attempt a simple transposition method. Kit, you and Greene take the letter C, make it an E, and transpose the whole message over those two letters, see what comes of it. William, if he likes, may join me in doing the same to N."

From the first, the simple solution did not hold. In the case of E, transposing the whole code up two letters in the alphabet yielded:

ADNVADVQNZAR…

Having the harder task, Lyly and Will took longer to come up with an equally unpromising transposition:

TWGOTWOJGSTKGOTAXNTWNTEAPNT…

As tempting as it was to try to create words out of an admittedly flexible written language, they eventually threw out their hopes of turning GOT, TAX, and TEA into a vibrant, coherent message.

That discarded, their hopes turned to frequency alone. But beyond the commonality of E, they could not say which letter was the next most-oft used. It led to a lively and somewhat enjoyable debate about the nature of language and expression.

It began with Greene throwing up his beefy hands and declaring, "English! Garbage language."

"Now now," said Lyly accusingly to Greene. "English is a proper tongue, fit for proper discourse."

"English is a boorish tongue, livened only by adoptions from Latin, Greek, and—"

"Don't say it!"

"—French."

Lyly was livid. "I hate the French *so much!*"

"Forget not, dear Greene," interjected Kit, "Spanish and Italian. We are indiscriminate stealers of tongues."

"Thieves of words, aye," agreed the corpulent critic. "Our own tongue is hardly fit to express loftier thoughts without them. There is a reason why men of learning use foreign phrases to debate grand ideas, and that is because our vernacular is spectacularly unsuited to high talk."

"Was Chaucer unable?" demanded Kit. "Was Spenser? Are you? Why then write plays in our native tongue, if it is so very vile?"

"Because it's where the coins are – grubby common coins from grubby common men speaking a grubby common tongue." But Greene was grinning – he was clearly fond of the lower classes, and abusing their cant was a sign of affection.

"It's no mistake that English is on the rise," exclaimed Will, interjecting himself into the debate. "It's a mark of independence. Latin is the tongue of the Pope, and English is now the language of protest. We have broken free from our European moorings and now must set sail to our own North Star."

This simple extrapolation seemed to take the three University men aback. Kit smiled, Lyly mused, Greene grimaced. In an effort to exclude him, the latter made his next remark in Latin. "How can we be independent from what gives us life? Aristotle, Plato, Catullus, Ovid? They are the North Stars of poetry. Cut ties with them and we are adrift!"

Will answered in the same tongue. "But Dante made his great poem in Italian, not Latin. *De Vulgari Eloquentia* – the eloquent vulgarity of his native tongue."

"Eloquence is lost on the vulgar," countered Greene.

"And Dante wrote his defense of the *vulgare* in Latin," added Lyly.

Deliberately Will changed back to English. "So you resort to inkhornisms to prove to the common hearers that you have a groats-worth of wit more than they?"

"If it is a war, I prefer inkhorn words to plainness, double meanings to single mindedness, eloquence to vulgarity. Victory lives not among the groundlings, but in the court!"

"Says the man who consorts with whores, thieves, and rakehells," crowed Kit in amused astonishment. "Do your low companions know you hold them in such disdain? And how do you defend earning your bread and beer through the language you despise?"

Greene shrugged this off, a mountain of trembling flesh. Visibly restraining himself from scratching his pox-ridden crotch, he said, "That I am a victim of my worldly desires has no effect upon my opinion. I write low things in a low tongue, that is to say my own, because when writing about the gutter, what better than the chamber-pot of tongues, English? But for airbourne notions, I prefer a tongue supported by the wings of the poetic angels that have gone before, scraping the clouds above."

"How did you become a playwright?" asked Will.

"By God's divine will, which is to say, by accident. I doubt you will credit it, but I have been known to tipple from time to time," — cries of 'No!'— "and on this particular morning I had been egregiously over-served, and then the moral-cripple of an innkeep threw me out of doors. I had injured my knee, which prevented me from walking away, so I took shelter in the lee of a particularly inviting hedge beside the road. Now, I am not one to suffer the vicissitudes of Fate without clacking my tongue back at Fortuna's capricious skirts. So I was loudly cataloging all the wrongs done me in my life when I was approached by a man. He might have been an angel, or Mephistopheles, but he was fair-spoken. 'I suppose you are a gentleman,' said he, 'and pity tis men of learning should live in lack.' I lamented that I was, in fact, as learned in my elbow as other men are in their whole bodies, and how was a man to provide for himself and his family in such a state. He replied that men of his profession get their whole living by employing the learned. I asked him his profession, and to my shock and chagrin, he declared himself a player! Where I had taken him as a gentleman, a man of substance. But players often ape their betters, and so become better themselves. But apes are, as we all know, without words. For these, the gibbering gibbons hired me to set down in ink what their tongues could mangle into something like art. Which means writing in English, that lowest of *langues.*"

"Not for long." Anger subsiding, Will found himself engaged in the debate for debate's sake. "The world changes, and English will soon become the new *lingua franca*, not in spite of its gutterly bastardization, but because of it. We adapt, we grow. So too our tongue. We are the beneficiaries of all that has gone before. Elyot gave us *education, dedication,* and *maturity.* Gilbert ransacks Latin to provide us with *paradox, external,* and *chronology.* What new Latin words are there? The poets we all revere created new words, but that was a thousand and more years ago. Its day is done, it is no longer vibrant, no longer alive. So too Greek, Italian, and French – they are all codified, they have no flex, no urgency. English is a living tongue, and young! We do not yet have all the words, but we will! Only when it ceases to grow, when there are rules and strictures, will it die! God bless England, and God bless the English!"

If ever he needed proof that adversity brought out the best in him, this speech was it. Kit and Lyly broke into spontaneous applause, and even Greene patted his beefy paws together. Kit turned to his friends with a look that said, *'See? See? He is one of us!'*

Greene was smiling wryly. "A point well-made. You have devoured and defeated the Devil's advocate. But you may lament the lack of codification. Such strictures would aid us in defeating your blasted cypher!"

They pored over the sequence of letters all that afternoon, but it refused to yield to their pressures.

The sole excitement came not from the page but the door. A thundering footstep on the stair had Will half-out the window when the portal burst open and a bear entered. Or so it seemed. But rather than recoil in fear, Kit rushed forward and fell upon the neck of the black-robed, black-bristled bear. "Watson!"

"Merlin!" growled Thomas Watson, the man of whom Kit had spoken so feelingly. His head was swathed in a black custard-coffin with a ridiculous black feather running transverse across the brim. Somehow Will was not moved to laughter.

"Here at last, another lover of Latin!" crowed Greene, wiping his rheumy nose upon his sleeve.

Watson stepped out of the embrace. "I've just come from Lincoln's Inn. The Benchers are debating *habeas corpus*, for fun. *Consuetudo, consuetudo, consuetudo!* Fit that I should leave the company of the law-makers to be embraced by the law-breaker!"

"Are you *amicus curiae,* or *amicus mihi?*" asked Kit.

"*Amicitiae nostrae memoriam spero sempiternam fore.*" Done quoting Cicero, Watson patted Kit's cheeks roughly. "So tell me, Merlin, what have you been about, little hellhound, that you have the whole city after your wagging tail?"

His speech was as rough as his appearance. He looked a man who would as leave strike as talk, hardly a jurist. But he overflowed with Latinate phrases (those inkhorn terms, as they were called). Will rather hoped against the renewal of debate between English and Latin. Watson looked to be a man who could win a losing argument with his fists, or the fine sword at his hip.

Kit told the tale, more excitingly this time, embellishing the perils and dareful doings. In passing he introduced Will, and Greene threw in a few caustic comments for spice. Will bowed, but Watson insisted on clasping hands, allowing Will to experience the aggressive squeeze of a man who challenged everything.

"Sir Francis certainly has the wind up, *ad absurdum,*" said Watson, hunching down over a stone malmsey bottle and a hunk of cheese. "I've worked for him a demi-dozen times, and I've never seen him so agitated. Zounds, he almost raised his voice! But if you've threatened one of his elaborate mousetraps, then aye, I can see where you'd say, '*Auribus tenere lupum.*'"

"Well," rumbled Greene, "while Kit's holding the wolf's ears, perhaps we can oblige him by removing the beast from off his back."

"Quite the contortionist, I," laughed Kit.

"Aye aye!" they all laughed. Watson was then shown the cypher, and Will had a fleeting moment of hope as the burly bristling brute bent his brain to the paper. He asked several questions, eliminating attempts they had already made. After just ten minutes more he shook his black mane of hair.

"Tis no use, fellows. This must be a substitution cypher, where letters are chosen at random. The encoder has a sheet with all the letters matched to their disguise, while the uncoder has its twin. Should we break one or two letters, there is no hope for the rest but by chance and the will of God."

"What's the symbol, then?" asked Lyly.

"Could be anything. A name? A number? The end of a line? There is no telling until you place your hands upon the code itself."

Kit looked to Will, who nodded. "Then that is what we must do."

Act IV
Cony-Catching

Scene One

London
26 July, 1586

The next day at dawn, in the London street known as Cheapside, Will stood feeling daring and nerveless. His eyes were upon a door halfway up the thoroughfare, towards Honey Lane. All around him the marketeers were selling their produce – live chickens, grey-looking fish, cabbages, and some limp carrots were among the most distinguishable. Cheap was a form of *ceap*, which Britons of old used as the word for market, and the cry "What d'ye lack?" reverberated around the whole neighborhood.

Crouched beneath an old lice-ridden cloak, a rude cap pulled over his head, Will watched a game of dice and wondered how on earth he had ended up here. The day before, dressed in his own clothes and arguing with the Wits in the White Hart, he'd still felt like himself. Now he was a shadow creature, in the company of thieves, pimps, and cony-catchers.

The debate had been over where to procure a copy of the code. "There are three we know of," observed Kit, thinking aloud. "Mary's secretary must have one. Walsingham must have one. And whoever authored the note must also have one, obviously."

The trouble was, of the two who they knew who had the code, there was no chance of laying hands upon them. Agents for both Mary and

Walsingham were hunting for Will and Kit, and would catch them long before they discovered the location of the un-cypher.

The author of the note, however, would have the key to the code in a far more accessible place. The only trouble being, they didn't know who that person might be. The only link they had was Gifford.

"Might not he be the mysterious author?" asked Lyly.

"If so, then why bear the note at all?" demanded Watson logically. "He might convey his message in person, free to come and go as he pleases from Mary's presence." Where Greene reeked of ale and tobacco, Watson reeked of danger, grimly reveling in this enterprise.

"Still, we should search his rooms," said Kit.

"Only if you want him to go to earth, Merlin," warned Watson. "Better by far to follow him and see who he contacts."

With a course of action decided upon, an argument grew – who should be tasked with the job of following the triple-crossed spy. Kit was furious at the instant exclusion of his name.

"We discussed this already," explained Will reasonably. "He knows you, both as man and girl. If he has even a hint that you're about, he'll run to Walsingham."

"Or else to his contact among Mary's men," replied Kit, "thus giving us the link we require!"

"It's a toss of the die," said Watson, taking Will's side. "Far better that I do it. He knows me not."

Now it was Will's turn to object. "Nor does he know me, and I have more at the stake."

"But I have been trained to the work," boasted Watson, with the same air of superiority evinced by Greene. "If we find the keeper of the key, we shall require guile, skill, and experience to remove it."

"Why remove it? One look is all I need," said Will with a significant look to Kit.

It was this truth that settled matters. While Kit could not directly participate in this enterprise, Will would be at its heart, with Watson nearby to advise.

The only trouble was that Will was not a Londoner, and had little idea how to blend in for lengthy stretches. At this concern, Kit looked devilish as he turned to Greene. "Is Cutting Ball about?"

Eyeing Will with newfound glee, Greene pissed himself with laughter. "For me, he will be! O, marvelous! I'd like to see you cheek him, boy!"

Having had no sleep the night before, Will and Kit had bedded down early in Watson's rooms.

"Now, my dear Will – tell all! Why did you engage in a duel of words with Greene? What prompted such madness? Do you have bias against the portly slobberers of the world? Or are you against success itself?"

"I misliked his manner." Will's answer was no answer at all, and deliberately so. Yet as he settled in to sleep, he was no longer able to ignore his past. Despite the strong determination to reinvent himself that had sent him north to Lancashire, he had to admit that just as he bore scars from the magistrate's lash, the scars of life were present as well, and far more durable. He could not escape his past – he was shaped by it, and could no more reform his inner self than he could change his features.

Greene's great and inadvertent crime had been to remind Will of the one man in all the world he most blamed for his troubles – his father.

For all of Will's life, he had been raised with aspirations to become gentle. His father's greatest wish was to be termed *armitro* – the bearer of a coat of arms. They had even gone so far as to craft a sign for their family.

But then his father's besetting sin had risen up to consume him. He had begun to indulge in a fashion he claimed suited his prospective status, and that indulgence had manifestly settled upon wine. As he descended into his cups, the family purse began not so much to dwindle as unravel, spilling coins into the sewer of vomit, stinking breath, grumbling, recriminations, near-starvation, all to feed the luxuriant pleasures of a momentary sating of paternal thirst.

And the worst of it was, he was encouraged! The whole town of Stratford had urged him on, because there was nothing so entertaining in the world as Will's father in his cups. They were not only laughing at him, but with him. Eyeball afloat in wine, he was a man of wit and humour, of charming hilarity, with a *bon mot* for every man and a song for every occasion. He was always and in all ways excellent company until that inevitable moment when he had to be carried home in a cart to his increasingly impoverished family.

It was the cause, the cause for so much of Will's disastrous state. The ruinous drinking of Will's father had left them all destitute. They had attempted every means to shore up the ditch he was digging for them, even forcing Will to marry their distant relation, Anne – who was desperate to wed, being imprudently impregnated by her father's groom. Thus young Will had found himself married to an older woman, claiming as his own the child of another man. As this was generally known, he was himself a laughingstock, and when she had further children, the laughter increased. To be fair to her, Anne was no whore, but she was desperately in love with a man far beneath her. Will could only hope that at least the son she had bourne was his, but he would never be sure. Little Hamnet looked like his mother.

On the cusp of becoming gentle, he had instead been thrust into the role of cuckold, of a bit player in his own life. Of the Foole. Was it any wonder that our Will fell afoul of the Law? Full of resentment at the life he had been forced to live, he had flouted Authority and been clouted for it. The young upstart with the Catholic family had been whipped in public for his crime – then committed a greater one, and fled before the world came crashing down upon him.

All this he kept within the hedge of his teeth. Kit was not to be trusted, it was clear. Nor were Greene and the rest. Will had to keep himself close to himself. It was a hard lesson, one he was learning over and over again: the appearance of openness is different than actual honesty. Given the chance, men would betray – it was in their natures. So give them no weapons, no tools, no chance to betray. One had to disguise one's true nature to survive. Hide in plain sight. Disappear.

Yet Will had inherited a most damning trait from his inebriate father. Not his bottomless thirst. Had it been that, Will might have been content, living forever as a drunken glover in Stratford. No, it was something much more galling, more insidious and devastating. He had inherited his father's ambition. In a fixed world, Will's black and deep desire was to be more than what he was. To achieve greatness. He had not been born great. He had hoped, in siding with Kit, that he might have found greatness thrust upon him, that circumstance and his stars might conspire to catapult him into the stratosphere of wealth and success, honour and gentleness.

But that was Foole's treasure. There was no Philosopher's Stone to turn his lead into gold. If there was to be greatness in his future, he must perform the alchemy himself.

First things first. He had to escape the executioner's axe that hovered over his neck like the Sword of Damocles. In which resolve, he rolled over and propelled himself into sleep.

It was perhaps two hours before sunrise when they were awakened by two men in rude clothes entering by a window in Watson's room. Both Will and Watson looked on distastefully while Kit clasped hands with the elder of the pair, who bore a sack upon his shoulders. "Cutting Ball! Well met."

"Oi." Cutting Ball was a squinty, shifty round-headed man with the jaw of a mastiff and the eyes of a drowsy hawk. His head was shaved – probably against the lice – but the shaving was inexpert and imprecise, leaving hither and thither patches of bristly iron hair.

"Will, may I present Cutting Ball. Cutting Ball, Will Falstaff."

Thus Will was introduced to the true Lucifer of London, the underworld figure known as Cutting Ball, commander of a rowdy, ragged rabblement of rakehells.

It was he who presented Will the low garments of the beggar, right down to the patched and stained hose. When Will asked to whom they had belonged previously, Cutting Ball merely answered, "S'a no port. E's doin' the 'empen dance at Tyburn. Get drezzed."

Swallowing, Will tried to curb his imagination as he put on a dead man's garments. "Cutting Ball," he ventured. "What's your Christian name?"

Cutting Ball studied him. "By the 'oly piss o' John the Baptist, what does Christ 'ave to do with a name? One name's as good as'a nex, an' I've earned Cutting Ball, 'aven't I? S'not a poxy gift from some ol' whore, but a name o' respect."

"Oh?" asked Will carelessly.

Cutting Ball grinned proudly. "When I was a lad, I was a bit careless wif me knife while liftin' purses." He shrugged, chuckling.

As most men carried their purses with their bodily valuables, within their cod-piece, Will suddenly understood the origin of the name. Dressing more quickly, he resolved to stop making stupid inquiries.

Cutting Ball handed him a rude sign with a loop of string attached. "Don this, eh?"

Will did as he was bidden, then read the upside-down words, *Licenced to Beggery, City of London,* followed by some initials and a seal. Will was now a member of the poorest class of men. An excellent disguise, if a humiliating one. Will suffered an unworthy suspicion that this idea had first belonged to Greene.

Next they went about disguising his features. "This be Beggar's Leprosy," explained the villain as he daubed Will's face with glue tinged with calf's blood and rye dough, then bound Will's face up in a tight scarf to make his face even more livid.

"So," said Cutting Ball briskly as he worked, "we's watchin' someone?"

Kit had given Will a complete – too complete – description of Gifford. The notion was to follow him throughout the day, observe his actions, and follow any man he made contact with. Hence the need for more than one pair of eyes.

Cutting Ball introduced his companion as Scarlet Dick, a sobriquet Will wisely left untouched. Scarlet Dick was younger than Will, but with aged eyes and the sallow skin of hard living. Dick carried a flat-tish, hinged box about three by three wide, and only a foot deep.

Kit bade them farewell, and Watson promised to check on them around noontime. Given the address for Gifford, the trio set up just before it, with the door over their shoulder.

"Shouldn't we be across the street? He'll see us."

"An' what if we're 'cross there and the crowds and 'orses 'ide 'im? No, best be 'ere, showin' what 'e 'spects t'see."

"And what's that?" demanded Will.

At a nod from his master, Scarlet Dick unhinged his box. Opened, it was like a table with low walls all around it, and a tall back wall with cloth stretched tight atop it. They placed it atop a tripod from Cutting Ball's sack, and took up residence behind it.

Will kept his curiosity in check, and was soon rewarded with an answer. After satisfying himself all was in place, Cutting Ball produced a pair of dice. He looked to Will. "Ye play?" Will shook his head. Cutting Ball chuckled. "Smart lad."

They had set up not far from the markets, and by dawn Will was again amazed at how full the streets were. The sheer number of people pressed into this tiny patch of land called London astonished the country boy in him. At once he saw the wisdom of being where they were. They could not help but see their quarry, but appeared to be facing out, not in.

It was discomfiting to be sitting out in the open. Will's sense of London geography was expanding, and he had a vague sense that Seething Lane was not so very distant – the Tower had been visible several times during the dark walk to Cheapside. But he told himself that in this disguise his own mother would look away from him before she recognized him. He had to resist scratching – until he watched everyone else scratch around him and decided to blend by giving in to the urge.

Meanwhile, he watched as Cutting Ball and Scarlet Dick plied their trade. Cutting Ball stood beside the open box, rattling his dice at passers-by. Every few minutes a patsy on the way to market would decide to double his funds with a quick throw. He'd toss the dice and either win or lose, completely honestly.

Scarlet Dick would arrive as if by sheer happenstance and take up betting as well. They would maneuver the patsy into betting on Scarlet Dick's throws, and soon he would find himself parted from his money. Then, if he was not clever enough to walk away, both Scarlet Dick and the marked-foole would bet against Cutting Ball's throws. Both appeared to lose money, but in truth Scarlet Dick was directing the betting, risking nothing at all. Then Scarlet Dick would feign anger and storm off, urging the patsy to do the same.

Over the course of the whole morning Will watched this process repeated, wondering how on earth they were winning. He'd tried the dice and assured himself that they weren't weighted.

"Normally we wouldn't let 'em win at all," explained Cutting Ball during a lull. "We'd clear off. But we need the spot, so we'll leave 'em somefin to sup upon."

"But how do you control the dice?"

Cutting Ball smiled. "Nex' time don' watch the fall. Watch the throw."

Will did, carefully noting how the two rogues gripped the dice. At last he perceived that they were picking them up the way they wanted them to fall, and that their 'throws' weren't actual rollings of the dice, but mere rotations, leaving the chosen faces upright. They disguised this by bouncing them off the cloth on the inner wall of the box top, or against the cloth-covered edges of the low walls below. The dice would bounce off, but never flip or roll. It was the impression of dicing, when in fact it was dropping.

Twice Watson ambled by, taking up the dice and playing Scarlet Dick's role for whatever patsy was at hand. They had agreed on a few signal words. To a querulous remark made to him, Will replied only, "Figs." This meant that they had seen no sign of Gifford yet. Watson would finish his part in the game, stalking off in anger at having lost. Men cleared a path of him, such was the ugly gleam in Watson's eye.

Will understood why Kit was equal parts admiring and wary of the man – even play-acting, he was fearsome.

At one point Will noticed another man in mean clothes eyeing them darkly. He pointed this out to Cutting Ball, who reacted immediately. "Oi! Clear off, ye clouted, flap-mouthed rabbit-sucker! We've got this patch this day!"

The man gave them the fig, but turned and stalked off. Cutting Ball laughed. "I know'm. A Ruffler."

Will wasn't sure he'd heard correctly. "Ruffler?"

"Aye. A Ruffler's one who's been t'war, and sees begging as too low an occupation. But 'e'll beat ye senseless for a groat."

"Are there lots of them?"

"Enough t'ave a name," observed Cutting Ball philosophically.

Will's curiosity was entirely piqued. With a conscious effort not to give offence, he inquired after the professions a London thief might employ. Cutting Ball puffed up like a peacock and held forth as loquaciously as any Oxfordian professor, pouring out knowledge that Will lapped up.

Setting aside the tiresome London cant of yore, Cutting Ball's list of scoundrels fell into two discrete categories – the Thief, and the Trickster. Among the Thieves were:

- The Rogue, a simple thief, a robber of houses or men.

- The Hooker, or Angler, a night-time scoundrel who carried a stave with a grand hook on one end, filching items through open windows when people are asleep.

- The Upright-man, likely a former servant, "skilful in picking, rifling, and filching." He was often as not putting on airs and, like the Ruffler, stole from other vagabonds. He was also often a pimp.

- The Prigger, that most detested of criminals, a horse thief.

Then there were the Tricksters, the men who played their parts like the players of the stage:

- The Coney-Catcher (the profession they were today engaged in), who employed games and confidence tricks to beguile money from unsuspecting victims.

- The Abram-man, a rascal who played his role *extempore* – he pretended madness, usually as an escapee from Bedlam.

- The Counterfeit Crank, a less inventive player than the Abram-man, feigning only the falling sickness.

- The Dummerer, a man who, as the name indicated, acted as if dumb and, if particularly skilled, deaf as well.

"Most Dummerers be Welshmen," observed Cutting Ball. "No one wants t'hear them noways."

"And how many of these have you been in your time?" asked Will.

Cutting Ball frowned, but in thought rather than anger. "Me? I've been a rogue, I was a mere lad then. I've angled and prigged. M'time as a pimp was by chance, an' really for the benefit of the doxies..."

They were interrupted by another mark, and Will watched the duo of skilled cony-catchers ply their trade. He was startled when he heard the door behind him open and footsteps on the stone stairs. He was just turning when a foot caught him in the shoulder and sent him sprawling. "Move, you rogues!" called a polished voice.

Will had only the briefest glance at the man as he pushed past. Gilbert Gifford was tall, with longish brown hair that fell straight like limp flax. He seemed to have a small nose, wide eyes, and long mouth, giving his face a glass-distorted look.

Will looked to Cutting Ball, already packing up the makeshift gambling table. Scarlet Dick appeared as if by magic to pick up the box and tripod, freeing Will and Cutting Ball to pursue Gifford.

"Then there be women," said Cutting Ball, carrying on their earlier conversation. It was as much a cover for their walking as actual conversing. "Doxies an' morts."

"Morts?"

"Whores," said Cutting Ball simply. "Autem-morts and walking-morts – married and not. Turned out by th'Upright-Men."

"Are all women in the business – forgive me, are they all, ah, women of purchase?"

Cutting Ball laughed sourly, not at the women but at Will. "Ye gots to lift the cant, lad. Women o' purchase, 'onestly. But no. There be Bawdy-baskets, oo gull serving wenches with knick-knacks so she can nick the knacks from the masters. But most're morts. Even wee tykes. Kinchin morts and kinchin cos. Soon ripe, sooner rotten." Will's country sensibility had him blushing at this, which made Cutting Ball bark out a laugh.

They followed Gifford from a distance, closing quickly when the man turned a corner, then letting him get ahead. He was ascending Fleet Street, and stopped in at a tavern for his luncheon. Feeling his belly constrict in sympathetic hunger, Will mentally tightened his belt and followed Cutting Ball to a post down the road, where they could see both front and back door to the tavern.

"So ye've gotten on Greene's evil side, 'ave ye?" asked Cutting Ball carelessly.

"Have I?" asked Will, eyes on the tavern.

"'E asked me t'give ye a rough patch."

Will nodded. "It's me own fault," replied Will, dipping his tongue into the street cant as a swimmer dips his toe in water. "He reminded me of someone."

"A lardy rake wif loads of brain but no sense?" asked Cutting Ball lightly.

Will laughed, then answered. "Yes, but wif less brain."

Cutting Ball nodded. "I knows 'im fer ought 'e is. Me sis is 'is doxy, which makes 'im family-like."

It took Will a moment to parse this, but then he understood Cutting Ball had a sister, who was both a whore and Greene's possession. Will wondered if Greene, among his many other faults, was an Upright-

Man. But he managed to hold his tongue, as he rightly feared Cutting Ball's enmity.

But for some reason, Cutting Ball had taken an evident liking to Will. Perhaps it was in the non-judgmental interest in the man's profession. Or perhaps it was a true-to-life myth of the honest confidence trickster taking a liking to a young foole. For whatever reason, the grubby thief had turned voluble. "An' 'e 'ad an open purse, when 'e was in funds, Greene did. Poor luck fer 'im 'is wife's cut him off. Though morelike 'e spent all she 'ad."

"Greene's married?"

"Aye, an' a good match it was, so they tell me. Fer 'im, at least. Doll, by name. Older woman, daughter of a country gentleman. She was wealthy, once. Doubt e's lefter two farthings to spark together. Nowadays, o'course, Greene's pawned sword and cloak. 'E couldn't even pay for the funeral of me nephew, 'is son. I had t'pay the parson to lay the boy down."

"I'm sorry," was all Will could think to say.

"Naught of a life, young Fortunatus had. But at least 'e knew his sire, which is more'n Greene's right son does." He took his eyes briefly off the tavern and looked to Will. " 'E's a good mate when the drink's flowin', but you watch 'im, Falstaff. You're right t'be *en guarde*, as they say. Sell ye out for a 'alf-pint of ale," observed the thief, sometime-pimp, and cony-catcher Cutting Ball. "Whoosy. There's our rabbit." Gifford was on the move again.

Following, Will was having trouble concentrating on playing his part. His mind was on Greene's history. Married to an older woman, he'd run off to London for adventure, leaving her with a child.

Too familiar a tale for comfort. No longer did Greene remind Will of his nemesis, his sire. He now reminded Will of himself.

Gifford's next stroll took him quite some distance, bringing him to a house near the magnificent Westminster Abbey – possibly the tallest building Will had ever beheld up close, and by far the most ornate.

Of course the original structure of Bishop Mellitus, he who had envisioned St. Peter standing ankle-deep in the Thames, was long gone. The monumental replacement had been started three hundred years earlier, and only finished seventy years since. The site of coronations and the final resting place of so many great Englishmen, Will knew that the faux-pilgrim Geoffrey Chaucer was laid to rest in a southern corner, making him the only English poet so honoured. *Typical,* thought Will. *England values war and bawdy songs above language.*

In his guise of a jaded beggar he was unable to play the gawker, so he merely stole glances as they passed it and headed down the street to Gifford's next port of call. There was a French flag waving over the house Gifford chose, and armed guards with the fleur-de-lis on their doublets.

"Oh fut," said Cutting Ball, stopping at the corner. They were in a rosy rich area, far from the comfortable bustle of inner London.

"You know the place?"

"No, but I ken what it must be. Tothill Street? Palace o'the French Ambassador, ain't it? Now 'ush!"

Silent as they passed it by from across the road, continuing to the end of the street, Will tried to decide what that meant. Did the French Ambassador have the other key of the cypher? That put a cloud over their plans.

The contrariness of Will's mind had him quoting French poetry at himself. He began with *'France, mère des arts, des armes et des lois'* and ended with selections from *Maladiction contra un Envieux.*

Unknown to him, this last was utterly appropriate. For suddenly there was a cry and a clatter in the street just ahead of them. Will tensed and ducked, his heart beating to break free of his breast, as a dozen men-at-arms came running towards them. Cutting Ball pushed him hard out of their way, and they thundered past to the house just behind them. Not the French Embassy, but another more modest abode on Will's side of the street. They put a heavy log to the door, bursting it in, and ran inside with swords drawn.

Mouth hanging open in shock, Will watched as one fellow in fine clothes remained without, waiting. The man was so fair his skin burned even on cloudy days. He was dressed well for a country squire, in a wine-coloured brocaded doublet with large silver buttons down the front. His creamy hose were thick and didn't bag. His curling red hair stood tall, like a puffy topiary brushed back from a chalky cliff. His trim red beard came to a stabbing point at the end of his chin, which somewhat ameliorated the limp lip whiskers, grown long to mask their sparsity. In the midst of all, he had a nose to cleave doors with.

Against all possibility, Will recognized this man. Sir Thomas Lucy – upstanding citizen, knight, Protestant, Catholic-hunter, Member of Parliament for Warwickshire, Magistrate of Stratford – and the man who had flayed the skin from Will's back with his own hand.

Will stood rooted like a great elm shaking in a tempest, unable to trust his eyes. What on earth was Lucy doing here, in London, on this street, on this day, not a dozen paces from where Will stood?

Will's answer came with the return of the men-at-arms. Two of them Will recognized as Lucy's own men. Between this pair came a new face in a skull-close cap and long black robes. He was perhaps thirty, and vaguely familiar to Will.

"Robert Dibdale," crowed Sir Thomas, aglow with dark satisfaction, "I arrest you in the name of the Queen, and do desire you to come patiently with us. Should you resist, I have warrant to gizzard you here and now."

Dibdale! He'd gone to Will's own childhood grammar school, the King's New School. But then Dibdale had gone continental, studying in Rome and Rhiems. Will knew he'd been arrested for Papal leanings at the start of the decade, but as he had not yet been made priest he was released. The last Will knew, Dibdale had returned to Rhiems to be frocked and mitered.

Clearly the devout foole had returned to England bearing his cross, hiding within a stone's throw of Westminster itself. Now he was run to ground by the hellhound from the blasted heaths of Stratford. Trust

Lucy to be on hand himself for the taking of one of his Warwickshire natives.

Dibdale now yelled out Catholic prayers, imploring his neighbours to come to his aid and help overthrow the heretics of England. Lucy stepped forward and struck Dibdale a cracking blow across the jaw. From experience Will knew that Sir Thomas preferred to administer justice with his own hand.

Swelling with righteous indignation, Will clamped his jaw shut so no oath might escape him. Yet such was the wrathful flame kindled in him that several men glanced in his direction, as moths might a sudden burst of fire. Those eyes included Lucy's, but his were the only ones that narrowed in startled recognition.

Will was on the verge of running. But that would give up the game. Instead he embraced his part. Bending low, he averted his eyes and stretched out pleading hands. "Alms! Alms, master!"

Sir Thomas approached, and Will made forward faster, as if hoping for coin. "Poor Tom!" he called, bending low and holding forth his arms. Recalling the urgent voice of Bedlam, he began to sing. "Pillicock, Pillicock sat on a hill! If he's not gone, he sits there still! Poor Tom! Poor Tom! Alms for Poor Tom!"

Sir Thomas squinted hard at the top of Will's head. Will could only imagine what it was that the bastard was thinking. If it were only a slight recognition, Will might escape. If Lucy connected Will's face to the deer and the whip, to the verse and the humiliation, then Will's goose was spitted and roasted. "Poor Tom?" begged Will, turning his face upwards and revealing the extensive faux leprosy.

A sudden, hard blow sent him sprawling. "No alms for ye, fellow! Not when you malign the good name of Thomas!" Will whimpered and cringed, making Sir Thomas laugh. "Off with ye, vagabond, afore I share this Papist's fate with thee!"

As the Malediction was still in his head, Will sang it even as he retreated:

Je prie à Dieu, qu'il vous doint pauvreté,
Hiver sans feu, vieillesse sans maison,
Grenier sans bled en l'arrière-saison,
Cave sans vin tout le long de l'été.

Will quickly scuttled back to the corner and around it, where an exasperated Cutting Ball waited for him. "What in the name of th' blessed Saint George's fucking tame adder were ye doin'?"

"Showing him what he expected to see," answered Will in a low whisper as they continued up the side street, away from where Sir Thomas' proud band was leading the prisoner away.

"An' what was tha' French bit?"

Will smiled grimly and translated:

I pray that the Lord gives you poverty
Cold hearth in the winter
Old age without roof
Barns bare of wheat, when autumn is ending
Cellars empty of wine
All the long summer through.

"So ye ken 'im?"

"Aye," said Will. "I ken him. And more, I owe him."

Scene Two

After watching Gifford return home via Goldsmith's Row, with its painted balconies and gilded statues, they waited in vain for him to emerge again. At nightfall Will and Cutting Ball finally retreated to the White Hart, entering by way of a rearward door. Kit was again in the front upper room, drinking with Greene, Lyly, Watson, and a woman who looked like Cutting Ball with hair. They were all singing:

Dronken, drunken, y-dronken –
Dronken is tabart ate wyne...

With biting sourness Will said, "Glad to see while I have been carrying hods in Egypt, you all've been toiling so diligent-like." He ached, itched, and hungered, owning only a belly-full of resentment.

Kit laughed with mawkish sorrow. "*Au travail, on fait ce qu'on peut, mais à table, on se force.* Watson came back and said you were on the hunt, your perch being empty and our bird flown. We've been all a-nerves for you and so attempted to quell their jangling with spirits."

The un-feminine female scanned Will from toe to top, a decided scowl set upon her jowls. "Be this he?" she demanded of her lover.

"Aye, Em." Greene's assent was more belch than vocal assent.

Emily Ball wafted a skinny finger at Will, wetting her chapped lips to curse him like a witch. "So you be the young cockerel that's been putting down my Greenery!"

Both itchy and titchy, Will's answer was short. "Mistress Ball, I assure you, I'm am no gardener, an' if I were, I would leave your greenery untouched, unplowed, and unremarked."

The entire room erupted, with Greene spewing wine from both nostrils as he choked upon outraged laughter. Will recalled too late that the woman's brother was both in the room and noted for his skill at castration. But Cutting Ball was laughing harder than the rest, which caused his enraged sibling to launch a flurry of clouts and slaps at his near-bald pate. Will took the opportunity to remove the worst of his disguise, but he kept his foul hose and shirt – he had no wish to transfer lice to his own clothes. Accepting a drink, he laid out for the eager crew what they had gleaned that day from following Gifford.

"The French embassy!" moaned Kit. "Fut fut *merde* fut fut! I may as well go back to France and ask Henri himself to give me the cypher!"

Watson was less dismayed. "Think, Merlin! If Gifford is indeed leagued with Walsingham, it is likely he is playing the part of intriguing with the French. I doubt the cypher is there – any message from the French ambassador would be carried through by means of the beer-barrel. We should continue to watch him."

Will had come to much the same conclusion, if only because no other option was available to them. Despite the prospect of more days following Gifford, Will felt his spirits rise. He had half expected to return to the White Hart to find it teeming with Walsingham's men, that he and Kit had been betrayed by Greene in exchange for a pot of ale. But apparently the bond of University was as strong as he'd been told.

They sent up for food from the landlord, who had also failed to betray them – a testament to how much Greene owed here. Will and Cutting Ball were given trenchers of meat and strong ale, and they ate in company. Em Ball had stormed out in a manner that would have made Huffing Kate proud, and so the University men returned to their favourite topic – abusing the plays and players of the age, bandying about names Will did not know. In this particular instance, they were relishing a lawsuit between theatre owners Brayne, Hyde, and Burbage.

"Brayne's widow wants her share of the Theatre, and Hyde and the Burbage boys mean to cut her out."

"Is that the Burbage who mangles the words of better men upon the Theatre stage?" asked Kit. "He of the pumpkin nose and cauliflower ear?"

"He has an excellent voice, if not a civil tongue in his head," observed Watson. "But in this case it is his brother and father who have seized the management of the Theatre." It took Will some moments to understand the Theatre was a physical place, not a reference to the art. "'Tis a good case the widow has, if it ever comes to court."

"Meanwhile the Burbage boy can inhabit any role of his choosing," groused Greene.

Watson nodded. "I hear he means to play the lead in every play. If he could, he would take upon him all the roles at once. I understand he even means to mount Kyd's Spanish Folly, it being praised so, and make it his own."

"There is a serious lack in the world," lamented Greene, "if such a play as that can draw so many ears. O, would some of that attention might be paid to a better painter of words!"

Suddenly Lyly rose, bearing the mantle of a man decided. "Fellows," he said, clearly braced to launch into a deep topic full of import, "I am of a mind to bend my quill to the writing of a play about a king. Not a foreign king, but an *English* king."

They all murmured appreciatively at his daring. No one had ever yet put to the stage a play about an English monarch. At once Will saw Kit growing mulish, his blood doubtless turning to jealous sludge because he had not invented this notion himself.

Watson, however, was grinning. "Bold! Daring! You will either be rich or be hanged." He sounded approving of either outcome.

"That will depend on the quality of the result," mused Lyly wryly.

"And your choice of subjects," observed Watson. "Which begs the question – who was England's greatest king?"

Every man present with a single voice: "Henry V."

"What," demanded Watson, "because he died before he could grow old?"

"He won the battle of Azincourt!" objected the multitude.

In typical contrariness, Watson remained unimpressed. "A great battle, a marriage, and an heir, then death – that's the whole of his legacy."

Lyly was eager for ideas, and proposed a question. "Let us look, then, at what our kings are famous for. Henry V, as stated, for Azincourt."

"Henry VIII – for marital folly and material fatness," laughed Greene, patting his own behemoth of a belly.

"No," said Will, oping his mouth for the first time. "For religion." There was a chorus of "Ayes," to that. Even Greene had to assent that the essence of Henry VIII was his change from Defender of the Faith to Enemy of God.

"I do not propose to write of our Queen's honoured father," said Lyly. "That might be a little close to home. Let us look further back."

"Richard *Cour-de-Lion?*" suggested Watson. "An English King in foreign lands."

"Or his father," offered Kit, "who married the French girl and nearly conquered the world, only to have his sons squabble over the pieces."

"If you admire conquerors, what of Edward Longshanks?" asked Watson.

Kit grinned. "I prefer his son, who is most memorable for his end."

Everyone laughed heartily at this *double-entendre* – Edward II had died with a blazing hot poker rammed up his posterior orifice, a scene made sport of by Geoffrey Chaucer's Wife of Bath.

Lyly snapped his fingers. "What of *his* son? Edward III ruled for five decades, and had far more than a single great victory. And he left an heir behind him – a weak-kneed philosopher, yes, but an heir. It is hardly his fault that his grandson was deposed. Victory at war, peace at home, a fifty-year reign, and an heir to follow him. My friends, I present to you Edward III, quite possibly England's greatest king in both daring and durability."

Greene waggled a pudgy finger. "Edward III began the Hundred Years War. It was up to Hank Cinq to end it."

"And leave us vulnerable to years of civil war here at home!" roared Greene. "English fighting English? Hardly better, I'd say."

"There were civil wars in the years between," Watson observed. "Henry's father being an excellent example."

"Which in turn begs another question," rumbled Greene. "What is the nature of greatness? I'd argue that Henry IV was a better king than the one he replaced, but Richard II was the better man."

"Do we then suppose that tyranny makes the better king? Are we to live in a Machiavellian world?"

"He was not mistaken," said Watson grimly. "'Tis indeed better to be feared than loved. Look at Richard III."

"Look at him indeed. The fear of him led to his deposition. And that fear most unjust! Rarely has a man been so maligned. Do not you agree, Morley?"

Kit shook his head, drawing every eye. But if they expected him to defend the wily Richard, they were disappointed. Instead he returned to Machiavelli's theme. "Why be either feared or loved, when you can be both. Look at good Queen Bess. We love her as we love a king, but fear her as we fear all women." There was a great hubbub of scoff-laughter at this, but he pressed on in seeming-earnestness. "My dear friends, from the moment of our birth we are positively dominated by women. Mothers, sisters, aunts, cousins, then wives, lovers, and daughters. Who here is master of his women? Who dares gainsay his mother, or his wife? No, Greene, your marriage does not count. Yes, you left her, you cad, but do not tell me that Em Ball does not carry your testes in a sack about her neck. A very small sack."

"Which reminds me," said Greene, "more sack here!"

His cup of wine was refilled as Kit pressed determinedly on. "These women – they are the tyrants of our existence. It was not always thus, but the changing times has put women into the roles of men – which makes women of us! Elizabeth and Mary are excellent examples – kings in petticoats. Who is more kingly than our Queen?

What monarch ever ruled in so absolute a fashion? Being a woman, she wears a fur glove. But there is a mailed fist beneath it."

"Mailed? Or male?" remarked Lyly with a smirk.

"Is it not possible," asked Will seriously, "that it is the role of monarch that brings forth these qualities from all beings, men and women?"

"If that were so," objected Kit, "would not the crown have made a stronger man of Richard II, or Edward deuce?"

Will persevered. "I mean to say, is it not likely that to be a successful monarch, one must show these signs and tempers, the steel and the resolve? That we deem them unfeminine is a fault in our character, not in theirs."

The Wits all gazed at Will as if he were dotard or heretic. Kit answered his philosophizing with real scorn. "Hardly! The fault, dear Falstaff, lies in the original sin! Eve's ambition damned the dickless, who are ever dragging men down to Hell with them!"

Will experienced the familiar feeling that he was out of step with the world. He wondered if this was how Sir Thomas More had felt – a Humanist, in a realistic world. It had always been thus. His mind was different from others, the paths his thoughts took diverged from well-trodden paths. It seemed that he leapt to conclusions and connections so far outside the norm that, if he spoke them aloud, no one knew what to say. Far from make him proud, he worried that there was something wrong with his brains. One could only receive so many blank stares in one's life before one began doubting one's sanity.

Yet this seemed a truth – it was not so much the difference between men and women, but a common cause in all humanity. To call what was admirable in a king abhorrent in a queen was mere bigotry, a blindness rooted in prejudice. Could not a woman be strong, and still be a woman? Weakness did not feminize men. It meant only they were weak men.

And was not ambition to be found in men as well as women? Why was not strength and leadership admirable across the board? It was on the tip of his tongue to say aloud, "I argue that our greatest king is a queen." But Will shied away from the stares, and in cowardice said no more.

"God save the Queen," said Lyly, and for a moment Will thought this most reasonable Wit might echo his thoughts. "But she has failed in her one duty – to provide us with an heir."

"She will never marry," proclaimed Watson. "That much, at least, is clear by now."

"And why should she?" exclaimed Greene. "Why welcome a man who will expect her to be a woman, when she so clearly is not?"

"Give her her Majestic due," said Lyly with dismissive fairness. "The realm is peaceful and prosperous."

"But for how long?" demanded Kit. "When will the Spanish come? Or the French? Without a king, we court invasion at every breath! We are at present ensnared in a mess borne directly of our lack of a king, and of an heir!"

"A failing shared by many other monarchs," observed Will.

Lyly pounced, hoping to return to the earlier subject. "Which is the best gift to leave to posterity? A great victory, lasting peace, or an heir?"

"A great victory," said Kit at once. "A resounding win over all the forces arrayed against one."

"An heir," said Watson, surprising the rest. In answer to their curious stares, he stroked his chin demonstratively. "Posterity should have some copy of my loveliness."

When the chuckles and mockery subsided, it was Greene's turn. He spoke slowly, with a grave smile. "I mean to have all three, myself. I shall go to my lasting peace victorious over convention. And I have at least one heir…" His eyes filled with tears, but who knew if they were for his dead son Fortunato, or for his living son whom he had left a pauper. The rest of the Wits looked away in embarrassment.

"For myself," said Lyly, "I prefer a peaceful legacy before I go to my eternal rest. I am not Hercules, and I will not burn my body to achieve immortality. I only ask for time and space to do as I like."

Kit rounded on Will. "Well, William? Which side to you come down on? What is the best gift to leave to the world?"

Will considered, and decided to reject all the other answers. "An idea."

Frowning for them all, Kit demanded, "I beg your pardon?"

"How many men have left something new behind them? How many have changed the world with their being? Far too few. One man in a million, perhaps. Hector. Moses. Joshua. David. The first Brutus."

"Aristotle," said Lyly, picking up the thread of Will's tapestry. "Socrates. Plato. Caesar. Virgil. Christ, certainly, though I suppose he had help. Marcus Aurelius."

"Constantine," said Watson, eager to join the game. "King Arthur. Charlemagne. Alfred the Great. Mohammad," he added, hoping to provoke his fellows.

But Greene was nodding, his jowls flapping as he mopped his eyes and rejoined the conversation. "Thomas a Becket. Dante. Chaucer. Caxton."

"Gutenberg, then," interjected Kit. "Tyndale. Martin Luther. Thomas More. Machiavelli. And I daresay every man in this room!"

"Yes!" Will was absurdly pleased that the others had, for once, understood the point he had been making. "Both ourselves and our creations are a debt owed to death. I submit the greatest legacy a man can leave behind is a new idea."

"And what idea, my dove, do you mean to leave behind, a posterior to posterity?" asked Kit, a daring twinkle in his eye.

Will shrugged and spread his hands. "How can I answer? I haven't thought of it yet."

Scene Three

London
31 July, 1586

A grey day, it did drizzle down dewy rain. There were fewer passers-by to lure onto Gifford's stoop, which afforded Will the chance to practice his hand at dropping dice. Five days of watching and trailing had, so far, afforded them nothing save Will's growing skill. Cutting Ball instructed him out of the corner of his mouth, so his words might stay with only them. Will had learned to pinch the dice together and drop them with a flourish of the wrist, so that they gave the appearance of rolling when in fact they only spun like a top.

But Gifford was off earlier this day, shoving and kicking past Will, Cutting Ball, and Scarlet Dick well before noon. As before, Will and Cutting Ball followed, leaving Scarlet Dick to pack up the table – or perhaps stay and earn a day's wage.

In a promising twist, this day Gifford was more furtive in his habits, cutting up alleys and down twisting side-lanes. He never ran, but he walked brisk-like and kept tossing squinny-eyed glances over his shoulder. Will and Cutting Ball split apart, taking it in turns to trail Gifford close. Twice Cutting Ball moved to the fore, advancing past their mark and trailing him somehow from the front.

Truth be told, there was no need for Cutting Ball to risk himself in this fashion. He could easily have opted out – there was no gain to be had from helping Will and Kit, and quite a bit of risk. It couldn't be only that he liked Greene. Nor did Will suppose that it was his own charm that had this rascal of the London underworld eager to aid them.

The only conclusion Will could come to was an odd one – patriotism. He asked if this was so, and Cutting Ball had actually flushed with embarrassment. "She's our queen too, ain't she?"

Respecting the man's privacy, Will let the question drop and refocused his attention on their prey.

They lost sight of Gifford once. But Cutting Ball was unperturbed. "There's n'a lane in London I doesn't ken." And sure as certain, a minute later they had spied their prey, who had taken a side-route parallel to their own.

While it was a nerve-jangling process, this boded well. Clearly Gifford was now meeting someone he should not and must not be seen with. Since he had visited the French in the open, morelike this was the person to whom he was betraying Walsingham. Which meant morelike this was the person with the key to the locked cypher.

It was hard to watch a man without looking at him. It was yet more difficult to traverse the street as a beggar without playing the part too broadly. The last thing they wanted was to draw attention to themselves.

Fortunately, Gifford seemed to be looking for men who looked at least as prosperous as he himself – in other terms, men likely to be in Walsingham's employ. With the aid of the rain, the beggar's rags made Will nigh invisible. It was almost worth the numerous raised bites on his legs and shoulders. Almost.

At last Gifford came to an inn. Will did not know the name, for Gifford entered by the rear. Alas, here the limits of his disguise became apparent. If he and Cutting Ball were to enter, they would be summarily thrown out again.

But it seemed luck was with them. It was near noon now, and the place was crowded. To stave off the chill of the rain, there were fires within, and windows were open to release the smoke – likely the chimney was less than adequate, and certainly not cleaned this time of year.

From the cover of a barrel in the mucky gap between the inn and its next-door neighbour, Will and Cutting Ball were able to peer through the rain's beaded curtain and examine the main floor.

Gifford was not there. "Damn."

"Secon' floor," guessed Cutting Ball.

Will was frustrated. "What if they leave separately? How can we know who he's meeting?"

"Can't. Unless…" A slow grin spread across Ball's face. Holding up a hand indicating Will should wait, he disappeared around the back of the house. He was gone nearly five minutes, and returned with a knowing look. Ignoring Will's questioning, he chivvied his charge across the street. They took up residence in an alley positioned diagonally from the front door of the inn, which Will saw was called 'The Hung, Drawn, & Quartered,' with a most graphic graphic to signify. As omens went, it was unnerving.

Cutting Ball seemed unperturbed. "Watch th'door."

"What did you..?"

Cutting Ball shook his head. "More'n my life is worth, and poor luck t'even name the deed. Jus' watch, neh?"

They waited, Will obediently focused upon the door. He heard some little noise within. Then his eyes were pulled from the portal by a plume of smoke rising over the back of the inn. The rain quenched it almost at once, but Will suddenly understood – Cutting Ball had committed arson, lighting the rear of the inn on fire. No wonder he didn't dare speak his crime aloud. Ever since the great fire of 1135, the city of London deemed arson an offense punishable by instant, immediate, and most intimate death – most likely in the form of the inn's namesake.

But the crime had the desired effect. The patrons of The Hung, Drawn, & Quartered all emerged into the rain at a run, only to stop in the street and look back at the ruin of their meals. Among the last to reach safety was Gifford, in the company of a man Will recognized at once. "Oh-*ho*."

"Know'm?"

"I do," replied Will, shrinking back into the lee of the alley's mouth. "His name's Savage."

Cutting Ball examined the huge ex-soldier carefully. "Suits'm. What ye reckon we should try?"

The answer was as obvious as it was unpalatable. "Follow him, find where he lives, and wait for a chance to search his rooms."

Cutting Ball deemed this sensible. It was well they had a plan of action ready, for the two men parted almost at once. Gifford seemed to want to talk, but Savage stormed away from him, glancing this way and that to see if he was being shadowed. Will remembered just in time to keep his eyes on the flaming inn, which was where all other men were looking. To the cheer of all, it seemed the fire had been more smoke than flame, and was already being extinguished – Cutting Ball knew his business. He'd smoked out the hares without burning down the forest.

Trailing Savage was a much more difficult business than following Gifford. He was watchful, and Will was an amateur. Worse, the prey knew Will by sight. After only three city blocks Cutting Ball shoved Will into a doorway just as Savage turned about and retraced his steps. Once the large man had passed, Cutting Ball hissed in Will's ear, "Get ye back t'the White Hart. I'll tell ye where 'e lands."

"But I—"

"Nay, I. This be a matter for professionals." Without waiting for acknowledgement Cutting Ball set off into the rain, leaving Will alone for the first time in London.

It was at once terrifying and liberating. He certainly recognized the wisdom of the move, and found Cutting Ball's orders shockingly courageous and honourable, if practical. It was a remarkable discovery, one that Will vowed there and then not to forget. There was more life in these low beings, in these clowns and vagabonds, these rakes and hellions, these criminals and idiots, than in all the respectable gentlemen of the court. Huffing Kate, Blacke Davie, Tarlton, Cutting Ball – these creatures positively teemed with spirit, overflowing the meager cups of their existence with their humour, their desires, their very essence. They were as worthy of immortality as the highest monarch born to the throne. For in them was the daily toil to survive, giving them a greater bond with the vast multitudes of human existence than a king might ever own. These low people were the stuff of high art – Comedy and Tragedy all in one.

Will considered returning to the Hung, Drawn, & Quartered to see if Gifford was still about, and thereafter following him at least back to some recognizable landmark by which he could navigate his way to the White Hart. But he sensed that the triple-traitor would now bear a more wary eye, and Will's own skill at shadowing was not yet so great he could manage alone. Instead Will turned left, then left again, and walked straight until he reached the best landmark in London, the Thames. This he traced, walking along with his rain-soaked scalp high as he took his leisure to soak in the city. He removed the bandage on his head and let the beggar's leprosy wash away, returning his features to their natural state, secure that no one would possibly recognize Will of Stratford.

Despite a nagging voice at the base of his brain that insisted he should return at once to inform Kit of his news, he felt he must embrace this chance to study his new city. It was remarkable how comfortable he felt here. For all its filth, vices, and dangers, London felt more like home than any place on earth.

The north bank of the Thames was wealthy, with mansions once owned by churchmen and now occupied by the New Men, men only recently nobled who had profited from Henry's split with Rome. Not wishing to be beaten away, Will crossed to the south bank at first chance, and strolled along with remarkable comfort. Across the water lay a city of congestion, clogged with men striving and toiling for advancement. Will perceived that over there lay the financial and religious heart of London. But here, on his side, was the carnival of delights those men required to make life endurable. Whores and bears, sport and gambles. And theatre.

He was tempted to seek out a playhouse, but the rain meant there was little chance of hearing a show. So instead he ambled up and down

Southwark, seeking its artistic heart. Twice he neared Borough High Street, home of the White Hart, but turned aside at the mouth of it, pressing on in widening gyres of exploration.

The narrow streets were sometimes cobbled, sometimes rough dirt. Houses crammed close, with furtive alleys between. Will had already learned to fight other men to maintain a closeness with the wall to keep the contents of jordans from splooshing over his head. Loud noises abounded – hooves and coach wheels, crying traders, brawling apprentices, scuffles between men who were perpetually half-sotted – London was not what you or I would term a city of sober pursuits. But for Will, it was one unending painter's palette of human colour. Scrubbed clean by the rainfall, it looked and smelled like a place ideal for creating one's self anew.

Which raises the question of creation, of the God-like act of making something from nothing. It might be argued that there is no new thing in all the world, that everything in creation has been created once already by the Creator, and therefore all is made. But reality is not perception, and the perception of newness makes a thing new again. Individually new, personally new. And if perception made a thing new to a person, might not that person make himself new to perception?

These thoughts carried Will about for hours. It was only the fear that Cutting Ball might return before him that made Will turn at last down Borough High Street, making directly for the White Hart's door. So confident was he, feeling so proud, so free, and so accomplished, that he did not duck his head, nor turn up the collar of his dirty sodden shirt.

They say beasts and birds know of impending upheaval, a disaster-sense that sends them flying for the hills. It is an animal instinct, almost beaten out of man and yet present at his core. Will's was too dormant, too buried, and it warned him too late, causing only a stutter in his step before the clarion-call of disaster descended upon him. Worse, the call came in a single word, one that had not passed his lips in six long months. Not since taking up the title Falstaff, a weak jest to hide his true surname...

"*SHAKESPEARE!!!*"

It is indeed a sorry state when the sound of your own name becomes a knell of doom. The name alone was a death knell, but the voice shouting it made death certain. His jaw transfigured into a wriggling hoard of maggots, his knees into water. Blenching and clenching every muscle in his body, he broke out into a sweat and resisted the impulse to turn. Perhaps if he played his part, the bastard might think he was mistaken.

"*William Shakespeare!*"

Too late. He'd already given himself away. His fearful pose was of a hind caught in the open. Entirely against his desire, Will turned.

Standing not ten feet behind him, at the very mouth of the gate to the wide yard, was Sir Thomas Lucy. His normally fluffy thatch of ginger was limply sodden, mournfully clinging for life to his pate. His pointed beard dripped from the sharp tapered end. But the face beneath it was suffused with the inner glow of a winter hearthfire as he regarded his prey.

Two men stood at Sir Thomas' shoulders. One was the same who had sworn before a magistrate that he'd seen Will poach a deer. The other was Dan Johnson, brother of a dead man in Stratford.

"O, how I have longed for this day," said Sir Thomas. "And let's have no more lunatic business, shall we? Try to die like a man."

Will drew himself up tall. Absurdly, at this moment his greatest regret was his attire. If he was to die, he didn't want to do it dressed in beggar's robes. "I'm not armed."

"An' if you were," said Lucy, laughing through his teeth, "would it make any difference 'tween us? You never knew foible from pommel."

"I knew your foibles for what they were, and are," retorted Will. "Sir Thomas Lousy."

Snarling and gnashing like a leashed hound, Lucy answered the ill-advised provocation by drawing his blade. "O, the mighty Shakespearean temper. I thought I had lashed it out o' you. But then you killed poor Johnson. Seems you nee'd another lesson."

"You would beat an unarmed man in the street?" asked Will. "Wait, scratch that. I know you of old. Of course you would. In fact, beating unarmed men is your favoured pass-time."

Flushed more crimson than his hair, Lucy raised his naked blade, fury etched across his pointed features. "Be warned! Atop the warrant for murder, there is a fair price upon your pate, Master Shakestaff. I could stab you through the liver and collect not damnation but praise and wealth."

Will nodded. "Your favoured means of gaining gold – the murder of innocent men." He was deliberately provoking Lucy, at the same time stepping aback into the gated yard of the inn, drawing Lucy closer while forcing the two merciless mercenaries in Lucy's train to gather near the gate entrance.

"Innocent!" cried Lucy with a sneer. "Plotting with Catholics to overthrow Her Majesty the Queen is hardly innocence! And do you deny breaking poor Johnson's pate and leaving him to die? I should let Dan here do the like for you! I knew I was right about you, Shakestaff. Or should I call you Quiverstaff, the way you tremble with fear at my approach."

"Call me what you please," answered Will. "I have already named you, Sir Too Mousey Lousey." He saw Lucy's hand twitch, but it was not yet enough, so he launched into the rhyme that had sent him running from Stratford six months earlier:

'*A parliament member, a justice of peace,*
At home a poore scarecrow, in London an asse,
If Lucy is Lousy and some folke misscall it
Then Lowsie is Lucy whatever befall it.'

Face purpling like an engorged thing, Lucy lunged. Just as Will had hoped. Twisting sideways the way Kit had taught him, he raised his right arm high. The point of the unbated blade sang past his chest and pierced the air just below his right armpit. Will's right arm was already dropping, wrapping itself about the blade. At the same moment Will's left hand struck Lucy on the wrist of his swordarm. The sword hilt came free, the blade trapped under Will's arm. In an instant he had it reversed and pointing up under Sir Thomas' chin.

> '*He thinks himself greate, yet an asse in his state*
> *We allow bye his eares but with asses to mate;*
> *If Lucy be Lowsie as some folk misscall it,*
> *Then Lowsie is Lucy whatever befall it.*'

Lucy's sword was a fine one, with a large double-ring guard and a grip of polished cherry wood. There was a raise to the centre of the blade on each side so that, if you stared at the point, it looked like a diamond. Sir Thomas was looking at it now, quite unaccustomed to seeing it from this vantage.

Will advanced a step, forcing Lucy to stumble backwards, chin still high.

> '*He's a haughty proud insolent knight of the shire*
> *At home nobodye loves, yet theres many hym fear.*
> *If Lucy be Lowsie as some folk misscall it,*
> *Then Lowsie is Lucy whatever befall it.*'

Lucy was turned chameleon, the purple dye of his flesh reverting briefly to white before turning the yellow of parchment as he stepped back and back from the point, seeking safety in his men-at-arms' arms. Pushing past him, the vengeful Johnson lunged as the perjurer darted around Lucy's other side.

Will parried first one, then the other, desperately seeking some advantage – his fencing lessons with Kit had not yet addressed fighting two men at once. He found himself wishing desperately for a longer sword, mentally cursing the Queen's own law on the matter.

During the early days of Elizabeth's reign, it had become the fashion to wear swords long. Meaning that actual sword blades kept growing longer and longer. Not only a decided advantage in dueling, where a longer reach meant better chance of victory, this was also a symbol of wealth and status – and, perhaps, a form of compensation?

But this fad eventually created quite the dilemma at court, as noblemen repeatedly whacked each other with every bow, every turn, every entrance, every exit. Finally the monarch, deciding enough was too much, issued a decree: henceforward there was but one length for swords – thirty-three inches. As Our Lord Christ had died at the age of thirty-three, this seemed the right length of steel for good Christian men to wield in the ending of other men's lives. And it lessened the number of bruised shins at Elizabeth's court. Swords were scrupulously measured, and if they were any longer than the granted thirty-three inches, the royal blacksmith confiscated the weapon and chopped it rudely to the correct length – the only acceptable form of circumcision practiced in Elizabeth's England.

Will ducked a swipe at his eyes while he blocked a thrust for his belly, which due to the duck put the incoming point at the level of his chin. He slapped the flat of the lower blade with his palm while his over-taxed sword leapt up to catch the cut descending towards his pate. In the rain he felt his hand slip a bit on the sword's grip. *Terrific. Perhaps I can cap the day by letting my blade go flying from my grip.* But halfway through his mental lament he flashed upon an idea, like lightning through the rain. On his next swing he allowed his hand to slip a second time, then a third, until he was holding the sword not by the grip, but by the round pommel on the end. This extra five inches made for ugly, clanging, unfinessed swordsmanship – the blade was harder to maneuver – but Will was able to stop retreating. With a longer reach, he could fend off attacks quicker and even get in a riposte of his own.

All the while he kept on reciting his verse in half-sung tones:

'*To the sessions he went and did sorely complain*
His parke had been rob'd and his deer they were slain.
If Lucy be Lowsie as some folk misscall it,
Then Lowsie is Lucy whatever befall it.

'*He sayd twas a ryot his men had been beat,*
His venson was stole and clandestinely eat.

If Lucy be Lowsie as some folk misscall it,
Then Lowsie is Lucy whatever befall it.'

His confident poem masked his fear. Lucy's men fanned themselves wider, moving to flank Will upon either side. In seconds one would have his back and it would all be over. "Kit Marlowe, where are you!?" he shouted.

There came an answering cry from above. *"Corpus delecti!"*

Will's combatants both looked up as Kit came hurtling down, sword in hand, and crashed atop the man to Will's left. Will took advantage and lunged at his rightward foe. The extra length of his sword by-passed Johnson's defence and pierced his right shoulder. Dropping his blade, the man staggered back with a grunt.

Kicking aside the dropped blade, Will whipped around to see Kit climbing up off the downed man who had broken his fall, as well as a bone or three in his own chest. Kit cocked his head and smiled. "New friends?"

"Very old ones. What kept you?"

"Didn't care to get wet," answer Kit.

"Shakespeare!" Lucy was at the gate, having confiscated a sword from a passer-by. Suddenly he frowned, perceiving the change in odds. Faced with two armed men, and with his own men down, he shook his free fist then walked backwards out of the yard in high guard.

Will advanced, regripping his sword in the common manner for better control. His tongue and teeth and vocality all conspired without his knowing it to chant:

'So haughty was he when the fact was confess'd
He sayd 'twas a crime that could not be redress'd.
Though Lucies a dozen he paints in his coat
His name it shall Lousy for Lucy be wrote.'

Will feinted right and left, making Lucy dance to block both sides. He deceived under Lucy's guard and pressed the tip of Lucy's own sword against the knight's chest.

'*If a juvenille frolick he cannot forgive*
We'll sing Lowsie Lucy as long as we live!'

With a trifling twist of his wrist, Will lopped off two of the dripping silver buttons, one above Lucy's heart, one below. It was all he could manage not to carve his initials into the knight's bosom. His eyes still upon Lucy, Will backed away, then swept into the most flourishing bow he could perform. Imagining the figure he cut, a beggar aping the Frenchified fashions of the courtier, he could not help but laugh.

The laugh drave Lucy to the edge of lunacy, eyes distended and teeth gritted. But Will and Kit were already dashing and splashing up the street. In seconds they had turned the corner, leaving Lucy behind – he wouldn't follow without more men at his back.

'*If Lucy be Lowsie as some folk misscall it,*
Then Lowsie is Lucy whatever befall it!'

Lucy shouted, "Run, coward! I know you, Will Shakespeare! You're a traitor, murderer, coward, and thief, and I'll be revenged!"

Shaking with equal parts terror and glee, Will called out, "Oh! And your deer was *delicious!*"

Scene Four

Will and Kit raced through the surrounding streets, leaping over oceanic puddles and between busy Londoners in a winding path to lose any other watchers – neither could be sure Lucy had been alone in finding them. Only when they were a mile away, tucked into an alley behind a slaughterhouse and shielded by a falling wall of water from the roof above, did they pause to assess their state.

"Why with you am I ever and always running?" demanded Will with genuine laughter. Humiliating Sir Thomas had made his soul buoyant. Before today, imagining the confrontation with Lucy, he saw himself playing the part of the terrified innocent. Instead he found that though his worst fear had been realized, his old life and his new colliding, he had faced it well and lived to fight another day.

"*Me?*" gawped Kit breathlessly. "That scene was none of my making! But I must declare that you excelled yourself, my dear! Gripping the pommel for reach! I've never seen that move before! Certainly I never taught it you. Had you seen it in a book?"

"No," said Will blandly. "It was my own invention."

"Is it so?" asked a delighted Kit, his labouring breath sounding almost like Huffing Kate's. "So there's more than mere mimicry in you after all! You, Will, are a Creator! I shall certainly be inducting you into the Wits."

Will's laugh became a snarl. "The Wits? Kit, you must know that we were betrayed! Sir Thomas Lucy, a man who knows me by sight and by name, arriving by chance at the White Stag? Impossible. Someone informed Walsingham, and he used what you told him about me to send Sir Thomas after me." Kit had the good grace to look abashed as Will added savagely, "And I know who the culprit was! That foul bag of guts, that knave cloaked in a world of tallow, that spherical receptacle of ale and emitter of foul gases, that fat fucking bastard—"

"T'wasn't Greene," said Kit shortly.

"T'was! He wasn't present to witness our arrest, was he?"

"No," admitted Kit. Will let out an ecphonesis of angry and delighted vindication, but Kit pressed on deliberately. "But neither were Watson or Lyly – I was quite alone on the second floor. Fortunate, in a way – if Watson had been there, there would be three dead men in our wake. But don't suspect Greene. I know he doesn't care for you as I do, but he was the last one out. Moreover, he left much against his will, Will. It was his woman who dragged him out by the ear just minutes before you arrived. She was most insistent…" Kit suddenly frowned, his thoughts catching up with his words. "*Fut!* Emily! A woman! I told you, never trust a woman! That harlot, that dripping gash!"

"Em?" marveled Will. "But surely not! Her brother could have been nabbed as well!"

"Cutting Ball can fend for himself. Besides, your man Sir Thomas doesn't care a fig for Cutting Ball, does he?"

"I suppose not," admitted Will. "He has only eyes for me. What now?"

"That depends, I venture, on what you discovered today."

"Ah!" Will had almost forgotten. "Gifford met with our dear friend from another, more violent land."

"Meaning Mr. Savage."

"Quite. Cutting Ball followed him to ground." Pressing his two lips tight, Will punched his own palm. "But damn it all, how will we meet Cutting Ball again to learn what he found?"

"By going to his home," said Kit. "Or such an abode as he haunts. There's little likelihood that Em would reveal *that* address to Walsingham. Our beloved Cunnus Ball would never inform on her Cutting brother."

Will was still not convinced of Em's guilt – he would much rather have placed the blame on the walking vat of putrescence called Greene. But Em had as much cause, if not more. Regardless, Cutting Ball's haunt was most likely safe.

Shivering from the damp, they tramped southwards, away from the Thames and the White Hart. Their route was cautiously circuitous, but the day was dark and as the heavens chose that afternoon to rip wide and spill their tears down amidst claps of thunder and ragged slashes of lightning, they were confident they travelled unobserved.

"Wait – is that the theatre?" asked Will at one point.

"Ay, the Butts. Seems an age ago, does it not?"

Indeed it seemed a lifetime past that he and Kit had stood watching *The Spanish Tragedie,* wearing near-clean clothes and not itching, with prospects of greatness before them. Had it been ten days? Indeed, had it only been an hour since he'd stood along the Thames feeling gay and hopefilled? How quickly a man might fall. Will was glad there was no glass about – he was afeared to see his reflection at present, that he might not recognize the man he had become.

At last they came to a warren of buildings that seemed held together more by determination than mortar. "Cheaply built for, cheaply rented to, and cheaply occupied by Helpless Poor," confirmed Kit. "This way."

Will eyed the doorway Kit was alluding to. "Must we?"

"Never fear, darling. There's not been a collapse in months."

Will had thought he had seen squalor in the streets. Here, however, among the rushes stained with every bodily fluid and several brews of original filth, he perceived he had not seen true poverty until now.

The poor in England were divvied up into three types: the Helpless Poor, the Able-Bodied Poor, and Vagabonds and Rogues. The first were said to be looked after by Justices of the Peace, who collected a modest tax called the Poor Rate. The second group were pressed into work to pay their debts, or else paid out of the Poor Rate in exchange for base labour. The third were clearly criminals – able-bodied men and women who preferred begging and stealing to actual work. These were subjected to stocking, flogging, and hanging on a regular basis – theft of anything with a value greater than five pence merited death.

This being the case, the scoundrels banded together to make it harder to accuse them of crimes – if criminality was rampant, what criminal could be caught? It was no mistake, then, that upon entering the filthy two-story building, they were challenged.

"Who be?" snarled a man out of the shadows – there was but a single candle straining to bring light to almost palpable darkness.

"Friends of Cutting Ball," said Kit. Will made to bow, but Kit caught his arm, and Will understood at once – no sudden moves.

"O aye?" said the gate-keeper. "What business have ye, friends o' Cutting Ball?"

"He's been about our business for near on seven days, but we've lost our meeting place and hoped to wait for him here."

The man made a dubious sound, so Will quickly added, "Is Scarlet Dick about? He knows me."

That brought a more interested grunt as a second shadow across the room moved. "Be that Will?"

"It be, Dick," said Will, wilting in relief. "Cutting Ball insisted he move alone, and sent me back to wait."

"S'all to rights, Danny," said Scarlet Dick. "Put away yer dags." Only then did Will learn there had been a pistol pointed at him. His breath came more shallowly as Scarlet Dick led them through a door and up some stairs. "This way," he said, oping a door where Will could have sworn none existed. They stepped through, and Will imagined they had passed into, not another room, but another world.

Here was a large room fit for, if not a king, then a modest country squire – neat and clean, swept and well-lit. Near a fireplace stood several chairs about a table. There were even rich hangings on the walls, and fresh rushes on the floor.

Pleasingly, Kit was as astonished as Will. "We are in a different building, yes?"

Scarlet Dick grinned back, revealing as many lost teeth as he had present. "Aye. Yon door opens into th'ouse rearwards. This is where us lot plan our games and spend our nights. We get the wenches in t'clean if they're na'bout they business. Ye can wait here. I'spect Bally-Boy'll be back in short order."

"Do you have any fresh clothes?" asked Will before Dick could leave. Not wishing to seem disdainful of his beggar's garb, he added, "We're soaked skin deep."

Handing them a candle, Scarlet Dick pointed to another room adjoining this one, then lingered to hear Kit and Will's awe-filled gasps. Here were a vast panoply of clothes – fine clothes, rich clothes, some far better than any Will himself had ever owned. Men's clothes and women's, boy's and girl's. There were wigs and fans, boots and shoes.

"We 'ave an agreement wif a company o'players," explained a delighted Scarlet Dick. "They gets t'keep their best threadlings 'ere, an' we gets t'use 'em fer inny busy-ness we gets abou'."

"A sound business arrangement," said Will, pushing past his astonishment and already stripping out of his clothes. He heard Dick hiss in surprise. "What?"

Scarlet Dick had noted the whip-marks on Will's back. "Ye've stripes."

"Yes," said Will. "In fact, I just encountered the man who gave them me."

"Didja kill 'im?"

"No," said Will. He marveled at the embarrassment in his voice. "I had the chance, but didn't."

Scarlet Dick shrugged. "I'll send up ale, shall I?"

"Please," said Will. "And thanks."

"Yes, thank you," added Kit to the disappearing Dick's back. Then to Will he said, lowly, "I think you have gained more credit with him with your striped back than ever we might between us with words." He turned then to the rows of clothes hanging on portable poles, fingering the cloth of each before making a decision. Will had already found a neat pile of hose and was exchanging his tattered ones for fresh.

"Do you think we could make up a fire?" asked Will, still shivering from the drenching.

He sensed Kit drawing close. "We could kindle up a way to warm ourselves, I daresay. I'm told that rubbing two hard sticks together can kindle a flame. The heat of friction…"

Exhausted and cold, Will was in no mood, and had a handy weapon. "Kit, I took lice from these clothes."

Predictably, Kit retreated as if faced with another Orsino. Will found a shirt that fit, which was really a matter of guesswork, as Kit was holding the candle. He took up a pair of boots, and even found a baldric to hang Sir Thomas' sword in. But he waited to find a doublet until Kit had made his own choice. He knew Kit well enough by now to be sure that if he picked one, Kit would want it for himself, whatever it was like.

In fifteen minutes they had transformed from ragged and bedraggled refugees into respectable young men lounging over ale and a hunk of cold ham before a low fire. *"Magna pars libertatis est bene moratus venter,"* sighed Kit. *A great part of freedom is a well-behaved stomach.*

Will, too, was content. Miraculously, his itching had ceased – perhaps the little devils had drowned. With the tap-tap-tap of rain pellets upon the roof, it made for a drowsy afternoon, and Will was about to give himself over to dozing when Kit mused aloud, " *'If Lucy be Lowsie as some folk misscall it, then Lowsie is Lucy whatever befall it.'* What does that even mean?"

Flushing with genuine embarrassment, Will shrugged. "Who knows? I was in high dudgeon when I penned it, and working to call him a louse in as many ways as my cluttered mind could muster."

Setting aside his platter of ham, Kit wiped his chin. "Shakespeare. Or Shakestaff? Which is your name?"

Will said nothing.

"Come. We have been companions for weeks, you and I. Surely by now you know me as well as any man alive. Am I finally to learn what sent you haring from your barrow?"

"What, and give you more cannonshot for future betrayals?"

Rolling his eyes theatrically, Kit beat his breast and mimed whipping his own back. "A moment of weakness, of desperation! If you have never been desperate, then judge me harshly. But if you have, cast no stones. Besides, if Sir Thomas knows your past, you may rest assured that Walsingham knows it all by now."

That was true. Will judged his reluctance and found it wanting. There was no longer any point in keeping back the story. But still it took effort to bring it forth. On his first attempt, the words lodged in his throat. He had to cough and start again. "I was convicted of poaching a deer in Sir Thomas' keep. One of his fellows back there declared he'd seen me. He lied, of course."

"You didn't poach it?"

"I did not say so," corrected Will with a nasty grin. "The lie was that he saw me."

Kit doubled with laughter, slapping his hip. "Oh-ho-*ho!* I applaud your daring, my darling!"

Will understood Kit's reaction, which arose from the nature of the crime. Deer poaching in the time of Good Queen Bess was not, as one might think, an act of desperation or poverty. Perhaps once, yes, in the days of the fanciful rogue of Sherwood, he named Robin of the Hood, poaching deer had indeed been a crime of hunger. But not so in modern times. There were other ways to put food on a table, and quite as many animals to choose from – hares, fish, moles even.

No, quite contrarily, the sport of sneaking onto the keep of some wealthy landed gentleman and plucking a deer right under his nose was a show of disdain, a flouting of that lord's authority. It was the game of youthful rebellion against the elders, a way to prove daring to their fellows and show contempt for authority.

Kit downed more ale, then filled their flagons to the brim. "Quite the hellkite! I trust you had just cause?"

Will quaffed off the top half of his drink, bracing himself – the next part was not so amusing. "More than just. D'you recall when we rode into London, the many heads upon the gate? There were two men familiar to me."

"Fellow poachers?"

Straddling sadness and anger, Will shook his head. "One was a simple lad, a school-fellow of mine, though some years ahead. John Somerville of Edstone. The other was called Edward Arden."

"And who was he to thee?" asked Kit, agog.

"My mother's kin. His father was her second cousin."

"Did you know him?"

"To speak to. He was a gentle man, with a kind word and open hand. I knew John too, but from school, not from choice. John was – touched. But Edward was a good man – Catholic, but good. The Ardens are Catholic, you see."

"Which is how you knew the sign that was our salvation from the carbuncled snout."

"Aye. My mother had a Catholic bible in the house, and oftimes there were *sub rosa* meetings. She did not try to raise me so, and we went to proper church every Sunday. That is, we did until my father had to stop going for fear of being attached for debt…" Noting Kit's interest in this subject, Will quelled his bitterness and continued with the story at hand. "Five years ago, Cousin Edward cast a protective wing over a runaway Catholic priest, a decent fellow named Hugh Hall. Disguising him as gardener, he kept Hall as his private priest. Unfortunately, Edward's daughter had just married this fellow Somerville, who took an interest in all things that grew – like treason. From what I understand, the seed was planted when the priest informed young Somerville of the contents of *Regnans in Excelsis*."

"Ah!" said Kit. This infamous document was a papal bull in which Pope Pius V excommunicated Her Majesty the Queen, thus freeing all Englishmen from the duty to obey her. Moreover, the *Regnans in Excelsis* was cited by Catholic rebels in England as proof that God was calling for the overthrow of Elizabeth. By any means necessary.

Shaking his head, Will continued. "Somehow that seed planted in the fertile yet fallow ground of Somerville quickly blossomed to a rose of regicide. As he was a numbwit, he was quickly caught."

"By Sir Thomas?"

"No, by some fellows in an inn – he was always talking to himself. Day and night, sometimes muttering in his cup and sometimes talking aloud, as if conversing with a dozen invisible magistrates. This particular evening as he supped in the main room he was talking quite forcefully of killing Her Majesty. I told you, he wasn't right in his mind – quite Poor Tom."

"And?"

"And it was Sir Thomas he was handed over to. Lucy then imprisoned Somerville's wife, his sister, his in-laws, and the priest. The priest was condemned out of hand. Edward and John were taken to London. We heard they were tortured, and trialed for treason. Somerville actually proved clever at the end, stopping his tongue by hanging himself before he could be executed. Whereas poor Edward met the full fate of a traitor, beginning with the evisceration and ending with his head upon a pike."

"He harboured a priest," said Kit.

"Aye. But he separated his faith from his country. He would never have raised hand against the Queen. And Sir Thomas knew it. But he's made quite a life for himself, and quite a name, hounding out traitors and Catholics. Bastard," added Will reverently.

A smile twitched Kit's lips. "So you poached his deer."

"Yes I bloody did! What a night that was. We didn't even eat it. My friends and I caught it, then delivered it to the town square to show the world what had been done. The next day I was arrested, tried, and flogged for it. That bastard Lucy had his bastard game-keeper lie, then the bastard judge let Sir Thomas do the whipping with his own hand, right in the town square. A dozen lashes with a flayed cord." Will's back arched as he recalled each one, and tears came to his eyes, just as they had then.

"Your father couldn't stop them?"

Will chose to ignore the probing question. "After the whipping, I penned that little poetic revenge mocking Sir Thomas. Poor stuff, but my brain was half-addled by the lash. Nonetheless, he was enraged, and vowed revenge."

Kit waited before asking the one question remaining. "He called you murderer. Whom did you kill?"

Will sank a little into himself. If Kit, who knew him so well, did not even question the idea that Will had killed a man, what would a jury say? "Ken Johnson. Lucy's man. It was late one night, and dark. I was carrying a drunk man home when he accosted us in the street. He wanted to quarrel over the verses abusing Sir Thomas." Will shook his head. "That famous Shakespeare temper. Next thing I knew, he was lying on his face, his head broken, and the offending log of wood laying beside him, covered in his blood. So I packed a satchel, kissed my wife and children farewell, and skipped off before Sir Thomas got another friendly magistrate to order me stocked, flogged, hanged, and probably crucified."

Will expected Kit to mock him for the comparison to the deified Christ, but instead Kit reared back in shock. *"Wife!?"*

"Aye. Anne. Another tale for another date."

Kit looked at Will as if the lice had taken possession of his soul, far less disturbed by the notion of Will Shakespeare, murderer, than by Will Shakespeare, husband. Finally he laughed. "You are a conundrum, my friend. Each time I sound your depths, I find you without bottom. Which is not to say that you don't possess one. In fact, you have the finest—"

The door opened and Cutting Ball came trooping in. "Master Ball," said Will, wondering if he should rise. This was, after all, Ball's house. "They told us we could…"

Cutting Ball waved this off. Seeing the fire, he plopped down before it, wrenching off his boots and sodden clothes. "Damn me, it's a wet day."

"The White Hart is lost to us," said Kit. "But you must know that already."

"Aye. I'll be 'avin' words wif me sister, 'ave n'fear."

"So it was Em?" asked Kit.

"Aye."

Sensibly not pursuing that topic, Will stabbed for the more pressing matter. "Were you able to follow Savage?"

"Aye. That big bastard's go' a cove in a Dep'ford inn. 'E wen' in, an' I wai'ed long's I could stan', buh 'e didn' leaf. I'll go back on th'morrow."

"I'll go with you," said Will. "Better if we don't let him know the code is missing. One look at it is all I need."

"But surely," protested Kit, "it's no longer safe for either of us to walk the streets! If Em has told all, Walsingham knows what we're about, and that the code matters! If he brings the plot to light—"

"Then there's nothing for us save condemnation and death," finished Will when Kit faltered. "You were right, it must be us. It is time to make arrows of our wood. Besides," he added, flushing with the hereditary anger that had given the first Shake Spear his name, "I think I might enjoy meeting Sir Thomas again, so much the worse for him."

Act V
The Play's the Thing

Scene One

Deptford
1 August, 1586

Bedecked in cloaks against the continuing drizzles, our dramatic downtrodden duo were waiting without the Savage den when the man emerged early the next day. They had discarded the beggarly guises, now that those were known to Lucy and, through him, Walsingham. They recognized the want for extra caution – Sir Francis knew they were pursuing Gifford's contacts, and might station men outside Savage's lair to lie in wait for them.

But, as Kit observed, "The argument against such a course is strong. What if Savage sees Walsingham's men and thinks they are present, not to protect him, but to arrest him? Sir Francis might well prefer to send along a message through Gifford – or purportingly from him – that we are in the game. If Savage should kill us, so much the better for Sir Francis."

A disconcerting notion from a devious mind. The worst part was that such sidelong thinking was now beginning to make sense to Will. "Best we do this at once, then, before anyone has a chance to warn anyone of anything."

" '*Tarry no longer towards thy heritage,*' " quoted Kit. " '*Haste on thy way, and be of right good cheer.*' "

The moment Savage exited the inn, Will and Kit crossed the road and entered. While Kit made arrangements for a light breaking of the fast, Will looked to Cutting Ball, seated to the far side against a wall. The man made to pick his nose with his left hand, holding up three fingers while the other two fiddled his nostrils. All three fingers pointed up. Savage's room was third on the left, on the second floor.

"We might be interested in a room as well," yawned Kit to the Kentish landlord.

"We're full up – ships in," came the apologetic reply. Their fine clothes bespoke wealth. "Ye might want to try Richard Bull's house up the road. They sometimes let out a room."

Damn, thought Will and Kit in unison. Renting a room was the best excuse to wander up the stairs, and in such a place as this, the key to one room might well fit every other door.

However, as luck would have it, they were seated at a table near the stairs. When the landlord retreated to fetch bread and ale from the back room, Will shed his dripping cloak, slipped off the bench, and strolled up the stairs as if in hunt for a chamber pot. No one took any note.

At the top of the stairs he began counting doors. The third on the left was the last of the short hall. He felt confident as he tried the door – Savage was definitely out. The hardest part would be finding the paper, and Cutting Ball had suggested several clever hiding places that cony-catchers oft used.

Squeezing the latch, Will pushed, but the door was locked. If it hadn't been, Will would have felt frightful it was a trap. He began trying the several pass-keys that Cutting Ball had supplied him. If those failed, he could slip out the window here and see if there was a close-at-hand window into Savage's room. Just below was a low thatched roof to a stable that might hold his weight.

But there was no need. The fourth key he tried turned over and the bolt released. Quickly Will stepped into the room, shutting and locking the door behind him. "Hello?"

There was no answering sound, so he prepared to search. First, though, he slipped off his boots – still damp, they would leave obvious traces. Then he oped the shutters on the window to his right. Damn. This grey weather was too dark, the window did nothing to illume the room. Finding a candle by the door, he struck flint to it, then proceeded to search.

His excellent memory allowed him to replace drawers and clothes exactly as he had found them, which was neatly. Savage was quite ordered in his living standards, perhaps due to his as-yet-unspecified martial background. He was also a sparing liver, keeping only a few personal objects beyond his clothes. All the better, it meant there were fewer things to search.

But there was no sign of a code-sheet among any of the clothes, nor in the heel of Savage's boots, nor tacked to the underside of a table or the truckle bed. It wasn't rolled into a sleeve, nor hidden within the wax of a candle. It wasn't in the chamber pot, already filled with Savage's nightsoil. In short, it was nowhere.

What if he has it upon his person? thought Will in despair. *Can we waylay him? Kill him? Surely that would alert our foes. Our many, many, many foes.*

Indeed, it seemed the whole world was set against them. From the servants of one queen to the spies of another, from Protestants to Catholics, from the French and Spanish to Blacke Davie and Em Ball, from Savage and Derby to Lucy and Walsingham. The only voices in their favour were criminals, scoundrels, rogues, fooles, and literary dilettantes.

But that wasn't true. There was one woman, a noble lady from a foreign land, who had inexplicably taken their side. He had promised to bring word of their success, if any. So far he had none to convey.

On the verge of giving up and retreating, aware of every creak and scrape without and below, Will decided to try once more. He returned to the first place he had searched, a leather satchel hung on the back of a chair. It had papers within it, but mostly promises of money, signed by a fellow called Babington. Will had never heard of him.

He was about to set down the satchel when a stray bit of thread hooked his eye. The stitching on one side was frayed. Loosening it further, Will found that the seam was not connecting the side-panel of the satchel to the back – that task was accomplished by several grommets hidden under the flap of leather. What this stitching concealed was a second skin of leather within the first. Teasing out the strands of thread, Will plunged two fingers into the flap.

His found it at once, a single piece of coarse parchment trapped between the layers of leather. Drawing it carefully out, fearful of smudging the ink, he held it gingerly to the candle's light and with bated breath beheld four simple rows of letters:

a b c d e f g h i j k l m
P K G B C I A R Q Z D N T

n o p q r s t u v w x y z
E Y X M F W O J H L U S V

Such aggravation over something so simple! Yet there were a few other scratches further down:

† - M
‡ - E

Two Es and two Ms? Ah, of course. The special symbols were shorthand. Already his mind was working to combine this paper with the message they had been labouring over for days. *Erarerpyad…* Will's brow developed sudden and deep furrows. *What language is that..?*

From below there was a loud clatter, as if someone had dropped an entire trencher of meat and two flagons of ale. It was Cutting Ball's signal of danger if Savage returned, serving to warn both Will above and distract eyes from Kit below.

Racing back to the satchel, Will carefully slid the paper within. There was nothing to be done for the stitching but tuck it into the seam. He hoped he had not overly disturbed it. He reached out to pinch the candle's wick, then changed his mind – the smell of smoke would betray his presence. Let Savage wonder if he'd left the candle burning.

Darting back to the door he plucked up his boots, then dashed to the near window. He swung the shutters outwards and pitched his boots onto the low stable roof just below. He followed them, poising himself on the sill long enough to pull the shutters halfway closed behind him. He heard a key turning in the lock. Heart-thudding, he swung the two shutters shut and dropped onto the thatch just as the door within opened.

Will should have scarpered and he knew it. But with the clouds louring overhead, the misty spits of rain, and the half-shuttered windows, he risked a single, slow peek through the slats.

It wasn't Savage. It was ruby-snouted Derby. He paused for a moment near the candle, frowning. Then he went direct to the satchel, found the concealed cypher, and held it to the flame.

Someone had indeed passed along a warning. Will's choice for it was Walsingham, trying to protect his own men by exposing Will and Kit's involvement. But fortunately Walsingham had to ensure the carrier-pigeon could not be retraced to his coop, else he might lose his whole flock. In the time it had taken for the message to be filtered through the various channels, Gifford to Derby and Savage, Will and Kit had struck with just seconds to spare.

Time to go. Will slithered off the edge of the roof and dropped into the stables, his stockinged feet splotching in the mud.

At once he was grasped from behind, and hand clamped over his mouth. He struggled until he heard a voice in his ear, "Will! It's me."

As Kit released him, Will whispered, "Derby's up there."

"I know," said Kit, passing over Will's cloak as Will struggled one sopping foot into his boot. "Cutting Ball disturbed the peace and I scampered out."

"He's destroying the cypher."

"Fut!"

Shod, Will held up a finger and tapped his temple. "Too late."

"Ha! Excellent." Kit kissed Will on the forehead like a pleased parent. "Then let us went."

They went.

"I could murther a drink." Kit collapsed into a hard wooden chair in Cutting Ball's secret house, whereas Will went straight for the pieces of rude paper that had been scavenged for their use. He spit in a cake of ink to loosen it, swirling the quill until it took. Then he wrote out the cypher just as he had seen it, and began applying it to the message. The special symbols were simple enough to decypher. M was *Mary*. E was *Elizabeth*.

"And the best part is they imagine they got to the code in time," observed Kit. "Your second sight is our secret."

"Unless Em told them that, too," said Will, distracted.

"I very much doubt Greene told her about your faculty. T'would seem too close to praise."

"True. There – finished." Will sat back and flexed his cramped wrist as Kit leapt up to read the words over his shoulder:

ERAPERPYADEMASMARYEUCSER
SELUOSELBONYNLOWOLLA
WSLLIWLLEHDNAERIFELIZA
BETHNOPUNWODENIARLLAHSSN
EVAEHEHTDRIHTGUAERTA
EHTTASEIDELIZABETH.

"Well," said Kit laconically, "it is not perhaps as exciting as I had expected."

"Another code!" cried Will in a fury. "A code within the code! Save for the names, we are no further along than before."

But Kit was laughing. "O, clever for its very simplicity!"

"What?"

"Don't you see? 'Tis a mirror. They just wrote the message backwards before encoding it. Hardly a code at all now, but for anyone attempting to break the letters – as we tried and failed! – an added layer of difficulty." Plucking the quill from Will's hand, he began to scratch words at the bottom of the page:

ELIZABETHDIESATTHEATREAUGTHIRD
THEHEAVENSSHALLRAINEDOWNUPON
ELIZABETHANDHELLWILLSWALLOWONLY
NOBLESOULESRESCUE
MARYSAMEDAYPREPARE

He had left enough space between every letter to put dots between the words. He did so now, with periods to denote the end of a sentence. The last spot in place, he withdrew his hand from the damning words, hissing through his teeth as if burned. The smile was vanished from his face, and Will felt himself begin to shake.

The message now read:

ELIZABETH·DIES·AT·THEATRE·AUG·THIRD.
THE·HEAVENS·SHALL·RAINE
DOWN·UPON·ELIZABETH.
FIRE·AND·HELL·WILL
SWALLOW·ONLY·NOBLE·SOULES.
RESCUE·MARY·SAME·DAY.
PREPARE.

Will and Kit sat as if thunderstruck, as if the very finger of God had reached down and electrified them with his presence.

"August Third?" breathed Will. "But that is only…"

"Two days hence," said Kit. "Damn and damn."

"What should we do?"

"I wish they were more exact. They waste a great deal of coded space on hyperbole. *Fire and Hell will swallow only noble soules.* Gunpowder, do you think? Or arson?"

Will did not much care at present for probing the wordsmithing of their foes. "Surely this is enough. We have the date and the place. We know Savage and Derby and the rest. Is it not possible that this is the information that saves us? If we take it to Walsingham, surely he will—"

"—put us to death and save the Queen, reserving the role of hero for himself. Or else simply cancel whatever play she's attending, removing the possibility of a plot. As we have learned, there is no knowing which way his slimy and agile mind will hop. Only that whichever way it is, it will aid us naught."

"But surely we are not the priority here! The Queen's life is at stake."

"Aye, and the Queen's men mean to have us both dead. There is a delicious irony in rescuing Her Majesty under the noses of the very souls who are too busy protecting her from us to do their proper jobs."

"Kit – Christopher – we cannot play at this."

Kit began to hop upon his bottom and clap. "On the contrary, that is precisely what we must do! The play's the thing, my dear! First, we must find what play she's attending, and where. Most often the players go to her, but once in a great while she attends the theatre in secret."

"Not much of a secret, if they know this far in advance," observed Will, gesturing at the code.

"Too true. Which means someone in her train is passing information to the Catholics."

"Or to France, or to Spain. There are too many pieces on the board to choose among them."

"An incidental truth. Certainly Sir Francis will smoke them out when this is all done. But it only aids my argument. We cannot give them warning, because the only way to deal with the traitors and enemies to the crown is to flush them out. Why are they circumventing Walsingham's line of rats – his beer barrel ploy – to make plans to assassinate the Queen? The answer must be, because they know they are compromised."

"Well, at least Gifford. This all hinges on him. He's the one circumventing the rat line, as you call it."

"Yes, my darling Godfrey is playing a long game, both sides against the middle. But who else might be involved, hm? Until we know, William, we must act on our own! You enjoyed Kyd's play-within-the-play device? Well, this will be the greatest *drama inter drama* ever devised! A trap to catch our savage bear and ruby-snouted beagle! We shall play the heroes!"

Kit's tone was triumphant, sure as he was that his logic was unassailable. But Will knew that his friend had constructed his flawed argument to fit his desired outcome.

Will's goal now was to preserve the Queen. Kit's was to play the hero. The two were not incompatible, but nevertheless remained quite distinct.

Scene Two

The next two days were spent in a frenzy of activity on the part of Will and Kit – most of which found them engaged in memorizing a play.

"It's as though I'm back at Corpus Christi!" exclaimed Kit happily, his paper roll in hand. "Except, of course, a failure in the oral examinations here means a stretched neck. Hm. If that were the case at University, men would likely learn more."

Will was too nervous to provide witty comments as he worked over his own lines. His was a smallish roll, barely the length of his forearm. "This is a ridiculous plan," he exclaimed for the hundredth time.

"What better? They will certainly be watching the crowd for trouble-makers, but whose eyes will be on the stage?"

"Everyone's!" was Will's exasperated reply.

"Precisely! And they will see two magnificent-looking young men in false beards and Portuguese attire, speaking poor lines so splendidly that they will never doubt we are the finest actors of the age! No thought to Kit Marlowe or Will Shakespeare! We shall be great tragedians, and the Queen herself will weep my death!"

It hadn't taken much to discover that the only public play performing on the Sunday, a day usually forbidden to such shows, was at the Newington Butts – none other than the infuriatingly popular *Spanish Tragedie*, by the upstart Kyd. So popular was it that it had gained a special exemption to perform on the holy day of rest. At one o'clock, weather permitting, the entire company would play one final time before the show closed and the cast moved on to their next drama.

Of course, no one was aware that the Queen was to be present. But it explained the exemption, and how this show had been scheduled so very far in advance. Without doubt the Queen would be there. And be attacked.

Kit's ludicrously dramatic plan was to pose as players, the better to have the run of the theatre without question, and so disrupt whatever plan Savage and Derby had in head to attack the Queen.

"Dags, for certain. 'Raine fire?' They mean to use pistols to fire up from the crowd and bring Her Majesty low. But from the stage we can see the whole crowd, pick out where the villains stand, and so disrupt them when they try."

"And how, pray, do we achieve this end? We cannot very well walk up to the Earl of Oxford's Men and demand parts, can we?"

"Absolutely not. In this, we require Wittier help."

And so they had all unexpectedly called at the questionable lodging of Greene and his mistress, Em Ball. The house was shabby on the outside, and disordered on the inside. Like Cutting Ball's secret rooms, it had nicer furnishings than one might have expected, but they were ill-used and ill-cared for.

It was Em who opened the door to their first-floor rooms. Seeing who it was, she was quick to close it again, but Kit's foot prevented that.

"Who is it, Em?" rumbled Greene, sounding only half-sotted as he stumbled forward. Seeing Will and Kit in the door he grew statue-still.

"Well well," said Will. "Good evening, Master Greene, Mistress Emily. Spent your thirty pieces of silver yet?"

Em spat at him.

"Venomous," observed Will, wiping at his doublet. "Just like the snake in Eden."

"And treacherous, just like Eve," said Kit.

"Alas," added Will, "Eve ate of the fruit of knowledge, whereas the fruit Em tastes of has fallen far from the tree." When she looked confused, he nodded to the crotch of Greene's hose. "That is some low-hanging fruit."

"It's not that my penis is small," rumbled Greene. "It's that my testicles are so wretchedly large."

Em balled up in a fury and shook her fist. "I'll 'ave ye, William Falsestaff! I'll roast yer manly bits 'n feed'em t'me cat!"

Will threw up his hands. "Oh no, please! Any pussy but yours!"

"Why ye..!" She went to strike him, but Greene forestalled her. It was then that Will noticed the bruises on her arms and face, hidden until now by shadows. Her lip had been split. Her left eye was puffed and mottled.

Yet Greene was all tenderness with her. "Now now, my lovey. Let me see what it is they desire. You run along to the next room."

"I'd rather she stayed," said Will. "So she cannot pass word of our whereabouts again."

"Oh, but if'n she did," said Kit with a nasty smile, "she'd be hanging her man as well. She knows it."

"That she does," agreed Greene. "Off with you, minx. Leave the men to talk."

Em Ball departed the room with a scowl that reached her very soul. She took up residence within a back room, there to listen through the thin wall, no doubt.

The moment the door had closed upon her, Greene said, "Lads, t'wasn't I who did you dirty. You cannot imagine how horrified I was to hear you'd been cornered, and how relieved when you escaped. Em told me it had been she, and as you see, her brother has already chastised her."

Kit seemed pleased, but Will swallowed and shook his head. Words and insults were one thing. But beating a woman was beyond his understanding. The rule of thumb was customary, to be sure – a man could beat his wife with a switch only as thick as his thumb, no wider – but it seemed utterly wrong. Perhaps there was a strain of Arthurian chivalry in his veins, or perhaps just enough humanity to believe striking a woman was unmanly. Also, what if a man owned an exceptionally large thumb?

Kit accepted Greene's apology, and Will nodded. They then went into the cause of their visit. Without giving details as to why (as Em was certainly behind the door with open ears), Kit said, "We require parts in The Spanish Tragedie the day after next. Small parts, by all means. But we must be on the stage."

"Very well. But why come to me?"

"Well, we cannot very well walk into the Butts and demand parts. We need to pretend to be players fresh from another house – somewhere in Cambridge would do – and given entrance to the theatrical scene by the most pre-eminent man of letters, Monsieur Greene."

"But the parts are set! How can I—"

Kit's eyes twinkled, and even Will smiled. "It is a part that only you can play. You must find two members of Oxford's company and drink them senseless. Put that girth of yours to good use and dare them to match you, cup for cup. Then, while their senses lie as in a death, you must make a great show of repentance and offer us up as their replacements!"

"But..." croaked Greene.

Kit cut across him. "Moreover, as we are both known to Kyd, you must keep him well away from us. Which means you must attend the play, and keep him beside you."

"But – but that means abasing myself to that turnip!" roared Greene in genuine horror.

"It does," agreed Kit. "All this depends on how badly pricked your conscience is at present. Your dame did us a dirty deed. You can mend it."

"And all it costs is your pride," added Will unhelpfully.

Greene pleaded with Kit. "You know what he'll demand! That I endorse his work! That I give him public praise!"

"If he values such a thing," supplied Will, but shrugged when Kit waved him off. Insults would not aid their cause.

"You must weigh your guilt over Em's betrayal against your distaste for Kyd, and see which side the scales come down upon."

From Greene's face, there was clearly no question. "Very well. But not alone! I'll drag Lyly and Watson with me! Let them share in our collegial downfall. Besides, Lyly knows that scoundrel the Earl of Oxford – he can be the one to suggest two strapping lads as replacement players. De Vere will heed him. Now, one more question – who pays for my sack? If I must endure Kyd, I must be drunk."

"Why not make Sir Francis Walsingham pay?" asked Will lightly, opening the door to leave.

Outside Kit rebuked him. "You ought not harp on so. T'wasn't his fault."

"Had it not been for your teachings and timely intervention, I would be playing a harp above the clouds, not harping on his fat guts here below."

"Then, for the sake of my teachings, let him be."

"For your sake, I will purchase his sack. Will that serve?"

Their next call, of all places, was to the Elephant, which they braved by the back door. Their visit within took several minutes, and was peppered with shouts and oaths and broken bottles, but finally acquiesce.

"We do seem to have a way with the women," observed Will wryly as they started the return trip to Cutting Ball's home.

"Yes," said Kit. "They seem all to want us dead. It is the way of the fairer sex. Bring me the head of John the Baptist!"

"We do this in the service of a woman."

"To undo another. Come, bid night descend and let us to our truckle beds."

They awoke the next day to find Em Ball waiting for them. Without a word of greeting, and under the harsh glare of her brother, she handed them both two rolls of paper. "These be fer ye. Me man's down wit' the 'air o'the dog. But 'e's played 'is part. Kept 'is word."

"I never doubted him," said Kit with a twinkling smile.

"Thank you, Mistress Ball," said Will as he took the paper from her, careful to keep all derision from his voice. He had moved from anger to pity. She scowled, but it was instinctive, and she frowned harder trying to discern if he was mocking her.

"Just make sure your man is recovered for his part on the morrow," advised Kit.

Em nodded jerkily at him, cast one more suspicious glance at Will, then departed.

"You were needlessly polite, William," said Kit.

Will made sure that Cutting Ball had exited before he said, "I don't like that she was beaten."

"Whyever not? Certainly tamed her."

"She was beaten yesterday and remained untamed. It was reason from us and love of her man that has her aiding us."

Kit shrugged, oping his roll in place of replying. Will did the same.

He had never before considered the extensive effort at having a play written out new for actors. Before now, always the plays he read were printed in books, or else in quarto sheets. How tedious, to copy out by hand the parts for fourteen actors and their prompter! To abate this wrist-wrenching abuse, some industrious producer had come upon an ingenious – and terrifying – method to ease that burden.

Instead of being handed a whole copy of the play, each actor received a rolled-up sheet bearing their lines. Once upon a time these had included no cue at all, simply the words the actor was to speak. A prompter would stand in the center of the stage with a full copy, pointing his baton at each actor in turn, letting them know when they were to begin their next part.

That method had eventually met with disfavour, it being a hindrance to the illusion of wit and daring that all actors prize. So a small addition was made to the rolls, with the last line directly preceding theirs being put in place. Each man had to memorize his part, then listen intently for his cue, the final line of another actor's speech that would launch the next. No actor ever read the play as a whole, and likely would never know the entire story until it was played upon the stage before a crowd on opening day. The key, it seemed, was to listen.

Kit informed Will that whenever a new play was to be performed, the company manager would descend to whichever tavern the actors called their own and distribute the parts by handing out rolls of parchment. The players would have a couple days to con their lines, be they many or few, the sheets containing their words attached end to end with glue. Actors often compared the size of their rolls – the thicker the roll, the larger the part. "One particular game is to unfurl your roll and see whose reaches to the farthest wall. Some reach there and back again!" He looked with dismay at his own roll, which was hardly three sheets long. "Villuppo. Which was he?"

"The man who falsely accuses Alexandro in the opening scene," said Will at once.

"Ah yes! I recall him. And you are..?"

Will read the name at the corner of the roll. "Alexandro."

"Ha! How very apropos. And I am to die, am I not? Excellent! Let us con these, then speak them aloud to each other so we will be ready on the morrow."

"Mustn't we rehearse with the rest?" demanded Will.

"Plays don't rehearse!" scoffed Kit. "The prompter will direct you to enter here, exit there, dance a little at this bit, and we're off!" The prompter was the man in charge, and the only whole copy of the play was in the prompter's book, where he could direct the actors from the wings of the stage.

To Kit's monumental annoyance, Will was able to set aside his roll and recite his words in just a few minutes. However Kit had a better flair for the accent, and was generally satisfied with his performance by the time supper arrived. Whereas Will kept pacing the well-appointed room until the sun was setting, practicing each line, each word, with the attention he had given tumbling and mimicry in his youth.

"Leave off, Will! You'll be fine. Better to be rested with a clear head on the morrow! We are to arrive at the theatre two hours before the performance, which is at one of the clock."

Will shook his head. "No. No, you rest. I'll step outside and take the air."

"Careful, my love," said Kit sententiously. "It would be a sorry state to be picked up by your friend Sir Thomas tonight when tomorrow holds promise of liberty, long life, and liberality."

"Careful I shall be," agreed Will.

"And see that you do not recite your lines in the street," advised Kit as Will threw on a light summer cloak. "You may be taken for a lunatic and placed in Bedlam."

Will laughed, but in a distracted way. "Well advised. Thank you. Back soon." He closed the door lightly behind him.

Several hours later Kit was awakened by Will's return. "What the devil hour do you call this? I was worried stiff!"

"You were worrying so hard your snores shook the walls," replied Will.

"I? Snore? Hardly." Will seemed much more at ease, which pleased Kit, who fell back into his straw-filled bed and curled his head upon his arm. "Tomorrow is the day – or is it today already?"

"Tomorrow, I think," said Will. "'Tis not yet so very late."

"Tomorrow," sighed Kit drowsily as he relaxed back into sleep's embrace. "Tomorrow, and tomorrow, and tomorrow…"

"Aye," agreed Will, settling into his own bed. "Tomorrow will salvage all our yesterdays."

Or, he did not add, cut off tomorrows altogether.

Scene Three

Newington Butts, London
3 August, 1586

Will and Kit reported promptly at the appointed hour of that most fate-filled day, already attired for the stage, with clean-shaven faces ready for their false beards. Kit asked for the Prompter, and was pointed towards a man leaning against a post of the stage roof, arms folded and eyes shut.

"Fut fut fut," said Kit under his breath as they approached the stage.

"What?"

"That's Henry Evans," said Kit. "Ah well, nothing for it…! Excuse me! They told us to report to you."

The man's eyes cracked open. "Who the devil be you?"

"Christopher Sly," replied Kit, relishing his latest false name.

"Will Lancet," replied Will with less audacity. His nerves were out in the open, his knees turned to water.

"Oh, the replacement players. A day for it, I guess. Conned the text, I hope?" Both Will and Kit said "Aye" and Evans nodded, wiping his lips and nose with his sleeve. "Very well. You enter at the third trumpet. Augie! Augie! *Augustine!*"

A grave man appeared from behind the central door's curtain, a man in his decline – he must have seen nearly thirty summers. "What ho, Hank?"

"These are your Alexandro and Villuppo for today. Take charge of them, will you? I have enough to trouble me with new hands."

The actor rolled his eyes, as if he had been better employed picking his nose than shepherding two new players. Still he introduced himself. "Augustine Phillips. I'm the Viceroy, so you enter with me, top of scene two. We enter from the lower stage right door – no no, *stage right!*" he corrected as Will started heading to his own right. Exasperated beyond measure, Augustine muttered about "fooles think because they can talk they can act…" while leading them to their place. "Wait here, I'll be back in a mo and then we'll run your lines." Shaking his head, the veteran player stalked away.

"That was a narrow escape," confided Kit. "Hank Evans used to run the Blackfriars – great friends with Lyly. He must be in hard circumstance to be acting as Prompter here. He could easily have recognized me. Actually, I'm rather disappointed he didn't…"

"This isn't going to work," said Will.

"Why did you not say so before?"

"I did say so before," hissed Will.

"Too late!" shrugged Kit as Augustine returned.

"Very well, let's run our part. Which of you is Alexandro?"

"I," said Will, swallowing and clearing his throat, then coughing softly. The man rolled his eyes once more, then launched into the first line of their scene, himself in the part of the Viceroy of Portugal – or, as they spoke it, Portingale. *"Is our embassadour dispatcht for Spaine?"*

"Two daies, my liege, are past since his depart," replied Will.

"And tribute paiment gone along with him?"

"Aye, my good lord."

"Then rest we heere a-while in our unrest; And feede our sorrowes with inward sighes, blather blather blather. You both may sit, Alexandro close to me, but Villuppo sit at some distance. I prattle on about my lost son before saying, *O, wherefore went I not to warre my-selfe? The cause was mine; I might have died for both. My yeeres were mellow, but his young and greene. My death were naturall, but his was forced."*

"*No doubt, my liege, but still the prince survives,*" said Will with more voice.

"*Survives!*" exclaimed Augustine, feigning surprise. "*Aye, where?*"

"*In Spaine, a prisoner by mischance of warre…*"

As they progressed, Augustine visibly relaxed, and when Kit spoke his part he began to smile. The scene itself was about betrayal – Kit's character blamed Will for the capture of the missing prince, when it was Kit himself who betrayed the lad. Will had already remarked several times how very like Kit to find himself playing a trickster and liar.

The scene finished, Augustine nodded. "Creditable. Very well, that's the end of us until Act Three, though you two will have to play ladies in the background – there are wigs and dresses for you. Just follow the others when they tell you and stay close to the stage wall. React to what you hear with your faces only – no gasps, no thrown up hands, and when you're motioned to go, go at once." He rubbed at his head. "Don't know why I'm the one has to tell you all his – bloody Hank and his morning naps. No wonder the Blackfriars sank. But anyway, I'll fetch you for your scene in Act Three."

They ran through this scene as well, as men run races or horses their courses. In that scene, the truth came out, and Kit was carried off to execution.

Finished, Augustine said, "Well spoke, sirs. Admirable, even. Now, if I may offer a word or three of well-intended advice – too many men ascending the stage feel the need to gesticulate, slash the air with their hands, make faces and signs, use their thumbs or slap their thighs. Alas, this does not only apply to neophytes, but to veterans of the boards as well. Speak loudly and clearly, and keep your hands still, so that when you do make use of them, it is to greater effect. And always remember, though your character addresses me, you must address the crowd. Do not feel the need to speak to me – *I* know what you are to say, *they* do not. Look at me only when it can elicit emotion from them – as with gestures, choose your moment, and they have more weight." He paused to consider, then smiled. "That is all, I think. If you lose your line, press on, and I'll assist as best I can. The rest, as they say, is a mystery." Laughing, he took them to don their false beards in the Tiring House.

It is a fact that when a man dreads a thing, time seems to speed up, drawing the dreaded thing ever nearer. So did the sands of the hourglass slip as though greased, and Phoebus' chariot race at breakneck speed across the sky, bringing the crowds into the theatre and the moment of decision relentlessly closer. Will knew not which he was the more nervous for – thwarting the plot on the Queen's life, or speaking his first professional lines upon the stage.

He was roused by a playful slap from Kit. "Come, William! The trumpets blare, and like Vespasian and Titus who ruined the Jews, we shall march in Triumph – not only over the arts, but over our woes, our foes, and our sorrows!"

The trumpeters were indeed pursing their lips and expanding their lungs, and in seconds the air was rent by the industrial bellow of cheap music. The play was off – and so too the plan to rescue one Queen and doom another.

The first scene with Revenge and the dead Don Andrea proceeded apace. With sweating palms, sealed throat, and watering eyes, Will listened to the characters of Lorenzo and Horatio each claim the honour of capturing the Portuguese leader, Balthazar. The King then spoke the words granting them equal credit and reward, though Balthazar himself made it clear it was Horatio alone who defeated him. Then together they exited.

"Now, while they're exiting," said Augustine, pushing Will forward with his shoulder as he entered himself.

Will had no chance to take in the crowd, for Augustine was already speaking his lines from the instant he stepped onstage, asking if the ambassador had been dispatched for Spain in thundering, commanding tones that drew everyone's attention from the players leaving to the players emerging. Five hundred pairs of eye shifted and fixed upon Augustine, Will, and Kit in their false beards and fine robes.

Will answered the query without thinking, and the one after that, then heaved a mental sigh of relief as Augustine's Viceroy launched into his lengthy speech of lamentable sorrow, bemoaning the loss of his only son. Remembering to sit when he was bid, Will settled himself on the stage floor. For the first portion of the speech, he kept his eyes focused on Augustine. But when the veteran player started to bemoan the *'folly of despightful chance,'* our friend decided to risk casting his gaze out over the sea of men just inches away from him. He could not help himself – if he could but espy the villain Savage among the crowd, or even Derby, Rookwood, and Brockhurst, he would know where their adversaries stood.

There was no sign of any such men. *Damn.*

Yet there were faces he knew. Among the groundlings stood Tarlton with his familiar, Bob Armin. Further away were Blacke Davie and Huffing Kate. Right close to the stage's lip were Cutting Ball and Scarlet Dick. Ball gave Will a nod and a wink, and Will had to resist a returning smile.

Next he risked a glance up into the top box, where the Queen herself had station, cloaked from view behind her courtiers, all in disguising robes. Will had already surmised that none of the players knew they were being seen by royal eyes, or that their words might be audited by Tudor ears. If her being here were public, she would doubtless be in the Lord's Box, above the stage. But that remained empty. No, arranged well in advance, this secret must have been between the theatre-owner and Her Majesty's staff. Though it must have been known to at least one more…

Will could not make out the features of the painted face in the far box, but he prayed for her safety. Recollecting that this great woman's survival rested largely upon his shoulders, he resumed gazing into the crowd.

Imagine the shock, the absolute, heart-stopping shock Will felt when his eyes drifted rightwards and, in a box not far from the Queen's, he spied Sir Thomas Lucy.

Now multiply that shock by an infinite factor. That's how Will felt when he recognized the man seated beside Lucy.

Fatter than Greene, with skin the colour of old parchment, broken veins in his nose and cheeks, hair in full retreat from the advancing forehead, yet with eyes all too familiar – Will had seen the very same orbs when looking in the glass backstage.

Sir Thomas had brought Will's father all the way from Stratford to hear the play!

The implications were monstrous, and invaded Will's thoughts in a jumbled tumbled torrent. *They knew I'd be here! Lucy brought him as a weapon against me! We are betrayed – again! There is no escape! How on earth—?*

Worse than his fear, he was flooded with anger at his sire, the giver of his life who was also its bane. Of course, to advance himself, John Shakespeare would betray even his own son.

But Lucy was actually watching the play, eyes upon the lamenting Augustine. Whereas the gaze of Will's sire was immovably fixed upon Will's face. *What are they doing here? Who told them..?*

Shaken by this unexpected appearance, Will missed his cue. Augustine repeated the final line of his speech, resorting to hair-tearing and near-shouts to gain Will's attention. "My death were naturall! But his was forced!"

Startled, Will spoke the necessary words, his eyes still upon his father, using the script to convey his own message. "No doubt, my lord, but still the prince your son survives."

"Survives!" cried Augustine. "Aye, where?"

Will's line was meant to be, 'In Spaine, a prisoner by mischance of warre.' But that did not serve Will's purpose. All thought of duty to the Queen or even risk of his life vanished in the red haze of anger at this man.

Instead of speaking his rehearsed part, Will stood. Gazing directly at the portly man in the side box, Will spoke, inventing both rhyme and meter from his own pure brain:

"He resides among his Father's fierce foes,
His life indebted to serve his Sire's fault,
Victim of his Blood, the source of all Woes
Man endures under the heavenly Vault."

There was a moment of understanding shared only by father and son, an intimate scene played before five hundred men. Will let the moment linger a breath longer, then, feeling Augustine's eyes upon him, added, "In brief, he's in Spaine, victim of mischance of warre."

Augustine looked fury at Will, which thankfully served the theatrical moment. "Then they have slaine him for his father's fault."

"That were a breach to common lawe of men," answered Will.

"They recke no lawes that meditate revenge," declaimed Augustine, relieved that Will was again adhering mostly to his roll. The change from "lawe of armes" to "law of men" was negligible, but had served Will's purpose.

"His ransomes worth will stay from foule revenge." Message conveyed, Will turned from his father and cast himself again into his part.

"No; if he lived, the newes would soone be heere."

Kit stepped forward to speak for the first time. "My soveraign, pardon the author of ill newes, and I'll bewray the fortune of thy sonne."

"Speake on," said Augustine, portraying the part of a concerned father. "I'll guerdon thee, what-ere it be. Mine eare is ready to receive ill newes, My hart growne hard gainst mischiefes battery; Stand up, I say, and tell thy tale at large."

"Then heare that truth which these mine eies have seene," answered Kit laconically, playing the earnest liar and condemning his rival to death. When it came his turn, Will was still so angry he had no trouble mounting the passion to shout, "O wicked forgerie! O traiterous miscreant!" His ecphonetic Os were marvelous ejaculations of fury and outrage.

Kit continued his character's lies, and Augustine was ready to command Will's death. "Thy ambitious thought shall break thy neck. Aye, this was it that made thee spill his bloud! But I'll now weare it till thy blood be spilt."

"Vouchsafe, dread soveraigne, to heare me speak!" shouted Will as guards closed upon him.

"Away with him! His sight is second hell!" roared Augustine. "Keepe him till we determine his death. If Balthazar be dead, he shall not live."

Hands clamped on Will's biceps. As he was hauled off, he glanced again into the stands above the groundlings. Now Lucy was looking at him with a frown of puzzlement on his brow. Clearly he had not yet recognized the character of Alexandro as William Shakespeare, but something was itching at his brainpan. Will wondered if this scene were to be replayed later in the day, with Walsingham's men in the part of the guards, and Augustine's roll of lines in Lucy's grip.

Off-stage, he had time to consider. How on earth had Lucy and his father come here?

Point - Lucy was in town, hunting Will, because of Walsingham.

Point - He must have summoned Will's father from Stratford. Why? As a weapon.

Point - They were here at the Queen's invitation, as it seemed by their proximity.

Point - If Sir Thomas knew Will was here, he'd have started shouting the moment Will stepped on stage.

Could it be mere chance? Had Lucy accepted the Queen's invitation, yet refused to leave old Shakespeare by himself, lest he go warn his importunate offspring? Could it be that simple? Will doubted he could be so lucky.

Augustine himself stepped behind the curtain moments later. Out of sight of the crowd, he gave Will a withering look, clicking his tongue in disgust. Kit waited until Augustine had stalked off to make his next costume change, muttering about "amateurs improving what needs no fix," then said, "What was that? Some extemporizing for the sheer joy of it?"

Will shook his head. "Sir Thomas is in the right-hand box – and he has my father with him."

The implications of this spilled upon Kit, thankfully without Will's surge of rage. "What can this mean? Lucy here I could fathom, paying court to the throne. But your father? They must know we were to be here! How? Greene? Em?"

Will shook his head. "I know not, but it matters not a jot. Our task is the same. Only we must achieve it before we are apprehended. I did not see Savage or the others. Did you?"

"No," agreed Kit ruefully. "And Savage especially should stand out among them. Even hunched and his head covered, his bulk marks him."

"And Derby's rosy snout shines like a beacon. Where can they be?"

"Perhaps they mean to come late?"

"With royal guards to get past? Even disguised, they cannot have. Besides, it is clearly oversold. No," said Will with certainty, "I feel they are here already, mocking us."

They were interrupted by trumpets as the King of Spain re-entered in the midst of the scene. At once beckoning hands urged Will and Kit into the Tiring House, where they donned dresses and voluminous wigs. They spent the next two scenes standing in silence behind the stage, waiting to enter with Bel-Imperia, the heroine of the play embodied by a stick of a boy with a lovely falsetto. All around them was movement, with musicians preparing their instruments and actors entering and exiting at break-neck pace. The only men idle were the stage-hands, large sailors who occasionally had to shift a table or a chair. Their real task would be manning the cannons at the end of the play.

It was the sight of the cannons that made Will pause. "Kit," he whispered. "The cannons."

"I was thinking the same," murmured Kit in return. "Turn them and fill them with shot, and poof, no Queen. Fire and Hell indeed." He called out to a stagehand. "Oi. Aren't those dangerous?"

The sailor scoffed at this. "Hardly! We have no shot, just powder. What harm is there in simple powder?"

The lad playing Bel-Imperia cocked his head. "And here I thought I was the ball-less one today."

"Ha. Ha. Ha," answered the sailor, raising a threatening fist to back-hand the boy. He returned to Kit. "Besides, we're not to fire today. Manager's orders. We've got some noble in the crowd afraid of the noise, and they paid extra so we'd not bang these off. Shame, but makes for a simple day. Which is good, with so many of my mates off."

"Oh?" asked Kit, more in passing than in genuine curiosity.

"Aye," said the seafarer. "Big French ship hired a host of stout British hands. Reckon the crew got the scurvy or sommat. Rare as 'tis, me mates were keen to find the job. I heard about it too late, or I'd've gone meself! Instead I'm stuck here, not even firing the cannons."

"So who are the other hands?" asked Will – the French reference had him on his guard. "And where are they?"

The sailor shrugged. "About. Most have already left – there's naught to do, when all's in place. One or two are still here. But as for who they are, I've no idea. Never seen them before."

"Not sailors, then?" asked Kit.

"Couldn't tie a knot between them."

It proved irresistible. "They could not knot?"

Will aimed a significant look at his companion, but Kit was leaving puns behind to latch on to another thread and follow it as Theseus did in the Labyrinth. "You say you have no shot. But ample powder, I imagine. It's not kept here, is it? I'd hardly want to be blown to pieces on my first day!" he added with a laugh.

The sailor laughed along. "Well, best you re-tire from the Tiring House, for all our powder is stored there—" he pointed up to the room above the Tiring House "—in the Hut. But fear not. There's barely half a barrel, not enough to blow you, me and these four walls down." The sailor chuckled at the thought.

Will said, "One of these non-knotters. Perchance did he have a bump on his nose as large as a young cockerel stone?"

"Aye!" cried the sailor. "And as red as my——" (We shall, gentle reader, omit that word, acknowledging that he was, after all, a sailor.)

Will and Kit both exchanged a glance, their minds in complete agreement. But before they could act, the lad in the fancy dress said, "Oi! We're on!"

And they dutifully followed him on-stage, remaining near the rear wall where ladies-in-waiting would stand. Under his wig, Will stole another look into the seats ringing the theatre, but neither his father nor Lucy were looking at him. Nor was there any sign of Savage.

Not that Will now expected there to be. He knew exactly where Savage and the rest were. It was amazing that he had not yet laid eyes on them, as close as they had to be. But likely they had done their work early and retired to out-of-the-way stations in the rabbit-warren of the backstage.

They were on-stage only moments before being shooed away by Bel-Imperia, who was about to have a love-tryst with Horatio. The moment they were out of sight of the groundlings, Kit said, "You know what I think?"

"I know what you think."

"I think they mean to use the cannons."

"I think so as well," agreed Will. "They arranged the ploy with the French ship for the stage-hands to find better employment and, like us, have taken the place of the missing men. They will surely use the cannons to fire into the crowd at the finish of the show."

"Then our answer is simple," replied Kit jauntily. "We shall spike the cannons!"

"We must also be sure they cannot use the powder," warned Will. "Even half a barrel must be enough, if rightly placed."

Kit nodded. "Wisely, wisely. We shall spike the cannons and douse the powder. Wet, it shall not ignite. Come!"

Together they hurried back to the Tiring House. The plan, such as it was, turned out marvelously well. Instead of entering the building to disrobe, they threw their dresses and wigs over the two cannons. As they resumed their false beards and floppy feathered hats, they surreptitiously used woodchips and mulch from the ground at their feet to gum the firing holes, where the linstocks would meet a fuse.

"By Saint Sebastian the pincushion," swore Kit furiously. "I need to carry a scroll in the next scene." He turned to the stagehand from before. "Do you imagine they'll have one in the Hut?"

"Oh aye," said the sailor carelessly, leaning against the wall of the Tiring House watching the younger men dress. "Go on and find one."

As he went up the exterior stairs leading to the Hut, Kit called back, "Will, be a friend and fetch me a drink. I'm positively parched!"

As Will grabbed up a skin of water, he watched Kit disappear into the upstairs door, hand upon his sword. They had both worn real ones, deliberately failing to exchange them for bated ones upon their arrival. Will raced after his friend, cursing himself for not thinking ahead – Savage and the others might well indeed be hidden in the Hut, waiting their moment to bring down the powder and murder the Queen.

But when he arrived at the top of the stairs and entered the dim storage room, only Kit was in sight. "No one?"

"No one at all," sighed Kit in relief, and Will realized with real warmth that his compatriot had thrust himself into danger in order to spare his friend. He smiled as he joined Kit in a hunt for the barrel. What a bundle of contradictions was Kit. But wasn't that true of all men? Of mankind itself? Great men determined to hold power sowed the seeds of their own destruction. Poor men showed more nobility in their crimes than great men did in their statecraft. What was the nature of Man, holding so much potential and so rarely achieving it? Striving to overcome their baser aspects, and yet at one and the same moment reveling in them. Mightn't there be some cause, some internal impediment that, once overcome...

"William, this must be it, no?" Kit had the lid off a small barrel, barely the height of his knee.

"Hmm," said Will uncertainly. "I thought it would be bigger."

"Said the whore to the bishop." Reaching down, Kit drew up a handful of shiny black grains. He let all but a pinch fall back through his fingers, then lifted his finger to his lips. "Saltpeter, certes. This is it."

Responding to Kit's beckoning hand, Will poured the contents of the skin into the barrel, dousing the meager contents. Kit swilled his hand about, making certain the whole mixture was unusable. Rising, he gave Will a glowing smile. "There! That's put paid to our Savage friend."

"I surely hope so," said Will, feeling equally giddy. Was it as simple as this?

Another blare of trumpets announced another entrance of the King of Spain. Will was thankful he had seen the show before, because their rolls contained no clue as to the order of the scenes. If the King was on, then there was but one more dramatic piece before he and Kit had to return to the stage. They raced down and Kit took a moment to clean his hands before they resumed their places backstage.

Kit was exultant, and yet – and yet, how could that have been the plan? If they had meant to use the gunpowder in the cannons, would not Savage or Derby have secured it before now? And where were they? Will could not help but fret.

The events upon the stage were no help. The King had departed, and now the treacherous villain of the play, Balthazar, was hanging and stabbing the young lover Horatio. His father and mother rushed upon the planks too late, finding their son dead and vowing revenge.

Augustine appeared beside them. He looked at Will. "No more flights of fancy, eh? Put these manacles on, and imagine them about your tongue as well." Will obediently donned the weighty metal shackles, allowing himself to be locked into them even as the grieving parents dragged their dead son off the stage. *Perhaps this is what Sir Thomas is waiting for. Saves him the trouble of binding me himself.* He heard the ghost address Revenge, demanding justice. Revenge's reply was that all things ripen in their time, and only require patience.

Instantly Augustine entered, with Kit and several actors as guards. Will remained behind, for his entrance came late in the scene wherein Kit's villainy was revealed and Will's life was spared. Will felt again the nerves, and quickly rehearsed his lines in his head. Shifting his weight back and forth between the halberd-carrying actors meant to be his guards, he let his eyes wander over the curtains and stairs of the backstage area. Caught by a slight movement, his eyes traveled up.

John Savage was ascending the steps towards the second level of the theatre. But instead of stopping, he climbed up a ladder and into a small hatch, through which his bulk could barely fit.

He was carrying a small covered lamp, full of fire.

Scene Four

Will was as a statue, a dumbfounded, horrified statue, his mouth hanging open like one who has been captured by the sculptor in that moment when the ruin of the gods is made clear.

Frozen in panicked wonder of what to do, he was utterly unprepared when two hands clamped on his arms, dragging him forward through the central curtain and out upon the stage. So bewildered was he that he had forgotten entirely the play. It was fortunate that he did not have the first line upon entering. One of the players in the guise of a Portuguese noble said, "In such extremes will naught but patience serve."

What do I do? What do I do? Savage could be meaning to murder the Queen this moment. Do I shout out? Do I warn them, and cause a panic?

Nay, thought Will at once. *That would warn Savage. We've stymied him, but he doesn't know it yet. And if we are wrong, if there's another method of killing the Queen, he might well be moved to use it if he's exposed. No, I must press quickly on with the scene, and follow him the instant I'm off the stage.*

All these thoughts flitted so swiftly through his head that barely had the noble ceased his speech when Will gave his answer. "But in extremes what patience shall I use? Nor discontents it me to leave the world, with whome there nothing can prevaile but wrong."

But I do not wish to leave the world, thought Will furiously. *I have something in me, inexpressible thought that, contradictably, longs to be expressed. I do not mean to die!*

The noble replied, "Yet hope the best."

Will picked up again at once, sharing the same line of verse with the noble. "Tis Heaven my hope. As for the earth, it is too much infect to yield me hope of any of her mould." He tried to catch Kit's eye, but the preening peacock had his back to him, playing to the crowd. Will's gaze then flickered to the box containing his father. The fat man seemed to be asleep. *Typical,* thought Will, blood thundering in his ears. *We are all about to die and he slips into a nap.*

In the part of Portugal's Viceroy, Augustine said, "Why linger ye? bring forth that daring feend, and let him die for his accursed deed."

Will rattled off the reply written by the playwright Kyd. It was apropos to the moment:

> *Not that I feare the extremity of death—*
> *For nobles cannot stoop to servile feare—*
> *Do I, O king, thus discontented live;*
> *But this, O this, torments my labouring soule,*
> *That thus I die suspected of a sinne*
> *Whereof, as Heavens have knowne my secret thoughts,*
> *So am I free from this suggestion!*

Heavens, thought Will, just as the word exited the fence of his teeth. *Heavens?*

But Augustine's Viceroy interrupted Will's nascent thought, saying, "No more, I say; to the tortures! When? Binde him, and burne his body in those flames, that shall prefigure those unquenched fires of Phlegiton prepared for his soule."

Will was dutifully bound to the stake for burning, the stake in this case being the stage-right pillar of wood. While most of the structure was open to the air, providing natural light, the area just over the playing space was covered by a roof. A roof with painted stars upon it.

Painted stars....

But it was time for Will to speak again, this time accusing Kit of treachery. He spoke rapidly, trying to propel the scene along. "My guiltless death will be aveng'd on thee! On thee, Villuppo, that hath malisde thus, or for thy meed hast falsely me accus'd!"

Swaggering close, Kit said, "Nay, Alexandro, if thou menace me, I'll lend a hand to send thee to the lake where those thy words shall perish with thy workes, injurious traitour, monstrous homicide!"

Damn your play-acting hide, Christopher Marlowe, cried Will's mind. *Stop lingering over your words! We haven't the time! Savage is above us this very instant, doing God in heaven alone knows what...*

Heaven. Again that word sparked some memory in Will. The message had read, *The Heavens shall raine down upon Elizabeth.* But that wasn't what was causing the itch at the base of Will's skull. It was something else, something theatrical. Something about the painted stars...

Will stole a glance upwards, and all at once the plan was clear. *Oh dear God. The Heavens...*

The other players brought real torches close to Will, threatening to burn him, and he did not need to act frightened, for he truly was. What fooles they had been! Why had they thought to do this themselves?

Just before they were to set Will aflame, the Ambassador arrived from Spain with news of the Viceroy's son, and a letter from his own hand. Augustine's character ordered Will's freedom and condemned Kit, demanding of him the cause of his deceit. Typically, Kit decided to treat the stage as his cow and milk his final lines for all they were worth:

> Rent with remembrance of so foule a deed,
> My guiltie soule submits me to thy doome,
> For, not for Alexandros injuries,
> But for reward and hope to be prefer'd,
> Thus have I shamelesly hazarded his life.

The shackles were removed from Will's right arm, but for speed the left remained in place. The Viceroy condemned Kit, who was led off-stage, then clapped an arm about Will's shoulder. "Come, Alexandro, keep me company!" Together he and Augustine exited the centre door.

Their parts were done. The now had only to re-don their dresses to be part of the crowd for the play's final scene.

But it was a scene Will knew he'd never enter for.

The moment they were out of the crowd's sight, Augustine tried to pay a compliment to Will, only to find the young man haring off towards his friend, a half-shackle still dangling from his wrist. Clicking his tongue, Augustine returned to the Tiring House.

Kit already had his doublet off and was pulling his gown over his shirt and hose as Will approached. "Well, that was an excellent! Though, if I may say, you spoke a shade faster than—"

Will cut across him. "Kit. Kit! The Heavens! The Heavens, man!"

"What are you..?"

"What did you say they called the roof above the stage?"

Kit's exasperated look hurtled at Will as if cannon-shot – this was hardly the time for theatrical ephemera. "Aye, they're called the Heavens, for heaven's sake. Now why—" His brain caught up with his tongue. "The Heavens!"

"'*The Heavens shall raine down upon Elizabeth!*'" exclaimed Will, quoting the coded message in final understanding. "'*Fire and Hell will swallow only noble soules!*' I saw Savage climb a ladder into the Heavens just before I came onstage."

Kit slapped a hand to his pate. "What blind beetles we are!" Not bothering to undress again, he lifted his baldric and slung it over his dress, settling his sword in place. "Come, Will, come! Pray we're not too late!"

They raced to the stage-left stairs and ascended at a run. Actors below made shushing sounds at the tromp of their feet. In seconds they reached the ladder and started to climb, Will in the lead. Behind him, he heard Kit say, "Thank the Bleeding Mary that we doused the powder. At least they'll not use the cannons."

But Will was now certain they had it wrong. The theatre's cannons and gunpowder did not come into the plan. Perhaps they meant to pistol the Queen from their high perch, raining the fire of bullets down upon her, as Cutting Ball had suggested. Perhaps they meant to set the whole theatre aflame, trapping all within. But then, why hide in the Heavens?

Will crawled through the hatch, Kit right behind. They had to bend their necks, for the Heavens were about a head shorter than either of them. Savage must have had to almost crawl.

They drew their swords, careful of the theatrical ring in the scabbards – they had to be silent. Elbow to elbow, they began to advance. The only light came by chinks and slats in the thatch roof. But there was a glow far ahead, around the struts and beams that supported the thatch. There was also some sort of rope-drawn wheel hanging in the middle of the Heavens, just above centre-stage. Will recalled Kit mentioning that this was the door for the *Deus Ex Machina*, the ancient God from the Machine who in theatrical tradition would descend at the end of the show to put all right. It was no longer fashionable to have such divine interference. Rather, spirits like Revenge watched men's affairs without altering them.

Pity. We could use a bit of divine intervention at the moment.

Creeping forward towards the light, Will barked his shin on something. Reaching down, he groped at it, feeling its shape. A short barrel, just like the one he and Kit had found in the Hut.

Oh dear Lord.

Eyes adjusting now, Will could make out more such shapes scattered about the low attic. This was more than half a barrel of powder. There was more than a barrel. There were more than a dozen barrels. There were perhaps thirty barrels, all marked with a chalked fish – the secret sign of Christ from the Roman days, when Christians were persecuted by the government. Clearly the Catholics had re-adopted and revived the old sign, using it for this purpose.

But these barrels held no fish. Will could see one of the barrels had its lid off, and right up to the brim glistened the reflective black of gunpowder. There was enough here to blow apart the theatre, the yard outside, and set fire to all the buildings beyond.

Will was about to point this out to Kit when they heard voices. Not the actors below, which they had heard all along. These voices were much closer, conveyed in whispers.

"What are we waiting for? Light it now, I say." This, by his voice, was Brockhurst.

"We mustn't until we're certain the Queen is safe," replied Derby. "A fireball like this will alert the whole countryside."

Until the Queen is safe? wondered Will, shooting a look to Kit, who shrugged.

"What could they do?" answered Rookwood. "Her Majesty is hours away, even by the swiftest horse."

Will and Kit shared a knowing glance. *Ah! They mean Mary.*

"Watch yourself, imbecile," came the low growl of Savage. "Jostle my arm again and we'll not fear the timing – we'll be past fear itself."

That chilling voice actually calmed Will's nerves some. So long as they had hope of surviving, they would not blow the whole theatre to ruins.

He felt the ruffle of Kit's skirts as his friend sidled forward for a better view. Ducking low, Will followed, and together they slunk until they cleared the central strut holding up the Heavens.

Standing at the far end, peering through a peephole at the crowd below, were all five conspirators – Derby, Rookwood, Brockhurst, Higgins, and the mountainous John Savage. In Savage's hand was that single, simple lamp, all alight.

"I say do it now," opined Higgins, with a conviction born of fear.

"We're in the third act," said Derby. "We should time it for the end of the play – no doubt the apostate pretender will come to the stage itself to commend the actors ."

"Did you hear the voice of those two players?" demanded Higgins. "I swear it was Falstaff and Marlowe."

"How could they possibly know?" demanded Derby. "I burned the code myself."

Higgins was dogged. "I'm just saying I think Brockhurst is right, we should do this now."

Shifting his weight, Will felt his boot scrape some gritty substance underfoot. Reaching down, his fingers came away with a pinch of gunpowder. There was a trail. He traced it back a step and surmised that it led from the door all the way to the barrel at the heart of the Heavens.

They mean to go to the stairs, light this floor-fuse, and then run as fast as they can. Sword in his right hand, Will raised his left to try and signal to Kit.

He had entirely forgotten the manacle, still hanging off his left wrist. The moment he raised his arm, it struck the blade of his sword with a resounding *clang!*

"What was that?" demanded Savage. "Quick..!"

Will thought to hide, but it was too late. Two steps from the foremost wall and Savage was in view. The light from his lantern exposed Will and Kit to their foes.

For an instant there was no movement on anyone's part. All remain as if turned to ice, standing, staring, studying. It was a moment of supreme communication, where words were utterly unnecessary. All was known.

Then Savage reached down to open the doors to the lantern's flame, where resided the blazing wick that would doom them all.

At the same moment Will lunged forward. "Kit! Quench that flame!"

They were of one mind, both stabbing their blades for Savage's hand. At the same instant the other conspirators dived at them, and all was chaos. Will was buffeted by blows and knocks. Stabbing Higgins with his sword, he swung his manacled left arm at Brockhurst, bloodying the man's face with the loose cuff. Amid the crimson spray, his eyes were still on the lantern, whose doors remained closed as Savage retreated from Kit's attack.

The glass panes of the lamp let through light, and that light now reflected off more blades. This was no place for proper fighting, and their swords were too long to be of much use. Whereas the daggers that Rookwood and Derby held were far more practical to the space, infinitely more dangerous.

Still, the most dangerous man was Savage, with the power to blow them all to Kingdom Come. Ignoring the rest, Will chased the light even as Savage backed away, moving among the barrels, skirting the fighting and edging towards the ladder where he could light the fuse and escape. The other conspirators shouted, "Wait! Savage! Not yet! Let us..!" For it was no part of their cowardly plan to die with Elizabeth.

But Savage was such a man that, if he thought all was lost, he'd surely resort to just that.

Will stabbed and slashed, keeping Savage's hand away from the lantern's latch. He could hear the scuffling sounds around him, and surmised that Kit was guarding his back. "Kill him, can't you?"

"I'm trying!" Will lunged again, and Savage parried with the lantern, making Will check his attack. If he broke the glass, he'd be doing Savage's work for him.

Hunched low, Savage was making for the hatch, dogged by Will's constant pursuit. But a blow from behind sent Will face-first across the wooden floor, his sword skidding out of his hand. "No! Oh God, no!"

Freed from pursuit, Savage reached the hatch. Before Will could rise he had the latch open and had removed a glowing ember – not the candle, but a coal nestled at the lantern's base. Ignoring his scorched fingers, he dropped it deliberately on the floor where the gunpowder was spread.

The black grainy substance sizzled and sparked, and for an instant all fighting ceased as every man present watched the glowing trail of gunpowder burn a path towards the barrels—

—and fizzle out. Either by the passing of Kit's skirts or in the scuffle of the struggle, the gunpowder fuse had been swept aside and dispersed. There was no longer a trail to the barrels.

Kit cried out in triumph as he wheeled about to stab at Rookwood, who took the point in the shoulder. The others now raced for the hatch, hoping only to escape.

But not Savage. Roaring, the great man surged back towards the centre of the Heavens, intent on plunging his open lamp into a barrel, any barrel, and blow them all to Hell.

Sword gone, Will used his bare hands to wrestle with Savage, who was far too strong for such an endeavor. His only advantage was that Savage dared not drop the lantern – not for fear of death, but rather of snuffing the flame. The beast kept trying to stretch his arm for the nearest barrel. Will flailed and pulled, but Savage's strength was great, and he warded off Will's hands at every turn, unfazed even by the blows of the dangling manacle.

The manacle! Will grasped the cuff in his right hand and, in the midst of their struggles, clamped it down hard on Savage's right wrist. He then heaved with all his weight, dragging the huge soldier away from the barrel, his feet scrabbling on the floor. Snarling, Savage yanked up hard, clouting Will's head on the low ceiling.

"Will!" shouted Kit. From his voice he was too away far to help.

Dazed, Will landed on his backside in the perfect centre of the Heavens. There was a barrel nearby, and Savage was reaching for it.

"Will! Stop him, you skinny bastard!" Kit was hampered by Derby, who had remained behind to see this deed through. Like Savage, the ruby-snouted villain preferred dying success than living defeat.

Will pulled hard, his free hand added to the chain to haul Savage back. But it was a losing cause. Slowly, inexorably, the lamp drew closer to the barrel of their destruction. Savage was laughing now, and Will had an instant of wondering what all this sounded like to the crowd below. Was it enough of an alarum? Had they cleared the boxes? Was she safe? He couldn't hold the beast back much longer…

"William, the rope!" screamed Kit. "Grab the rope!"

Rope? Yes, there was a rope, attached to a winch and wheel, the great pulley for the *Deus Ex Machina*. Will grabbed it without thinking why. Then he saw the lever on the floor, and he understood what had to be done. Hauling back once more with all his might, he held Savage back long enough to kick out with his booted foot and drive the lever from closed to open, releasing the trap-door.

The floor fell away, and like Lucifer, Will was cast out of the Heavens in a blaze of fire.

Scene Five

Thankfully the players on the stage below heard the scuffling and were therefore looking up when the Heavens opened, giving them time to scatter before all Hell fell upon them.

One hand wrapped in the rope, Will fell through the trap, dragging Savage down after him. The fire came only from the cloud of gunpowder scattered on the floor, which ignited as it touched the passing lamp. Not an explosion but rather an instantaneous singeing that burned away the hairs on Will's arms and blackened his face.

He had more pressing concerns. In a moment he would land on his back on the stage floor, possibly a crippling blow, only to have Savage land on top of him and finish the work. A sourly wry voice in his head said, most unhelpfully, *At least I won't suffer.*

There were screams from the crowd of spectators, and applause – they believed this was part of the show! *O, what a show*, thought Will, bracing himself. *No repeat performances for me. My first day on stage, and my last.*

A split second before he hit, the rope in his hand jerked upwards, and him with it. Now it was Savage who was falling, while paradoxically Will was headed in the opposite direction. They passed each other, making senseless sounds of fear and rage.

"WILL!"

Looking up, he saw Kit working the winch, hauling him back heavenward. *Bless you, you vainglorious, arrogant, brilliant man. I owe you my…*

Will's arm was wrenched near out of its socket as all of the still-manacled Savage's weight pulled him back down. The winch-wheel was ripped from Kit's grip, and Will was again falling earthwards. Only now it was Savage on the bottom, cushioning Will's fall.

Not that it was much of a cushion. The man's muscles were like iron, and Will felt the breath driven from his lungs as together they crashed to a heap on the stage floor.

Through bleary dancing eyes, Will saw the lantern land a few inches away, its flame snuffed out. He sighed, thinking to himself, *It's over.*

That was when the mountain beneath him shifted.

Savage rose to his feet, dragging Will behind him in afterthought, as if unaware of the weight on his arm. Upright, Savage took in the sight of the people, all still living, and heard the continued scuffling above. Regaining his breath, he staggered a step, pulling Will off-balance with him.

The watching crowd was not yet panicking, wondering if this was some wonderful part of the play. But some among the groundlings knew this was nothing written by Kyd, that Savage was no actor. Tarlton and Armin surely recognized the man, as did Blacke Davie. Cutting Ball had followed him in the rain, and described him to Scarlet Dick. They now pressed forward, hands upon the hilts of their swords.

Slowly Savage came to his senses and realization set in – they had failed to blow the powder. But there, in the box at the back of the crowd, sat a painted woman muffled in a voluminous cloak. *"Sic semper tyrannis!"* Bellowing, he charged for the lip of the stage, ready to trod upon heads until he could reach the monarch and tear her with his bare, bear-like hands.

Dragged forward in the giant's surge, Will clutched at the stage-right carved pillar that supported the Heavens, checking the assassin's attack. Only as he was yanked back did Savage notice the drag on his wrist, and the cause. "You!"

"Aye, I." Will's eyes went, not to the Queen, but to his father's box. Lucy was standing, shouting, "Traitor! Traitor!" But the senior Shakespeare was still seated, his bulk straining forward at the rail as he watched his son's imminent death. *This is your fault…*

The massive murderer heaved his arm, yanking Will free of the post, and suddenly he was dangling before Savage, who punched him straight in the face. It was rather like being struck with a ham wrapped around a brick. Already dazed, Will saw the Heavens dancing before him, and could not tell if he was looking at painted stars above or his own private universe.

"Whathewhahuh?" said Will unintelligibly. Blood poured down his face and clogged his throat. Between blows, Will desperately cried out, "Gunpowder! In the Heavens! Gunpowder!" Savage stopped his mouth by hitting it. He expected Savage to keep pummeling him until he was dead. Which surely would not be long.

Finally the crowd realized this was no act. Screaming and shoving in their panic, they pressed for the exits. The royal guards at the back of the theatre tried to beat their way forward, but were pressed back by the weight of humanity.

There were guards around the royal box, now shedding their disguising cloaks and producing swords. Standing on the rail of his box, Lucy was shouting, "Shakespeare! Shakespeare, you devil!" Did the idiot think Will was party to this assassination? *Am I here to bleed on the Queen?*

Seeing the theatre vomiting forth its patrons, Savage was faced with a choice: kill Will, which would be thoroughly pleasurable, or kill the Queen, which would gain him eternal fame. Duty and fame won over pleasure. Dragging Will after him, Savage again made forward, planning to leap off the stage and race for the monarch, only to find himself facing the blades of London's best fooles and villains. With a thousand souls pressing back the honourable protectors of the realm, it was up to the dregs of London to face the Savage.

"Back, ye wee beastie!" cried the aged Tarlton, leaping spryly upon the stage's thrust.

"O no, devilish Savage," cried Armin, right behind his mentor. "Back ye go!"

"Save a piece for me," shouted Blacke Davie, who was almost of a size with the brutish assassin.

"Oh-ho!" crowed Thomas Watson with appreciative relish at the bulk of their foe.

But it was Cutting Ball who cried patriotically, "You'll not touch a hair on Her Majesty's head!" His blade sliced the air, which hissed at Savage with scorn.

Savage began to swing at them with his free fist. Tarlton ducked and dodged, Armin rolled and kicked, Cutting Ball hacked and slashed, Blacke Davie swung. Together they went on poking and feinting Savage back and back, towards the centre of the stage. Flung this way and that, used as a fleshly shield, Will could not help be reminded of Orsino the baited bear, surrounded by ferocious mastiffs.

Only this time Will was shackled to the bear. Through bloodied lips he said, "I have tied you to the stake, my friend. Now you must fight the course."

Savage glanced up to where the Queen was being pushed out an upstairs door. His prey was slipping away. "You fooles! Death to the Queen!" He swung Will into the nearest blades, which blessedly for all posterity drew back at once. With his free hand, Savage struck Blacke Davie such a clout that the big brute sank to his knees. "Owitch!"

"Davie!!" The scream came from the Pit as Huffing Kate flung herself upon the stage and began beating and clawing at Savage's face. He struck her, too, knocking her sideways onto her lover.

The others moved in. Watson was laughing as he feinted and looked for an opening. "The London commons with one voice say, No," he taunted, misquoting his own translation of *Antigone*.

In answer, Savage took Will's chain in his free hand and with his whole body he began to spin. Barely having found his feet a moment before, Will was lifted off them again and whipped round and round like a doll, his feet warding off his friends and allies.

"Aaaahhhhh!" The pull on Will's wrist was tremendous, and he feared his hand would be torn off by the force. His free hand came up to grab the chain, releasing at least a portion of the pull. He felt his legs strike other men, and tried to pull his knees up, but that just allowed Savage to spin faster.

Finally Savage stopped turning, himself made dizzy. The others had all backed away, lest their swords do harm to Will. Cutting Ball called out, "Give it over, big fellow! She's gone!"

Staggering, Savage glanced up to see that this was so. His face a rictus of rage, he drew Will in close and took hold of his throat in his free, beefy hand. "I'll do for you, at least!"

"Gahhack—kkgk—pduh," said Will, turning purple, his vision reducing slowly to a pinpoint in each eye.

And so I die, thought Will. And to the world, I die Falstaff. No one will ever remember there was once a man called—

"*SHAKESPEARE!!!*"

All eyes (including Will's bulging and puffed orbs) turned upwards as Kit Marlowe dropped from the trapdoor above and swung along the rope in a magnificent show of flamboyance. Kicking his legs, he landed upon the Lord's Balcony and stood, sword held high, his fine boots sticking out from beneath the skirts of his player's gown. With a flourish of the blade, a laugh, and a smile as wide as all outdoors, he leapt from the balcony, swinging at the dumbfounded Savage below. His heels connected with the big man's jaw, Savage's hand opened of its own accord, and Will felt air rush into his lungs.

Kit's blade was next to strike, the true edge slicing the big man along the shoulder. "Like an eagle upon the bear!" cried Kit in self-delight.

The arc of his swing brought him around for another attack. Neatly avoiding Savage's outstretched hand, Kit released the rope and dropped to straddle the giant's neck. Banging down with his sword's pommel on the villain's crown, he used his free fingers to poke Savage in the eyes.

"Alive!" called Kit to the onrushing others. "Alive! He must stand trial!"

Heeding this command, everyone leapt upon Savage. Will watched from the floor as they abandoned blades to use fists, elbows, knees, and feet. There was Tarlton, using an old wrestling trick to make Savage's knees buckle. There was Blacke Davie smashing his fists into Savage's kidneys. There were Scarlet Dick and Cutting Ball kicking him in the back and groin, respectively. There were Watson and Armin hanging off the free arm, holding it down with their whole weight. And there was Huffing Kate, clawing at any skin she could reach, possibly doing the most damage.

Above them all perched Kit, continuing to bash the pate, box the ears, and heel-kick the chest of their mighty foe. "By five-hundred thousand million cartloads of devils," cried he, "may the plague take hold of your whiskers!"

Will did his part, too, putting all his weight towards holding back the shackled arm. *Fall! Fall! Why won't you...?*

Finally, down upon his knees, Savage released a groat's worth of noisesome air, vibrated as if struck by lightning, then began to sway. Kit leapt lightly to the earth, and Will rolled aside to avoid the mountain of flesh falling upon him. Everyone else stepped back to watch the big man finally pitch forward onto his face. The planks of the stage floor shook as he landed, bounced, and finally settled into a heap.

There were grins among the bloodied and bruised faces. But they were all too lost for breath to cheer their victory.

Nor did they have time. No sooner had Savage fallen but the royal guards flooded the stage, swords and halberds bared. Exits were blocked and shouts were made, consisting mostly of the word, "Stand!"

Will tried to stand, but found his legs would not support him. Kit came to his aid on the right-hand, Tarlton on the left.

"Where's the key?" demanded Kit, fumbling with the shackle.

Oddly enough, it had remained in the lock this whole time. A simple twist and Will was free to rub life back into his extremity. There was a nasty groove dug into his left wrist, and most of the skin had been rubbed away, loosing yet more of Will's blood.

"Derby?" he asked through thick and bleeding lips. "The others?"

"Fled down the ladder," replied Kit. "I sealed the hatch behind them before transforming myself into the god of the machine. By Saint George's dripping lizard, was that not an entrance!?! Ha!"

"I shall never forget it for all my days. I am grateful – to you all," Will added, smiling at the others, who were even now staring at the tips of the guards' halberd. Will glanced down to Savage. "Best hope he doesn't wake."

"Indeed." Kit stooped to fasten the loose cuff about Savage's other arm, only to discover a sword's point hovering an inch from his nose.

"I'll have those cuffs, boy," said Sir Thomas Lucy. "They belong on the traitor still standing." The point flicked again. "William Shakespeare, I arrest you in the Queen's name! The charge is treason."

Beyond thought or even anger, Will merely nodded. It was up to the others to roar forth in outrage, which they did.

"Are ye mad?!"

"How dares't thou, false knave!"

"Fut that and fut all!"

"Where were you when this bastard…?!"

Armin flung a coin at Lucy. "There! Buy a fit of mirth for a groat, and leave us be!"

"Who be you, then?" demanded Tarlton.

"Sir Thomas Lucy, magistrate and Member of Parliament," said the furious knight. "And you are all to be hanged!"

"No!" shouted two voices from the depths of the theatre. One was a woman's, the other a man's. Will could not say which surprised him more – the cry from the woman in the muffled robes, or the one from his father.

His corpulent sire was still stuck in the same seat he'd occupied during the show. It was the regal woman with the painted face who was drawing closer, having re-entered the theatre once her guards had charge of the place.

Everyone broke their legs to her, stepping backwards in obeisance. She surveyed them, then said to Lucy, "What is the charge?"

Sir Thomas looked perplexed. "The charge? Why, the attempted assassination of Her Majesty the Queen!"

"How can that be, when the Queen is not even present?" Throwing back her muffling cowl, the lady revealed herself to them all. Though the resemblance was quite uncanny, she was clearly *not* Queen Elizabeth. Younger and slightly taller than the monarch, with pointed ears and a secret smile, she spoke with the faint trace of a Scandinavian accent.

While guards and rascals alike stared in amazement at the lady, Kit turned an outraged glare at Will. He returned Kit's anger with an apologetic shrug. "I could not, in conscience, allow Her Majesty's life to be risked." He turned to Helena of Snakenborg, Marchioness of Northampton, wife of Sir Thomas Gorges, and Lady-in-Waiting to her Majesty the Queen. "Though when I brought you my message, I did not intend it should be you that took her place, my lady. You risk too much."

"No more than you, Master Falstaff," replied Lady Helena. "Or is it Shakespeare now?"

Will bowed unsteadily. "Like an actor, I will be whoever the moment requires. Now I am your servant, my lady."

It was a shame there was no longer an audience, for the scene that unfolded was like none other ever played upon the stage. The rogues were glancing warily about for a chance to escape. The guards were entirely uncertain from whom they were meant to be taking orders. The Wits tried to live up to their self-given title. Kit was both elated and furious, and the colours of each quilted his skin like a rainbow.

"I don't know who you are," snarled Lucy, misliking the deceit that had him breaking a knee to a woman not his monarch. "But William Shakespeare is guilty of a litany of crimes, both past and present."

"And you are guilty of ingratitude. It was my invitation that brought you here today." Lady Helena smiled wanly. "In the hope of effecting a charming scene of reconciliation. Is it not to be?"

So that was the answer. She had heard about Will Shakespeare from Walsingham, and wanted to bring father and son together. Will stared at his sire, who stared dully back.

Lucy had no interest in a touching scene. "He is my prisoner, and I shall take him back to Stratford to be flogged and hanged. If not for treason, then for heresy – and murder!"

"No!" shouted John Shakespeare, loud enough for everyone else to finally take notice of him. Ironically Lucy's threats had achieved the lady's desire. The fat glover pressed his way along the upper stands and finally pushed his way down the stairs to the edge of the stage. "He's innocent! It was—!"

"Peace, father!" shouted Will, finding his anger. "Peace, you mumbling old foole! What are you even doing here?"

"I came to rescue you from my own sin, son," rumbled the corpulent father. "Sir Thomas, this can go on no longer. It was I who—"

Again Will cut across his sire. "Go find your cups, old man! You don't talk sense without a keg or two of sack in your bladder!" He turned to Lady Helena. "I appreciate the intent, my lady. But alas, I'm afraid I am so charged, as Sir Thomas states. He has the right to take me."

But the lady shook her head. "I think that you do not belong to this man, or any other. I think you are a woman's man. That woman is the Queen. Ah, see – here is her representative now."

All eyes turned to the central doorway, where at that moment four guards were making way for a man dressed all in black, save for the white ruff about his throat. His grave expression and drooping eyes made him seem sleepy, but the voice that emanated from Sir Francis Walsingham's throat was as sharp as a knife.

"You all –" said he, punctuating each word, staring at each man in turn, "—have much to answer for."

Though most of the dozen recipients of this fearful man's stony gaze had the good grace to look abashed, three did not. Savage, because he was still less than conscious. Lady Helena, for it had been she who had summoned Sir Francis to this place at this time. And Kit Marlowe, who had been rehearsing his relaxed attitude for this confrontation for days now.

"Before we press on, could we all step outside?" asked Kit gaily. "There are a dozen barrels of gunpowder over our heads, and all this heated talk is likely to explode more than tempers."

This sound suggestion was embraced by all, and quickly the theatre was abandoned for the open air.

"I'm not through with you," hissed Lucy in Will's ear as they exited.

"But I, Sir Thomas, am entirely through with you," replied Will. He gave a warning glance to his father, who had the good grace to stay silent for once in his life.

Outside they encountered Old Shakespeare's doppelganger, Greene – the son of John Shakespeare's spirit, if not his flesh. But such was the flesh between the elder Shakespeare and the unrepentant Greene that between them God above could have formed five men and a small child.

Lyly was with Greene, and between them was the playwright, wringing his hands and weeping openly.

"You can't deceive me, Kit Marlow!" shouted Kyd, shaking his clenched fist in the air. "You did this – all this! – just to *ruin my play!*"

Kit smiled serenely as he passed. "Not at all, my little lamb. That was but an added bonus."

Will could not help but laugh.

Scene Six

·

"Wait wait," said Will. "Slow down, in Heaven's name, man – *who* was arrested?"

"Sir Anthony Babington," repeated Skeggs.

"And who in the name of the bleeding winking Christ on his cross is Sir Anthony Babington?" demanded Kit.

"He's the villain," replied Thomas (not-Peter) Phelippes the goat-man.

Will rubbed his temples. "Christ, my head aches."

It was the next day. Will's wrist had been bandaged and his other wounds tended. After extensive questioning, their companions had all been released, upon which they had all taken to the Elephant and celebrated their glorious achievement the live-long night.

Will and Kit, however, had passed the night in adjacent cells in the Tower. Will was uncertain if he was grateful for the separation. Certainly, if they had shared a cell, Kit would have had more time to utter complaints.

"I cannot believe you did not tell me!" he'd fumed through the bars. "Our one chance to impress the Queen—"

"Impress her how? By endangering her very life? By risking all that England is?"

"By showing her our daring! Our panache!"

"You're merely angry she did not see you perform upon the stage."

"Well, yes, 'tis a truth, now you mention it," Kit had admitted before returning to his theme. "I cannot believe you didn't tell me!"

"It was you yourself who suggested I become better about keeping my secrets."

"Not from me!"

At dawn they had been brought to the house on Seething Lane. Now they sat in the company of Walsingham's men, Skeggs and Phelippes. Forced to nursemaid Will and Kit, the agents had been given permission to explain at least the core elements of the plot, the details of which were making Will's head ache.

Kit, too, was having difficulty following the story. "I say again, by the light of Lucifer's bedtime taper, who is Sir Anthony Babington?"

"Babington was the axis of the plot to free Mary and kill the Queen," repeated Skeggs.

"Fut that!" cried Kit in furious denial. "Savage was the man. And Gifford!"

"Gifford," said Phelippes slowly, "was working for us."

"In the sense that he carried out the duties he was paid to perform," retorted Kit. "But he was also working across you to conspire to murder the Queen."

"There's no proof of that," said Phelippes.

"There's the note I copied from him to Mary! The coded message saying exactly where and when the assassination of Her Majesty was to take place!"

"In his own hand?"

"Well – no," admitted Kit, frowning. "But nonetheless—"

"That's hardly conclusive."

"We saw him meet Savage," said Will. Kit nodded vehemently, pointing at Will with both forefingers.

"He was paid to meet with Savage," said Skeggs. "He reported the contents of those meetings the same day they took place."

Kit bit his lower lip hard so hard it threatened to burst. "I say if you bring him in here, today, you could have a full confession."

"That would be difficult," said Phelippes, "as he left for France five days ago."

This news cooled the atmosphere. "Oh did he? And that isn't evidence of his guilt?"

"Or possibly evidence that he sensed you two idiots following him," sneered Skeggs, "and decided to run rather than risk his life to your blundering attentions."

Kit was about to reply hotly, likely to the effect that they would have saved the Queen Herself (had the Queen Herself actually been present), but Will cut across his friend. "What about Derby, Rookwood, and the rest?"

"Escaped," said Skeggs sourly. "We found Higgins and Brockhurst, both wounded – I presume by you? They had gone to a barber for doctoring before they fled London, and we took them. But Derby and Rookwood got clean away."

"Probably across the Channel already," observed Phelippes.

Less than concerted by this news, Will returned the central point. "Back to this Babblerton fellow."

"Babington," said Phelippes.

"Aye, him. What was his part in all this?"

As Skeggs and Phelippes explained, the thrust of the story was this:

The plot against Elizabeth had grown out of a pair of separate but equally dangerous plans. The first involved a Spanish invasion with the purpose of deposing Elizabeth and replacing her with Mary. The second was a plot by English Catholics to assassinate Elizabeth.

"Both plots were coaxed and fueled by Mary's chief agent in Europe, Charles Paget," said Skeggs. "Seeing a confluence of desired outcomes, Paget began to consolidate the two plots, joining Catholic, French, and Spanish interests. The Catholics wanted Elizabeth dead, the French wanted Mary on the throne, and the Spanish wanted Mary to then wed their king."

Phelippes took over. "At the behest of the French, a Jesuit priest called Ballard came to England the previous year to stir up the Catholics and prepare them to rise. This past March, he met with your friend Savage, who assured the priest that English Catholics would raise arms so long as they had support from France and Spain. But that wasn't enough – Ballard needed a member of the gentry. So he found a young man – hardly older than you two fooles – called Anthony Babington to organize and lead the English Catholics against Elizabeth."

"And you knew all this?" demanded Kit.

"From Gifford and others like him, yes," admitted Phelippes.

"Then why not arrest them all?" asked Will in perplexity.

Skeggs looked at Will as if at an utter imbecile. It was Kit who supplied the answer. "Because it was not those men they were after."

Neither Phelippes nor Skeggs said anything. The latter looked slightly uncomfortable.

"Who, then?" demanded Will.

Kit's gaze was shrewd. "As long as she's alive, Mary Stewart will be a barrel of powder waiting for a spark. So Sir Francis decided to let this little plot play out. That's why he allowed the notes to pass so freely in and out of Mary's comfortable prison – so he could read them, and let her incriminate herself in writing. Irrefutable, entirely damning writing." Kit turned to Phelippes. "Who were the messages written to, this Babington?"

"The damning ones, aye," replied Phelippes. "I deciphered them myself before they were allowed to pass on into Mary's hands. Babington wrote that while six of his friends were murdering Her Majesty the Queen, he and a hundred of his followers would ride to rescue Mary."

"And that was supposed to be yesterday?"

Phelippes shrugged. "We did not know the date. It was never in the messages."

"But it *was* in the one that Savage sent through Gifford," mused Kit. "If he was working for Babington, why would Savage go around him? Why circumvent the system? Clearly they didn't think it was compromised, else Mary would never have committed herself in writing – as I take it she did?"

Skeggs glanced to Phelippes, who nodded. "Yes, at last. This is evidence even Her Majesty the Queen cannot ignore. Mary has signed her own death warrant for certes." He sounded almost proud.

"Then why would Savage risk all to pass along a message this Babington knew nothing about?"

Skeggs continued to look uneasy, and Will began to sense why. "When were these damning letters written?"

"A fortnight and more since," answered Phelippes.

"So you've had the damning evidence for two weeks, but you've not acted to arrest anyone."

"We were waiting for them to try it, to smoke them all out. We didn't yet have all the names of the conspirators." Phelippes was straight and tall as he spoke. But Skeggs avoided looking at either Will or Kit.

Kit was amazed. "An astonishing risk, if you didn't know when, where, or how the deed was to be done!"

"Hardly," scoffed Phelippes.

Skeggs said nothing. Watching him, Will said, "It wasn't going to happen, was it?"

"Excuse me?" said Kit.

"Babington. He'd lost his nerve, hadn't he? That's why there was no date set. He was putting it off. He didn't mean to go through with it, did he? So what did you do? Put pressure on him? Try to make him act? Savage sensed this and decided to put the plan into motion himself, without telling Babington. He sent the message through Gifford giving the exact date and method of the assassination to Mary. Babington didn't know, did he? What did Savage do, send a message on Saturday that Sunday was the day, and Babington better move? By then it was too late for Babington to do anything but keep his word." Will's temper, always dangerous, was growing warm again. "You risked the life of the Queen, and arrested a man who might have changed his mind. Did he even try to rescue Mary yesterday?"

Skeggs looked down, and now Kit saw what Will had been seeing – guilt.

"He wrote treasonous letters," insisted Phelippes. "That's enough to hang him."

"Will," said Kit in a musing voice, "do you know what skill my friend Thomas-not-Peter here has, that I neglected to mention? He is an absolute master of the forge."

Will glanced at Phelippes, confused. "Blacksmithery?"

"Wordsmithery. Not the creation of something new, as you or I might make. But rather the replication of something already made. He is a forger."

That hit home. Will saw it in Skeggs' fallen face.

Kit pressed on. "How much of what Babington will be accused of did he write himself? In your rush to hang Mary, have you also entrapped a man who might have walked away?"

Phelippes was unrepentant. "He wrote enough that I shall not lose a jot of sleep over his death."

"Words are not deeds," said Will.

"No. But words do have the power to make a life. And end one."

At that moment Walsingham's Welsh secretary appeared. "Sir Francis is ready for you."

Will and Kit were again ushered into Sir Francis' study, and again there was an unseasonable fire blazing in the large stone fireplace. Will noted at once that the windows had been completely replaced, with sturdier frames.

"Will Shakestaff and Christopher Morley, Sir Francis," announced Walter Williams.

Sir Francis was standing behind his desk, hands clasped at his back, gazing out the windows into the street below. Without turning he said, "Thank you, Walter. That will be all."

The steward bowed and exited, closing the door softly behind him.

Having not been bidden to sit, Will and Kit remained upon their feet. Will shifted his weight nervously inside his boots and wondered what was about to happen.

David Blixt

Walsingham stood for what seemed like hours, but was no more than two minutes. Very theatrical, thought Will. Twice Kit oped his mouth to provoke some response, and twice Will stopped him.

Finally, in a slow, deliberate tone, Walsingham said, "What shall I do with you two?"

"I know what you *should* do, Sir Francis," said Kit boldly.

Walsingham turned sharply. "Oh, I know what you *think* I should do, Mister Marlowe. You think I should fall upon my knees and thank God in His heavens that you were here to save the realm. You think I should heap you with praise, honours, and gold. Mostly gold. You think I should even whisper in Her Majesty's ear about a possible knighthood for yourself and your friend here."

"You disagree?"

"I do. Your meddling nearly under-mined a wall of evidence I have been building for over a year. Before this, Marlowe, you were guilty of mere sodomy, which sadly afflicts half your fellows at Corpus Christi."

"And a great many professors," added Kit with a smile. "I could name them…"

"But now," said Walsingham, sweeping on, "you have committed treason – yes yes, don't argue, you have! You have assaulted soldiers, knights, and even my own person. You have destroyed government property. You are guilty of kidnapping, theft, and horse-theft. You have incited riots and street-brawls. And you have dressed in women's clothings, against the use of nature."

"We have *ben lyke the lytel bee*," agreed Kit.

"Moreover, you, Christopher Marlowe, have aided and abetted this man, William Shakestaff, a man who, if I am to believe Sir Thomas Lucy, was born a Papist and can produce no evidence to preclude his continuing adherence to the evil of Rome. He, too, has gone about in unnatural dress, corrupting the minds of the youth of Lancashire. He has certainly committed slander after being convicted of the poaching of a deer belonging to the local magistrate – the aforementioned Lucy – and on top of it all, Lucy asserts that Shakestaff here is guilty of murder." Walsingham addressed Will for the first time. "Is there anything in this that you wish to contest?"

All Will could think to say was, "Shakespeare."

"Eh?"

"My name is William Shakespeare."

"Ah. So noted." Sir Francis smiled coldly. "Is that your only objection?"

"No. I mean to say – none of that is true. Or if there's truth in it you have turned its worst face to the light."

"Truth has but one face, Master Shakespeare. The lighting should not matter to an honest man. Do you wish to address any of these charges directly?"

Will thought for a moment, then shook his head. "No, sir."

Walsingham nodded smartly. "I thought as much. Most fortunate for you, then, it is clear to me that Sir Thomas is an idiot. You did not kill the groom. It was most probably your father, who I'm told is a drunkard."

Kit turned to stare as Will flushed with emotion. How? How could Walsingham deduce in seconds what the Law had not in months? And what would it mean? Vindication for the son, damnation for the father?

Walsingham smiled thinly. "I see I am correct. Gratifying. What was the cause? No doubt a provincial argument."

"No," corrected Will. "A drunken one."

The curl of Walsingham's lips turned from up to down. "Too common, I'm afraid. And certainly well-documented. John Shakespeare's petition for a coat of arms was withdrawn, I understand, because he drank away the price. Your future, your chance to be a gentleman, swallowed by a father's thirst. Yet, rather than have your importunate sire branded a murderer, you fled, letting the suspicion fall upon you and thus sparing your father's life." Walsingham shook his head. "Which marks you as more of a foole than Marlowe here – a sentimental foole, which is the second most dangerous kind there is."

Kit could not resist. "The first being?"

"A zealous foole. Which brings us," said Walsingham with a newly brisk air, "to Mister Savage. The very definition. He has survived his injuries, which is just as well for you two. If he were dead, we might well have needed to put the pair of you on trial in his place."

"Alongside Babington," said Will in a neutral tone that was yet somehow accusing.

"Yes, alongside Babington. You object?"

Will summoned all his bravery. "A man should be judged for his actions, not what is in his head."

"Should not we then judge your father by his actions? Why is he spared? If that is too close to the bone, let me ask, is not writing an action? If so, we are all accord. Babington put treason down on paper."

"Would he have ever done so if you had not prompted him to it, and provided the means?"

"Doubtful," admitted Walsingham frankly. "But circumstances should not matter to a man of principle."

"If one side is willing to forego their principles altogether, then what have we become?"

Walsingham waved a hand. "Fascinating as this discussion may eventually become, it is sadly irrelevant. The plot is not credible without someone of noble birth. That someone is Babington. His fate is certainly set with a seal. Yours, however, I have yet to wax."

Kit said, "Sir Francis, you know what you plan to do with us. You've known since before we entered the room. So please end this tortuous catting-and-mousing and tell us, that we may get on with living or dying, whichever it may be."

Walsingham was silent for a moment. Then he seemed to be distracted by something that lay upon his desk. He lifted a handbill for 'The Spanish Tragedie'. "Tell me, gentlemen – do you plan to continue a life in the theatre?"

Will and Kit exchanged surprised glances. "Is there a correct answer?" asked Kit.

"It is my hope that you will answer with an affirmation. Both of you."

"It was my understanding you detested the theatre."

"No," said Walsingham firmly, "in that you are quite mistaken. I detest theatre *people*. Actors, stage managers, playwrights – all scum. But theatre? I have a more-than-healthy respect for the theatre. Yesterday has but solidified my interest in all things theatrical. There are few more efficacious tools to alter the mood of the people, shape their opinions, than the theatre."

Sir Francis turned his full attention to the felonious pair before him. "It is my desire that you both remain in London, involved in the arts. In exchange for this small service, I shall – arrange matters. There will be no knighthood, no royal audience, no gold, no honours. There will be your lives, for as long as I see fit to prolong them." He faced Kit. "Mr. Marlowe, you have proven uncontrollable. I do not mean this as a compliment. So instead of giving you paid work, I will require from you information, and the occasional service. Should you provide these to my satisfaction, then you will be paid, in due course. And you may also be allowed to attain your degree, if you like. But only in furtherance of my goals."

Walsingham turned the embers of his coal-black eyes upon Will. "You, Master Shakespeare, will remain in London. I have conversed with Sir Thomas, and convinced him that so long as you are in London, you are under my eye. Should you venture outside the city without my leave, a message will be sent winging to him that you are to be arrested, tried, flogged, and hanged. There is no question of you returning to Stratford, I'm afraid. You are now a Londoner."

Will could scarcely believe his luck. Had Sir Francis realized his words were not threatening, but rather liberating, he might have taken a different tack. Under orders from Her Majesty's government, Will was not to be allowed to return to a wife who regularly cuckolded him; to a father who shamed and ruined him; and to a town too small to appreciate him. Instead he was commanded, under penalty of death, to pursue the life which most appealed to him. A theatrical one.

Still, he had to be certain. "Does this mean, sir, that we are not to hang?"

"Hang, Master Shakespeare?" repeated Walsingham, eyes alight with chilling amusement. "No. It means you now belong to Her Majesty the Queen. Body and soul."

Epilogue

Walking down the steps of the house in Seething Lane into the bright August air, Will felt his newfound freedom in his joints. He could stroll in the open air without fear of reprisal, arrest, or execution. He was in exile, true. But exile from Hell is not a burden.

"Well, my Will," said Kit, rubbing his hands together, "it all turned out right, did it not? Surely, it was a trifle more convoluted than I anticipated—"

"A trifle!" Incredulity raised Will's voice a whole octave. "A *trifle!*"

"—but all's well that ends well, neh? Oop! I seem to have spoken too soon."

Standing by the gate were four men. At their forefront was Sir Thomas Lucy.

"So," said Sir Thomas coldly. "You continue to survive. The luckiest man alive."

"So it seems," said Will with unforced brightness. He noted that his father was among these men – such bulk was unconcealable. But he avoided the old man's gaze, focusing instead upon Lucy. "How kind of you, Sir Thomas, to bid us well."

Lucy scowled. "I know not what Catholic witchcraft has allowed you to pull the wool over Walsingham's eyes. But I see you clear, Will Shakespeare."

"A poet!" cried Kit, applauding.

Will shrugged. "A poor one. He's missing two beats. Add an iam for an iamb."

"If he likes, we can offer him those beats," replied Kit with a taunting smile.

Sir Thomas' hand dropped instinctively towards his reclaimed sword before he caught himself. "I've come to tell you, if you ever return to my jurisdiction—"

"—you'll have the flesh off my back." Despite his broad smile, Will's eyes were colder than the moon. "Oh, hang about. You've done that already."

"It'll be the noose for you."

"The goose?" answered Will loudly. "I'll not goose you, Sir Thomas Lousey! You are not a man of parts."

"Can I be his goose?" asked Kit eagerly. "Because this goose bites."

"Switch and spurs, switch and spurs," cried Will.

Mocked so mercilessly, Lucy resorted to his final weapon. Turning to the elder Shakespeare, he said, "Say farewell to your son. Certes you will never lay eyes upon him hencewith."

And so, for the first time since he had rushed his drunken, murderous sire home and fled Stratford forever, Will Shakespeare came nose to nose with his father.

The old man was sober. At least, his heavy mouth-breathing did not reek of sack. But the eyes had long since lost their luster, and the skin had ceased to be taut. There was shame, and sorrow, and wrath, and pleading. But no fire.

"Have you aught to say to me?" demanded Will.

The fat man's many chins wobbled as the senior Shakespeare sought words. Finding none, he settled for putting a hand on Will's shoulder. "What shall I tell Anne?"

Will almost laughed. "Tell my lady wife that I am detained in London, indefinitely. She needn't visit. But tell my children their father will make the family name proud."

The old man took the insult well. Or perhaps he was so immune to injurious words that it passed him by. Regardless, he asked only, "How? As a glover?"

"No, John," replied Shakespeare, heaping further disdain upon the patriarch by calling him by his Christian name. "As an actor. A writer. A creature of the *theatre*."

The elder Shakespeare had nothing more to say. No word of thanks for saving his life by taking the blame, no word of regret or of shame. He merely looked blankly at his son, prolonging their mutual discomfort. This was very like the pregnant moment in the Heavens before the brawl - so much to say, yet nothing worth saying.

Finally Will looked to his sire and said, "You know me not, old man."

Sir Thomas signaled his men to mount. It took John Shakespeare several attempts to heave his girth into the saddle, and his son did not move to assist. A minute later the Stratfordians were turning the corner, heading out of the city. Out of Will's life. Forever.

The scene left Kit utterly bemused. "Hmmm. Awkwardness abounds. Shall we drown the taste of mixed feelings with mixed spirits? I know a pack of men anxious to drink us well!"

Will laughed. "I doubt they've waited."

It was a goodly walk to the Elephant, but with Kit's eager gait they were passing through the door in just a quarter hour. Sure enough, the whole pack was present, from Watson to Tarlton. Their cheers also carried sighs of dismay, some quite real – both Greene and Huffing Kate had, for their own reasons, half-hoped Will and Kit might have been, if not hanged, then at least racked.

Yet soon even their sour moods were mended by the general good cheer. Kit, of course, insisted upon changing into finer clothes, and then the festivities commenced in earnest. Airy barbs flew, goodnatured breathy bullets of the brain, and slowly the Elephant and Castle became a blaze of revels. Greene recited a labourious poem in Latin:

Meum est propositum
In teberna mori,

Minum sit oppositum
Morientis ori,
Ut dicant, cum venerint
Angelorum chori:
'Deus sit propitious
Huic potatori!'

Despite the sentiment, Will smiled. Greene had summed up his own life, and that of Will's importunate *pater*:

I would die where I would dine,
In a tavern to recline;
Then would angels pray the glibber:
'God have mercy on this bibber!'

Kit made several overt overtures to Will, some mocking and some less, and Will was pleased to find himself able to banter back in equal spirit and ribaldry. There would be time enough now to explore that side of himself as well. London promised everything the wide world had to offer.

Soon there was music, and singing, which is how all good Comedies should end – with a touch of sorrow, a few bruised feelings, and much foolishness. And a marriage! Always a marriage! This was the joyous dance and revel that ends the play, everyone wiser than before. And who was it being wed that night? Not man and woman, but man and idea. Or perhaps man and place. You be the judge, as everyone else is far too busy singing.

You can see them, can't you? Even at the remove of hundreds of years, you see them as they are – real, breathing, full of life as they sing:

Ah, Robin, jolly Robin
Tell me how thy leman doth
And thou shalt know of mine.

Kit kneels and sings the first verse, making Will the object of his desire:

My lady is unkind, perdie,
Alack, why is she so? (cried the others)
She lov'th another better than me
And yet she will say no.

Ah, Robin, jolly Robin
Tell me how thy leman doth
And thou shalt know of mine.

The music rises, with Tarlton himself on the lute, and Armin on the fife. Greene takes up the next verse, pulling Em Ball into his lap.

I find no such doubleness
I find women true;
My lady loveth me doubtless;
And will change for no new.

Ah Robin...

Cutting Ball and Blacke Davie are improvising drumbeats upon the table, Scarlet Dick is slapping his cheeks in rhythm, as Kit replies gaily:

Thou art happy while that doth last
But I say as I find,
That women's love is but a blast
And turneth like the wind.

Ah Robin...

Huffing Kate, Em Ball, and the other tavern wenches are adding surprisingly mellifluous feminine voices and hilariously inappropriate *Alleluias* to the chorus, to great effect. Armin drops his fife from his lips to sing:

If that be true yet as thou say'st
That women turn their heart;
Then better speak of them thou may'st
In hope to have thy part.

Ah, Robin…

Kyd and Greene and Lyly and Watson all bellow out the chorus, then Kit sings again:

Such folks shall take no harm by love
That can abide their turn;
But I alas can no way prove
In love but lack and mourn.

Ah Robin…

All this combines to create one of those moments when all life seems to have built to this. When all that is behind is forgotten, all that is before is promise. A Golden Moment, of which there are so few.

Inspired, Will cannot not help himself. He stands and, pulling Kit nose to nose, boldly sings the final verse:

But if thou wilt avoid thy harm
This lesson learn of me:
At other fires thyself to warm
And let them warm with thee.

Will kisses Kit full on the mouth, to the jeers and cheers of all.

Ah, Robin..!

Mors sine Morte,
Finis sine Fine

Clearly this should be the end. In one of Will's plays, it would be. But this is a novel novel, so we add an epilogue to our epilogue.

For days after, as the mingled shock and relief fades, Will does not quite feel at ease. There is a thing unfinished, incomplete. Loose threads dangling from the sleeve God had knit for him. But he cannot put a name to it.

Then comes a note, unsigned, ordering him to be at Fleet Bridge at noon the following day. Raising the note to his face, he scents just a hint of fresh lavender.

Slipping out of the cheap rooms he now shares with Kit, he goes to the rendezvous alone. Arriving, he is part of a modest crowd, quickly growing. It's soon apparent why.

Just at noon, Her Majesty, Elizabeth Tudor, Queen regnant of England and Ireland, sometimes called the Virgin Queen, Gloriana, and good Queen Bess, exits a large carriage and begins to walk towards the bridge.

Will knows not where she is going, nor does he care. He is moved just to be standing here. A small, unworthy part of him longs to cry out over the rest of the shouting, clapping crowd and say, "I am Will Shakespeare, lady, and I saved your life and realm." But the impulse was no more than that, and he was glad in his heart that he found restraint.

She passes not far from where he stands. Walking in her train is the Lady Helena, no longer bedecked in Queenly robes, looking quite herself in her best court finery.

He does not know that she has seen him until, unheard by all save he and the Queen, she says his name. Elizabeth pauses as she passes, glancing into the crowd. As her eyes find him he bows to her, low and without flourish.

She looks him over from heel to head, then gives a single nod. In an instant, she is gone.

But Will knows he will forever be marked by that moment.

Her Majesty's Will.

FIN

Post Script
an Historicall Apologie from the Author

This book is entirely silly.

Yet, despite bending and twisting history, I've never actually *broken* it that I'm aware of. I set a rule that, accepting a ridiculous premise, the story would adhere to the facts as we know them. I reassure myself that both Will and Kit would have done no less – and probably a great deal more.

The question of Shakespeare's 'Lost Years' has been an intriguing mystery for as long as men have studied him. Why did he leave Stratford? How did he get from Stratford to London? What was he doing in the years between?

My answer is as simple as it is absurd. He was employed by Walsingham, the original 'M'.

Yet absurdity is often rooted in truth. That Marlowe was one of Walsingham's agents is generally accepted, though it is commonly held that his clandestine work really began after *Tamburlaine* was produced, that daring and heretical play having lowered the boom on poor Marlowe's head. And it is uncontested fact that at Marlowe's death, a former agent of Walsingham was present. That agent was Skeggs, also called Skeres, who was intimately involved in – what else? – the Babington Plot.

The Babington plot has long been a footnote in the grand drama between Elizabeth I and Mary, Queen of Scots. Walsingham entirely controlled the imprisoned Mary's communications, and prodded and poked Babington until they had enough incriminating evidence that even her cousin Queen Elizabeth could no longer ignore the charge of treason. After months of suspicious messages, Walsingham's code-breaker Phelippes made an addition to the last inbound code that doomed Queen Mary. Though under today's laws this was most probably entrapment, Walsingham was striving to protect his monarch. By providing Mary the means to communicate with the outside world, he gave her just enough rope to hang herself and thus remove the one problem that Elizabeth refused to face.

Of course, none of that is really of matter in this story. I've clearly taken a tangential, parallel, and oblique look at the Babington Plot, using none of the actual key conspirators save Gifford and Savage. I've always thought that the most maddening part of being a spy is having no idea what is going on, so I chased that notion here, possibly to indifferent effect. As a huge fan of Ian Fleming and Tom Clancy, I'm always amazed at how Bond and Ryan are ever able to stumble across the correct tidbit of info at just the right time. So I decided to write a story where the important piece of information never quite reaches our heroes. Really, as spies go, these two are quite terrible. It's a miracle they survive. Like the old saying goes, it's better to be lucky than good.

As for all the talk of religion, I only point out that it was the hottest issue of the day. The religious back-and-forth of yesteryear explains Britain's current attitude towards religion, which mirrors the American military's old 'don't ask, don't tell' policy, akin to sticking fingers in one's ears and shouting, "La la la la la la I can't hear you!"

In literature, we see a great deal of kings and lords, queens and ladies, but seldom do we see Tudor culture from, shall we say, street level. For this story I've tried to populate London with the real people of the time. Huffing Kate, Tarlton, Black Davie, Cutting Ball and Em Ball – these were all real rogues in Shakespeare's London. We know that poor Cutting Ball ended his days at the end of a rope, and before 1590, but without an exact date I was more than happy to let him survive into my tale, and possibly beyond.

The only important characters that come not from history are Derby, Rookwood, Brockhurst and Higgins. The latter two are theft from another series, but the first pair are my own creations – which is why they get away. It's not that I have plans for them, *per se.* It's only that a good author always leaves a door open for future stories. Or so I'm told.

Though I am deeply indebted to many scholarly works, I hesitate to mention them as I don't wish to embarrass anyone by associating them with this dreckish tale.

My first victim is, of course, Stephen Greenblatt. His amazing book WILL IN THE WORLD gives wonderful colour and detail to a vague outline of a possible life for the wayward playwright. As the joy of this kind of work is in the details, his book is a treasure beyond treasure, and provided quite a bit of fodder for my fancy.

The next unfortunate soul to whom I owe gratitude is Robert Hutchinson, for his book ELIZABETH'S SPY MASTER, a grand overview of Walsingham's life and career, wherein all the Babington details were gleaned, and this story was born.

Then there's THE ART OF SHAKESPEARE'S SONNETS by Helen Vendler (so sorry, Helen!) and Park Honan's CHRISTOPHER MAR- LOWE: POET & SPY (forgive me!). At least I did not manage to man- gle Ross W. Duffin's SHAKESPEARE'S SONGBOOK, as it's difficult to wreck direct theft.

I decided not to read Antony Burgess' A DEAD MAN IN DEPT- FORD until after I finished this novel, which was all to the good. I might have stolen whole pages – nay chapters! – outright, or else thrown my hands up and run from the project entirely (some might now be wishing I had). Nonetheless, I've acted as the most dastardly of the Elizabethan playwrights and stolen from him – not his take on Babington, which was entirely different, but rather his oaths, which are the most vibrant I've ever read. Match the language of the man who invented the Droogs? I cannot. If you are reading this afterword in advance of the story, first, shame on you, and second, I urge you to throw this volume into the bin and go find a copy of that book instead. It is a far superior novel, in every way.

I owe Dorothy Dunnett a deep apology for recycling her research into the period's poetry and presenting it in the mouths of lesser creations. For the poems themselves, look to THE LYMOND POETRY, edited by Elspeth Morrison.

There is a subtle domino-line of homages here that have nothing at all to do with Shakespeare or Marlowe. I deliberately styled this novel after ANOTHER FINE MYTH by my old friend, Robert Asprin. I was a kid when I stumbled onto the comic book detailing the Myth-adventures of Aahz and Skeeve. One day in the comic shop I asked the owner, Norm, when the next issue was coming out. He pointed to the bearded man behind me and said, "Ask him. He writes them." Over the next several years, Bob was incredibly tolerant of my pestering calls and visits, and I got a lot of wonderful Myth swag and, better, an inside look at the writing process. His books were a wonderful parody of Fantasy novels, but also of the Hope-Crosby road movies, which I also watched while writing this. The characters of Brockhurst and Higgins are my happy thefts from Bob's first book. Bob died in 2008, and I miss his voice and sense of humour more than I can say. Also the inside jokes about Ann Arbor, my hometown.

In this age of interweaving media, it's important to remember what the cutting edge means for disseminating information was in other times. There were no personalized websites (like, say, www.davidblixt.com). Nor were there twitter feeds (such as @David_Blixt). Nor blog pages (like, for example, themasterofverona.typepad.com). The printing press was still new, town criers were still in use. But if one wanted to reach a large audience with an important message, what better way than the theatre? Which is why Walsingham was so taken with it. He detested players and playwrights, but nonetheless saw the power inherent in the stage. Today you know he would have film-makers in his pocket, and have government subsidies of blockbuster films. But alas there is no modern Walsingham. Which is a shame, as I am perfectly willing to be bought.

I must thank Steve Pickering, Alice Austen, and Kevin Theis, my compatriots at Shanghai Low Theatricals, for their kind aid and acid advice through the various stages of this piece. Steve posted the early chapters and hounded me for the later ones. Kevin in particular came at me with reams of notes as to how to actually make the mess of ink I had spilled funny. And Alice, an amazing novelist in her own right, lifted me with kind praise. Seriously, Alice writes books so subtle, so marvelous, so complete, I want to give up scribbling altogether. And the harridan writes incredible plays, too. It's simply unfair.

Thanks to Tara Sullivan, Melanie Schuessler, Joseph Radding, and Bart Williams for their excellent notes. As per usual, all mistakes are entirely mine.

As ever, I owe a lot to fellow author MJ Rose. If you're reading this, it's likely you heard about it because of her. So go buy her books! They'll certainly be better than this.

The best question to ask an author is, "Who do you read?" Let me point everyone towards Dorothy Dunnett, Bernard Cornwell, Colleen McCullough, and Patrick O'Brian. Robert Asprin I referenced above. I'm also fortunate enough to have rubbed shoulders with some of my favorite authors, among them the aforementioned MJ Rose, as well as Sharon Kay Penman, C. W. Gortner and Michelle Moran, to whom I owe incalculable debts, both for their words and for their kindnesses.

If you haven't read them, do yourself a favour and pick up their books now.

While I adored Rob McLean's original cover, with a surprisingly fetching Matt Holzfeind in Elizabeth MacDougald's lovely dress, for this edition I commissioned the amazing and hilarious Jay Fosgitt to draw a new cover and some internal art (again inspired by Bob Asprin, and his work with Phil Foglio). Jay came through in a trice, whipping off utterly hilarious images in the span of just two days. Check out his comic book work - he's a rising star in that firmament, and to be cherished.

To Rick Sordelet, Broadway powerhouse and story-telling genius, I offer my friendship and my thanks. His heart is bigger than all outdoors, and his whole family is just like him. Thanks, Rick!

My most sincere appreciation is to the woman who makes this possible, not least by her insistence that we do in fact lead somewhat normal lives, but mostly by her very being, her presence in my life. Jan, I love you.

In May of 2017, this novel was transformed into a play by my old friend Robert Kauzlaric. That play was produced by Lifeline Theatre in Chicago, and directed by another longtime compatriot, Christoper Hainsworth. The script is available, both for reading and for production.

Lifeline Theatre's mission is to adapt literature for the stage, and they do it superbly well. Rob adapted Neil Gaiman's Neverwhere and Wilkie Collins' Moonstone. Chris adapted Terry Pratchett's Monstrous Regiment. Both have acted and directed there, and I could have wished for no better hands to shape a play based on my novel about the theatre.

Myself, I was surprised to be invited to participate in that production, as the violence designer. "Because the author saddled us with a ton of fights," remarked Chris. So I was allowed to be there as the show was cast, and to have the run of the rehearsal room. It was a delightful exercise in keeping my mouth shut. Every now and again I would whisper to Rob, "I really miss this line," though equally often I would suggest cutting something. A play is not a novel, it has different needs. And Rob and Chris did a magnificent job of transmogrification, an alchemy turning my lead into gold.

So naturally, I stole from it. There are a few lines added into this edition from the play, written either by Rob, by me, or by one of the actors in a beautiful moment of improvisation. So congratulations! You're holding the very best of the best. Or the best of the worst. You can decide.

When this was first printed, I threatened to return to our unlikely pairing of unlikelier heroes. That book is in progress now. I'm still fiddling, but the premise will be clear from the sneak peek on the next two pages. Enjoy!

As promised, Will and Kit will scribe again.

Ave,
DB

A Sneak Peek at Fire At Will

It is generally understood by poets, if not princes, that the machinations of comely Fortune proceed by Laws. Not the Laws of Nations, nor the Laws of Man. Rather by older Laws, drafted and enacted in the Endless Dark before Creation.

You will recognize them, I am sure. The Laws of Irony are quite powerful. So too the Laws of Gravity. First up, then down again. As with apples, so with men.

Science bestows the Laws of Attraction, and of Diminishing Returns. Often the aforesaid Laws of Irony link those two.

Yet the most intricate Law governing that fickle temptress is the Law of Unintended Consequences. The Creation itself was a result of this Law, for the Creator was simply weary of finding His slippers in the dark, forever barking His shins on the nightstand. Once Light was formed and his feet were shod, the rest was mostly afterthought.

In the affairs of man, this Law might run thus:

Say you have a Catholic king, perhaps a Spanish one, who is exhorted by Rome to invade an heretical isle and overthrow a queen who protests too much – not only virginity, but also the nature of her faith.

Say this king is disinclined, because should he succeed, the crown will pass to the Virgin Queen's imprisoned cousin, whom we'll call Scots. Thus his only way to take the isle's throne would be to marry the

Scottish lady, and thus court misfortune (she being quite unlucky in her husbands, one of whom was quite literally exploded). Besides, the Holy See in Rome, while adamant, is niggardly in terms of financing the expedition. The Spanish king politely refuses.

Now say that, during a previous misadventure, a pair of witty idiots had all unknowingly exposed an intricate plot to kill the Virgin Queen, implicating the Scots Queen in the sordid business. The affair might even have a name, one which rhymes with Blabbing Tongue, particularly apt. Our dramatic duo might feel a quite understandable inclination towards chest-puffage and peacock-walkage, full of pride at their remarkable achievement. All well and good.

Ah, but here is our Law at work! Entrapment not being then arguable, the Scots Queen is led to her death for her hand in the plot. Thus there is now no Catholic heir to the throne of England to oppose our Spanish king. It follows that the profit of any invasion would not be for some third party, but for the Spanish King himself.

The Spanish king re-inclines himself, and orders the building of ships.

Many, many ships.

Thus it was that, all unknowing, Will Shakespeare and Kit Marlowe unleashed the Spanish Armada.

Dear reader,

We hope you enjoyed reading *Her Majesty's Will*. Please take a moment to leave a review, even if it's a short one. Your opinion is important to us.

Discover more books by David Blixt at
https://www.nextchapter.pub/authors/david-blixt-historical-fiction-author

Want to know when one of our books is free or discounted? Join the newsletter at http://eepurl.com/bqqB3H

Best regards,
David Blixt and the Next Chapter Team

Author Biography

Consistently described as 'intricate,' 'taut,' and 'breathtaking', David Blixt's work combines a love of theatre with a deep respect for the quirks and passions of history. His novels span the early Roman Empire (the COLOSSUS series, his play EVE OF IDES) to early Renaissance Italy (the STAR-CROSS'D series) up through the Elizabethan era with this volume, HER MAJESTY'S WILL. He has recently completed a novel on the life of reporter Nellie Bly.

An Artistic Associate of the Michigan Shakespeare Festival, David continues to write, act, and travel. He has ridden camels around the pyramids at Giza, been thrown out of the Vatican Museum and been blessed by Pope John-Paul II, scaled the Roman ramp at Masada, crashed a hot-air balloon, leapt from cliffs on small Greek islands, dined with Counts and criminals, climbed to the top of Mount Sinai, and sat in the Prince's chair in Verona's palace. But David is happiest at his desk, weaving tales of brilliant people in dire and dramatic straits.

Living in Chicago with his wife and two children, David describes himself as "actor, author, father, husband. In reverse order."

https://www.davidblixt.com/

Other Books from David Blixt

Novels

The Star-Cross'd Series
   The Master Of Verona by David Blixt
   Voice Of The Falconer by David Blixt
   Fortune's Fool by David Blixt
   The Prince's Doom by David Blixt
   Varnished Faces - Star-Cross'd Short Stories by David Blixt

The Colossus Series - The Roman/Jewish Wars
   Colossus: Stone & Steel by David Blixt
   Colossus: The Four Emperors by David Blixt
   Colossus: Wail of the Fallen by David Blixt

Her Majesty's Will by David Blixt
Eve of Ides -- A Play by David Blixt
Fighting Words by Blixt, Girard, Kirby, & Leoni

Her Majesty's Will
ISBN: 978-4-86751-441-2

Published by
Next Chapter
1-60-20 Minami-Otsuka
170-0005 Toshima-Ku, Tokyo
+818035793528
20th July 2021

Lightning Source UK Ltd.
Milton Keynes UK
UKHW012103221222
414357UK00004B/110